I0632980

THE GIRL IN THE WIND

IRON ON IRON

BOOK TWO

GREGORY ASHE

H&B

This is a work of fiction. Names, characters, places, and incidents either are the product of the author's imagination or are used fictitiously, and any resemblance to actual persons, living or dead, business establishments, events, or locales is entirely coincidental.

The Girl in the Wind
Copyright © 2023 Gregory Ashe

All rights reserved. No part of this book may be reproduced in any form, stored in any retrieval system, or transmitted in any form by any means—electronic, mechanical, photocopy, recording, or otherwise—without prior written permission of the publisher, except as provided by United States of America copyright law. For permission requests and all other inquiries, contact: contact@hodgkinandblount.com

Published by Hodgkin & Blount
https://www.hodgkinandblount.com/
contact@hodgkinandblount.com

Published 2023
Printed in the United States of America

Version 1.06

Trade Paperback ISBN: 978-1-63621-067-4
eBook ISBN: 978-1-63621-066-7

1

"I'll have my phone on," Theo said. "We both will."

Auggie bit back a comment.

"In case there's an emergency."

"We don't actually expect an emergency, by the way." Auggie sent Theo a smile. "If that needed to be said."

"That's why I said in case."

This time, Auggie bit back a sigh. He didn't think anyone noticed; the Hazard and Somerset home was a maelstrom (SAT word) of chaos.

"We're going to have a great time," John-Henry Somerset said. The chief of police—and Auggie and Theo's friend—cupped the back of Lana's head.

"We're going to play Fillies," Lana said. The words were flat, almost affectless, one of the lingering effects of the terrible car accident she'd been in as a toddler. The leg brace was another. She was ten years old now, which was hard for Auggie to believe, with long dark hair that came to her shoulders. She had none of Theo's features or coloring—in fact, at a casual glance, she might have looked more like Auggie's biological daughter.

Emery Hazard looked at Theo. John-Henry's husband was a former police officer turned private investigator, and it didn't matter how many barbecues and baseball games Auggie went to, the unsettling weight of those amber eyes never changed.

"Fillies," Theo clarified.

Evie, Emery and John-Henry's daughter, looped through the room, being pursued by a scruffy puppy—when Auggie had asked what kind of dog she was, Emery had glowered and said, "Mutt." Evie was four, almost five, and she had John-Henry's features, although, like Lana, she was dark where John-Henry was blond. As she ran, she screamed, "Biscuit, Biscuit, Biscuit!" The dog didn't have any problem keeping up with her—in fact, most of the chase seemed to consist of the puppy jumping up to put her paws on Evie, at which point Evie squealed and pushed the dog down to run some more.

"Come here a minute, you maniac," John-Henry said, catching her with one arm. "Do you remember Lana?"

Lana smiled and ducked her head.

"Lana came over to play."

"We're going to play Fillies," Lana mumbled.

"She said—" Theo began.

"Biscuit is chasing us," Evie said. "Come on!"

Then, latching on to Lana's hand, she pulled her into a stumbling run. The brace made Lana's gait uneven, but Evie was smaller and younger, and Lana matched her stride for stride. Biscuit charged after them, yapping, and jumped. Both paws connected with Lana's waist, and she went down with a crash.

Theo started forward.

Before he could reach their daughter, though, Lana was back on her feet, laughing and pushing Biscuit away, while Evie shouted, "Come on, come on, she's getting us!"

"Her brace—" Theo said and took another step.

Auggie caught his wrist, and when Theo looked at him, he gave him a lot of eye contact.

After a moment, the tension in Theo's arm eased, and a rueful smile parted his beard.

"Knock it off!" The shout came from Colt, Emery and John-Henry's son. The teenager was as tall as Emery now, and although he wasn't their biological child, he had Emery's startling straw-colored eyes. He also had a thundercloud of hair, which he was—Auggie had been informed—trying to grow out. And about which, on pain of death, Auggie had been told to make zero comments. "Pops," Colt complained from the living room, "she won't listen to me."

"Evie," Emery said, "listen to your brother."

The girls stampeded past them again, screaming with laughter.

Theo smiled, but his eyes had that familiar tightness at the corners.

"Come in for a minute," John-Henry said. "Do you have time?"

"Our reservations—" Auggie began.

"Yes," Theo said. He followed John-Henry deeper into the house. Auggie watched them; when John-Henry said something about Lana's bag, Theo passed it over. Slowly. Like he was cutting off his own arm.

Emery stayed with Auggie, and he was watching too.

From farther back in the house came the swell of more voices, and after a moment, Auggie said, "Full house."

Emery made a face.

"You're coming with me," Colt said. He appeared in the opening to the living room for a moment, Evie slung over one shoulder, where she was giggling uncontrollably. "We've got to make your lunch. First day of school tomorrow. Lana, you can be in charge of the snacks."

"First day of school?" Auggie asked.

"Preschool," Emery clarified. "She's got one more year before kindergarten; late birthday."

"I love snacks," Lana said, and she took Colt's hand as he carried Evie toward the kitchen.

"He's really good with kids," Auggie said.

For a moment, the change in Emery's expression was like watching sunlight catch glass. Then it was gone, and he scowled at Auggie. "Don't you have a regular babysitter?"

"I heard that," John-Henry called from the living room.

"I'm not objecting to watching Lana," Emery shouted back. "I'm pointing out a logistical reality of parenthood. They should have an on-call babysitter who has been properly vetted."

"We do," Auggie said. "She got arrested. Cocaine. She sold all of Theo's beard balm on eBay."

For a moment, curiosity peaked in Emery's expression. Then it flattened out. "I am surrounded by aspiring comedians."

He turned and headed toward the living room.

"She was very good until she tried to harvest our organs," Auggie said as he went after him.

As they reached the living room, Biscuit—presumably bored now without the girls to chase—rushed toward Emery and began to bark at him. The scruffy little puppy was barely the size of a football, and Auggie grinned in spite of himself as the little thing locked her legs and began to tell Emery off.

Emery, being Emery, crouched and said, "Keep it up, and I'll make you into a handbag."

Biscuit whimpered and shot off into the kitchen, where she circled Colt's ankles and darted dirty looks at Emery.

"She's mad because you won't let her sleep with me," Colt said. He stood in the kitchen, visible through the opening that connected the two rooms, supervising Lana and Evie as they crammed a lunchbox full of goldfish packs.

"She's a dog. She sleeps where dogs sleep, in her crate."

"Dogs can sleep with people. I asked Dr. Leon. Dr. Leon, can't dogs sleep with people?"

Until that point, Teancum Leon had escaped Auggie's notice, which Auggie guessed was probably the idea. The wildlife vet, with his bushy hair and wild eyebrows, was hunkered down in an armchair, a book held in front of his face, obviously trying to pretend he hadn't heard.

"When Dr. Leon is your father, he can decide which animals are allowed to piss and shit in your bed. How does that sound?"

"Actually, most animals wouldn't—" Tean poked his head up above the book, and for a moment, Auggie was reminded of a wild animal testing the air. Then Tean ducked back out of sight.

"Hi, Tean," Auggie said.

"Hello."

"Is Jem around?"

"In the kitchen."

"He's smart," Emery said in an aside to Auggie as he headed toward the kitchen, "but zero social skills."

"Hmm," Auggie said in what he hoped was his most noncommittal tone.

The kitchen, it turned out, was the center of the madness in the house. Lana and Evie gabbled over each other as they focused their attention on loading the lunchbox with fruit snacks—only minimally supervised now by Colt. The boy had turned his attention to the other men in the room. To one man, in particular.

North McKinney had a thatch of blond hair, and he was built big and muscular in a way that made Auggie, even as an adult, feel a twinge of envy. In a gray tee that said BARNEY'S FISH AND CHIPS, he slouched against the cabinets, a beer in hand. "—you could paint it yourself, but that's a lot of work. And you've got to decide if you're going to spend your money on that, or if you want to save it toward the next one."

"Definitely the next one," Colt said. Lana tugged on his hand, and Colt made a dismissive noise without pulling his gaze away from North. "So, like, I should change my own oil, right?"

"Not this again," Emery said.

"You don't change your own oil?"

A flush rode Colt's cheekbones. "Uh, I mean, Pops said—"

"Because he doesn't know how."

"I know how," Emery said. "But I'm not interested in spending half a day doing a job I can pay someone else to do for forty dollars, thank you very much."

"Half a day," North said. "If it takes you half a day, you don't know how to do it."

"Maybe, um, you could teach me?" Colt's blush intensified. "I mean, I know you're busy, so, like, not right now—"

"He can't teach you because he doesn't know how," Shaw said. North's partner was wearing a black leotard and, probably only because North had insisted, baby blue shorts that only minimally covered his junk. He had cornered Ashley, Colt's boyfriend, and he broke off from whatever he'd been saying to speak over his shoulder. "One time North said he was going to change the oil, and it was hours and hours, and I went out there, and he'd taken off his shirt and he was all hot and sweaty and there wasn't any oil anywhere. So, I said—"

Colt's eyes darted to Shaw and then back to North. To North's chest, actually, if Auggie weren't mistaken. Only for a heartbeat. Emery must have noticed too, though, because the muscles in his jaw stood out.

"I know how to do it, for fu—" North shot the girls a look. "I know how to do it. I can show you."

"Seriously? That would be dope. Ash, did you hear that?"

Ashley didn't appear to have heard, though, because he was currently trying to wriggle free from where Shaw had trapped him. Shaw was talking nonstop—the only part Auggie understood was "Would it help if I summoned my Patronus first?"—but when Ashley slid a few inches farther, Shaw's arm shot out to block the escape.

"Good fucking Lord," Emery said under his breath. "Excuse me while I go blow my brains out."

"Not that one." The voice belonged to Jem Berger. Tean's husband worked in real estate, although Theo had said on more than one occasion that he didn't believe that story. Auggie wasn't sure what he thought; Jem was a puzzle. Clearly savvy, keenly trendy—although he skewed more toward vintage stuff, not really Auggie's vibe. But every once in a while, Auggie caught a glimpse of something else, like laughter or amusement that didn't quite line up with what was going on, and he wondered what he was missing. Right then, Jem was bent over John-Henry's phone, shaking his head. "No, definitely not. You're already fighting a losing battle in the ass department. Those are going to make you look like you're lugging around a couple of sacks of flour."

"Gee," John-Henry said, "thanks."

Jem flashed a grin, a hint of his slightly crooked front teeth making an appearance, and swiped on John-Henry's phone a couple of times. "What about these?"

"Uh." John-Henry seemed at a loss for words. "They look…young."

Jem burst out laughing. "We'll get them in this khaki color, and we'll go a little longer because I don't think you want to wear them above the ankle. I'm telling you, this is the pair."

"What are you guys doing?" Auggie asked as he worked his way across the kitchen.

"Bankrupting me," Emery said.

John-Henry flashed his husband a smile before saying to Auggie, "A little wardrobe update. Jem is really good at this stuff."

"He's motivated by existential despair, he told us. He wanted Tean to tell us about Sartre."

"To be fair, I'm motivated by existential despair about everything," Jem said. "We all are. Right, Tean?"

Tean's voice floated back from the living room: "I'm not listening."

"Let me see what you're getting," Auggie said, taking his place next to the men. "Ok, hold on, I know you said khaki, but what if you went for this one, a little more neutral?"

John-Henry said, "I like it, but Jem said—"

"No, he's right." Jem nodded. "Closer to the natural color. It's even better."

"And let me guess," Emery said from where he was picking an abundance of fruit snacks out of the lunchbox. "They cost sixty dollars."

The beat lasted a moment too long.

"Yes," Jem said. "Sixty dollars."

Emery paused. "How much are they?"

"I'd better check on Tean."

Jem slipped out of the room before Emery could catch him.

"John?"

"I, uh, better help."

And then, somehow, Auggie was alone.

"How much?" Emery said with that tone like he was picking each word carefully because the sentence was going to end in a murder.

"You know," Auggie said, "I actually didn't see."

Emery's silence seemed to grow by the second until he finally said, "I am going to remember this."

Auggie offered a smile.

"Did I mention that we charge for babysitting?"

"No," John-Henry called from the other room, "we don't."

"Speaking of which," Auggie said, and he tried to check his watch, only he wasn't wearing one—because, well, he never did. Emery snorted. "We'd better get going, Theo."

"Right." Theo scratched his beard. "Let me just check on Lana—"

"She's fine," North said, gesturing with his beer. "She and Evie ran that way."

Theo looked in that direction.

"They had a bunch of kitchen knives," North said. "And they were running with scissors. Oh, and I think they were dousing each other with gasoline."

Theo shot him a dark look, and North smirked.

"It's ok if you have a third nipple," Shaw was saying to Ashley, who had now gone wide eyed and looked, frankly, a little desperate. "But it's not ok to lie about it."

"Not ok to lie about it," North said. "Look who's talking. I find you tits up in the bathtub, so blitzed you keep asking if your legs are balloons—"

"Balloon animals," Shaw said. To Ashley, who was trying to slide away again, he added, "I thought they were those little sausage dogs."

"—and you tell me all you did was have tea with Master Hermes."

"It was tea! It had the little mushrooms in it!"

"Those are 'shrooms, dumbfuck!"

Ashley made a break for it, his bare feet slapping the boards as he escaped.

North squinted at Auggie. "What product do you use in your hair, Short Round?"

"Uh."

"It's North's eyes," Shaw said. "They're starting to go."

"Do you want to try that again?" Theo asked. "Maybe call him Auggie instead of a nickname that's borderline racist?"

But North's smirk just got bigger. "Daddy wants to play."

"Ignore them," John-Henry called from the next room. "North's being an asshole because he's bored."

"Language," Emery shouted as he scooped goldfish out of the lunchbox. "Am I the only one in this fucking house who remembers there are fucking children here, for fuck's sake?"

"Come on," Auggie said, catching Theo's arm and leading him into the living room. Theo, of course, kept his gaze on North until they'd left the kitchen.

To judge by the volume, Colt and Ashley and the girls were upstairs. Colt roared, "Because I'm a monster and I'm going to eat you," and Ashley shouted, "Come on, come on, in here," and Evie and Lana squealed with delight. Jem perched on the arm of Tean's chair, combing fingers through his hair while Tean tried to read, and John-Henry was flipping channels on the TV.

"Thank you again," Auggie said.

"No problem," John-Henry said. "Pick her up whenever you want."

"Not whenever you want," Emery said from the kitchen. "It's a fucking school night, which I already had to fight with Colt about. Tonight it's about seeing Ashley. Last night it was about that fucking back-to-school party. Fuck me. One more fucking excuse to get tanked in a fucking cornfield."

"Ten o'clock curfew, Peewee," North called to them. "Actually, make that nine."

Theo's expression flattened.

"Leave it," Auggie whispered.

"Oh, hey, before I forget." John-Henry dropped the remote on the sofa. "A girl named Shaniyah came to the station. She dropped your names, wanted to interview me about a boy who'd gone missing."

"Wait, really? Is it—do you think it's related?"

The question brought a stillness broken only by the buzz of the TV. A week ago, the eight of them had found themselves drawn into the hunt for a killer. In the process, they discovered a criminal organization operating in the region. One branch of their operation seemed to include theft or robbery, and they had found, among the stolen jewelry and IDs, a class ring from Wahredua High School.

"I don't know," John-Henry said. "That's what I wanted to ask you."

Auggie glanced at Theo.

"She's one of my students," Theo said. "Shaniyah. She's going into her senior year, and she's been working with Auggie on a digital media project for her college applications."

"And she needs to interview the chief of police about a missing boy?" Tean asked, his book now forgotten in his lap.

"I don't know about that," Auggie said. "The project is a collection of videos, but they're about social media use among teens—you know, TikTok challenges, BookTok, lip synching, cringey fails, the whole range."

"What are cringey fails?" Emery asked.

At the same time, Theo began, "What are—"

"Pops," Colt groaned from upstairs before roaring again like a monster. "I've told you like a million times!"

"She hasn't said anything to me about a missing boy," Auggie continued. "What boy?"

"I don't know," John-Henry said. "I was in a meeting, and by the time I got out, she was gone."

A question hung at the end of the sentence, and John-Henry was looking at Auggie in a way that reminded him that, even with the buddy-next-door smile, John-Henry was still a cop—and an extremely good one.

"I swear," Auggie said. "Shaniyah hasn't said anything to me about anything like that. Not even remotely. She was down the other day, you know, upset. But that was because she didn't get a big scholarship she'd applied for. She didn't tell me she was going to change her project, though."

"Because if she had," Emery said, "and you two were planning on playing Lone Ranger—"

"How could the two of them play Lone Ranger?" North asked. "Isn't there just one Lone Ranger?"

"One of them is clearly Tonto—"

"We're not doing anything of the sort," Theo said. "Neither of us knows what Shaniyah is asking about, and we certainly didn't have anything to do with it."

The second floor rumbled with heavy steps and mock growls.

"Have you—" Auggie restarted, but he didn't know how to ask about what they had found at the Cottonmouth Club. "It's been a week."

"Nothing," John-Henry said.

"We have jobs, remember?" Emery said. "We've been working on it, but it's going to take time."

Theo looked at Jem and Tean.

"We're still trying to run something down," Jem said. "Anything, really, but we've been trying to work the wildlife trafficking side."

"We haven't made much progress," Tean said.

"We haven't made any progress. But we're not giving up. And we've still got some time. Tean's working remotely, and my job is flexible."

"Ours isn't," North said. "Some of us actually have to go to work."

"I'm sure watching dentists get blown by their mistresses is an incredibly demanding calling," Emery said.

"Look who's talking," North said. "Same job, bozo."

"And it is hard, Emery," Shaw said. "Sometimes they pull the curtains. And sometimes the dentists cry a little bit. And one time, one of them was—" Shaw mouthed, *Getting a hummer.* "—and his wig fell off. Oh my God, and one time my wig fell off! That was right after I fell on one of the mistresses."

"How did you fall on a mistress?" John-Henry asked.

"Sure," North said. "Great. Let's all give him exactly what he wants."

"I was wearing these polar bear feet—imitation!" The last part was a rushed assurance to Tean, whose eyes were huge. "And they were in this English basement—"

"What the fuck is an English basement?" Emery asked.

"I'll pop popcorn," North said. "We'll be here all day."

"—and it looked like she was doing something, you know, interesting, like, um, her technique, so I thought I should probably see with my spiritual eye—"

"He forgot the telephoto lens and humped his way right over the rail," North said.

"While North was getting his banger mashed," Shaw said with what might have been a note of vicarious pride.

"I was not—"

"He said this guy had hands that could crush walnuts."

North's face was turning a startling shade of purple.

"He couldn't sit down for a week. Well, he couldn't sit down front ways. That was before we were dating."

"What does—" Emery began.

At the same time, North shouted, "What the fuck does 'sit down front ways' even mean? I could sit down just fine, and Rodrigo didn't mash anything, since my sex life is now public fucking record." He snapped a look around the room, seized Shaw's arm, and said, "We're leaving. We'll be back when we can."

"John-Henry, my Pepsi—" Shaw tried.

But North dragged him toward the front of the house. Shaw's giggles came back to them for a moment, and then the door shut them off.

Emery rubbed his face. "God fucking damn it."

Laughing, John-Henry rubbed his shoulder. "Don't worry; they'll be back when they can."

Emery dropped his hands to give him a betrayed look.

"We need to get going too," Auggie said. "Listen, I'll ask Shaniyah why she wanted to talk to you, but in the meantime, is there something we can do? I mean, the class ring?"

John-Henry shook his head, but Emery was the one who answered. "We're working on the Cottonmouth Club, trying to figure out who's operating out of there. Tean and Jem are taking the animal angle, and North and Shaw are going to see if they can get a line on anything moving through St. Louis. There's nothing you can do right now without getting in the way."

"We didn't get in the way last week—" Auggie began.

"That's fine," Theo said. "We'll let the professionals handle it."

When they were in the Audi, driving away from the house, Auggie had to wrestle with the argument he wanted to start. Finally, he managed to swallow it, and as they drove toward Moulin Vert, he managed to say, instead, "Lana's going to have so much fun."

Theo nodded. He was staring straight out the windshield.

"She's going to be fine, Theo. Evie adores her, and she's got a house full of people who are going to make sure nothing happens to her. Colt and Ashley might need a three-day weekend to recover after this, but everyone's going to be fine."

"I know." Then Theo's mouth softened, and he said again, "I know. I'm sorry; it's hard to turn it off sometimes."

Auggie nodded and rubbed Theo's knee.

"They're going to have fun," Theo said.

"She loves other kids," Auggie said. "And I don't know if I've ever seen her run like that."

"She has to be careful—" Theo stopped.

Auggie rubbed his knee some more while they drove.

He didn't mean anything by it, not really. It just came out. "It's cute, isn't it? The—I don't know, the dynamic, I guess. At Emery and John-Henry's house."

"Cute like an insane asylum."

Auggie slapped his knee lightly. "It's busy, sure. But it's...warm. It's—" Full, he wanted to say, although that sounded like he was pitching a '90s sitcom. But it was the right word, that sense of fullness, of a house brimming with life. "It's happy."

Theo made a noise that could have meant anything.

"Didn't you think it was cute, watching Evie and Lana together? Or, God, Colt with his little sister?"

It was the wrong thing to say; Auggie felt it as soon as it left him. Theo pushed his hair back with both hands and looked out the windshield. He didn't knock Auggie's hand off his knee. He didn't do anything dramatic. He didn't need to.

"That's not what I meant," Auggie said.

Theo nodded.

"I was just saying."

"I know what you were saying," Theo said. The sunset caught his eyes and turned them into hard little mirrors. "I thought we weren't having this conversation again."

2

The end of the first day of school always found Theo exhausted. The transition from the peace and quiet—relatively speaking, anyway—of summer to the demands of performing for a live audience for seven and a half hours every day wasn't an easy one. His throat had that mild burn that would last for the first week, and his body ached in new places from being on his feet. Even the classroom smells of whiteboard markers and Axe body spray and Clorox wipes were threatening to turn that little pinprick of discomfort into a full-on headache. On top of all that, the beginning of the school year had been unusually stressful—a few months before, on the last day of school, an active shooter had entered the building. Which meant this year began with extra nerves, extra wariness, and extra assemblies.

By the time Theo made it to his final class period—which was, by some twist of fate, also his plan period—all he could do was sit and read *The Cardinal Nation* and *Bleacher Report* and pretend he was going to get back to work in a couple of minutes.

Not that there was much to do; he'd planned out the first few weeks of school, and he had plenty of time to print off the reading packets for *Much Ado about Nothing*. It wasn't a play the tenth-graders normally read, but this year, the community theater was putting on a production. Many of the students—maybe even all of them—would never have seen live theater before, and so the plan was to read the play, watch the movie, and then take them to see it performed. By then, Theo thought, maybe they'd understand the overall plot.

He was toying with the idea of getting tickets to a Cardinals game. He could offer Auggie a weekend in the city as a kind of apology for last night. Not that it had been an argument. They never had arguments anymore, not really. Not that it had been anything except a tense moment, an uncomfortable few seconds, and then they had both moved on from it. Without talking about it. The way they always did.

The door opened, and Principal Wieberdink stepped into the classroom. She had one of those milky complexions that might have been good genes and that definitely involved good makeup, and she wore her dark hair in layers. Auggie said her clothes were expensive, and Theo could testify that she certainly dressed, well, more professionally than a lot of the staff. He hadn't once, for example, seen her come to work in a sports bra like Danika Greer, the health teacher slash water polo coach.

Theo waited for the usual check-in—how was the first day, all that stuff. Instead, though, Wieberdink said, "Dr. Stratford, I need your help."

"Sure." Theo straightened in his seat. "Is something—"

"Do you know Shaniyah Johnson?"

"Yes."

"Great. I need you to help us look for her."

"I'm sorry, I don't understand. Did something happen?"

"What happened is that Shaniyah's first- and second-hour teachers apparently did not think taking attendance was an important part of their jobs." Wieberdink's usual glacial reserve had melted a little. "A point about which I will be happy to remind them. In the meantime, we don't know if Shaniyah is in the building, or if she's playing hooky, or if she even came to school at all today. Her aunt and uncle insist that she's here, and they want her found."

"Uh—" Wieberdink shifted her weight, and Theo locked on to the reality of the moment. "Right, I'll start looking. Are you—"

"I've got to get Bobby Porter out of the Gator, which he is currently trying to drag race on the track. Find Shaniyah, Dr. Stratford, and bring her to my office."

Then she was gone, and from the clip of her heels, she was just shy of running.

It wasn't exactly unusual for a first day—there was always some kind of minor disaster. And students did love to steal the four-wheeler, which was kept in the athletics shed with minimal security. But it did strike Theo, like the echo of an off-key note, that it was Shaniyah who happened to be unaccounted for. And they'd been talking about Shaniyah the night before.

He locked the classroom behind him and started moving through the building. He worked his way down the hall, checking the electrical closet— the door was still locked—and then the staff bathroom—also locked. Wahredua High School was one of those buildings that had grown in stages, which meant it was, speaking politely, a maddening fuck-up of a maze, even if you'd been working there for years. And with those stages of construction had come odd nooks and crannies, unused corridors, forgotten architectural irregularities.

A giggle came from nearby, and Theo changed direction, heading for an alcove tucked off the main hallway, where the custodial staff often stored unused desks and chairs, and where every year they caught kids vaping (and before vaping, smoking). Maybe not so forgotten, Theo thought as the giggle came again, louder.

"Yeah, I work out." That was a boy's voice. He wasn't speaking loudly, but he wasn't whispering either. Someone else said something that Theo couldn't hear, and the boy laughed—a low, even sound. "A couple of hours every day," he answered. "Go on. Here. Yeah."

When Theo came around the corner, the boys didn't notice him, not at first. One of them sat on one of the spare desks, his legs spread, an arm curled to show off his biceps. The gray gym shorts didn't leave any doubt about how much he liked the attention. He had olive-colored skin under a deep tan, hair worn long on top with a hint of curl, the sides tapering to a skin fade. Probably, Theo thought, so nobody got the wrong idea.

The other boy Theo recognized, although he didn't know his name— black motorcycle pants, a tight black tee, a quiff of mousey hair. He was ultra skinny, which Theo thought was partially a choice, and he was running his hand over the first boy's arm.

"What's going on here?" Theo asked.

The skinny boy about jumped out of his motorcycle pants, whirling around to face Theo, red blotches moving into his cheeks. The boy with the biceps showed a flash of surprise, but he recovered quickly. He changed his posture on the desk and adjusted himself, but that was all—more like he was being polite than like he'd been busted.

"What's going on?" Theo asked again.

"Nothing," Biceps Boy said.

Theo looked at the skinny boy.

"Nothing," he mumbled.

"Names," Theo said.

"What were we doing wrong?" Biceps Boy asked.

"You're not in class. How's that for starters? What's your name, please?"

"My teacher doesn't care."

"Your name."

The boy smiled. It was a good smile, with straight, white teeth, and none of the usual adolescent uncertainty. "Keelan Vasquez-Mendoza. It's got a hyphen."

Theo glanced at the skinny kid.

"Trevor Cohen." He looked like he was about to cry. "Please don't tell my dad."

And the worst part was that he looked genuinely terrified. After a moment of silent deliberation, Theo jerked his head toward the hallway. "Next time, it's a phone call."

Trevor sprinted away, but Keelan was slower, sliding off the desk, adjusting himself again, straightening his t-shirt. None of it was anything Theo could point to as insubordination or disrespect, but none of it was accidental either. All the alpha bro arsenal of movements telescoped onto a teenage boy. He'd learned it from his father, Theo guessed. Maybe an older brother. Keelan made eye contact as he passed Theo on his way to the hall. Not a challenge, not exactly. A statement. It was a surprisingly adult move, as though this were his decision, and he were still in the process of assessing Theo. It was the kind of thing, in Theo's opinion, that made people wonder why teachers didn't murder students more often.

Theo trailed Keelan until the boy stepped into a classroom, and Theo made a note of the number; he planned on talking to Ms. Singleton about her wandering student after school.

And still no sign of Shaniyah. He continued his search. He couldn't check the girls' bathrooms—he wasn't dumb enough to try that without a female staff member accompanying him—but he did call through each doorway, asking if Shaniyah Johnson was in there. His next stop was the theater, which had a separate exit from the building where students often came and went—went was the more popular choice—without being noticed. In theory, the exit was fire-alarmed, but the school was old, and the alarm on the door had a mysterious way of not working as it should.

When he reached the vestibule, Theo stopped and listened—it was another favorite place for kids wanting to sneak a moment together, and the memory of stumbling onto Trevor and Keelan was fresh in Theo's mind. But he heard nothing, and after a moment, he tried the doors. Locked. His key let him inside.

The theater itself was cool and dark, with only the footlights and LED strips on the aisles to keep him from total blindness. He listened again, but still nothing. When he turned on his flashlight, he waited for movement, the sounds of escape. Nothing came. He made his way across the theater and checked the fire door, which appeared to have made it through the first day of school intact. Then he hopped up onto the stage and headed behind the curtains. The backstage hallway—with the dressing rooms, the prop storage, the access to the catwalk, the stairs to the orchestra pit—was another favorite of wanderers and skulkers. Nominally, it was supervised by the theater teacher, whose classroom had a door onto the backstage hall, but—

Through the lite set into the classroom door, Theo had a direct line of sight to the teacher's desk. Dalton Weber, the theater teacher, sat there, looking out through the same lite Theo was looking in.

Theo and Dalton had never hit it off, even though they worked in the same department, even though they were both gay in a small, conservative town. Even though, for that matter, Dalton was good at his job—he was a talented director, and outside of school, he often directed productions at the community theater, including the upcoming staging of *Much Ado about Nothing*. Theo wasn't sure why they'd never clicked. Part of it was that he found Dalton's appearance off-putting. When Dalton was standing, he was too tall to pass for Pat Sajak, but they shared a look—shrunken, almost gremlinish features; a hint (more than a hint) that he did a lot of upkeep with creams and masks and peels. His hair dye looked like the color that had rubbed off an old belt, and Theo remembered, in a staff meeting, the way Dalton had moved his hands—a kind of Bruce Vilanch-esque campiness that was so stereotyped that it had the ring of authenticity. And part was that something had always felt off to him about Dalton, although he couldn't point to anything in particular.

Right then, Dalton had his hand to his mouth, and, in his other hand, a prescription vial. There shouldn't have been anything strange about the encounter. Maybe a slight awkwardness, both of them a little surprised. But Dalton froze. It lasted only a moment, and then he shoved the prescription vial into a pocket, and he dry-swallowed the pill in his mouth before looking back at Theo. Under the fluorescent lights, his face was bloodless.

Theo turned, following the backstage hall away from the classroom. An odd, secondhand embarrassment attached itself to him, and he found himself walking with his head down, his shoulders hunched. He had grown up around people who hid their pills when you walked in on them, people who startled when you came into a room unannounced, people who thought—at the beginning, while there was still hope—if they could act normally, naturally, everything might be all right. Theo had been one of those people himself, and he knew the tricks, and he knew the way the mind twisted and contorted and tried to protect itself.

He might have hurt his back, Theo thought as he walked faster. He might have had surgery over the summer. It might not be a painkiller at all; maybe it's for high blood pressure, or maybe it's cholesterol. Hell, maybe he's got a headache and a sore throat like you do. But Theo walked faster because he knew it wasn't any of those things, the way you knew yourself—and didn't—in a mirror. And he walked faster because something inside him was waking up from a long sleep, stretching tight muscles, raising its head. The first one was the best, when it had been so long, when the rush was something your body still remembered and it was like thirst, when you knew you needed it—

Theo hit the crash bar at the end of the backstage corridor and emerged into one of the school's main hallways. Sunlight flattened him, and he had to blink. For a moment, it was almost like vertigo. Then shouting made him turn, still trying to adjust to the brightness of the dusty, summer-lit hall.

"I heard you the first time!" It was a woman's voice, the tone riding a knife's edge between frustration and aggression. "And I'm telling you, she's here!"

A man spoke in a hushed voice: "It's been a long weekend."

"She's doing this to embarrass me! Shaniyah, get your butt out here!"

A man and woman came into view, trailed by Principal Wieberdink, who wasn't quite unprofessional enough to wring her hands, but was sliding a bangle up and down her forearm instead. The woman was tall, built large, her Afro gathered in a hibiscus-print wrap. The man was big too, his hair in waves, with a well-trimmed beard.

"Shaniyah!" the woman shouted.

"Please," Principal Wieberdink said, "classes are still in session—"

Theo changed course, heading toward the new arrivals; already, the shock, the rippling echo, the spike of need—they were fading, like something he'd forgotten. In an hour, he'd probably be able to laugh about it.

Before he could take more than a few steps, though, his phone buzzed. Auggie's name showed on the screen, which was strange; Auggie never called during the school day. Messages, yes. Sometimes, when he was bored, an unending stream of them, often with GIFs and memes Theo could only partially decipher. But not calls.

"Hey, uh, this is weird—" Auggie sounded out of breath, his voice wound tight. "—but did you borrow my laptop?"

"No. Why?"

"You didn't move it or anything?"

"Of course not. Auggie, what's going on?"

"Shaniyah!" the woman shouted. "Get out here this minute!"

"Listen, we've got kind of a situation here. Shaniyah's missing. Can I call you—"

"I think we've been robbed." Auggie stopped like he was hearing himself. "My laptop's gone, Theo. I think somebody stole it."

3

Before Theo got home, Auggie still had enough presence of mind to hide the surrogacy papers. Not hide. Put away. Out of sight. Because he'd just been curious, that's all.

Then he did another circuit, the whole house, room by room. He lifted cushions from the couch. He pulled Theo's recliner out from the corner. He opened drawers, and he took out pots and pans. A part of his brain was running one line of commentary: Lana could have moved it; Lana picks stuff up and carries it around, and it ends up in the weirdest places. Like my keys. Like my slides. Like that photo of her at Disney World. And, at the same time, another part of his brain was saying, Please let me find it, please don't let Theo show up and find it, actually, yes, please, as long as somebody finds it. He carried with him, a leftover from that double major in English, the idea of irony as an equivocal statement. He was also aware—and here it was personal expertise talking—that he sounded batshit crazy.

The lock turned at the front of the house, and the door opened. Steps came down the hall. Theo looked tired the way he always looked after the first day of school; people who didn't have kids (or who weren't domestic partners, aka shacked up, aka living in sin with a teacher) forgot how significant those transitions were. Back to school in August. Back to school in January. Back to school after spring break; Theo always spent that week in March looking like he was hungover, and the kids were even worse. But he was still Theo, with the flow of strawberry-blond hair combed back, with a little more silver in his thick beard, with the gingham framing the lines of his shoulders, with quads and glutes for days. The man still knew, after all these years, how to fill out a pair of chinos.

"Are you ok?" Theo asked.

Of course. First thing. Because he was Theo.

Auggie's laugh sounded a little raw, even to him, but he nodded. "Are you?"

"Me?"

"First day?"

Theo shook his head like the question was a gnat buzzing around him. "Where's Lana?"

"She's still at school. God, I'm sorry; I should have said something."

Theo shook his head again, but his shoulders slumped, and he sank down onto the arm of the sofa.

"Sorry," Auggie said again.

"You don't have to be sorry, Auggie." It took a few more seconds, though, before he uncurled his fingers and ran one hand along the back of the sofa. He got up, his stiff knee slowing him, and came across the room. Then he hugged Auggie, kissed the side of his head, and tightened his arms until Auggie made a sound he'd once heard a dog make when Fer, at eleven years old, had tried to pick it up around the middle.

"It's got to be here, right?" Auggie asked, surprised to hear the threat of tears in his voice. "I feel like I'm going out of my mind. God, we're going to find it, and then I'm going to feel even worse. I shouldn't have called; you rushed home, and you were worried about Lana, and I should have waited—"

"Hey, hey, hey." Theo loosened his grip enough to let Auggie move back. He raised his eyebrows, and after a moment, Auggie rolled his eyes and shook his head.

"If it's here," Auggie said, "you have to spank me."

The arch of Theo's eyebrows became a little more pointed.

"That's it. That's what's got to happen."

"Uh huh."

"You can't weasel out of it. You can't make excuses. You can't make up some alternate system of penalty blow jobs."

"It's not entirely clear to me, this whole thing that's happening right here, but you realize that in this hypothetical situation you've imagined, you're the one getting spanked, and you're also the one telling me to be more...hard core about it?"

"Yes, Theo. I'm very well aware of it, thank you. Because the last thing I need is a candy-ass swat on the bum; I can't do everything myself."

Theo was quiet for what felt like a long time before he murmured, "Good God."

Auggie grinned, but it felt like one of those water features, the kind he'd thought about getting Theo for his desk, the thinnest sheet of water catching the light as it ran over a cut of black stone. After a moment, Theo touched the corner of his mouth, and Auggie leaned into the cup of Theo's hand.

"You've got backups," Theo said.

Auggie nodded.

"And it's all on the cloud."

Another nod.

"And it's an expensive laptop, but it's not irreplaceable."

"There goes the new sofa."

"So, it's fine, right?"

Auggie nodded again. A part of him knew Theo was right. A part of him knew that, in the grand scheme of things, losing his laptop—stolen, a voice inside his head corrected; it had been stolen—wasn't the end of the world. But it had been the disorientation of not being able to find it, and then the frustration, and then, as doubt grew, the flicker of fear growing alongside it. This was their home. Someone had been inside their home. And Theo. He would have to tell Theo, and that had been fuel for his fear.

"Why don't I start in the office—" Theo began.

But a knock at the door stopped him, and a hint of color came into his cheeks.

Auggie blinked. "Did you—"

"Well, you said we'd been robbed."

"Right."

"Was that the wrong thing to do?"

"No, no. I guess—I don't know." Auggie broke the circle of Theo's arms and started toward the front door. "No, that was—I should have thought of that."

When he got to the front door, John-Henry was there: blond hair a little less mussed than on the weekends, a professional smile in place, dressed in his uniform in total disregard for the simmering August heat. Behind him, two uniformed officers were getting out of a patrol car—a Black woman, Nickels, and a white kid, Yarmark.

"Hi, Auggie," John-Henry said. "Mind if I come in?"

Auggie stepped back.

"They're going to take a look around the perimeter of the property," John-Henry said with a nod for Yarmark and Nickels. "If that's ok with you."

"Yeah, of course, but—" Auggie couldn't finish the question, but what he wanted to say was, *Isn't that a lot?* "Yeah," he said again. "Of course."

He led John-Henry back to the combined living room and kitchen at the back of the house. Afternoon sunlight brightened the space, and in the quiet, the babble of the creek made its way through the balcony doors. Theo had loosened his tie and stored his laptop bag, and now he sat on a stool at the counter, his bad leg kicked out the way he did when it was bothering him.

"Do you want to sit down?" Auggie asked. "Do you want a beer? You can't have a beer because you're working. Do you want a soda?"

"No, thanks."

Auggie dropped onto the stool next to Theo. John-Henry stayed standing, and Auggie had a moment of memory that was like vertigo: he was twentyish, still in school, and facing down an angry John-Henry Somerset, one who was a detective, and a good one, and one who wasn't Auggie and Theo's friend. Maybe Theo felt it too, because his hand came to rest on Auggie's thigh.

"First of all," John-Henry said, "I'm sorry this happened to you. It's important that you know that you didn't do anything wrong. Having your home violated can bring up a lot of feelings, so don't be surprised if right now you're having a hard time managing your emotions. If you need to take a break, or if you find yourself getting overwhelmed, just say something, and we'll take a step back."

He waited until Theo nodded.

Auggie said, "Does the chief of police do this for every burglary?"

Theo tsked and squeezed Auggie's thigh.

But John-Henry gave a small smile. "The chief of police does this for his friends. Why don't you tell me what happened?"

Theo looked at Auggie.

"Nothing happened," Auggie said. Both men were still looking at him, so he laughed. It was like too-tight strings on a violin. "I mean, I couldn't find my laptop. And—I don't know, I still can't find it." He laughed again.

John-Henry didn't laugh, though. He nodded. "Have you looked everywhere?"

"Yeah, of course."

Another of those small smiles. Friendly. Warm, even. "I have to ask," he said wryly. "Sometimes people surprise you. They surprise themselves, I should say. One guy, he found a book of stamps behind a line of VHS cassettes; he'd put it there for safekeeping and forgot all about it."

This was why he was so good, Auggie was starting to realize—the thought buzzing at the edge of his awareness. He'd known, already, that John-Henry was smart, funny, even kind. But this, right here, was one of the things that made him an excellent chief, as well as a great detective.

A rap at the glass slider that led out onto the deck made Auggie jump. Yarmark stood there.

"Be right back," John-Henry said.

He stepped out onto the deck and shut the door behind him—careful, Auggie noticed, to touch the handle as little as possible. Just in case, Auggie guessed. After a few moments of conversation, he stepped back inside.

"Officer Yarmark noticed some security cameras around the exterior of the house."

Theo shifted on his stool, a half-glance sliding to Auggie. "Yeah." And then, because he must have felt some kind of explanation was necessary, he continued, "We're far enough out here—I mean, we turned off the notifications because we get so many deer." He stopped again. In a different voice, he said, "I'll check right now."

"What are they looking for?" Auggie asked.

"Anything that might suggest a break-in." John-Henry tipped his head toward one of the bookcases. "Is that camera functioning?"

That, Auggie decided, told him a little more about John-Henry, because the camera was tucked behind some books and a little bust of Shakespeare. Somebody might spot it if they were in the room long enough, and John-Henry had been over plenty of times as a friend, but it wasn't the kind of thing you'd notice unless you were looking for it. Had trained yourself to look for it.

"No," Theo answered for him. "We got them when Lana had a sitter here, and then we turned them off once she started going to school."

John-Henry nodded.

Auggie felt his face heat. "We should have them on, shouldn't we?"

"Auggie, I told you: you didn't do anything wrong."

"But that's the whole point of having cameras, to have them on. Like, on a schedule, even. For when we aren't home."

John-Henry nodded, but it could have meant anything. "Why don't we talk about your day? Theo, you were at school, right?"

Theo nodded, but his attention was fixed on his phone, where he was reviewing the clips recorded by the exterior cameras. "Got there, uh, about eight."

"Seven forty-five," Auggie said. "He's always early."

"And you?" John-Henry asked.

"After I dropped off Lana, I went to the gym. I picked up some groceries." Auggie tried to run through his day in his head. I stopped for a smoothie, he thought. I dicked around in a bookstore because I was avoiding work and I wanted to find something nice for Theo. Was that what he was supposed to say? He settled for "I ran some errands. When I got home, I used my tablet to catch up on some clients' feeds, just making sure everything posted, the content was what we'd agreed to—" He nodded toward the tablet on the sofa. "—so, I didn't notice the laptop was missing until I went into the office to do some editing."

Another nod. "What time did you go to the gym?"

"I don't know, maybe eight thirty? Nine? I wait until people have gone to work so it's not as crowded."

"Which gym?"

"The Y."

Another of those unreadable nods. A hysterical laugh rose in Auggie's throat, and he had to clamp down on it. It was so unreal, all of it, that it was making him think of job interviews, of all those opaque responses, never knowing if you'd said the right thing or if the other person was thinking you were a fucking moron. This was why I never got a real job, he wanted to say, and then he thought of John-Henry and Theo hearing him say that, the looks on their faces, and the wild laughter surged up inside him again.

"God damn it," Theo said.

Auggie glanced over. On the screen of Theo's phone, a figure dressed in black was fumbling with a window on the side of the house. It slid open easily, and the figure climbed inside. The camera continued recording for another fifteen seconds, but nothing happened, and then the clip ended. Theo played it again.

Someone came into our house, Auggie thought. Someone was inside our house. He tried to rally, tried to focus. The angle made it hard to tell how tall the person was—average height for a man, a slender build. But it could have been a woman. Auggie couldn't see enough to tell if the breadth of the shoulders, the shape of the hips suggested anything more. Someone came into our house, and they weren't even trying.

Theo's knuckles were white around his phone.

"I'm going to be right back," John-Henry said. "Theo, would you send me that video, please? And then I'd like you to see if you can find the recording of when this person left."

John-Henry stepped out onto the deck again, and the door clicked shut behind him.

Theo's chest rose and fell. He tapped the screen harder than he needed to.

"I don't remember," Auggie said. "I don't remember if I opened that window."

"Auggie."

"It might have been me. It was probably me."

Theo tapped the screen again.

"But I don't know the last time I opened that window."

"It doesn't matter," Theo said. "That's not important."

Auggie opened his mouth, but he had no idea what to say to that.

"Which window is that?"

The words were the first indication John-Henry had come back, and Auggie struggled to piece together a timeline: what had John-Henry heard, how much, what had they said.

"The office," Theo said. "Auggie's office."

"Our office," Auggie said. "We share it."

"Right," John-Henry said and stepped outside again.

Theo had found the video of the burglar leaving. They exited through the same window, tugged the window down, and walked away from the house. A black bag hung from one shoulder. After they left the camera's field of view, the recording ran for another fifteen seconds and stopped.

"They wore gloves," Theo said.

"Theo, if I left that window open, I'm sorry."

"In and out in three, four minutes."

"I only open it on nice days; we haven't had a nice day in forever."

"Break-in happened at...seven after nine."

"It's been too hot to open the window."

"So, they either knew your schedule, or they were watching, or they got lucky."

"Theo!"

Theo's eyes focused on him. "What?"

In the office, the window slid open, the sound carrying through the stillness.

"Theo," John-Henry called. "Auggie."

Theo still wore a question on his face.

Auggie pushed off the stool and headed down the hall.

John-Henry and Yarmark looked into the office through the window. John-Henry was finishing what sounded like a brief set of instructions about processing the window for evidence. Then he said, "Could you double check the office?"

"The laptop's not here," Auggie said.

"I know. But I'd like you to see if anything else is missing."

The air floating through the window smelled like fresh-cut grass and the new mulch Theo had laid down over the weekend; it was hot, and sweat prickled on Auggie's forehead, his cheeks, in the hollow of his throat. He shut the window, and John-Henry gave a thumbs-up and headed toward the front of the house.

"What's going on?" Theo asked from the doorway.

"We're supposed to see if anything's missing," Auggie said.

The weight of Theo's silence told Auggie that he'd been asking something else, but Auggie put his head down and started looking.

By the time John-Henry joined them, Auggie knew at least one more thing was missing.

"My external hard drive." He pointed to a spot behind the desk, where the mare's nest of cables from the docking station kept company with dust bunnies and what looked suspiciously like—but couldn't be, because Auggie was so careful—Doritos crumbs.

John-Henry squatted to examine the spot Auggie had indicated. He nodded and asked, "Do you know the make and model?"

"Yeah."

"We'll need you to provide that, plus the information for the laptop."

"What are we supposed to do now?" Theo asked, his voice hard and flat.

John-Henry held up a finger and excused himself. They saw him through the window, conferring with his two officers again. Nickels was writing something down. When he returned, he said, "Let's move into another room. Is there anything from the office you want to take with you? I'd like to close it off until they can process it."

Auggie looked at Theo. Theo shook his head.

In the living room, they sat again, but this time Theo and Auggie took the sofa, and John-Henry an armchair. Back straight, hands on knees. This wasn't the guy who watched the Cardinals with Theo and asked Auggie to toss him another Coke. Auggie could hear himself repeating the thought, could hear himself caught in it. But it was like watching something ghost along behind this John-Henry, an impression of movement that followed him when he turned his head. My life, Auggie thought. My old life. He wanted to giggle. The bad old days. And they're back, and that John-Henry is back, and that Theo will be back too.

"This person," Theo said, "they didn't show up on any of the other cameras."

John-Henry nodded.

"If you get a print, you can find them, right?"

"Maybe. A print would be helpful."

"It looked like they were wearing gloves."

John-Henry nodded again.

"This wasn't a random break-in," Auggie said. He hadn't put the thoughts together, hadn't strung them out into syllables like that, until right then. "Was it?"

"What do you mean?" Theo asked.

But John-Henry only gave Auggie a considering look.

"In the office—my watch is still on the desk, and there's a Bose speaker on the bookshelf. I bet if I check the top drawer, there'll still be loose cash—I toss it in there sometimes when I get home and go straight to work."

"I think there are reasons," John-Henry said, "to believe that someone was looking for something in particular."

"What?" Theo looked from Auggie to John-Henry. "His laptop? His hard drive? What do they want? I mean, no offense, Auggie, but it's not like you've got military secrets on there."

"Who would be interested in stealing those materials?" John-Henry asked.

A laugh escaped Auggie. "Nobody. You're talking about a competitor, is that it? Like, a rival or something? Nobody. I'm good at what I do, but I'm not doing anything that a bunch of other agencies aren't also doing. Nobody—and I'm not exaggerating—would come all the way out to the middle of nowhere to steal a few TikTok stitches and the outline for a hard seltzer campaign."

"Keep thinking about it," John-Henry said. "It might be someone local. A kid who cuts the grass—"

"I cut the grass," Theo said.

"—someone who cleans the house, maybe neighbor kids."

"You saw that video. That wasn't a neighbor kid. And a cleaning lady doesn't dress in all black, sneak in through a window, and steal Auggie's laptop and hard drive."

"I understand—"

"She would have taken cash, and she would have done it while she was here cleaning."

Auggie shifted on the sofa, his shorts whispering against the upholstery. He encircled Theo's wrist with one hand; the muscles and tendons there were iron.

"It would be helpful," John-Henry said in what Auggie was coming to remember as his chief-of-police voice, "if you could put together a list of anyone who's been in the house in the last two weeks. The last month would be even better. I know this is frustrating, and it's frightening, and it's upsetting because your home has been violated, and you don't feel safe." And then he was John-Henry talking again. "I know, Theo. Auggie. I really do. Ree and I have been through this, and it's awful. I'm sorry there's nothing I can do. I can have some uniforms sit outside tonight if you'd like, and I can ask them to cruise the street more frequently."

"We're a hundred yards back from the road," Theo said. "You can barely see the house for all the trees. At night?"

"Theo," Auggie said.

But John-Henry gave them an understanding smile. "Think about it. If there's something else you'd like me to do, I'll do it. Ree and I can split nights over here if you want."

Theo shook his head. His jaw was set, and behind the beard, his cheeks were flushed. He wasn't looking anyone in the eye.

Auggie finally realized he was going to have to answer. "No, you don't have to do that."

"If you change your mind, call. Any time." John-Henry's smile crooked slightly. "I'll even throw in Jem and Tean, no extra charge."

Auggie laughed, and it felt like they were all doing one of his skits, like somebody had written out each agonizing second of this. He could practically hear the directions: you're being supportive because that's who you are, the supportive boyfriend, but our real goal in this scene is to make everyone feel awkward as fuck.

Maybe John-Henry felt it too, because sympathy washed over his features, and he squeezed Auggie's shoulder as he stood.

"Wait," Auggie said. "What about Shaniyah?"

"What?"

"Shaniyah. Theo's student." Auggie glanced at Theo, who at least seemed to be paying attention to the conversation now, although his face was a blank mask. "She didn't show up for school today."

"Do you think she might have broken in here? She'd been in the house more than once; would she have known that window was unlocked?"

"No, she didn't—she's missing, right? And then someone breaks in and takes my laptop and hard drive, and I mean, I was working on a video with Shaniyah."

John-Henry was silent for several long beats. "From what I understood, her project had something to do with social media and teens."

"But you said she came to the station. You said she was asking about a boy who went missing. And now she's missing. And someone broke into our house and took my gear."

"And you believe it's all connected?"

The question was so careful, so noncommittal, that Auggie had to swallow a scream. "It doesn't seem like a big coincidence to you?"

Instead of answering, John-Henry asked, "Theo, what do you think?"

Theo shook his head.

Auggie opened his mouth, but before he could say anything, John-Henry said, "I talked to Shaniyah's aunt and uncle; they're her legal guardians. And they told me that she's not really missing, she's just lying low, trying to get attention." He held up a hand to forestall Auggie. "I'm not saying I believe them, but I'm saying right now, I've got limited options because when I pressed them, they said she's probably on a bus back home, some little town in Kansas, and she'll call when she's ready to come back. It puts me in a difficult position; the guardians aren't concerned, and all I can do is ask my officers to keep an eye open."

"But—" Auggie gestured at the office.

In the quiet that unfolded, the sounds of Nickels and Yarmark moving through the house filtered into the living room.

"It's a good thought, Auggie," John-Henry finally said. "I'll keep it in mind, and I'll ask around. If I turn anything up, I'll let you know."

Which, Auggie thought from behind the wall of stunned disappointment, was cop talk—very polite cop talk—for *you've got to be kidding me.*

"In the meantime," John-Henry said, "I'll have a couple of officers stationed here tonight. You'll see them walking around, so don't bash them on the head, please." He softened the words with a smile. "I'm going to recommend that you make sure the windows and doors are locked when you leave the house—"

Auggie couldn't hold back the wince, and he couldn't bring himself to look at Theo. Under his fingers, Theo's arm was still stiff, muscles clenched.

"—and that you turn on the alerts for the exterior cameras, as well as activating the interior cameras when you're asleep or away from home." Another smile. "I know it's an inconvenience. I know it's not fun. I know it's not fair, having to worry about things like that, because of someone else's bad behavior. But once those things are part of your routine, you'll hardly notice them."

Theo still hadn't said anything, and Auggie realized, again, he would be the one to speak. "Thank you." It sounded so awful, like they were still saying their lines, so he worked some moisture into his mouth and tried again. "Thanks, John-Henry."

He squeezed Auggie's shoulder again, and the three of them headed for the front of the house.

"I meant what I said." And now John-Henry's eyes darted to Theo, their gaze quick and assessing before returning to Auggie. "If you need anything, call me."

Auggie nodded.

"Yarmark and Nickels will let you know when they're finished. And they'll clean up when they're done." The last part was delivered in a louder voice.

"Roger that, Chief," came Yarmark's twentysomething enthusiasm.

Nickels didn't make a noise, but Auggie thought he detected a psychic sigh.

John-Henry gave them a real smile, a commiserating one, and then he was gone.

As soon as the door had closed behind him, Theo set the deadbolt. Then he started down the hallway and ducked into the bathroom. He checked the window latch and came back to the hall.

Auggie followed.

Theo skipped the office because Yarmark and Nickels were still busy, but he went through the master suite again, checking each window. He didn't look at Auggie.

"I'll do upstairs," Auggie said.

Theo shook his head. He didn't run into Auggie on his way out of the bedroom, but only because Auggie drew back, flattening himself against the wall to make room for him. To make room for his anger was more like it. For the massive rage that hung around Theo now.

He checked the slider in the living room.

"Do you want a beer?"

Another of those tight shakes of the head.

"I can go get Lana."

"No."

Auggie's eyes stung. "I'm sorry about the window. I'm really sorry. I didn't think—I mean, it's been weeks since I had it open. I could have sworn I locked it."

"But you didn't," Theo said, as he went for the stairs. "Did you?"

4

By lunch the next day, Theo was dragging. He'd snapped at two tenth-grade girls who wouldn't stop talking, and he'd published the wrong unit on Canvas, so the kids had all seen the quiz they were supposed to take at the end of the unit, and when a junior boy had muttered something about Theo's mood, Theo had sent him to Wieberdink's office without an explanation.

He ate at his desk, alone, in a grainy haze of exhaustion. He kept thinking he heard a high-pitched note, like maybe overnight he'd developed tinnitus. The red of the digital clock glared back at him, and he thought, It's only eleven-thirty.

After a bad evening, he'd spent a worse night on the sofa. It had been dramatic, which was a grown-up way of saying it had been childish. It had been petty. And, worse, it had been spiteful. All of it done to punish Auggie because that was, perhaps not so conveniently, the best way to punish himself. It had all been horrible, everything from the supreme dickishness of walking the house and checking the locks, making sure Auggie knew what he was doing, to the stilted carnival-house pretense of normalcy when Theo finally got home with Lana.

When it had finally been time for bed, sleep had seemed like a mercy, but, of course, it hadn't come. He'd lain there, on the beautiful mid-century sofa that Auggie had agonized over, smelling the fading scent of the leather, under a throw that managed somehow to leave him both too hot and too cold at the same time. And he had been forced to stay there, victim to his worst nightmares—an intruder coming into their home while they slept, a gun, no, a knife, Lana's screams, Auggie's bloodied body crumpled on the floor. That had been his night: exile to his own private hellscape, population one. And now, trying not to get mustard in his eyes as he rubbed them, Theo thought maybe he deserved worse.

It wasn't Auggie's fault; the rational part of him knew that. It wasn't anybody's fault, but it most certainly wasn't Auggie's. They both used the office. They both occasionally opened the window, although Auggie, still a California boy at heart, relished mild days. If Theo were being totally objective about it, he could admit that it was more likely Auggie had been the one to open the window. And it wouldn't have been out of character for Auggie to have left the window unlocked; he wasn't absent-minded or careless, but those things weren't a fixation for him, the way they could become for Theo.

Even last night, in the grip of terror and fury, a part of Theo had known it wasn't Auggie's fault. But the need to lash out, the need to externalize that pain rather than dying from it—which was what it felt like—had been too much. And now, eating a hastily made turkey sandwich (the turkey slimy because, of course, Auggie usually made him a sandwich, and Theo had grabbed the old stuff without realizing it), he hurt in all sorts of new ways.

When he and Auggie had been dating and then living together, when Theo had still been so...reactive, and when it seemed like every year sent them tumbling into a new disaster, he had understood, at some level, that Auggie wouldn't put up with it forever. Auggie was patient. And Auggie was kind. And, in a way that still left Theo occasionally breathless, a kind of gut-punch surprise that caught Theo when the realization came on him unawares, Auggie loved Theo. But the thought remained, still surfacing when the fear came, and Theo had to struggle to master it: Auggie wouldn't put up with it forever.

Before he could think about it anymore, he took out his phone and called.

Auggie's tone was guarded. "Hey."

"Hi. Oh shoot. Did I call at a bad time? Are you in a meeting?"

"No."

"Oh. Ok."

In the hall, a boy shouted, "Dank!" drawing the vowel out, and a chorus of laughs followed. Theo's skin felt tight, and sweat had started under his arms.

"Theo—"

"So, I'm really sorry about last night. And the afternoon. About the stunt with the windows—I mean, God, it's not your fault we left one unlocked. All of it. I was totally out of line, and I feel awful about it. I know this isn't an excuse, but I want to explain that I was in a really bad place." He took a deep breath. "And I know I'm responsible for my actions, and I'm responsible for what I say and do, even if I'm—scared is way too small a word, so can I say fucking terrified?"

Some of the restraint in Auggie's voice relaxed. "Not when you're in school, you can't."

"I'm at lunch. Swearing is fully allowed at lunch. You should hear the other teachers let rip." He took a breath. "Auggie, I'm so sorry."

"I know."

"I'm—I'm so mad at myself. It's just, things have been good, right? And then, last week, everything got turned on its head. And then—I mean, I kept thinking, 'What if they'd broken in while Auggie was home alone? What if they'd broken in while we were asleep? What if Lana had been there?' I couldn't turn it off." Sweat dampened the fabric of Theo's button-down, and he knuckled his forehead. "Not trying to make excuses, I swear. I shouldn't have done what I did, and I'm sorry."

"I know you're not trying to make excuses, Theo."

"What can I do to make it up to you?"

"You don't have to make anything up to me. You apologized; I forgive you. I know yesterday was…a lot. For all of us."

"I'm not happy with how I acted."

"Well, I'm not thrilled about it either, but you don't need to keep beating yourself up. You got grumpy, stomped around, and checked the locks. I think I can survive an episode of that. You should try yelling; Fer's got yelling down to an art."

For a moment, Theo had to squeeze his eyes shut. Because he heard it in Auggie's voice: the work he was doing, patching things over, making sure everything was ok again. And because he knew last night had been so much worse than stomping and grumbling. And because he could remember—to a degree, anyway—the way he had felt drunk and blind, his world contracted to the tunnel of his fear and anger, like someone else was behind the wheel and steering him headfirst toward disaster, and Theo couldn't stop it.

But that was wrong. That was false. He could stop it. He hadn't; that was what made it worse.

"Knock it off," Auggie said. "I can hear you beating yourself up all the way over here."

"Sorry," Theo said, surprised by the thickness of his voice.

"Why don't you leave early? Take a half day. You didn't sleep. I know because I didn't sleep; I heard you moving around all night."

"Oh God."

"You have very sticky skin apparently. Or something is seriously wrong with that sofa."

In spite of himself, Theo laughed.

"Come on," Auggie said. "I know it's the second day of school, but they'll understand."

"I'll stick it out. But I appreciate it."

The next question waited in the air between them, but Theo couldn't bring himself to ask it.

Maybe Auggie heard it, though, or a version of it because he said, "We've gotten through bad things before. We'll get through this."

It was an opening—all the opening Theo needed, anyway. "Someone was in our house, Auggie." His throat tightened. "In our fucking house."

Auggie didn't say anything. In the hallway, the boys were back, accompanied now by the sound of a ball bouncing against the linoleum.

When Auggie spoke, all he said was "I know."

"Do you really think it's connected to Shaniyah?"

Another of those fraught silences. "I don't know how you want me to answer that."

"I want you to tell me what you think."

"I don't know. I guess I think it's a lot of coincidences." And then the words spilled out of Auggie. "I mean, we found that class ring, and then Shaniyah shows up at John-Henry's office, wanting to ask about a missing boy, and then Shaniyah doesn't come to school, and nobody knows where she is, and somebody breaks into our house to steal my computer and hard drive." Auggie stopped, and when he spoke again, it was like he was struggling to put on the brakes. "That's what I'm thinking."

Theo tore a piece of crust from the forgotten sandwich. "You're saying this has something to do with the Cottonmouth Club?"

"I don't know if it does."

Theo let out a noise.

"All right," Auggie said. "I think it might."

"DeVoy is dead." To Theo, the man was only a name—someone Jem had gotten caught up with, someone who had led them to the snarled knot of violence the week before. "He was the one who had the stolen IDs, the drugs, those trafficked animals, right? They were in his van. And now he's dead."

"And he parked his van inside the Cottonmouth Club's garage," Auggie said. "And someone else at the club killed him."

Theo wiped his hands with the napkin. "Nothing says we're right, assuming the break-in at our house was connected to Shaniyah—connected to anything." Auggie's silence was something to fall into, and Theo heard himself saying, "We live on a secluded street. There are people—people who need money." Addicts, the clinical voice in his head observed. Junkies. Say it. You know all about that, and Auggie's not a fool. But Theo couldn't finish the sentence, and the silence swallowed him.

When Auggie spoke again, his words were surprisingly gentle. "We don't have to do anything. Emery and John-Henry are looking into it. And Tean and Jem. And North and Shaw, when they can take time off from being jackasses." Theo heard the attempt at a joke, but he couldn't respond to it. After a moment, Auggie said, "Nobody expects us to do anything."

Theo shuffled papers on his desk.

"Theo, we don't have to go."

"No. We don't have to."

The bell sounded, signaling the five-minute passing period for students to return to the classroom.

"Come home," Auggie said. "Get some sleep."

"If it's something specific to the high school," Theo said. His throat felt stiff, his tongue anesthetized and fat and heavy. "Something they might not notice. Or understand."

In his mind, he walked his nightmares again: Lana screaming, Auggie broken and bloodied.

"I called the Johnsons," Auggie blurted.

"What?"

"This morning. After you left. I called them, and I pretended to be a social worker from the school, and—and they told me not to call back, everything was fine, Shaniyah was fine, she was visiting family in Kansas. And they were lying, Theo. I know they were lying. I checked her TikTok; she hasn't posted anything since Saturday. Don't be mad."

Theo let out a sigh. It might have been relief. It was something, anyway—an externalization of what was happening inside, the stretching of old muscles, a part of him waking up. The pleasant discomfort of shaking off stiffness.

"Theo—"

"Will you go with me?"

Voices swelled in the hall; the babble moved toward the classroom.

"What—" Auggie began.

"Tonight?"

"To the club?"

"Just to look around. Get a feel. Emery and John-Henry can't go back; they're already too well known, and Jem and Tean have gotten made."

Gotten made. A part of him heard those words and knew they were back, the bad old days, and a part of Theo was awake again, a part with glittering eyes and a savage restlessness that he realized, now, had never fully gone to sleep. "North and Shaw are back in St. Louis. There's nobody else. I'm going to look around, that's all. But I'm not going to do it if you tell me not to, and while I'd like you to stay with Lana—"

"I'll go."

The worst part, Theo knew, was not knowing if he had done it on purpose, if that final combination of words had been him pulling the trigger, or if they had been the truth, or a slip. Or some combination of all three. Pulling the trigger, he thought. God, please not that.

"I'll find someone to stay with Lana," Auggie was saying. "Is that ok?"

"Perfect," Theo said. But that wasn't right either, so he said, "Thank you." He hesitated, and the classroom door opened, a noise and bodies spilled into the room. "I've got to go."

He wasn't sure what he heard in Auggie's silence. Maybe he heard an echo in the darkness. The bad old days.

5

"Augs," Orlando said as he flipped Lana upside down, "tell him to quit worrying."

Lana giggled helplessly as Orlando gave her a gentle shake.

"That's not good for her spine," Theo said.

Auggie put a hand on Theo's arm, and he stopped, but Orlando must have gotten the message because he set Lana upright again.

She immediately started tugging on his hand. "Come see my room, come see my room, 'Lando, come see my room."

Orlando had been Auggie's roommate, and then, after a weird—and failed—attempt at romance, his friend. He had heavy brows, dark scruff, and a lantern jaw. In college, he'd been ripped with muscle, and now, in his young adulthood, he'd thickened a little, in a way that looked comfortable and good on him. Part of that, Auggie knew, had to do with having a chef for one of your romantic partners. He was grinning at Lana now, pretending she was jerking him off his feet.

Theo rolled his eyes.

"Thank you for doing this," Auggie said. "I thought Drake was coming with you."

"Nah, somebody called in sick, so he's back at work, and Nat's out of town." Lana gave another vigorous yank, and Orlando laughed and stumbled with her. "You guys go. We're good here, right Lana?"

"We're good!" She broke out in giggles again as Orlando scooped her up and spun her.

"Orlando—" Theo started, but Auggie squeezed his arm, and he stopped again.

"Call us if you need anything," Auggie said and towed Theo out of the house.

The drive took them almost an hour and a half, and after a few weak attempts at conversation, they passed the time in silence. When they arrived,

GREGORY ASHE

Auggie slowed and did a loop of the half-full parking lot. Loose stone crunched under the Ford's tires. Theo's Focus was less conspicuous than the Audi, and, since they had removed the license plates, it had even less of a chance of leading people back to them. Auggie guided the car into a stall and parked.

At night, under a yellowing streetlight, the Cottonmouth Club could have been any other building on any other stretch of country road. It was low and rambling, a pole-frame structure with corrugated steel panels for walls and roof. The paint was a quiltwork of different colors, jobs begun and never completed, colors discontinued, everything faded in the sun. Where an illuminated sign should have hung over the street, the holder was empty, but the name was spelled out on the side of the building. Some of the letters were missing, but you could fill them in where, over the years, they'd discolored the galvanized steel.

Auggie had picked a Wrangler t-shirt and the jeans he wore when they visited Theo's family—over the years, as the Stratfords had become more familiar with him (if not more accepting), Auggie had learned that family time could consist of anything from extended family prayers to shoveling shit, literally, in the barn. It paid to dress accordingly. He'd added a trucker hat with the words FRESH MILK across the front, a gift from an influencer bro after Auggie had helped him salvage a tanking account. Theo's eyes had crinkled at that, and it had been the first time in two days that something had seemed normal.

In the passenger seat, Theo wore jeans and a raglan tee and boots. His beard and hair were the same as always, but something looked different about him. A hardness to his face, maybe. Maybe more. The way he carried himself. Auggie remembered it, kind of. There was a part of Theo's life he had only glimpsed, a place and a time behind a swinging door. This Theo was still Auggie's Theo. But also not. Not entirely.

"Do you want to wait in the car?" Theo asked. "Or do you want to go inside?"

Because Theo was a teacher, it was both a genuine question and, at the same time, a trap. Teachers knew how to do shady shit like that. Auggie took his time answering.

"I think it makes more sense for me to go inside." When Theo glanced at him, Auggie continued, "Two sets of eyes are better than one. We can split up. Cover each other."

Theo made a noise that could have meant a million different things.

"Also," Auggie said, the word a slow exhale, "I think we need to be realistic about, uh, who they might be interested in."

42

This time, Theo's gaze stayed on him.

"Jem told us he saw them forcing a drunk girl through a back door. And, I mean, it's a strip club. And if Shaniyah was right, a boy disappeared, and now Shaniyah is missing."

Theo's laugh didn't sound like a laugh, not if you knew him. "I'm too old?"

"That's not what I'm saying. I'm saying that's why both of us should go in. Separately. Because someone might approach me who wouldn't approach you. And vice versa. And that's why we need to keep an eye on each other."

"Targeting," Theo said.

Auggie looked at him.

"What you're trying to say is that we know who they might be targeting. And you're going to make yourself a target."

"Theo—"

"So we're both clear on what's happening."

"That's not—"

"Is that the plan?"

"I understand that there's a lot to be worried about here, and I'm going to be careful—"

"Is that our plan?" When Auggie didn't answer quickly enough, Theo said, "Ok," and got out of the car.

"God damn it," Auggie said. He clutched the keys, digging the teeth into his palm, and started counting to a hundred as Theo headed inside the club. For a moment, Theo was outlined by the streetlight, detail obliterated until he was only a shape. Then he was through the door and gone.

Auggie kept counting. And swearing.

When Auggie got out of the car, the night air was shaggy with summer, and he instantly wanted another shower. The smell of old smoke and fresh weed came to him, along with something else, the nose-tingling chemical burn that he was pretty sure was meth. In the cab of a truck a few stalls down, a lighter flared. The effect was like a photo flash: an impression of deep-set eyes, the dash of cheekbones, the glint of glass. And then darkness again, and the hint of smoke curling against the windows.

Inside, Auggie had to wait in a vestibule while a heavyset man in a black polo carded him. That part, Auggie hadn't counted on. Theo probably hadn't been carded. This guy would take one look at Theo, at that beard, and wave him through. Auggie would probably still be getting carded when he was forty. A few weeks before, at the Piggly Wiggly, a pimply teenager behind the register had called his manager to check Auggie's ID. Auggie could tell the little wiener had thought he'd busted Auggie. That's right, boner, Auggie thought. Trying to buy a six-pack of White Rascal to party with my boys.

The bouncer handed back Auggie's ID without a word, and Auggie twitched aside the curtain and entered the Cottonmouth Club proper. Jem had described it to them, and to be fair, his description had been accurate: the sludge of brownish light, the tables spotted with water rings, the private booths behind velvet curtains, the bar with bottles catching the light like cat eyes. The air was arctic compared to outside, stinging with the scent of cheap alcohol and even cheaper body sprays.

The stage, of course, was designed to draw and hold your attention. Two white girls—one skinny, and one heavier—were walking around a pole, doing identical versions of a stiff-hipped strut. They both had hair fried to white blond, and they both wore nothing but bikini bottoms with a few bills sticking out. An old white guy, his hair roostered up in back, had dropped his trousers in front of the stage. It looked like he was going for his dick, but a couple of no-necks in matching black polos grabbed him under the arms and dragged him toward an exit. At another table, a pouchy guy was huffing and shaking his head, obviously in some sort of argument with the other men. As Auggie watched, the man snapped something to his companions and pushed away from the table. Nobody seemed to care about that either.

Nobody looked at Auggie. Nobody dropped a glass in shock, or gasped, or screamed. He wasn't sure what he'd been expecting—not that, a part of his brain insisted, but, at the same time, maybe something. His heartbeat was hammering so hard in his ears that he couldn't make out the music, and he forced himself to take a deep breath. Somebody bumped into him from behind and swore, and Auggie stepped out of the way. A middle-aged, moon-faced man with a silver belt buckle stepped into the club, glaring at Auggie before he continued toward the bar.

Ok, Auggie thought with a giggle rising inside him. I'm doing great.

The crowd was mostly men, mostly white, and if appearances were to be trusted, mostly blue collar or working poor. Some of them—a kid with big hands and a cowlick, for example, with hay still clinging to his boots—probably worked on the farms in the area. It took Auggie a moment to spot Theo; he'd taken a seat at the bar, and he had a pint in front of him, head down: universal body language for fuck off and let me drink. He looked like any other guy in the joint; if Auggie hadn't known him, he never would have picked him out of the crowd.

Auggie, on the other hand, was painfully aware that he didn't blend in. He wasn't the only brown guy in the room, but the others looked like they were probably laborers—and, if Auggie had to guess, based on the realities of this part of the world, probably migrant workers. There was an older man, dark from the sun, in a faded Cali t-shirt that didn't hide how painfully thin he was. There were a couple of hard-thirties guys, maybe brothers, who had the same look of men who made their living outdoors. Maybe not brothers, Auggie decided after another moment of considering them, but with the kind of closed-off attachment of people who know they are outsiders and have banded together. A few others, sprinkled here and there throughout the white crowd. But not enough that Auggie wouldn't stand out. The Wrangler t-shirt. The jeans. The clothes looked like what they were: relatively new, and perfectly clean. Fuck, he wanted to say, what was I thinking?

But he was committed; if he left now, he'd be abandoning Theo. So, Auggie picked an empty table near the stage—and, more importantly, close to the hall that led to the bathroom and, hopefully, an emergency exit—and navigated through the room toward it.

He dropped into the seat, pulled down the brim of his trucker hat, and stared into the middle distance toward the stage. It took a few minutes, but his pulse slowed, and the ocean's rush of blood in his ears quieted. The music was Rihanna. "Birthday Cake." And when Auggie recognized it, he couldn't help the crazy grin that spread across his face. A waitress swooped in, with washed-out eyes and chipmunk cheeks, and Auggie ordered a shot of Jose Cuervo and a Bud Lite. She smiled automatically, not even really seeing him, and drifted away again. Look at me, Auggie thought, blending in.

Yeasty breath blew across his ear, and a voice said, "You're not supposed to be here."

Auggie jerked upright in his seat. He twisted, but at the same time, a man came around the table into his field of view. Rockabilly hair, an orange spray-on tan, a golden cross the size of a paperback swinging from his neck, the guy could have been anywhere from twenty-five to forty-five. His arms and legs were thin, but under his white polo, he had a potbelly. The polo had a little lizard, and the little lizard had a little grin, and Auggie thought it looked like the grin on this guy's face.

"Let me guess," he said. "You know you're not supposed to be here."

Auggie didn't look over at the bar, but he wanted to. He kept his gaze on the man in front of him. For a lot of his life, Auggie had thrived on this, excelled at it. Knowing what people wanted from him. Knowing how to give it to them. That part of him was still there, still ready to come forward. Some days, he had to fight to keep it buried. Like a mask. Or, as he had often thought of it, a cutout figure, something to stand in his place. Cardboard Auggie.

He went for goofy. "Am I that obvious?"

"Kid," the guy said and laughed.

Kid, Auggie thought. I can play kid.

The man dropped into a seat too heavily, catching himself with a hand on the table at the last moment. In the other hand, he was carrying an empty glass, and the smell of hops and malt rolled over Auggie. Underneath the spray-on, his face looked flush, and his eyes struggled to track Auggie, as though Auggie were deking and juking instead of planted in a straight-back.

"Kid," he said again through that yeasty cloud. "You look like that joke about the nun."

Kid, Auggie thought. Eyes a little wide. Brow furrowed. Only a trace. Because he was still scared. But curious, too. God, he was curious.

"The bike's got no seat," the man said. "And she says, 'I was a virgin when I started.'"

He burst into laughter. The cross slid over his polo, light winking along the gold. The lizard with his little smile stared back at Auggie, so Auggie laughed too. A little. He was confused. He tried to paint that into the sound. He was just so confused.

"Gid," the man said and stuck out his hand. His skin was tacky with drying beer.

"Gus."

"Gus. I like that." Gid sat back—a little too far, the chair wobbling before he caught himself on the table again. He hitched a thumb behind him, where someone had turned a black light on the stage. A different woman was dancing, and handprints glowed ultraviolet on her skin next to the white string thong she was wearing. When she bent over to say something to a hawk-nosed man, the inside of her mouth lit up like a fungal colony. Gid was still looking at Auggie, still hitching his thumb. "You ever seen titties before, Gus?"

Auggie didn't have to answer that because Gid was laughing so hard about his own joke.

"Lemme guess." Gid leaned in. "You never been anywhere like this before?"

Auggie shook his head.

"Didn't think so. Lemme break it down for you."

He smiled, then—white, even capped teeth that must have cost a fortune—and Auggie caught the vibe. He'd grown up with big brothers, had seen them (especially Fer) go through that phase where they had to explain everything to you, even if you already knew it. Maybe especially if you already knew it. He'd dealt with agents who wanted you to think they were your buddy, at least until they didn't need you anymore. He'd heard, more times than he wanted, an aging bro in an expensive suit explain Auggie's career to him—usually, right before Auggie fired him. More recently, he'd had to deal with corporate types, the ones who talked to Auggie like he'd been born with his head on backward. All of which meant Auggie had a lot of practice at nodding and looking interested.

"Let's see, let's see." Gid sucked his teeth. "That's Martha over there at the bar. We call her Big Martha."

"She's not that big."

That earned Auggie an indulgent chuckle. "She's got a daughter named Martha too. Don't mess with Martha or any of the other women working here, the ones who aren't dancing, I mean. They don't appreciate it, and the rest of us look out for them." He touched the heavy cross around his neck without seeming to think about it. "Martha, you are worried about many things." He said it like it meant something, and then he laughed.

Auggie smiled and drank some beer. His phone buzzed, and he ignored it. When he shifted slightly in his seat, Theo came into view, shoulders tight as he hunched over his phone.

"Now, this place has some pretty rough customers," Gid said. "So, you want to watch your manners while you're here. You don't bother anybody, and nobody'll bother you. You cause a fuss, though, well…" He let it trail off. "You don't have anything to worry about, though, because you've got me, and I'm looking out for you."

"Yeah, man," Auggie said with an internal eye roll. "Thanks."

"Some of these assholes, pardon my French, they don't know who they're talking to sometimes. They don't know one fucking thing they're saying, pardon my French."

And that was it, Auggie understood. That was the key that unlocked this whole bizarre encounter. The disagreement that Auggie had witnessed, Gid pushing back from the table in a huff, his stooped posture and scurrying movements—he'd gotten run off, tail between his legs. And then he'd seen Auggie, spotted his chance to be the big man again, and locked on to him. Which was great and useful and all that until it wasn't.

Glass shattered, and laughter erupted over the music. On the far side of the room, a sharp-jawed woman looked down on a man. He was on his knees, shaking his head, one hand on an empty chair like he was still thinking about getting back up. Blood and beer made a web on the side of his face; Auggie knew it was beer because the brown glass of the bottle littered the floor. The man seemed to consider the possibility of standing for another moment, and then he dropped to the floor and didn't move.

More laughter erupted from the woman and a circle of cronies. Auggie had lived in Wahredua long enough to know the type: a man with a red and black swastika tattoo on his arm; a man in a biker's cut, the denim covered in patches Auggie couldn't read from a distance; a man with a shamrock on his neck—prison ink, Auggie guessed.

The woman, though, held his attention. Auggie had a good sense of people, and right then, he could tell she owned that little knot of bodies. She wore her blond bob gelled, and her Carhartt shirt and jeans were clean but well worn. Same for the boots—silver tooling, but plenty of miles on them. She didn't do any dirty work, not with those boots, but she dressed like she might. That was interesting.

"You don't want her to catch you staring," Gid said, the moistness of his breath on Auggie's cheek. "Ingra would cut you open before she let you near her, and then she'd let her pack of dogs fuck you to death. How's that sound for a night on the town?"

Auggie dropped his eyes and shook his head. But he sensed the opening. Toying with his glass, he risked a look at Gid before letting Gid catch him and pulling his eyes away. "Is, um, there anybody else I should watch out for?"

Gid snorted. "Me, dumbass. I'm the dangerous one here."

Auggie risked another look, this time with a half-smile. But Gid was trying to look dangerous, so Auggie let the smile drop off his face. He wondered if a big, dramatic gulp would be too much—he figured for Gid, probably not. He gulped.

Satisfaction glimmered in Gid's eyes. He twisted in his seat, waving his arm to catch one of the waitresses; after one of them nodded at him, he dropped back down and looked at Auggie. "Anybody you should watch out for? Kid, what are you, eighteen? Nineteen?" Auggie opened his mouth to protest, but Gid spoke over him. "Look, I don't care how you got in here. If you're cool, everybody else will be cool too."

Auggie nodded.

"And if you're smart, you can meet some important people. People who might be able to help you."

"Like you."

Gid burst out laughing. "Fuck yeah, like me. Or like Eric, even though he's being a jackass tonight." He nodded toward the table where Auggie had witnessed the earlier disagreement. One of the men was dark-haired with zaddy vibes. He was talking to a blond guy who looked like a walking advertisement for CrossFit. Whatever disagreement had happened earlier, the two men seemed past it. "Eric's the kind of friend you want even if he is an ungrateful turd sometimes. And Jace—well, you want to know about dangerous? Trust me, you don't want to get on Jace's bad side."

Eric, Auggie thought. Jace. Ingra. Gid. He had a good eye for faces, and he studied the men for another moment. As though sensing the attention, the blond man—Jace, Auggie guessed—raised his head and glanced over. His eyes flicked past Auggie to Gid, and his expression darkened before he lowered his head and said something to the other man—Eric.

"What do you think, Gus?" Gid laughed again. "Glad you met your buddy Gid?"

Auggie nodded.

"Let's get you a girl, how about that? You seen any of them you like?" Gid fumbled a fat leather wallet out of his pocket and tossed it on the table. "You ever had a lap dance? God, I bet you're just going to squirt the first time you get a cooze rubbing on you. What about Celeste, you like her?"

The woman with the glow-in-the-dark mouth smiled vacantly down at the stage as she did another twirl.

"I heard—" Auggie stopped. He wet his lips, and then, like he was bracing himself, dashed off some more of the beer. "I heard you can do other stuff here. I heard they've got other stuff you can do." He let a beat pass and blurted, "With a girl."

The music changed. "Cherry Pie." A drunken whoop went up from a big, bearded man near the stage. Auggie wondered if they'd plucked the playlist from the internet, if that's how they did this. There couldn't be somebody DJing this shit.

Gid's bleary gaze sharpened. "What kind of thing?"

Auggie didn't have to feign nervousness. He squirmed in his seat. His phone buzzed again, and he wrapped his hands around the half-empty glass of beer, flexed his fingers, wrapped them tight once more. "I don't know." He looked down at the table. "That's just what somebody said." He weighed the risk and then said, "My friend, Shaniyah told me that."

But if Gid recognized the name, it didn't show on his face. "Oh yeah? What'd they say?"

Auggie shook his head.

"Go on," Gid said.

"That if you want to…do something," Auggie said. "Something different." He raised his eyes and went for challenging—only a heartbeat, but direct. "There are girls other places, you know. I didn't have to come here if I just wanted a girl."

Gid stared for another moment. Then he sagged back, laughing. "You want to cork her from behind or something? Christ, kid, you've got no idea the kind of shit you can do. You got no idea."

Auggie looked down again, but he gave a stubborn shake of his head. He could feel the ice buckling beneath his feet; one wrong step, and the whole thing would fall apart.

"Oh yeah?" Gid chuckled. "You know what you want, huh? You get on the internet, and you watch a little porn, and you know what puts the ram in your rod. Kid, you don't know shit. Come back in ten years. Come back when you've made it past second base, Christ's sake." It looked like Gid might have stopped there, but his face was flushed, his eyes beer bright, and that energy Auggie had sensed, that need to soothe his own ego, spurred him on. "You know the right people, have the cash—wild doesn't even begin to describe it. Last weekend, we had the back room, this pretty little thing, you wouldn't believe the sounds—" He cut off, staring at Auggie, and the color drained from his face. Music pounded. A woman was screaming to make herself heard, saying something about chicken wings. But through the din, a silence ballooned between Auggie and Gid. Weaving slightly, Gid pushed himself back from the table and mumbled, "Not really your scene, kid."

Auggie nodded. He tried to think nothing. He imagined emptiness and tried to let it fill his face.

"Gotta hit the head." Gid worked a few bills out from his wallet, dropped them on the table, and gave Auggie another wide-eyed look. Then he lurched away from the table.

Auggie counted to five in his head. Then he turned, making the movement as casual as he could. Down the hallway that led to the restrooms, Gid was talking to a brown-skinned man who might have been Auggie's height. Young, Auggie thought. But old eyes. A ridge of scar tissue marked his neck. Gid was saying something in a low voice, shoulders hunched, wiping his hands on his pants.

Auggie slid out of the chair and started toward the door.

Out of the corner of his eye, he saw Theo raise his head and cast a glance over at him. Auggie jerked a nod, and Theo dropped off his stool. When Auggie glanced back, the short man with the scar stood at the mouth of the hallway, watching Auggie. Their eyes met. Then the man started after him.

Auggie walked faster. Not quite a run, not yet, but he kept his head down and moved. He passed through the curtained vestibule, nodding at the bouncer as he went. A wall of damp Midwestern heat met him, with the smell of trampled clover and puke and hot engines. He still wasn't running, but the gravel sounded like slush under his footsteps. He couldn't leave Theo. Maybe circle around, maybe the back entrance. The sound of the gravel was so loud Auggie couldn't hear anything else. He worked his phone out of his pocket, saw the series of unread messages from Theo, tapped one to open the thread. Tried to tap. His hands were shaking, and he missed.

A hand caught his arm.

Auggie spun around, bringing up a fist.

"It's me!" Theo released him. "Auggie, what—"

Auggie pushed Theo aside to get a look back at the club. For a moment, in the darkness, he couldn't see anything. And then he saw the outline: someone standing in a pocket of shadow, watching them.

"Get in the car."

Theo nodded, already moving, one hand taking Auggie's arm again as he hurried them toward the Ford. Auggie dragged the keys out of his pocket.

No one came after them. No one shouted. No one fired shots into the air like this was *The Dukes of Hazzard* (which Auggie had been forced to watch, more than once, on a visit to Ma and Pa Stratford).

But when Auggie checked the rearview mirror on their way out of the lot, that silhouette was still there: a curve of red, a slash of yellow, three dimensions given shape by the bar's weak light. Someone stood there and watched them leave.

6

When the bell rang at the end of the day, the only way to stay alive—the only guaranteed way—was to stand near the wall. If you survived Pamplona, if bulls weren't enough, try Wahredua High, Theo thought. Kids flooded the hall, and Theo clutched the stack of copies to his chest and braced himself against a locker. Lacrosse boys stretched across the hall to whack each other with their sticks. A girl with braces held her backpack like a shield. A big kid with floppy hair in a *Simpsons* t-shirt pumped his arms in finest power-walking fashion. And then, ten seconds later, the halls were empty again.

"Mother of Christ." Auggie's voice floated down the hall a moment before he came around the corner. Some of his hair was sticking up in back. "A little pixie cheerleader got her shoulder under my ribcage."

Theo grinned as he smoothed down Auggie's hair.

"Swear to God." Auggie looked back the way he'd come. "She did it on purpose."

"Kids these days."

"Fucking savages."

Theo arched an eyebrow.

"Oops," Auggie said. "Are teachers still allowed to spank naughty students?"

"It's called corporal punishment, and yes, actually, they are in Missouri. As long as the parents allow it."

"Are you kidding me?"

"Do you think we could get Fer to sign off on it?"

"Can you wait until next time we see him in person? I kind of like the idea of watching him have a stroke when you ask him for permission to discipline me."

Theo decided that was a good time to return to the classroom. He also decided (with what Auggie probably would have called the wisdom of age) to ignore Auggie's laughter.

It had been a long day after another sleepless night; Auggie had been sure that no one had followed them, and he had insisted that, with the license plates removed, no one would be able to identify the Focus. And Theo had agreed—at least, the rational part of his brain had agreed. He had seen no sign they were being followed. He had questioned Auggie, at length, about his conversation with the man who called himself Gid. The names Auggie reported meant nothing to Theo, but he recognized the descriptions of the men and woman from the club. Nothing pointed to immediate danger. Nothing suggested a clear threat. Even Theo and Auggie's quick exit from the club had been based on nothing more than intuition—Auggie's sense that Gid had realized his mistake in letting too much slip, and the fact that Gid had spoken to another man who had followed them out of the club.

By daylight, it didn't seem like much. They had tried to get some information. They had learned—well, maybe something. Maybe nothing. The fact that a place called the Cottonmouth Club had a back room wasn't really a surprise. The most interesting thing was that Gid had panicked after his comment about the previous weekend, but even that might not have meant anything.

But.

Theo had spent the night jerking awake at every sound. In the small hours, he had removed Ian's old service weapon from the safe, taking care not to wake Auggie, and he had waited for dawn with the gun on the nightstand next to him. In the early morning shadows, Theo kept seeing the man with the scar, the one who had followed them out of the club. Now, with the afternoon dragging on him, he could believe it might have been nothing—maybe the guy had picked that time for a smoke.

Sure, said a voice inside Theo's head. Right after Gid pointed out Auggie.

He leaned away from that thought; he didn't trust his judgment. You're tired, he told himself. You're worked up. You're spiraling, and when you spiral, you blow things out of proportion. He tried to do what he'd worked on in therapy: wait, hold on, breathe through the discomfort—which felt less like discomfort and more like the first fever of panic.

It didn't help that the first week of school was hell, relatively speaking—a combination of students adjusting to new routines, new sleep schedules, and new people (specifically, Theo), while Theo was also trying to learn names, reconfigure seating charts on the fly (after today, Brock and Johnny, who had spent all of third period trying to outdo each other with fidget spinners, would no longer be sitting next to each other), and remember why he had thought it would be a good idea to start the semester with *Much Ado about Nothing*.

"Oh my God," Auggie said, picking up one of the packets from Theo's desk. "Don't tell me you're going to show them that movie with the butts."

"It's twenty seconds at the beginning, Auggie."

"It's a lot of butts."

"Thirty seconds, tops."

"White butts."

An important part of a relationship—maybe the most important part of a relationship, Theo considered—was the selective ability to ignore your partner.

"So," Auggie said, toying with a staple, "hi."

Theo paused in the middle of sorting the sixth-period exit tickets. He glanced up.

Auggie had big, brown, doe eyes. When he wanted to.

Sighing, Theo came around the desk. He kissed his boyfriend. "So. Hi."

"I came to check on you."

"I thought there was something about a spanking."

A grin flashed and burned itself out. "You didn't sleep last night."

"I slept all right."

Auggie rolled his eyes. "You have to be quieter next time you get out your gun, then."

Theo didn't say anything to that.

"Maybe don't swear so much when you're checking the load."

"God damn it."

"Like that."

Theo rubbed his eyes. The school's silence was unnatural after a long day of shouting and talking and backpacks banging into chairs. He thought he could smell fresh toner on his hands.

"Do you really think we're in danger?" Auggie asked.

"I don't know. I don't...trust my judgment right now."

Auggie was silent.

When Theo lowered his hands, Auggie was studying him. "I'm not having a nervous breakdown," Theo said. "If that's what you're wondering."

"I think if you were going to have one, it would have happened while I was still in college."

That startled a laugh out of Theo, and Auggie grinned.

"If you say we weren't followed," Theo said, "if you say nobody can identify us, I believe you. But I'm worried there's something we missed. If Gid recognized Shaniyah's name, if he thought he told you too much, if he went to tell that other man about you, and that's why it looked like he was following us—" He cut off, unable to finish the sentence.

"Then they could have gotten stills of us from the security cameras," Auggie said. "They could be showing them around, asking about us. It wouldn't be too hard to find us. We don't exactly blend in."

"I blend in fine, thanks."

"Theo!"

"It's not your fault, babe. You're too good-looking."

Auggie rolled his eyes, but he was blushing—still, after all these years.

"I'm not sure how many other people were wearing a hundred-and-eighty-dollar sneakers in the Cottonmouth Club last night, though."

Auggie opened his mouth.

"Something to remember."

"Rude!"

"The next time you go to Walmart to buy a Wranglers tee to impress my dad."

"Double rude! How dare you?"

Theo couldn't help his smile, but the easiness of the moment couldn't last. "I don't know what to do now, Auggie. The Cottonmouth Club is a dead end; even if there is a connection to the missing kids, we can't go back there, not after the possibility that we've been made."

Auggie nodded. "I really don't think he recognized Shaniyah's name. I know that doesn't mean anything—there's a dozen other ways Shaniyah could have gotten involved with someone at the club, someone besides Gid, and he wouldn't have known about it. But I agree: if we had a chance at the Cottonmouth Club last night, I blew it."

"You didn't blow it. You did what we went there to do, and you got some information."

"Yeah, some random names that aren't connected to Shaniyah in any way." When Theo glanced at him, Auggie shrugged. "I had free time today. I did some googling."

"God, you're amazing."

Auggie's shoulders relaxed, and his face opened. It wasn't youth, although Auggie was still young. It was...vitality. It was the way dogwood buds opened even though the winds could still be freezing, white curls of life and hope the world was ready to shred.

It was also kind of fun, Theo had to admit, now that he knew how to do it. Fun and, well, hot.

"Tell me," Theo said.

"The woman, Ingra, she was up for possession a couple of times, and she did a year in prison for assault with a deadly weapon—a knife. There's a stub of an article about it from a Joplin newspaper that folded a few years ago, but they're still on the Wayback Machine." To Theo's unasked question, he said, "Internet Archive. Anyway, that was ten or fifteen years ago, but she doesn't look like she's softened."

"Kind of the opposite. You got all that from her first name?"

"It's not a common name. If I were guessing, based on the area and those details, I'd say the Ozark Volunteers."

Theo shrugged. "Sounds about right. Could be something else—a motorcycle club, maybe."

"Eric is too common a name, especially if you're a handsome white guy with a square chin, so I didn't get anywhere, and nothing with Jace either. But here's the thing: when I tried different combinations with Shaniyah's name, nothing came up."

"All right. So, we keep the Cottonmouth Club in our back pocket. Maybe there's a connection, maybe not—if there is, we're not going to find it right now." Theo scratched his beard. "I guess we could go talk to Shaniyah's aunt and uncle. It's strange to me, the way they came in hot about Shaniyah not coming to school yesterday, and then they immediately clammed up."

"The word is suspicious."

"Maybe. You see a lot of strange things with parents and guardians. But you're right, they might be hiding something."

"Maybe they know something about the club, some kind of a connection we don't know about."

Theo nodded.

"The only problem," Auggie said, "is I already tried talking to them once, remember? And the aunt ripped my head off."

"I'm Shaniyah's teacher—"

"And I was pretending to be a social worker from the school."

"Right. I meant to talk to you about that."

In a rush, Auggie said, "That's not really the point. The point is, being from the school didn't help. If anything, it shut them down even faster."

"So, what?"

Auggie lifted his head, and a moment later, Theo heard the voices moving down the hall toward them. "Don't be mad—" Auggie said.

"Interesting choice of words while I'm still thinking about that social worker thing."

"—but I got us some backup."

Colt stuck his head through the door. "Um, hi? Dr. Stratford? Mr. Lopez?"

"Please call me Auggie. For the millionth time, Colt. I'm literally begging you."

"Mr. Hazard says he can't," Ashley said. "It's not because you're not cool, Mr. Lopez."

"Why don't you call me Auggie?"

"Oh no, Mr. Lopez. My parents would shi—um, crap a brick if they heard me do that."

"Your parents aren't here right now—" Auggie began.

"Consider how that sounds when you're addressing two minors," Theo said.

Colt snickered.

"Your dad has been a bad influence on him," Auggie said. "He never used to say stuff like that."

"Hello, Colt," Theo said. "Hello, Ashley. Dare I ask what you're doing here?"

"He'd be mean, sure. Like one time, we had this epic fight because I washed my face."

"You washed your face. I'd just cleaned the bathroom, and fifteen seconds later, it looked like you went in there with a firehose."

"But he never sniped like that."

"You let the soap dry on the mirror."

"You like projects! You're always looking for things to do around the house!"

The whole thing was cracking Colt and Ashley up, of course; the two numskulls were falling over each other laughing. Auggie was grinning too and doing a poor job of trying to hide it, and Theo had to admit that even he felt better. Well, also an echo of outrage at how Auggie had treated that mirror, but better. Like that tunnel vision had opened up some. Like he could think again.

"They don't have a lot of time," Auggie told Theo.

"Oh shi—shoot," Ashley said and checked his phone.

"Football," Colt said with that particular mixture of brashness and insecurity that so many teenage boys operated under—saying *football* like it was no big deal, and, at the same time, the biggest deal in the world.

"You guys made the team," Theo said with a weary smile. "That's great. Look, we don't want to keep you, but I'm not sure—"

"We're trying to track down Shaniyah Johnson," Auggie said.

Colt and Ashley traded looks.

"Do you know her?" Auggie asked.

"Well, yeah," Colt said.

Ashley nodded.

"Do you know where she is?"

Colt shook his head and looked at Ashley. Ashley said, "No, Mr. Lopez."

"How well do you know her?" Theo asked.

"Just, you know," Ashley said and shrugged.

"We know who she is," Colt said.

It was hard not to, of course—that was what neither boy said. In a town like Wahredua, in a school system this size, it was hard not to know everybody, especially by the time they got to high school.

"She moved here last year," Ashley added.

Colt nodded. "I don't think she has, um, made many friends."

"Is there anybody she's close to?" Auggie asked.

"Maybe."

"She had a boyfriend," Ashley said.

"They weren't dating," Colt said.

"Bruh, yeah they were."

"No, they weren't. They were hanging out, that's it."

"Lorcan told me they were dating."

"Lorcan?" Theo asked. "Lorcan Matthews?"

Colt nodded.

"Do you know him?" Ashley asked.

"Duh," Colt said. "He just said his name, didn't he?"

"That doesn't mean he knows him."

"I know who he is," Theo said with a glance at Auggie. "He and Shaniyah are friends?"

The boys agreed on this point.

"He's in that group that's, like, obsessed with Pops." Colt rucked up his backpack, annoyance mingling with pride in his face. "You know who I'm talking about?"

Theo did—and, to judge by the grin on Auggie's face, Auggie hadn't forgotten either.

"I could message them if you want," Colt said reluctantly.

"That would be great. Thank you."

Colt shrugged and looked away, but he was smiling.

"Do you know if anything had changed in Shaniyah's life?" Theo asked. "She's a good student, but I know that's not always the full picture."

The boys traded a look and shook their heads.

"How are things at home for Shaniyah?"

"I don't know, Mr. Lopez," Colt said with another shrug.

But Ashley said, "Danna told me her aunt is pretty mean to her. The uncle is all right, but the aunt hates her for some reason."

"Danna didn't know why?"

Ashley shook his head.

"Did you hear anything about a new person in her life? Maybe a new partner or a friend?"

"We don't, like, talk to her."

"We see her at parties," Ashley said. When Colt shot him a look, though, Ashley shrank down, face reddening. "Um," Ashley added. "Like, good parties. Like good kids. Like—"

"Bruh," Colt said.

Ashley shut his mouth.

Theo decided now was time for one of his favorite teaching tactics: wait.

Colt broke after fifteen seconds. "She, um, can get a little wild. With drinking and stuff. Not that we do. Drink, I mean. Or anything."

Ashley was nodding enthusiastically.

Auggie was looking like he was trying not to burst out laughing.

"She doesn't always seem happy." Colt hiked his backpack up again. "But, I mean, we really don't know her."

Ashley checked his phone again.

"Do you need to go?" Auggie asked.

"Um, no," Colt said, but he glanced at Ashley. "It's ok."

"They need to go," Theo said. "Thank you, guys, for taking time to talk to us. If your coach is mad that you're late, tell him I kept you after. He can chew me out instead of you."

Relief blossomed in Ashley's face. "Thanks, Mr. Stratford."

"It's Dr. Stratford, dumbass," Colt said.

"I know! I just said mister by accident."

"You should know he's a doctor; you had his class all year."

"Bruh, I said I know!"

They made their way to the door, which now involved a lot of shoving and laughing, but then Ashley stopped, warding off Colt's hand, and looked back.

"If it's, like, about Leon—" Ashley broke off, and he didn't even seem to notice when Colt moved closer, his shoulder bumping Ashley's. "Do you think somebody's killing kids at school?"

"What do you mean?" Theo asked.

At the same moment, Auggie asked, "Who's Leon?"

"Leon Purdue," Ashley said. When Theo and Auggie didn't react, he looked at Colt.

Colt said, "The boy who disappeared."

Auggie glanced at Theo, and Theo shook his head.

"I thought—" Colt stopped, eyebrows knitting together. "Pops said you guys were working together on a video or something."

"Yeah," Auggie said slowly.

"That's what she's been doing," Ashley said. "Everybody knows about it. She never stops talking about Leon. She's doing all these interviews, recording everything."

"What do you mean, he disappeared?" Theo asked. The name was vaguely familiar, although he didn't think he'd had Leon in any classes.

"He's gone," Colt said.

"A trucker took him," Ashley said.

"Bruh, we don't know that."

"That's what Damir said."

"Yeah, but that's like a rumor. You have to have evidence."

"It might not have been a trucker," Ashley informed Theo and Auggie, like this was breaking news. "Noelle Sutton told me he moved to LA to do porn." Then, correcting himself so fast the words were a blur: "To become an actor."

Colt put a hand over his eyes.

Theo fought the urge to check Ashley's grade from the previous school year. He was having a hard time believing he'd given him an A. Maybe it was a deficiency in how the gradebook categories were weighted. Maybe it was something simpler; maybe the math had been wrong.

"Do you know Leon?" Auggie asked.

The boys shook their heads.

"He's a year older," Colt said.

"And super weird," Ashley put in. When Colt elbowed him, he said, "What? He is."

"I don't think someone is targeting high school students," Theo said. "But if that changes, we'll talk to Chief Somerset."

The set of Ashley's shoulders softened, and he smiled. "Cool. Thanks, Dr. Stratford."

Colt echoed his thanks, and a moment later, the boys' voices were fading down the hall.

"I can't believe you called him Mr. Stratford," Colt was saying.

"Bruh!"

"Seriously, you're so dumb sometimes."

"Like two weeks ago you said, 'Yes, sir,' to Ms. Wesley."

"Shut up! You were distracting me!"

"Der, yes, sir!"

"I'm going to tell your dad you're being mean to me."

For some reason, that broke both of them up laughing again, and after another moment, Theo couldn't hear them anymore.

"America's future," Auggie said with a grin.

"We don't exactly come off looking much better." Theo shook his head. "I can't believe we didn't think to ask them about Shaniyah's investigation."

"In our defense, they're not exactly star witnesses. But yeah, let's not tell Emery and the others about that."

"God no." Theo sat at his desk. "Does that line up with your view of Shaniyah?"

"What? Oh. I mean, I guess. Or, I should say, it's not out of line. I mean, you know what Shaniyah was like—polite, happy, enthusiastic. I guess at some level, I knew that was the face she put on for adults, but I didn't really think about it. Does it surprise me she got a little wild at parties?" Auggie was silent, considering his own question. "Actually...no. It doesn't. I knew kids like that in high school. And in college, as a matter of fact. They're really high-achieving, super smart, all of that, and the other stuff is a way to blow off some steam, let their hair down, that kind of thing."

Theo nodded. "That's what I was thinking too."

"Did you know she didn't have friends?"

He hesitated before answering. "It's hard to say. She was quiet in class, but like you said, she was very social with adults. Last year, I saw her for one hour every day—it's easy to assume that she just didn't click with the people around her. I guess I didn't really think about what her life was like outside the classroom."

"Or at home," Auggie said.

Theo didn't say anything to that. He hooked the phone from its base, keyed in a number, and held the receiver to his ear.

Auggie cocked an eyebrow.

"I don't want to hear about this later," Theo said. "So, either you promise, or you leave the room."

"Oh my God."

"I'm serious, Auggie. This is never to be mentioned again."

"Ok, now I'm curious."

"Promise—"

On the other end of the call, a woman's voice said, "Registrar."

"Hey, Denise." Theo couldn't help it; his voice slid up a little, warmed, softened. "How's it going?"

"Oh my God, Theo. The first week, am I right?" She laughed. "We've just got to make it to Friday."

Auggie strolled over to the phone. Theo shook his head, but Auggie gave him wide-eyed innocence and, like a little shit, reached over and punched the button for speakerphone.

"Please tell me you're coming out with the Mamas," Denise said—now on speakerphone. "You've got to. We're not taking no for an answer."

"Denise, one sec," Theo tried.

"Hey Denise," Auggie said. "Auggie here—Theo's partner."

"Oh my God, Auggie!!!!" Theo could practically see extra exclamation points in the air.

"I'm just going to take this off speakerphone," Theo said.

But Auggie grabbed his hand before he could reach the button. "You've got to tell me who the Mamas are."

"The Margarita Mommies! We go to Charo's every Friday—you've got to come, Auggie, they've got the best margarita! They call it Mommy's Little Helper, and oh my God, Theo can drink two of them!"

Theo looked into the eyes of the man he loved most in the world and mouthed, *No.*

Auggie, of course, looked like he was about to die from pent-up laughter. "Oh, yeah, I'd love to come."

No, Theo mouthed again.

"You couldn't keep me away."

Denise was squealing with excitement. Auggie tapped a button to mute their microphone while Denise babbled details about the next meetup of the Margarita Mamas, and then he said, "Is this the mandatory staff meeting you have once a month after school?"

"Auggie!"

"Fine, I'll ask Denise."

"No!" Theo took a breath. "It's not the staff meetings. I wouldn't lie to you. And I've only gone a couple of times because you have to be social in a school or you get a reputation. These people hold grudges!"

Auggie seemed to consider this. Then understanding clicked in his face. "Oh my God."

"No."

"Oh my God!"

"It's not what you think—"

"In May, Theo. In May. When you were loading up all those guns and you said you were going shooting."

"I didn't say I was going shooting!"

Auggie's eyes got huge.

"I let you believe I was going shooting," Theo muttered. "There's a difference."

"Theo."

"Don't judge me."

Denise, meanwhile, had moved on to describing the apps and 'sserts. "—Theo's favorite is the s'mores nachos, of course, but I don't have to tell you that—"

With a warning look for Auggie, Theo unmuted their microphone and said, "Denise, sorry to break in like this. I have kind of a weird question."

"Oh!" Her voice became playful. "Auggie, Theo loves the hot gos'!"

Auggie was biting the collar of his tee now, blinking back tears of laughter.

"Uh, yeah," Theo said. "So, a couple of students just told me about a boy named Leon Purdue."

"Yeah?"

"They said he disappeared. Is that right? I mean, that seems like kind of a big deal. Why didn't I hear about this? You figure there'd be a staff meeting at the least, so we knew what to say to kids."

"Well, he's gone—" A hint of confusion filtered into her words. "—but he didn't disappear."

"What do you mean?"

"He got emancipated last spring. You know, as a minor. And then he dropped out of school."

"You're sure? These kids made it sound...dramatic."

A little laugh. "Sure, I'm sure. I processed all the paperwork, didn't I? He got emancipated, and then he dropped out. That's pretty much it."

"Do you know anything about his family? Anything about his home life?"

"Why? What'd those kids tell you?"

Theo forced his tone lighter. "Something about a serial killer targeting teens."

Denise burst out laughing. "Oh my God, you've got to tell the Mommies about that."

"Yes, Theo," Auggie said at a frankly unnecessary level of volume. "You have to tell the Mommies."

It had been a long time since Theo had given Auggie a dead leg. It was nice to know he could still do it.

"Theo?" Denise asked as Auggie hopped on one leg, breathing through his teeth as he held back a shout. "Is everything ok?"

"You know what, Denise? Everything is fine, actually. Right now, it's fine."

"Because it sounds like someone got hurt. Did you stub your toe? Oh God, did you hit your funny bone?"

"All good over here," Theo said, smiling at Auggie, who was alternating between scowling and massaging his thigh. "Thanks for the hot gos'. I've got to run."

"Oh, before you go, Auggie: about Friday—"

Theo disconnected the call.

"You son of a bitch," Auggie said. "I'm never going to walk again."

"I think we already had a conversation about bad language and spankings, didn't we?"

Auggie doubled down on the scowl.

"So, Leon disappearing isn't quite as...dramatic as Colt and Ashley made it sound." Theo frowned. "Are we even sure he disappeared? Or do these kids all think he did because he dropped out?"

Auggie limped in a circle. Moaning. Dramatically.

"Enough." Theo caught his arm and sat him on the edge of his desk. He took Auggie's thigh in both hands and began to rub. "You realize this is why people like bullying you? You give them exactly what they want."

Auggie looked up from under fluttering lashes. "But Dr. Stratford, it doesn't hurt right there. A little bit higher."

Theo made a disgusted noise and let go of Auggie's leg.

"Should I lie face down on your desk?" Auggie asked from under those thick, dark lashes.

"You're going to hell."

Of course, that only made him laugh.

"This has been very productive," Theo finally said to his still giggling boyfriend. "I'll see you at home."

"No, no, no, wait." Auggie composed himself. "So, Leon Purdue drops out of school in the spring, right? But Shaniyah didn't start investigating his disappearance until recently. Why?"

Theo shook his head. "You're sure she didn't say anything to you about any of this? She didn't show you any clips, or talk to you about ideas for an investigation, anything?"

Auggie gave him both eyebrows this time as he rubbed his thigh.

"Sorry," Theo said. "I know. I'm just frustrated."

"Me too. Honestly, the amateur investigation thing isn't a bad idea; I wish she'd talked to me about it."

"Do you want to think about rephrasing that?" Theo said. "If my memory serves, every time we got involved in an 'amateur investigation' —"

"Don't do air quotes. Air quotes are petty."

" —it ended very badly, Auggie. Usually for you."

A look Theo couldn't parse crossed Auggie's face; his hands, still massaging his thigh, slowed. "What I meant," he said like someone building a bridge in thin air, "is TikTok investigations are actually…well, hot right now. That's kind of a gross way to describe it, but you know what I mean."

"You're kidding me."

"Not at all. It's not really investigating, actually, but that's what people call them. For the most part, it's speculating. People do a video—maybe with a clip from news footage, a still from a video, a photograph—and they analyze it, or they point out something they think the police missed. Usually, it's bonkers stuff, you know, totally far-fetched theories, or connections that would be impossible to ever prove. But people eat it up. If Shaniyah's doing something like that about a boy from her own high school, well, it might actually be better material for scholarships, portfolio submissions, that kind of thing."

"It sounds like a lot of people 'creating content' —"

"What did I just say about air quotes?"

" —out of someone else's pain and suffering."

"Which is super shitty," Auggie said. "Yep. But *Dateline* has been doing it for a lot longer, and *Forensic Files*, and Truman Capote, and before that there were the penny dreadfuls, and the broadsheets —"

"All right," Theo said, and it sounded a little like a growl.

Auggie smirked.

"Do you have anything else you'd like to add?"

"Just thinking about those enriching nuggets of knowledge that an English major provides."

"Fuck me," Theo said and rubbed his eyes.

But when he opened them again, Auggie was still smirking. Then the smirk faded, and he said, "You know what I'd like? I'd like to see whatever

Shaniyah has put together in this investigation. Maybe that would give us an idea of where she's been—or where she's gone." Then horror snowed across his face. "Shit!"

It hit Theo at the same time. "You think that's what somebody's looking for?"

"I don't—" Auggie spread his hands. "I mean, Theo, I swear to you, she never said a word to me about this investigation into Leon. And if she dropped any content, I didn't see it."

"But if someone is trying to cover something up—if someone is trying to hide something—they may not know that. They might think, because you were helping Shaniyah with the video, you had copies of the recordings."

"But Theo—I mean, it was a summer project with a girl who didn't have many friends. How would somebody know I was helping her?"

Theo shook his head.

"Whoever it is," Auggie said, "they're dumb as rocks."

"What? Why?"

"Because nobody keeps everything on a hard drive anymore, Theo. It's all in the cloud. That's the whole point of the cloud."

"Have you—"

Auggie shook his head. "But I'm going to look through every damn file tonight, you'd better believe it. God, I wish I could watch those interviews Shaniyah recorded, the ones Colt and Ash were telling us about."

Theo opened his mouth, and then the idea came. "You think she kept everything on the cloud?"

Auggie was silent for a moment. "I don't know. Probably, yes. In some ways, it's becoming the default. But I guess I can't say for sure."

Theo grabbed the phone from his desk again. "Want to pay me back for that stuff about Denise?"

"About the Margarita Mommies, you mean?"

"Answer the question, please."

Auggie's face became earnest and innocent. "What question? What stuff with Denise?"

This time, it was definitely a growl.

"I'm just having such a hard time remembering. The specifics—"

"Yes, Auggie. The stuff with the Margarita Mommies."

"Oh, that. Sure, sweetheart, love of my life, my treasure. How can I make it up to you?"

Theo gave him the stink eye. "Prepare yourself for the role of a lifetime."

He dialed the district's tech department, which consisted—as far as Theo knew—of three desperately unhappy people in a dark room somewhere. He had the vague idea that, in some way, corn nuts were involved.

A man answered on the third ring. "Help Desk, this is Roger."

"Hi, Roger. Theo Stratford here. I'm calling from Wahredua High. I've got a student trying to log in to her Chromebook; Shaniyah Johnson forgot her password."

"It's been like this all day," Roger said.

"I know."

"Every year, this is how it is."

Theo made a noise that he hoped sounded sympathetic.

"Put her on."

Theo wrapped one hand around the handset and whispered, "You're up."

"She?" Auggie hissed.

Theo shrugged.

"It's bad enough asking me to be a teenager, Theo, but she?"

"Tick-tock, love of my life."

Auggie yanked the phone from Theo. He went very still for a moment and glared at Theo—the kind of glare, Theo imagined, many a husband from *Dateline* had received just before they shuffled off this mortal coil. Then, in a surprisingly high voice, Auggie said, "Hello?"

That was pretty much all it took. Auggie made a few understanding noises, and then he said, "Wildcats with an eight, got it. Thank you."

Then, because August Paul Lopez couldn't ever seem to help himself, he did a schoolgirl giggle and hung up.

"I want the best sex of my life," Auggie said, stabbing a finger in Theo's direction.

Theo blinked.

"For a month."

"Like, non-stop?"

"Oh, you're a comedian now?"

"I noticed you added a giggle at the end."

"And I want to be taken out to a nice dinner. And I want you to—to do something nice for my mom. Cut her grass or something."

"Cut her grass. In California."

"You owe me, Theo! After that debacle? You owe me big."

"I thought you were making up for that stuff with Denise."

"And I want you to do something…inventive. A move. I want you to do a sex move I can tell the Margarita Mommies about."

"I'm having a hard time telling if you're serious."

"I don't know either, Theo! It depends on how good the sex move is!"

That, Theo decided, was a good point to turn his attention to his laptop. He brought up a new tab and signed into the school's educational cloud account under his own name, long enough to look up Shaniyah's user ID. Then he logged out and logged back in, this time using Shaniyah's ID and the newly reset password.

In her cloud storage, one of the primary folders was labeled LEON PURDUE.

"Hot damn," Auggie said.

"You should probably use your Shaniyah voice," Theo suggested. "You know, in case this thing is voice-activated. Oh my Christ, Auggie!"

While Theo checked to see how much hair Auggie had ripped out, Auggie elbowed him out of the way and sat at the laptop. He began to click, browsing the subfolders and files. As Theo discovered—to his disbelief—a complete lack of blood from his savaged scalp, he noticed that the majority of the files were…well, strange. Screenshots of social media accounts that apparently belonged to Leon Purdue. Screenshots of a Spotify playlist. Screenshots of students, some of whom Theo recognized. Stills of Wahredua High School, of a brick bungalow, of a trailer park. The raw material, he decided, of a TikTok investigation—images that Shaniyah could edit into her own work where necessary.

Then Auggie opened another folder. This one held videos. He studied the contents for a moment, and then he clicked on the most recent one.

It began with footage from the Wahredua High School commons, where students were eating lunch. It looked like any other school day, but Theo guessed it had been in the spring, before school let out for the summer. A Black girl with enormous lashes was laughing, looking down and away from the camera, when shouts erupted. The camera swung toward the disturbance. Kids moved outward in an expanding ring, knocking over chairs, bumping into tables, tripping over backpacks. They were all trying to get away from a fight: two boys, one swinging wildly as he came after the other, who was trying to shield himself while retreating. For a moment, it looked like that might be it—Theo had seen enough school fights to know that, for most boys, that initial release of testosterone was usually all the gas they had in the tank, and the fights ended almost as quickly as they began.

Not this one. The attacking boy kept coming, screaming—not words, not as far as Theo could tell, but a kind of preverbal fury—and throwing giant haymakers and roundhouses that looked great but weren't worth shit when you didn't have any control over them. The retreating boy kept trying to get away, but then he stepped on something, and he slipped. He lost his balance and fell, and the other boy threw himself on top of him, and even over the excited babble of the crowd, the sound of meat striking meat carried clearly. Theo had just long enough for two observations: the retreating boy had been blond and skinny, dressed in black; his attacker had been muscular, with a good base tan, and a face Theo recognized. He was the same boy Theo had run into while looking for Shaniyah—the kid who had been playing patty-cake in the stairwell, the one who had called himself Keelan.

Before Theo could process that fact, though, the clip ended, and another one began—a compilation, Theo realized; they were watching several different videos that Shaniyah had edited together, probably so they would be easier to share in a single social media post. In the second video, the light was so low that for a moment, Theo couldn't tell what he was looking at. Then the camera panned, and he realized he was inside a theater—not the school theater, but clearly a theater. The stage was lit from overhead, and he got the impression of a set, complete with a balcony. Someone was screaming, "—the fuck is wrong with you? Get back here you little shit! You're going to pay for that!" A blond boy dressed in black ran out from behind the set, sprinting toward the wing. He disappeared behind the stage curtains, and a man let out a scream of rage. The camera followed in a mad chase, the video wobbling and bouncing. Then the video stopped in front of a door, and Theo had just long enough to read the plaque next to it: TRAP ROOM.

The video ended as abruptly as the first one, and a third began. This one, like the others, appeared to have been recorded on a phone, and it was clearly a party: music pounded, and the lights were low, and Theo guessed he was looking at the infamous back forty, the field (and woods) where Wahredua teenagers had thrown parties since Theo had been in high school. He knew because he'd been to a few of them, back in the day. A flickering bonfire sent light and dark rippling over everything, giving them tiger-stripe glimpses of the party—isolated slashes of visibility before shadows closed in again. A boy in a Cardinals jersey was trying to set up a beer bong. A girl in Daisy Dukes and a white sports bra was trying to do a Jell-O shot off another girl's breasts. A boy and a girl were grinding together to the pulse of the song. In the background, a girl, clearly drunk, was trying to do what looked like a dance. As Theo watched, she lost her balance, took a stumbling step, and almost fell. Her cutoffs slid off her hips, and she wasn't wearing any underwear. Then, if Theo wasn't mistaken, she farted and fell over.

He decided, once and for all, if he ever got caught up in any sort of *Freaky Friday* situation, he would kill himself rather than be a teenager again.

Yelling cut through the music, and once again, the camera spun toward the source of the noise. For a moment, Theo couldn't see anything as the camera tried to adjust to the movement and the shifting light. The man in the tiger-stripe light was short—maybe even shorter than Auggie, Theo thought, which felt a little like a betrayal—and white, with dark hair. He was waving his arms, a can in one hand. Beer sloshed and arced; where it caught the light, it looked like a spray of glitter. The tiger-stripes shifted again, and Theo could make out more details: the strong jaw, the wavy hair. It wasn't just the light, Theo realized; the camera was moving closer.

" —fucking faggot—" the man shouted.

"Who the fuck are you?" That voice didn't sound familiar, but Theo recognized the skinny blond boy from the previous two clips. "Who the fuck do you think you are? You're nobody, you're a fucking nobody!"

The man launched himself at the boy, and the boy leaped back. The man fell short, tripped, and went down, but he got his arms around the boy's feet. The boy screamed, kicking and thrashing. Then the tiger stripes moved again, and the video ended.

A black screen showed, and then Shaniyah's voice spoke: "Today, we're finally going to learn the truth about what happened to Leon Purdue."

Then nothing but the black screen. A second passed. Then another. Auggie wrapped a hand around the mouse.

And then a final image appeared: a screenshot, this one of a message thread from a phone. The contact information said PIECE OF SHIT, and a string of texts were displayed. They were all from the sender, without any replies. *Don't you dare post that video.* And, *Give me that video.* And, *You'd better fucking delete that video.* More like that, on and on. And then one final message: *I'm going to kill you, you bitch.*

7

They tried Shaniyah's house first, but nobody was home. Or, Auggie thought as they waited on the porch, nobody wanted to come to the door. Empty houses had a feel, and this one didn't feel empty. Someone's in there, Auggie thought, watching the sidelites for a hint of movement. Someone's watching us.

Eventually, though they retreated to the Audi.

"We've got to turn it over to John-Henry," Theo said. "All of that stuff."

Auggie nodded. "And tell him what?"

"I was hoping to avoid the part about impersonating Shaniyah so we could access her private files, if that's all right with you."

"No, I mean, what are we going to tell him about the Cottonmouth Club?"

Theo shut his mouth. Then he said, "We don't have to tell him anything."

Auggie nodded.

"What's there to tell?" Theo asked. "We didn't learn anything. Gid didn't react to Shaniyah's name. It's not like it was an exhaustive investigation, and they already have that place on their radar."

Auggie nodded again.

"I don't know," Theo said. "What do you think we should tell him?"

"Honestly? I have no idea."

When they called, though, it went to voicemail.

Auggie left the message. He did his best to keep it short and sweet, laying out the conversation with Colt and Ashley and their mention of Leon Purdue, as well as the dead-end visit to the club. He didn't fib, not exactly, when he got to the part about Shaniyah's videos, but he did…glide over the details. If John-Henry wanted to assume that Auggie had come across those files in a shared cloud drive, that was perfectly all right with Auggie. He ended the message with a request for John-Henry to call him back. Then, in his personal cloud drive—where he'd stored copies of all of Shaniyah's files—he created a share link and emailed it to John-Henry's personal address.

"Ok," Auggie said. "Our duty is done."

Theo slumped in the passenger seat, staring out the window.

"Theo?"

"It's not a priority."

"What?"

"Shaniyah's disappearance. Her uncle says she's back in Kansas, but I'd bet money that's just Cleve covering for her. He did the same thing when I had her in class—he always had an excuse if her work was late, if she was tardy, whatever. And that means nobody's looking for her, not really."

Auggie waited a moment. "We are."

"What are they going to do? Look at those videos and tell us that's kids doing kid stuff."

"Is it?"

Theo turned his head then, blue eyes hard. "Don't do that."

"Ok, fair enough. I don't think it's kid stuff. It feels weird to me. Seriously weird. Even just now, knocking on the door, that felt weird."

Theo grunted. "Somebody was in there."

"Right? I mean, something is wrong. That's what I think. What do you think?"

Theo scratched his beard, his gaze shifting to the passenger window. The Audi's air conditioning whispered moderately cool air through the car. Outside, the afternoon sun came down so hard that even the little patches of shade looked like they were melting.

Theo took out his phone. He navigated through the school's online learning management system until he found Leon's record from before he had withdrawn himself. There was a phone number for the boy's father, and Theo placed the call.

"Hello?" The man's voice was even, professional. The kind of guy who answered calls from unknown numbers, Theo guessed, because of work.

"Mr. Purdue?"

"Who's this?"

"My name is Theo Stratford. I'm a teacher at Wahredua High School, and I wanted to talk to you about Leon—"

"Fuck off. And don't call me again."

The call disconnected.

Eyebrows raised, Auggie gave Theo a look.

"Well?" Theo said.

"My professional opinion?"

Theo nodded.

"That was weird as balls."

Theo nodded again, tapping the phone against his hand. "I think we need to go to Leon's house."

Auggie nodded and shifted into drive.

It was a brick bungalow that had seen better days: the tuckpointing crumbling, the white paint peeling back from the trim, one doglegged downspout twisted around like somebody had kicked it. It sat in a neighborhood of similar houses—the yards gone mostly to crabgrass and clover and bare, yellow earth; chain-link fences bowed and sagging; carports and two-track parking pads empty at this time of day. Under one of the carports, a sectional sofa in olive upholstery was set up around a kerosene heater. When a gray-striped tom moved under the sofa, poking his head out to stare at them, Auggie startled.

Theo didn't laugh, of course, because he was Theo. He did catch Auggie's arm, though, and say, "Keep driving."

Auggie craned to see what he'd missed, but Theo squeezed his arm, and Auggie kept going.

"Ok," Theo said.

Auggie parked at the side of the road. Then he twisted around.

On the porch of Leon Purdue's house, two women were arguing. Or rather, one woman appeared to be arguing. The other woman appeared to be doing an impersonation of a mannequin. At that distance, Auggie couldn't get more than an impression that they were both white. Theo popped his door, and voices rolled in.

"—just want to check!" That came from the woman who was shuffling backward. Auggie figured that's why he hadn't seen her on his first glance; the porch was deep, and it looked like she was slowly giving ground, moving backward toward the steps. "Why can't I just check?"

If the other woman said something, Auggie couldn't hear it. She had her arms wrapped around herself, and she stayed in the doorway.

"It's my personal property!" the first woman screamed. "It's not fair! You're not being fair!"

The second woman shut the door.

For a moment, the woman on the steps did nothing. Then she fumbled with a little black crossbody and took out a phone. She tapped the screen a few times and held it up, studying the screen, obviously trying to get the best angle. Then she started talking.

"So, update, I'm having a really bad day. See this house behind me? The woman who lives there, Elise—that's Elise Purdue—she's a total bitch. I just want to see if some of my personal property is there, and she won't let me. And you guys, I'm just having such a hard time right now." She sounded like she might be crying. "You guys know how hard I'm working on this, but, like, it's just so hard. I mean, I just want to—I just want to do something really bad right now, but I won't. Narcissism is, like, something you can't cure. All you can do is learn how to manage negative tendencies. But, like, you guys, I'm just really struggling right now." She was definitely crying by the end.

She hit end, and the crying stopped. After a few taps, she locked the phone and put it back in the crossbody. Over her shoulder, she called, "I'm going to come back with Merlin, you cunt," and then she pranced down the stairs. She got into an enormous white Kia Telluride, and a moment later, subwoofers boomed. Auggie thought it was a nice touch that she shot away from the curb at approximately forty miles an hour—spoiled teenager meets *The Fast and the Furious*.

"If I have to hear an impassioned speech about the evils of social media right now," Auggie said, "you're sleeping on the couch for a week."

Theo grinned as he got out of the car.

The house looked even worse when they reached the porch. The ceiling was cracked, and the strands of fairy lights strung overhead were green with algae. It looked like, at some point, the porch had been put into service as temporary storage, but that temporary storage had turned permanent: cardboard boxes, drooping and bulging from age and humidity, held cans of motor oil and hedge clippers and a three-foot-long neon sign of the St. Pauli girl.

"This is probably that important personal property she was trying to get back," Auggie said.

Theo shushed him and knocked.

This house, like Shaniyah's, had the same kind of artificial silence.

Theo knocked again and called, "Ms. Purdue? My name is Theo Stratford. I was wondering if I could talk to you about Leon for a moment."

A full minute passed. And then the deadbolt clunked, and the door swung open.

Auggie's first thought was that he might have been wrong; she might not be white. Her skin had a faintly yellowish cast that suggested another possibility, at least. Her hair was long and straight, and freckles ran across her cheeks and the bridge of her nose. Auggie put her somewhere in her thirties, and he figured when she'd been younger, she'd probably been pretty, but never beautiful.

Her gaze flicked to Theo, then to Auggie, and then away. She framed herself with the door, one hand clutching it like she was going to have to slam it shut, and she wanted to be ready. "Yes?"

"Theo Stratford. I'm a teacher at the high school. This is my partner, Auggie."

"I know who you are."

Theo smiled. "You do? Have we met?"

She shook her head, but she still wouldn't meet their eyes. "Leon talked about you."

"I don't think I know Leon either."

She shook her head again.

"Are you Leon's mother?"

"Elise Purdue." She held out a limp hand. "Pleased to meet you."

Not a dead fish, Auggie thought as he took her hand. Worse. Like he was squeezing the fingers of somebody in a coma.

"Could we come inside and talk for a minute?" Theo asked. "I've got a few questions."

Elise hesitated. Her hand opened and closed around the door.

"It'll just take a minute," Auggie said.

Her shoulders collapsed, and she nodded and retreated into the house.

They followed her into the kitchen, which wasn't what Auggie had expected. The linoleum was a speckled brown that had to be almost as old as the house, and the wallpaper—pink rose of Sharon—had yellowed. The smell of boiled starches and ground beef met them, and the air was almost as hot as outside.

She gestured to a Formica table and two yellow plastic chairs. "Go ahead. I've been sitting all day."

Auggie opened his mouth to offer her his seat, but Theo gave a tiny shake of his head, and Auggie settled into the seat next to him. Elise took up position leaning against an ancient Whirlpool refrigerator. She wasn't a big woman, but the fridge rocked under her weight, and the motor's pitch changed slightly.

"He doesn't live here anymore," Elise said abruptly, chafing her arms in spite of the heat. "He moved out. So, if he's in trouble, you need to look for him somewhere else."

"No, it's not like that," Theo said. "I'm not sure if he's in trouble, actually. Leon doesn't live here anymore?"

She shook her head.

"When did he leave?"

"A few months ago."

"Do you remember when?"

A tiny shrug that might have meant anything.

"Mrs. Purdue," Auggie tried, "maybe you could help us understand what happened with Leon."

She shrugged again. She was wearing a polyester polo with the 7-Eleven logo and polyester slacks, and she looked like all that polyester might be giving her a heat rash; she scratched at her neck and immediately folded her arms again.

"Mrs. Purdue—"

"He's not here, like I said. So, if you want to know what happened, you can ask him yourself." Her eyes came up—not to meet theirs, but settling on the yellow Formica. "He dropped out of school, that's what he told me. In case you didn't hear, he's emancipated. So, if there's some kind of problem, you've got to talk to him about it."

Auggie studied her, the way she hugged herself, the way she made herself smaller. Then he said, "Mrs. Purdue, we need your help. Actually, a girl needs your help. Will you do that? Will you help us?"

She squirmed, tightening her arms across her chest. But she finally said, "I don't know."

"A girl from school is missing," Theo said. "Shaniyah Johnson. We heard that she'd been looking into Leon's disappearance."

For the first time, life sparked in Elise Purdue. She gave a weird, wheezing noise that might have been a laugh and shook her head. "Disappearance. I told her—she came here, and I told her he wasn't gone. He just moved out. That didn't matter to her; she would have talked all day if I let her." Her gaze drifted to the Formica again—not quite to their faces, but daringly close. "Leon said you're gay."

"That's right," Theo said.

She nodded. Something changed in her body. She was silent for a moment, and then she scratched her side, and the only sound was her nails rasping against polyester.

"Is Leon gay?" Auggie asked.

She nodded.

"Is that why he left?"

"He left because his dad and I got a divorce."

"Was that in the spring?"

She shook her head.

"When did that happen?" Auggie asked.

"Last year."

In the silence that came after, he could imagine some of it—what must have happened, in the months following the divorce, so that a judge would emancipate Leon.

"Do you know where Leon is living?"

"With a friend."

"Who's that?"

She shrugged.

"Do you have an address?"

Another shrug. She thumbed at her cheek.

"When was the last time you talked to Leon?"

"He came by a few weeks ago."

"Why?"

It was the way she hugged herself tighter, the way her eyes tried to fall through the floorboards again. "Just to visit."

So, Auggie thought, he wanted money. Or he wanted something.

"And you haven't talked to him since?" Theo asked.

"He doesn't like talking on the phone. He likes to text."

"When was the last time he texted you?"

Her nails rasped against the polyester again.

"Could you check?" Theo asked.

Elise pushed off from the refrigerator and crossed the room. From a hook near the door, she took down a massive purse and, after a few moments of fumbling around, pulled out a phone. She checked it and put it away and wrapped her hands together and stared at them. You could tell something about a person from their hands, Auggie thought. Hers were rough, the knuckles red.

"When did he text you?" Theo asked.

"June."

For a moment, Theo didn't seem to know what to say.

"That's more than a few weeks," Auggie said. "That's almost two months."

She shrugged.

"Did he come by a few weeks ago?" Theo asked.

"It might have been longer."

"Before or after he texted?"

One more in that infinite supply of shrugs.

A hint of color came into Theo's cheeks.

Auggie decided to speak first. "Maybe you could tell us about Shaniyah. You said she wanted to talk?" He got nothing, so he asked, "What did she want to talk about?"

"Leon."

"What did she want to know about Leon?"

That seemed to stir something again. "Where is he, where'd he go. I told her he moved out. She just kept talking. She wanted to see his room."

Auggie resisted the urge to look at Theo. "Would you mind if we took a look? It might help us, you know. Nobody knows where Shaniyah might be, and I know it's a longshot, but we'll try anything at this point."

"It's just a room," Elise said, but she stepped through the opening to a hallway, and that seemed like an invitation.

They followed her up a flight of stairs. Family photos hung on the wall: Elise, growing younger and younger as they moved up the steps; a man with a strong jaw and dark, wavy hair who grew younger with her; and a boy who must have been Leon.

In the most recent picture, he might have been fifteen or sixteen. He was taller than his dad, and he was thin in a way that Auggie couldn't quite pin down—it might have been the way a lot of teenage boys were thin, but taken together with the bleached blond hair, the black shirt and the ripped black jeans, it struck Auggie as that emaciated look fetishized by some gay men. He had several tattoos visible on his arms, but Auggie couldn't make out what they were in the photo.

The second floor of the bungalow was really more of a half-story—a single low-ceilinged room with dormer windows that looked out the front and back. The twin bed had a body pillow shaped like a half-peeled banana. Black booty shorts with rainbow trim hung off the back of a chair. A matching rainbow headband lay on the floor. Fairy lights had been stapled to the sloping ceiling, with an ancient bedsheet tacked over them like an improvised canopy. It was a child's attempt to make a bad place better, and something inside Auggie broke as he took it in.

"It's just a room," Elise said again. And then, "I've got to go to work."

"Who was that woman?" Theo asked. "The one who was here before us."

There was still steel in Elise Purdue, somewhere, at some level because the question struck another spark. "Ambyr."

The way she said it told Auggie something. "And who's Merlin?"

"Merlin's my husband. My ex-husband."

"What did she want?"

"She wanted to cause trouble. That's all she ever does. She says Leon owes her money. She deals drugs, did you know that?"

"No," Auggie said, "I didn't." But he was thinking about what she had said on her stream, about trying to get her personal property back. "Did she and your ex-husband get together—I mean, would she know Leon? Have any contact with him?"

"I'm sorry, but I've got to go to work."

"If we could get Leon's number," Theo said. "Before we go."

She gave it to them while they stood on the porch, the swampiness of the summer day submerging Auggie again. Then she started to close the door.

A thought struck Auggie, and he held out a hand. "Did she record the interview? Shaniyah, I mean. When she came to talk to you. Did she record the conversation on her phone?"

Elise moved one shoulder and shut the door.

They made their way to the Audi, and Auggie started the car and rolled down the windows. Sweat broke out across his forehead, under his arms, down his back. He turned the vents toward him and fanned himself with one hand.

"I should report her," Theo said. "I should call child services."

"She doesn't have a child anymore, Theo. Leon's emancipated."

"He's a kid, Auggie. He shouldn't be out on his own, living God knows where. You heard her—she can't even keep track of the last time she saw him."

Auggie nodded.

"Why the fuck didn't anyone report her?"

"She's obviously had a hard life. I think she's probably done the best she can."

"It was really fucking good, wasn't it?"

Auggie put on his sunglasses.

"Somebody should have reported the whole fucking situation," Theo said, the words verging on a shout. "What the fuck were his teachers doing? What about the neighbors? Somebody knew, Auggie. Somebody fucking knew and didn't care enough to say anything."

Auggie let the words fade. Then he said, "That fucking room."

For a moment, Theo looked like he might shout again. Then he nodded, wiping his forehead.

"Want to try Leon's phone?"

Theo placed the call, and a recorded message told them the number was no longer in service.

"Is this—" Auggie stopped. "Should we call John-Henry again?"

"It's a little late for that, don't you think?"

"I know you're upset about—well, about everything, but Theo, let's be realistic: even if someone had called, even if someone had seen something they could report, something they could substantiate—"

"More than his pathetic bedroom, you mean?"

Auggie took a breath. "What would have happened? Best-case scenario, he would have ended up in the system, probably in a group home. You know there aren't enough foster care parents—"

He had already passed the flash point when he caught himself; for a single moment, before Theo took control of his emotions, fury blazed in his face.

"That's not what I meant," Auggie said. "That's not where I was going with this."

Outside, the world was a heat shimmer of empty asphalt and concrete.

"I'm sorry, I didn't mean—"

"There's nothing to tell John-Henry," Theo said. "Unless you saw something in there I didn't?"

It was a question. And a challenge. And it was a kind of verbal shove, like Theo wanted to get things going.

Auggie shook his head.

"Fine," Theo said. "Let's—"

But his phone buzzed, and he picked it up and frowned at Emery's name on the screen. He answered on speakerphone.

"Get your asses over to the ice plex," Emery said. "Now."

"We're in the middle of something—" Theo said.

"I don't care. Because of you two, I'm currently an accomplice to a felony. I believe the charge, when the dust settles, will be kidnapping."

"What—" Auggie began.

"Just get over here. Fast."

8

The ice plex hadn't existed in Wahredua when Theo had been growing up—not that his dad would have driven them into town to go ice skating. Hockey wasn't the Stratford sport of choice, and the Stratford boys certainly wouldn't have been allowed to skate purely for fun—or for performance, God forbid, like a fairy. The Stratford boys played football, basketball, and baseball. Wrestling was an alternative to basketball if you were Jacob, but Jacob had always gotten special dispensations like that because Jacob was the eldest and because he was, in the ways that counted, so much like their father. Not that it had mattered in the end, Theo thought as they pulled into the parking lot for the massive structure. In the end, no amount of sports had changed what Theo had been. Hell, maybe he should have done wrestling. Maybe he should have sprung a boner and humped somebody's leg in the middle of gym. It might have saved him some time.

"I know you're mad at me," Auggie said in that joking-not-joking voice he had started to use more and more often lately. "But could you not take it out on the car?"

Too late, Theo realized he was gripping the door handle hard enough to make the plastic squeak. He forced himself to release it, and he dropped his hands in his lap. When the anger got this bad, he felt like he was standing at the bottom of a well. Down, down, down. Up above him, was light and clean air and that sense of spaciousness, but here, at the bottom, everything contracted to a circle. Like a tunnel. Like the barrel of a gun. Everything had to make its way across that great distance: Auggie's voice, the whisper of cold air across his face, the feel of the tremor in his hands, the one he was trying to hide.

What is going on with me, he thought across that vast distance. What's wrong? It was a question he had been asking a lot in the last year.

He forced himself to say, "Sorry."

Auggie nodded and eased the Audi into a parking stall. The lot was three-quarters full. Late afternoon balanced on the cusp of evening, but the sun still broke hot shards of light across the glass and chrome in the lot. This time of year, the light and heat had their own weight and density, pressing in, trying to fill every available space. A mom—Theo thought she was a mom—in a mauve jumpsuit was shouting at a kid as she picked up her sunglasses. The kid, five years old, maybe six, hung his head, a miniature hockey stick hanging from one hand. Theo knew how it had gone. The kid had been trying to have fun. It had gotten out of hand. A bad day tipped into something worse. The yelling started. And later—when it was too late— perspective, guilt, maybe even disbelief. Why did I react so strongly? How did I let it get so far out of hand?

"I'm sorry, Auggie."

"It's ok. I shouldn't have said what I did."

Theo closed his eyes. It took him a moment to clear the lump from his throat and say, "It's not your fault. You can say whatever you want; I shouldn't lose my temper like that."

"You were upset," Auggie said. "It's ok."

"I was upset," Theo said like he was reading something back. His part in this. His lines.

Auggie laughed softly, and then his fingers were at Theo's forehead, brushing back a few sweat-damp strands. "Knock it off in there, you two."

He ran his fingers through the flow of Theo's hair, the movement slow and careful. Theo smiled in spite of himself, eyes still closed. The aches of two nights' bad sleep, the pounding at the back of his head, the fear and then the bitter backwash after the adrenaline was gone. He realized, with a kind of distant surprise, two things: he had climbed out of that dark pit (been dragged out by Auggie was, maybe, a better way to put it); and he was about to fall asleep.

"You two?"

"My Theo," Auggie said, "and the one who comes around to beat up on him sometimes."

Theo smiled again, helpless even at the pain of it.

"Don't make me come in there," Auggie said.

"Oh my God," Theo murmured. He forced his eyes open, blinked a few times to clear them, and found Auggie.

He never stopped being amazed. Sometimes the amazement was further back, hidden by day-to-day things. But always, forever, the amazement was there: Auggie helping Lana put together the Fashionista Fillies wardrobe; Auggie taking Lana down to the creek to catch frogs while

Theo pretended to read on the deck and listened to the two of them laughing; Auggie staggering out of bed and into a pair of joggers, sleep-deprived the week Lana had the flu, taking every night shift so Theo could work.

"What?" Auggie said.

He was beautiful, too. That was part of the amazement; Theo would have been lying if he tried to deny it. He had lied, for a long time, about the effect Auggie had on him. Lied to himself most of all because it had been so frightening. To feel these things, to feel them so strongly, when grief had been a black snow wintering over arousal and desire. The crew cut, the dark brown eyes, the body that had taken on a man's muscle, every line sharp because he was twenty-five and because he worked harder than anyone Theo knew and because, in a weird way, it was still part of who he was, even if Auggie had convinced himself he'd let that part go.

"What?" Auggie asked again, prodding at Theo's grin with one finger.

"I'm remembering the time you put both legs through one leg of your joggers."

Auggie burst out laughing, his face coming alive. "Oh my God, I was so tired."

"Auggie, I'm sorry."

"I know." Those eyes found Theo, held him. "It's ok, I promise. I'm not made of glass. And you didn't even yell at me or anything."

Theo rolled his eyes.

"Compared, say, to the time Lana and I brought the sensory table inside."

"It wasn't the bringing it inside part. It was the sand in our new carpet part."

"I remember hearing something about that."

"Do you know how hard it is to get sand out of carpet?"

Auggie's smile had gotten bigger. "When was the last time you ate?"

Theo shrugged. "We had first lunch today."

"So, ten-thirty? They should be legally required to call that breakfast. It's been, like, eight hours since you've eaten something, and I know you haven't slept." He paused, his fingers carding Theo's hair again. "Do you want to talk about it?"

"No. I don't know."

"Like a poet," Auggie murmured.

Theo grinned in spite of himself. "I don't know, Auggie. I don't know why it hit me so hard. I mean, we've seen worse. But—" He almost said *lately*. He almost said, *But lately, I can't seem to handle anything*. What he said was, "I don't know."

Auggie was quiet as he combed Theo's hair. "You're such a kind person. You're so protective. You want everyone to be safe and cared for."

"I've got a funny way of showing it."

Auggie rapped on his forehead.

"Hey," Theo said.

"I told you two to cut it out."

He went to knock on Theo's forehead again, and Theo caught his arm with a mock glower. "You know older men divorce their younger partners at much higher rates, right?"

Auggie flashed him a smirk. "Lucky for me, I've gotten very good at sex over the years. Come on, Daddy can buy me a hot dog and a Coke from the concession stand, and I'll be a very good boy for the rest of the day."

"I'm talking rates of seventy, eighty percent."

Auggie opened the door and in an unnecessarily loud voice, camped, "Come on, Daddy, I'm starving!"

"The murder rates are higher too," Theo told him.

Auggie got out of the car, laughing silently.

Inside, the ice plex reminded Theo of other large athletic facilities he'd been in, only kept about twenty degrees colder. The shock of stepping into the chill, after the brief walk across the broiling parking lot, was like a polar plunge. In the lobby, people mingled, lugging skates and pads and sticks and those massive rolling bags that were the sign of a true hockey player. The familiar mixture of ingrained sweat and body odor and cleaning products battled for dominance. They must have arrived just as the rink was being turned over, because a herd of moms and kids were shuffling toward the doors. On the rink, what appeared to be the Pee Wee version of adult hockey was taking place—a menagerie of middle-aged men in expensive gear were taking the ice, shouting to each other as the sound of metal slicing the ice filled the air. One jabroni had managed to get himself caught in his own jersey, and he was skating backwards as he tried to disentangle himself. On the jumbotron overhead—which wasn't all that jumbo, and maybe was more of just a regular tron—what appeared to be a blooper reel from some long-ago Ice Capades was playing. As Theo watched, a man on the screen spun a woman by her heels before losing his grip and sending the woman flying off camera—and presumably, off the ice.

"Do you know how handsome you are?"

Theo turned his attention back to his partner. "Thank you?"

"No, I mean, you're handsome in general, but do you know how handsome you are when you're grumpy?"

"You know, sometimes these places have a daycare center, somewhere you can leave your kids."

"I'm being serious, Theo. About the grumpiness. It's doing something for me. Well, I mean, it's always done something for me. Do you remember when I used to show up at your house, before you were ready to admit your undying love for me and you acted like you were annoyed—"

"It's coming back to me."

"—and just like now, you'd get this little furrow on your forehead, and your jaw gets tighter—oh my God, yes, exactly like that."

And, of course, he just laughed when Theo tried to smash him into the boards.

Emery had texted them a room number, and they passed the rink and moved into one of the service hallways. For the moment, Theo and Auggie were alone, and they hurried down the hall, watching the numbers as they went.

"What do you think this is all about?" Auggie asked. "Kidnapping?"

"I don't know. Honestly, I don't want to know."

"Guess we're going to find out."

Theo didn't answer that; he didn't have to, because the next door was the one they were looking for. It wasn't remarkable—it was a metal door painted light blue, like every other door in the hallway. Theo motioned for Auggie to wait as he listened. He thought he heard voices, but he couldn't make out words. When he tried the handle, it turned.

The room appeared to be a maintenance closet—several push-behind floor scrubbers lined one wall, and a utility sink was mounted with a bottle of orange Ajax soap next to it, and metal shelves held bottles of cleaning solutions and replacement scrubbers for the machines. All of that registered only briefly before Theo's attention fixed on the shitstorm happening at the center of the room.

He recognized Keelan: the dark tan; the hint of curl to long hair that was faded on the sides and back; the muscles under that layer of puppy padding. The boy wore a sweatshirt and mesh shorts and calf-length socks, and it was obvious he'd been exercising—practicing, a part of Theo's brain corrected—and hadn't yet had a chance to shower. He was sitting in a chair, and to judge by the remaining duct tape, he hadn't been sitting there voluntarily. Not initially, anyway. He also looked pissed.

Emery leaned against the shelves, hands in the pockets of his jeans, a strange expression on his face—somewhere between blind, murderous rage and what Theo was tempted to call pride. His amber eyes lighted on Theo and Auggie before darting back to the teenagers huddled at the back of the room.

There were four of them, and they were clearly caught in their own emotional dilemma of fear and pride. Theo and Auggie had...experienced Emery's fan club over the summer, and not much seemed to have changed. Arthur was tall and beanpole thin, wearing an honest-to-God pocket protector; Stevie had their hair in a butch cut and was wearing a jumpsuit with a Top Gun patch on the chest; Lorcan looked like he might be stuck at five-four forever and was the only teenager Theo knew who had ever come to school in spats; and last was Dot, in her orthodontic headgear, intermittently activating a stun gun so that it sparked and snapped. Keelan flinched when the gun went off, but he didn't look over his shoulder.

"What the hell?" Auggie whispered.

"These guys are psycho—" Keelan started to stand.

"Sit down," Emery snapped.

Keelan dropped back into the seat, paling under his tan.

"Yes, exactly," Emery said, still staring at the kids. "Would you like to explain what the hell you've done? Feel free to start with the kidnapping and proceed from there."

"This is why I said you probably weren't a police officer," the beanpole said.

"And for the last time," Emery said through gritted teeth, "I most certainly was a police officer."

"Because a police officer would know that kidnapping involves taking a person against their will to another location—"

"Which you did," Keelan said. "I was changing in the locker room!"

"—whereas false imprisonment simply involves the act of restraint, limiting a person's movement to a restricted area."

"Yeah, that!" Keelan shouted.

"Be quiet," Emery said, the words cold and snipped off. Then, heat blooming, he turned his attention back to the beanpole. "You seem to be operating under the delusion that because you coerced this boy at gunpoint—"

"At stun-gun point," the girl said, and the stun gun zapped the air. Keelan jolted again. His eyes were huge.

"At any kind of gunpoint!" Emery's voice had a slightly unraveled quality. "God damn it, you made me forget what I was going to say."

Arthur made a sympathetic noise. Auggie choked—and then Theo realized it was smothered laughter.

Emery's face turned a shocking red.

"I'm going to step in here," Theo said, "because I have no idea what's happening, and because I think John-Henry would hold me responsible if Emery had a stroke. Will someone please tell me what's going on?"

Everyone started talking at once.

Auggie whistled, and the sound cut through the noise.

Throwing him a thankful glance, Theo said, "Keelan, let's start with you."

"They're crazy!" Keelan put his hands on the arms of the chair, as though he might push himself up, but when Emery made a noise deep in his throat, he let his hands fall again. "They broke into the locker room and told me they were going to zap me with that thing if I didn't do what they said! Then they made me come in here, and then they taped me to the chair, and that guy showed up. He wouldn't let me go! I'm going to sue the shit out of all of you!"

"I cut the tape and told him he was free to go," Emery said. "I also suggested that other adults might be interested in the contents of his bag." He nodded toward the hockey bag snugged between a pair of floor scrubbers. "Coaches, for example. Athletic directors. The police. A wide variety of people have a vested interest in the abuse of controlled substances."

"I told you, they're mine," Keelan said. "My mom has to get the prescription filled, that's all."

"I'd like to meet the physician prescribing ten milligrams of diazepam to a teenage boy."

"It's for my anxiety."

"Sure," Emery said. "But you're still here, aren't you?"

Keelan shot him a furious look, one that Emery returned unfazed.

"And why did you kidnap Keelan?" Theo asked the Breakfast Club.

"Falsely imprison," Auggie said. Then, with a grin for the Butterscotch Kids, "He wasn't a cop either."

Dot and Stevie laughed, and Arthur nodded like he'd suspected all along. Only Lorcan looked slightly horrified.

"Thank you for that," Theo whispered.

"Answer the goddamn question," Emery said.

"Colt asked us to," Arthur said.

"Not, you know, in so many words," Dot said.

"We had to make an inference." Stevie cast a shy look at Theo. "We learn inferences in ninth-grade Language Arts."

Theo was starting to feel something akin to the horror on Lorcan's face.

"Explain," Emery said.

"Lorcan was showing us his typewriter—" Dot began.

The look on Auggie's face was priceless.

"—and Colt and his boyfriend showed up—"

"They're so dreamy," Stevie said. "Especially Ash."

Arthur stood a little straighter. "What were their projects for the science fair last year?"

"Anyway," Dot said, "they wanted to talk to Lorcan about Shaniyah, and then they told us you guys were looking into Leon's disappearance too—"

"Interesting," Emery said, "how that wasn't shared with the rest of us."

"We called John-Henry," Auggie protested.

"—and then we figured out if you wanted to talk to Leon, you definitely wanted to talk to Keelan, since Keelan killed him, so maybe he killed Shaniyah too—"

"What?" Keelan sat up so quickly that, for a moment, Theo wondered if Dot had gotten him with the stun gun. "I did not!"

"Be quiet until you're spoken to," Emery told him.

"—and then we decided it would be best if we helped you out."

"Mr. Hazard frequently needs our help," Arthur said.

"I do not frequently—" Emery began.

"Emery, for God's sake, they're children," Theo said.

A sharp vee of color spread along Emery's cheekbones, but he stopped talking.

Dot fiddled with her headgear. Stevie looked like they desperately wished the jumpsuit had pockets. Lorcan played with the hem of his shirt. Only Arthur looked around, eyes bright, clearly still waiting for approval.

"A few things," Theo said. "First of all, I'm glad you were willing to help, especially with something so important."

"Of course," Arthur said. "We're much smarter than most adults, so it's important for us to help."

Theo let that one hang for a moment. "Second, I want you to promise me right now you won't ever kidnap anyone again."

"Falsely imprison," Auggie said.

Theo managed to bite back what he wanted to say, but he scratched his beard as he looked at his partner.

"Helping," Auggie said. "It's important for us youngsters to help."

"You're not that young," Arthur said. "Thirty isn't young."

In that moment, staring at Auggie's face, Theo decided he was, perhaps, a very bad boyfriend.

A startled laugh escaped Emery before he put a hand over his mouth.

"But—" Auggie said, his eyes searching the room before coming to rest on Theo. "How—"

"It's ok," Theo said.

"But—"

"I know. It's ok."

"We won't do it again, Dr. Stratford," Stevie said.

"What's the big fucking deal?" Dot asked. "We're helping with a murder investigation."

"I understand that you were trying to help," Theo said. "And I appreciate that. But you also have to understand that there's a limit to what you can do, and that when you go beyond that limit, you not only put yourselves in jeopardy, but you compromise the investigation itself. Does that make sense?"

"For example," Emery said, "by committing a felony."

"Did you consider that we might have wanted to ask some questions about Keelan before he knew we were interested in his relationship with Leon? Or that by bringing him here at gunpoint, you've made him much less likely to cooperate? But the biggest reason is your safety; you put yourselves in danger, and Emery and I don't want that."

Dot looked like she wanted to argue about it some more, but Stevie gave an unhappy nod. Arthur, of course, opened his mouth, but he shut it again when Lorcan whispered, "Dude."

"Do you want me to get rid of them?" Emery asked.

"No, we've got a few things to ask them," Theo said. "I want to talk to Keelan first, though."

He took a moment to study the hockey player. The boy looked angry, yes, and perhaps even uncertain. But he didn't look scared, and he didn't even look too...unsettled was the best word Theo could come up with. Keelan met Theo's gaze without flinching, which was strange, because often teenagers, once they'd been caught by an adult—the way Theo had caught Keelan on the first day of school—were quick to make themselves accommodating. Even stranger, though, there wasn't a challenge there, either.

"You're welcome to start wherever you'd like," Theo said.

"Start what?"

"Everything connected to Leon Purdue."

Nothing changed on his face. "What?"

"That's not the right answer," Emery said.

"What happened between you and Leon?" Theo asked.

Keelan shrugged. "He's the kid who disappeared, right?"

"Try again," Theo said.

"I don't know what you want me to say, Dr. Stratford. He was in my grade. Yeah, I knew him. But he's gone now, and it's not like we were close."

"I'll be curious to know if you can continue to play any sports once we turn those pills over to your athletic director," Emery said.

Keelan clenched his jaw.

"Come on," Auggie said, "show him the video."

Theo glanced at Auggie, and Auggie nodded.

So, Theo showed Keelan the video from Shaniyah's cloud drive. He didn't show him all of it, only the clip of Keelan and Leon fighting in the commons.

"I understand that you feel like you need to protect yourself at this moment," Theo said. "But please believe me: the best thing you can do for yourself is tell us everything right now. Two kids are missing, and if you're involved, even the slightest bit, it's going to be worse for you when we have to uproot your life looking for answers."

Keelan stretched in the chair, the movement carrying him away from Theo; then he dropped back into the seat, and he began to play with the severed strip of tape around one arm. "Ok. We had sex."

Dot's eyes grew huge.

"I'm guessing that was a secret," Auggie said.

Shrugging, Keelan flipped the tape back and forth. "It's not like we were in a relationship. And yeah, I didn't go around telling people. Neither did he. It wasn't anybody's business."

"That's a pretty big secret," Emery said.

Keelan shot him a surprisingly dismissive look.

"What?" Theo asked.

"His own kid is gay. It's twenty-twenty, man."

"So, what?" Auggie asked. "I know times are different, but you're saying it wouldn't have mattered at all? Not to your coaches or the other players on your team? Not to the guys you hung out with at school? I've lived here a while, and I have a hard time believing that."

"Like I said, we didn't go around telling people."

"Did Leon want to tell people? Did he say something to the wrong person? Is that why you fought?"

"You don't get it. If Leon tells somebody, you know what I'm going to do?" He didn't wait for an answer. "I'm going to say he's a lying faggot, and that's the end of it."

"And people will believe you?" Theo asked.

THE GIRL IN THE WIND

"Why wouldn't they?"

Auggie grimaced, and Emery's face was a thundercloud, but neither man said anything.

"How long has this been going on?"

Keelan hesitated and then shrugged again. "Eighth grade. We were at the same sleepover. I could tell he wanted to."

"And?"

"And what?"

"That's a long time to be friends with benefits, or whatever you want to call it," Theo said. "Did the relationship change over time?"

Keelan grinned. There was nothing mean in it; he looked honestly amused. "You mean, did we fall in love?"

"Did you?"

"Look, I'm not big on labels. I like sex. It's easy with Leon; he likes giving head, and I like getting it. That's all."

"Don't be ridiculous," Emery said. "I saw that video, and that's not the way two people fight if there isn't some seriously fucked-up energy between them."

Keelan clenched his jaw again and looked back at the tape.

"What changed?" Theo asked.

"He wanted to move in."

Theo traded a quick look with Auggie and saw his own confusion mirrored there.

"What?" Auggie asked. "Like, live with you?"

Keelan nodded. "His parents got divorced, right? And they're both worthless anyway, so Leon got himself emancipated. And then he asked if he could live with me until we graduated." Keelan let out a disbelieving laugh. "He kept talking about it like it was this great idea. Kept telling me how I'd like it, you know, with him being in the other room. Like that's what I cared about."

"What does that mean?" Theo asked.

"Leon—" For the first time, embarrassment mingled with the bravado in Keelan's voice. It startled Theo, a reminder that the teen, no matter how cool and confident he played it, was still a child in many ways, and he was uncovering layers of his sex life to total strangers. "I mean, it's sex. He's fun because he's really into it, and that's, you know, hot. But it's not like he's the only one."

"And having him there, in your house, that might have cramped your style," Auggie said.

Keelan shrugged, but he gave a half-nod.

"How'd Leon take it?" Theo asked.

"He shot his mouth off," Keelan said. "He told me he was going to tell everybody about us. Fine, I didn't care; I told him what I told you. Then he came up to me at school. He asked me again, right there in the hall. I mean, Jesus, like he had no brains. I said no again, and he told me again he was going to tell everybody. I told him to get lost. I mean, I told him to fuck off. And then he walked right up to me and my friends at lunch, and—" He cut off, shoulders hunching, and yanked ferociously at the tape.

"When was this?"

"May. Pretty much the end of the school year. And then that crazy girl came to school with a gun, you know, and nobody cared about a fight. I swear to God, they just forgot about it."

That was easy for Theo to believe; the school shooting in May—which had ended, thank God, without anyone dead—had disrupted everything. Coming back had been hard enough, even after three months. He couldn't imagine anyone had wanted to worry about a run-of-the-mill fight in the commons.

"What about your parents?" Emery asked.

Keelan sank lower in the chair. "What about them?"

"What do they think of Leon? What did they think about the fight? What did you tell them when Principal Wieberdink called them?"

"They know we're friends," Keelan said. "I told them he wanted to move in and wouldn't take no for an answer. Mom didn't want him living there anyway."

"They don't know about the sexual component to your relationship," Theo said.

Keelan looked up, and he met Theo's gaze again. "It's none of their business."

Theo thought about that, about how much was wrapped in that statement—not the least part being that somehow, Keelan had conducted years of sexual encounters at home without his parents knowing. Or perhaps, Theo corrected, without them acknowledging that they knew.

"Did you see Leon after the fight?" Auggie asked.

Keelan hesitated. Then he nodded.

"When?"

"Over the summer. He texted me."

"When in the summer?"

"I don't know. I can check on my phone."

"Your best guess," Emery said drily.

Keelan drew his phone slowly from the bag, as though expecting a trap. "June 20. It was a Saturday."

"And?"

"He wanted to hook up. Well, he said he wanted to apologize, but I knew what he meant." Keelan stopped. Something crossed his face, and for a moment, the child appeared from under that mask of confidence again. Then he was the cool hockey bro again, the words falling out of his mouth like he couldn't care less. "I didn't even reply; I didn't want to deal with him again. But he kept texting, and you don't know Leon, do you?"

Theo and Auggie shook their heads.

"He's funny. He can be, I mean. And he kind of talked me into it. He had his own place, he said. I could come over; we didn't have to go to my house. That was new. I thought maybe he was for real."

"And you went?" Emery asked.

A hint of color rose under Keelan's deep tan. "Yeah."

Emery's sound of disgust carried through the utility room.

"What happened?" Theo asked.

"It was this shitty apartment complex out by the tracks. I don't know, it felt sus, and I drove around a couple of times. I started thinking it was a prank, or maybe he was trying to get back at me. And then—" He stopped, and the child was there again. He licked his lips. His eyes went from Emery to Auggie to Theo. "Am I, like, going to get in trouble because I didn't tell anyone?"

"Tell anyone what?" Theo asked.

"I saw this guy walking into the building. The one Leon had told me, the same address, I mean. And I don't know if it was him, but it looked like him. And I freaked out. I drove home. And Leon texted me and said not to come over, we'd have to do it later."

"Who walked into the building?"

Keelan shook his head. It took him a moment; Theo could see it in his body, the way Keelan braced himself. "Mr. Weber."

Auggie's brows wrinkled. Emery swore under his breath.

"Dalton Weber?" Theo asked, and the question sounded stupid as it hung in the air. He saw in his mind again that sliver of the classroom through the window, Dalton's hand sliding into his pocket, the brown vial. "The theater teacher?"

Keelan ducked his head and nodded.

"You're sure—" Theo started to ask, but he stopped and made himself say instead, "How confident are you that it was him?"

"I don't know. It looked like him." And then, the words bursting out: "It was him."

"Did you see him after that?" Emery asked. "Leon, I mean."

Keelan shook his head.

"Did he message you?" Auggie asked.

Another negative.

"You haven't had any contact with him?" Theo asked.

"No way," Keelan said. "That was too freaky. And then I heard he left town, you know. I heard he went out to California, that's what somebody said, and I figured that was ok. That was probably better, you know?"

For what felt like a long time, there didn't seem to be anything to say. Staticky music came from the hallway, Whitesnake playing over a cheap speaker, and then it faded. Theo thought he could hear the hum of the fluorescent's ballast. He made himself rally his thoughts.

"What about Shaniyah?"

Keelan glanced at him.

"Shaniyah Johnson," Theo clarified.

"What about her?"

"Did she approach you?"

Keelan's brows drew together. "Like, to hook up?"

"Jesus Christ," Emery said.

"What? I don't know what you're talking about!"

"Did she interview you about Leon?" Theo asked. "She was looking into his disappearance. She had that footage of you and Leon fighting in the commons."

Keelan shook his head.

"You're sure?" Auggie asked.

"I'd definitely remember that. She never talked to me about Leon."

"Did she contact you at all? A DM maybe, something you didn't respond to?"

Keelan shook his head again.

Theo glanced at Auggie, who made a face and nodded. When Theo checked Emery, the dark-haired man made a sharp gesture with one hand.

"If you think of something else," Theo told Keelan, "please let us know."

Keelan gave him stone-faced unconcern.

"And if we have any questions, we know where to find you." Theo waited a moment, but Keelan's expression remained smooth and untroubled. "You can go."

THE GIRL IN THE WIND

With a final dirty look for the Scoobies, Keelan grabbed his hockey bag and padded toward the door. It clicked shut a moment later.

"You should have taken a DNA sample—" Arthur began, but when Emery looked at him, he stopped and tried to turtle inside his shirt.

"Now," Theo said, "the four of you."

"We were trying to help—" Dot began.

Theo held up a hand, and she stopped. He counted to ten in his head. Auggie, he noticed out of the corner of his eye, was trying to keep a straight face. "Tell me about Shaniyah."

Arthur, Dot, and Stevie looked at Lorcan.

"What?" he said and plucked at his shirt.

"You two were dating," Stevie said.

"We weren't dating; we were just hanging out."

"Fuck that noise," Dot said.

"You told me," Arthur said, "Shaniyah was, quote, 'the *terra nova* of my Magellanesque voyage of sexual discovery'."

"Dear Lord," Emery muttered.

"Theo was my *terra nova*," Auggie said.

Theo decided maybe he wasn't such a bad boyfriend. He decided maybe Auggie constituted a perpetually extenuating circumstance.

"Probably because you were a virgin," Arthur announced. "Did you choose him because he's so much older than you and therefore sexually experienced?"

Theo had never seen Emery Hazard choke on his own spit before, but it was hard to appreciate it when he himself was in the process of dying. Auggie, God damn him, only widened his eyes as a huge grin stretched across his face.

"If we could focus, please," Theo somehow managed to say. "You and Shaniyah were involved, Lorcan. It doesn't matter what you call it. I'd like you to tell us what you meant earlier when you said you believed Keelan had killed Leon and Shaniyah."

The four Encyclopedia Browns stared at each other.

"Let's start with Shaniyah," Theo said. "You think something bad happened to her?"

Three sets of eyes swiveled to Lorcan, and he swallowed. "Well, yeah."

"Why?"

"Because she disappeared."

"Nobody else seems to think she's gone," Auggie said. "Her aunt and uncle said she went back to Kansas."

"She didn't go back to Kansas," Dot said. "She fucking hated Kansas."

Stevie shook their head. "She definitely wouldn't have gone without telling us."

"Even after she broke up with Lorcan," Arthur said. "She would have told us."

"Is that right?" Auggie asked.

Lorcan spread his hands—a small, helpless gesture. But then he said, "She's not posting anything. And she doesn't reply to texts."

Theo knew there were explanations. She'd been sent back to Kansas as a punishment. She'd had her phone taken away. But he didn't say any of that; all four kids practically vibrated with fear, and it had driven them to do something stupid—brave, maybe, and in a weird way, admirable, but undeniably stupid. "What do you think happened to her?"

The kids traded looks again, and Arthur said, "Someone killed her, of course."

"Why do you think that?"

"Because she was investigating another murder, of course."

"Cut it out with the 'of course' business," Emery said.

Arthur flushed, but he said, "It's obvious that whoever killed Leon would desire to keep the killing secret. Shaniyah was investigating Leon's disappearance. She was going to post about her search on TikTok. She conducted several interviews—everyone at school knew she was looking for Leon. But she never posted any of her videos, and now she's gone."

"Why," Auggie asked, "do you think Leon is dead?"

The silence had the disbelieving quality that Theo associated with teens mentally asking, *How stupid can you be?*

Stevie answered, "Because everyone knows he is."

"Uh huh. But how does everyone know that? Were you friends with him too?"

"Oh God no," Dot said.

"Not because he was gay," Arthur said, "in case you were worried about that, Mr. Hazard."

"I was not."

"Because he was a self-absorbed asshat," Dot said.

"In what ways?" Theo asked.

"Everything was about him. He loved making a scene. He always had to be the center of attention. I swear to God, Dr. Stratford, in the middle of Lifetime Fitness once, he started singing 'Let It Go' and twirling just because he was bored."

"He could be pretty mean," Stevie said. "You think he'd be, you know, an ally, but he'd say stuff about my hair, about my clothes."

"He called me Oscar Mayer," Lorcan said. "He'd say it really loud because it always got the other kids to laugh."

"Does anyone have any proof that he's dead?" Theo asked. "We know he was emancipated—"

"Isn't it obvious?" Arthur asked. "He was killed by Mr. Weber to cover up an illicit sexual relationship, of c—" He managed to cut himself off, but not before a pair of amber eyes glittered in his direction.

Dot burst out, "I heard he was at a truck stop, and there was a man at the truck stop, and that man had a hook for a hand, and he followed Leon into the bathroom and did this with his hook—" She mimed slicing it across her own belly. "—and Leon's guts spilled out into the toilet, and the man with the hook used the little point to pull out his eyeballs, and that's how the police found him, only they didn't know it was him because of the eyeballs." She stopped, turned bright pink, and seemed to shrink inside her headgear. "That's what I heard, anyway."

"A man with a hook," Emery muttered. "Fantastic."

"All right," Theo said. "Thank you. Is there anything else you'd like to tell us?"

Arthur frowned. Lorcan shook his head. Dot considered her stun gun. Stevie flicked the tab on their jumpsuit's zipper.

"Did people know about Leon and Mr. Weber?" Auggie asked.

Surprise flickered on the faces of the Breakfast Club. Lorcan finally said, "No," and the others shook their heads.

"All right," Theo said. "If you think of anything else, please let us know. And in the meantime, if you think there's someone we should talk to, or you believe someone knows something about where Shaniyah or Leon might be, please tell one of us."

"Call Mr. Hazard," Auggie said.

"Do not," Emery said.

"Anytime. Day or night."

"Go on," Theo said. "Get out of here."

The kids shuffled out, each one offering a muffled goodbye to Emery as they passed him. Then they were gone. Emery wore a bemused look, but when he noticed Theo looking at him, it snapped off.

"Well?"

"I don't know," Theo said. "We learned a few interesting things."

Emery grunted and pushed off from the wall. "So, what's this all about? That class ring we found last week? You believe this has some kind of connection to the Cottonmouth Club?"

"Hard to say," Auggie said.

"Right now," Theo said, "we're looking for a couple of missing students. That's all."

For some reason, that made Emery smile—an icy, knowing glitter of teeth, as though he'd been the only one to hear a joke.

As they let themselves out of the hallway, Auggie said, "I'm kind of surprised you let that happen. The kidnapping thing, I mean, with your little ducklings."

Emery's eyebrows stitched together, and he said, "By the time they called me and told me what they'd done, it was too late to stop them, and it seemed like an opportunity you might not get again." He must have heard the unasked question because he said, "John takes a narrower view of this sort of thing."

Angry voices rose at the end of the hall, moving toward them.

"That boy Keelan is a regular piece of shit," Emery added as they started back toward the rink. "Colt never came out and said anything, but I watched that boy at a baseball game last spring. He kept trying to get Colt alone—any chance he got when Ashley wasn't around, he shot toward Colt like an arrow. I think I've got an idea why now." He turned his head, as though shaking off the thought, and then glanced at them. "What are you going to do now—"

John-Henry Somerset, in his uniform as chief of police, came around the corner. His features were locked in professional neutrality, but Theo had known him long enough and well enough to recognize the tamped-down anger. Close at his heels was a miserable-looking Colt, and then, trailing farther back, Keelan, accompanied by a man and a woman.

The woman was clearly Keelan's mother: the same olive skin, the same dark hair—hers, clearly, had been curled and styled sometime before dawn. She wasn't wearing a cheerleader uniform or tennis whites, but you could practically see them ghosting along behind her. She was holding Keelan's arm and staring straight ahead.

Theo took the man for Keelan's father, and it was clear where Keelan had learned how to carry himself. He had to be in his late thirties, but he wore a ball cap backwards and diamond—presumably, fake diamond—stud earrings. His mustache and stubble looked like they had to be trimmed hourly. He looked good, in a sleeveless workout shirt and shorts. He also looked like he was having a midlife crisis.

"You don't have to hold his arm," he was saying to the woman. "He's not a kid."

Keelan's eyes were hooded and fixed on the middle distance.

"Jesus Christ, he's practically an adult," the dad said again. "Are you going to put him in a stroller?"

"He is not an adult," the mom said.

"It's my night with Kee," the dad said. "Why don't you take off, and I'll handle this?"

"Handle this? Handle this? You let him get kidnapped!"

"Falsely imprisoned," Auggie murmured.

"If you'd done what you were supposed to once, Ray, just once, you'd have been waiting for him when he came out of the locker room instead of staring down the shirt of a girl who's still in high school."

Keelan, for his part, just moved in a straight line: walking when his mom pushed, stopping when his mom pulled.

Then John-Henry reached them and said, "Really?"

Emery opened his mouth.

"Say something, Ree. Go ahead."

Emery shut his mouth.

"What about you?" John-Henry asked Theo. Then, to Auggie, "You?"

Auggie shook his head.

Colt looked like he was about to burst into tears. "Pops, I didn't know — I just thought Lorcan and them —"

"It's all right, Colt," Emery said. "You didn't do anything wrong."

"No," John-Henry said. "He didn't. Apparently, he is the closest thing I have to a responsible adult in this family." He took a deep breath, pinched the bridge of his nose, and let the air out slowly. Then he said, "Do I have to handcuff you, or can I trust you to drive yourselves to the station?"

9

Auggie had never sat in the chief of police's office before. He wasn't sure he liked it. The office itself was fine: it had John-Henry written all over it, from the tastefully modern desk to the oh-so-slight disorganization of files spread next to the keyboard, to the framed photos of Emery, John-Henry, and Evie—and now, one that had clearly been taken over the summer at a beach, with Colt. When John-Henry had sat them in here, he'd pulled the blinds on the windows that looked out on the station's bullpen, but sounds filtered in through the glass: men and women talking, the rattle of the copier, a ringing phone. The smell of burned coffee soaked the air.

"So, if we go to prison," Auggie said, "I won't be upset if you don't want to share a cell."

Theo tried to smile, but it was like muscle memory, there and then gone. His eyes were seeing something Auggie couldn't see.

Auggie took Theo's hand. This got him a glance that seemed almost startled, as though Theo had forgotten he was there.

"It's going to be ok."

Theo nodded.

The door opened, and John-Henry stepped into the room. The color was high in his cheeks, and he moved stiffly, without the usual ease and grace Auggie associated with him. He sat, back straight, and shot a look at the files on the desk. He closed them. He set them aside. He looked up again.

"John-Henry, we're really sorry—" Auggie began.

"Be quiet, please," John-Henry said. And this wasn't the guy who flipped burgers at the grill—poorly—to make Colt laugh, and it wasn't the guy who raced Evie and Lana around the backyard, and it wasn't the guy who got sent into the living room to pick up his socks, and who laughed and shook it off, when another guy might have felt like he had to put on a show for the guests.

Auggie stopped talking.

For a moment, John-Henry seemed to struggle with what to say. What came out, hard and low and furious, was "What were you thinking?"

Theo's head came up.

"Do you want to explain it to me?" John-Henry asked. "He's seventeen. He's a minor. He was being held against his will, threatened—"

"No one threatened him," Theo said.

"—and interrogated by a gang of misfits with an excessive regard for my husband. That's kidnapping—"

"False imprisonment," Auggie said with a weak smile.

John-Henry's palm cracked against the desk. "I told you to be quiet."

"Don't talk to him like that," Theo said.

"It's ok," Auggie mumbled, but his face was prickling, and he had to blink rapidly. "Theo, it's fine. We both need to be quiet."

"I'm going to ask you one more time," John-Henry said, "if you want to explain why you've decided that vigilante justice—"

"Give me a break," Theo said.

"—is an excuse for you to commit a felony—"

"You know that's not what this was."

"—against a child! You should know better, God damn it! You were married to a fucking police officer!"

Theo shook his head, lip curling.

"Do you have something to say?"

It was like watching something fall away: a mask or a disguise, like one of those dramatic Shakespearian moments of unveiling, when you realize a boy was a girl, or a statue was a woman, the kind of thing that seemed both true and real and, somehow, at the same time, so silly—because of course she was a woman, and not a statue. The real Theo sat there now, hands wrapped around the arms of the chair so tightly that his knuckles popped out, and he didn't look like a teacher, and he didn't look like the guy who wore those horrifying red shorts to cut the lawn, and he didn't look like the guy who had once tried to leave the house in two different shoes because he'd been so caught up in parsing a sonnet. This man was muscle and fury and barely leashed violence, and Auggie felt that same disbelief-yet-belief, that of course this was Theo, this had been Theo the whole time.

"You didn't have a problem when we helped you at the summer camp," Theo said. His voice was still even. A stranger, maybe, might have said he sounded calm. "You didn't have a problem when we bailed you out last weekend."

"That was different."

"Sure."

"We didn't have another choice."

Theo laughed, and the sound was darkly hollow. "You and Emery really are a match, you know that?"

John-Henry's features tightened.

Auggie spoke first. "We all need to calm down. Right now. We're friends, right? John-Henry, you know we weren't trying to scare or hurt Keelan. We didn't ask those kids to do what they did, and we didn't like it. But we did need to talk to him, and we took the opportunity when we had it. Theo, you need to take it down by a magnitude of ten. Right now."

John-Henry opened his mouth. He closed it again. Color filled his cheeks under the perfect gold of his tan, but he rubbed his forehead, and, after a moment, closed his eyes. Theo shook himself once, like a dog. He unwrapped his hands from around the arms of the chair. His fingertips, Auggie noticed now, were bloodless.

"Ok," John-Henry said. "Ok." He opened his eyes. "Keelan's parents are not happy. To say the least. You're lucky, though, that Keelan isn't saying anything. All they know is that you guys were talking to him, and he seemed freaked out."

"He's not saying anything," Theo said, the words sounding like they were coming from somebody else, "because he doesn't want to get busted for possession."

John-Henry let out a breath and nodded.

In the distance, the fax machine screeched.

"Let's try this again," John-Henry said. "What's going on? I got the message you sent me, but I want to hear it from you."

So, they told him: Shaniyah's planned TikTok investigation into Leon's disappearance, the videos they'd found in the cloud, the fight between Keelan and Leon.

When they'd finished, John-Henry said, "All right."

"What do you mean, all right?" Theo said. "Did you hear what we just told you?"

"I heard you, Theo. I'm trying to figure out what to make of it." He was quiet for a moment, running one hand along the edge of the desk. "You told Ree that you're not sure if this has something to do with the Cottonmouth Club."

"We can't prove there's a connection," Auggie said.

"But that's what's going on here; we found that class ring, and then a kid doesn't show up for school. I'm not stupid." John-Henry flashed them a tired smile. "Don't hold me to that."

"It's a strange coincidence, though." Auggie moved forward in his seat. "You see it."

In the lull that followed, a man's voice echoed clearly from the bullpen: "What got your Jockeys in a wad?"

Theo let out an amused noise. "Was that Foley?"

"He doesn't grow up," John-Henry said. "He just gets older." He was silent again, and then he said, "I understand that you're worried about a missing student."

"Two missing kids," Theo said and held up two fingers.

"But that's the problem, Theo. I'm not trying to be difficult or a hard-ass, but can you see it from my side? You want me to investigate; I understand that. But I've got nothing to prove that these kids are missing. Leon Purdue is emancipated. He can go where he wants, do what he wants. If he wants to pick up and leave without saying goodbye to anyone, he can. That's his right. I'll ask around—and I'll have a chat with this teacher, see what he says. But if I'm being honest, I've got to tell you that I think you're overreacting. The same thing goes for this girl. Shaniyah's aunt and uncle said she's fine. Why would they lie?"

"You didn't see them at the school," Theo said. "The first day of school. They weren't just angry. They were scared."

"And Lorcan and the others, they're convinced something bad happened to her," Auggie said.

"Yes," John-Henry said, "but they're also children. Come on, think: there are a lot of possible explanations. The easiest one is that she got her phone taken away. We took Colt's phone away one weekend, and Ashley literally showed up on our doorstep because he thought Colt had died. That's not an exaggeration."

"It helps that they're so cute together," Auggie said.

John-Henry's face softened, and a shadow smile touched his lip. "That kind of wears off after a while. They're less cute after they've ruined two Saturdays' worth of gardening because they were wrestling in those stupid sumo suits."

"What about the break-in at our house? What about that?"

Spreading his hands, John-Henry gave him a helpless look. "Auggie, if you think that's connected, I believe you. You and Theo are smart. I trust your judgment. Tell me where to go or what to look at, and I'll do it. Right now, though, all I've got are Keelan's angry parents. They can smell blood in the water; if Keelan starts talking, we're going to have a much bigger problem to deal with. I don't think you realize how big of a problem, especially for you, Theo."

Auggie didn't need the threat spelled out. Theo was a teacher; if there was even a whiff of inappropriate behavior between Theo and a student, it could mean being fired—or worse.

"So, what are you telling us?" Theo asked. It was still that stranger's voice. "Stop investigating?"

"If I told you that, would it make any difference?"

"Are you going to arrest us?"

"God, Theo, could you work with me a little?"

"I don't understand what you want me to say. There are two children out there, and they're missing, and something is seriously wrong. And nobody seems to care about that, not even you."

"Theo," Auggie said.

"I'm sorry it seems that way to you." John-Henry leaned forward, elbows on the desk. "We all went through a lot last weekend—"

Theo shook his head and looked away.

"—and I know you feel a responsibility for these kids—"

"Someone ought to."

The only tell was the slight pause in the flow of John-Henry's words. "—but I do think the best thing for you and Auggie to do is wait until we know more. Ree and I are looking into the Cottonmouth Club. Tean and Jem are trying to figure out who's moving wildlife through there. North and Shaw are going to be back soon, and they're going to start looking into everybody connected to that operation, background checks, finances, all of it. We'll figure out what's going on. And then we'll deal with it through proper legal channels."

Theo nodded. "And in the meantime, two kids are out there, and they might be hurt, they might be victims, they might be going through the worst possible things you can imagine, but they're just going to have to wait."

"Theo, that's not what he's saying," Auggie said.

"I'm trying—" John-Henry began.

"But that doesn't bother you."

"What is going on with you?" Auggie whispered.

John-Henry still wore that calm, almost relaxed professionalism, but when he spoke, his voice was tight. "For someone who cares so much about children, Theo, you don't seem to have any qualms about putting them in danger."

"We didn't ask Dot to put a stun gun on Keelan," Theo said.

"I'm talking about Colt and Ashley. I'm talking about my son." John-Henry pushed back from the desk and stood. "I think we're done with this conversation."

"John-Henry, we're sorry," Auggie said. "We never meant to get Colt and Ashley involved, and we definitely didn't mean for anything else to happen."

"I've said what I needed to say." John-Henry looked at Theo, and Theo met his gaze. "Do you want to add anything?"

"No," Theo said. "We're done here."

Auggie opened his mouth to apologize again, but before he could, Theo grabbed his arm and dragged him from the office.

10

They drove in silence. What passed for rush hour in Wahredua was over, and the city had settled into the dinnertime lull. The streets were quiet, and in the west, the sun hung on the horizon, a smoldering red. They passed a Taco Bell, where a girl with blue hair was trying to ride a unicycle in the parking lot, pancake makeup melting in the heat. They passed Muffler King, where some poor schmuck was cooking alive inside a foam suit shaped like a muffler, waving a sign to entice prospective muffler customers. They passed a park, where a red-faced man was trying to coax a red-faced child down the slide. The child was screaming his head off, and Auggie thought, Same.

Theo broke first, saying, "If you'll drop me off at school, I can pick up Lana—"

"What is going on with you?"

Theo didn't say anything, but his shoulders sagged.

"What happened back there?" Auggie asked.

Breathing out slowly, Theo worked fingers through his hair. Auggie had seen Theo hungover—not often, because Theo was so responsible, and, on top of that, he had some sort of built-in, country-boy tolerance for beer that verged on death-defying. But a few times. Enough that Auggie was struck by the similarities: the slowness of Theo's movements, the drawn look of his face, the half-closed eyes. Which was strange because Theo hadn't been drinking. But then, everything had been strange that day. Everything.

They stopped at a light, and a Chrysler 300, black, rolled up next to them. The windows were tinted. Music thudded. Even with the windows closed, Auggie caught a whiff of a joint.

Theo said, "I don't know."

The light changed, and the Chrysler sped away, engine roaring. No license plate. That was a nice touch, Auggie thought.

Instead of Market Street, Auggie cut through one of the neighborhoods close to the river. Even with rush hour over, Market Street still might be a snarl at this hour—families trying to get to dinner, or trying to get home from dinner, or people who were already heading out for a drink. The houses in this neighborhood were a mixture of brick and frame construction, a lot of Arts and Crafts homes like Emery and John-Henry's—low-pitched roofs, deep overhangs on the eaves, exposed beams, wide porches, lots of windows. In those windows, warm light. Against that light, families moved back and forth.

"I'm sorry," Theo said. "I lost my temper."

Auggie nodded. He wasn't trying to peep—he was trying not to look at Theo, which meant looking anywhere else—so when he saw the woman in the window, he felt a flash of guilt, like he'd somehow invaded her privacy. She was Black, leaning over the kitchen sink, laughing: head thrown back, the lines of her neck exposed, a pearl earring like a comet when the sun caught it. A man came up behind her, arms wrapping around her waist. He was laughing too.

"Auggie," Theo said.

Auggie turned to him. If anything, Theo looked worse than Auggie had first thought. The color in his face was bad, and he had sweat at his hairline, even though the air conditioning was going full blast.

"Are you on something?" Auggie asked.

Theo leaned back. He wrapped a hand around the seat belt. He swallowed once before he said, in a thick voice, "No."

"Are you using again?"

He shook his head, and this time, his voice was steadier. "No."

Auggie let out a breath. He wanted to touch his eyes. He wanted to stop the car. He wanted, in a weird way, to laugh. Ten and two, he told himself. Hands on the wheel.

"I wouldn't lie to you about that," Theo said. "I've always been honest with you."

"I didn't say you were lying."

"You're thinking it."

"Oh yeah? What else am I thinking?"

And because Theo was, for the most part, mature, and good at relationships, and an excellent communicator, he said, "Uh." And then, with perhaps the quickest recovery in the world, he added, "That's not what I meant."

Auggie wrestled with the next words. He wanted to say, *You know what I'm thinking? I'm thinking I don't know what's going on with you. I'm thinking I*

107

don't know what you're going to do, or how you're going to act, not lately. I'm thinking I don't know what's going to set you off, and since I don't know, I have to worry about everything. But he couldn't say that. He couldn't say any of it. Because, of course, how would Theo react?

"I'm sorry," Theo said. "That wasn't the right thing for me to say. Will you please tell me what you're thinking? I can tell you're upset. I'm sorry for how I acted with John-Henry; I...I shouldn't have reacted so strongly. I wasn't even angry at him, you know? It was everything, all of it. Seeing how Leon had been living. The fact that nobody seems to care if he and Shaniyah are alive—"

"You need to stop saying that." Auggie fought for control of his volume and won. In a more even voice, he said, "I want you to stop saying that, ok? Because it's not true."

Theo pushed his hands through his hair again. They went over a badly patched pothole. They passed a Midas. The spinning sign had gotten stuck halfway around so you couldn't read any of it. Theo nodded.

Then, in a voice much more like the Theo Auggie knew, he said, "Talk to me, Auggie. Please?"

All the possibilities spun in front of Auggie, like some sort of horrible roulette wheel. Which one will make him start shouting? Which one will make him shut down? Which one will make him scared, because scared is the one thing Theo can't ever allow himself to be?

"I don't like what I saw back there."

Theo nodded.

"In John-Henry's office."

"Ok," Theo said.

"He's our friend, Theo."

"He wasn't acting like our friend. He shouted at you. He was starting to get threatening."

"Threatening? John-Henry?"

"You saw him."

For a moment, Auggie didn't know what to say. The best he could come up with was "Right now?"

"He slapped the desk. He screamed at you."

I can't do this, Auggie thought. He was surprised by the voice. By how clear it was. By how much it sounded like him. I can't do this again.

Maybe Theo heard something in the silence too because he said, "I was keyed up, that's all."

Auggie nodded.

"I know he's our friend. I know he wasn't actually, you know, coming after us."

"He is our friend, Theo. He's a good guy. Our families spend so much time together. We trust him with Lana. We've been through some really bad stuff with him."

"I know."

"He would never threaten me."

"I know."

"And if he did, I can handle it."

"I know."

"Do you?"

"Yes, God, of course." Theo wiped his eyes; they looked dry and red. "I just wasn't thinking clearly, that's all."

Auggie spun that roulette wheel of possibilities again. This time, he got "You need to sleep."

A rocky attempt at a laugh. "God, yeah, I do."

"And eat, Theo."

"I'll pick something up for us on the way home."

Auggie nodded. There didn't seem to be anything left to say.

But Theo reached over the center console and took Auggie's hand from the steering wheel, wrapping it in his own.

"You could handle ten John-Henrys," he said.

Auggie rolled his eyes and tried to get his hand free.

Theo kissed his knuckles. "You could handle a million John-Henrys."

"He's too pretty. I'd go for the money-maker; that's his weak spot."

"Auggie, I am sorry. It's been a bad couple of days, that's all."

"I know."

Theo kissed his hand again and kept hold of it, and Auggie decided to let him.

They drove for a couple more minutes. They merged onto Jefferson, north of the high school and the government buildings, where houses perched on either side of the road and strip malls broke up the blocks. A Lincoln humped their bumper for a quarter mile and then, ignoring the double yellows, swerved around them and sped off. Theo's body tightened the way it always did around that kind of driving, but a moment later, he had relaxed again.

"Auggie," Theo said, craning to check the street behind them. "We passed the school."

"Yeah."

"My car."

"No, sir," Auggie said. "You're exhausted. We'll pick up Lana— together—and we'll grab some dinner and head home. Then you're going to sleep." Before Theo could protest, he added, "I'll take you to work in the morning."

Something indecipherable worked its way across Theo's face. After a few seconds, he said, "Thank you."

Lana's after-school center was located in one of the strip malls on this stretch of Jefferson, which, when Auggie and Theo had first been looking at options, had been a major turnoff for Auggie. But Kidz Academy—in spite of the Z, which had been a major turnoff for Theo—had impressed both of them. It occupied half of the strip mall, and on the inside, the paint was new, the carpets clean, and the toys and furnishings had all looked well maintained. They had a good staff to student ratio, and they even had an occupational therapist on staff who helped tailor the level of support the children with special needs received—in other words, as Auggie could put it, so Lana could be hell on wheels in her leg brace.

Auggie parked, and they got Lana. She started talking the minute she saw them, and while Theo listened to her tell them about her day— apparently she'd learned a new dance, which meant Auggie was going to be spending a lot of time helping Lana record it for TikTok—Auggie apologized to Terese, who apparently had drawn the short stick and been stuck with Lana until Theo and Auggie could pick her up.

"It's a three-strike policy, Mr. Lopez," Terese said, shouldering her bag as she locked the door. "Parents have to pick up their children on time."

"I know. We know. We're really sorry, and it's not going to happen again."

That didn't seem to be good enough for Terese, because she looked like she wanted to explain again to Auggie—perhaps more loudly this time— the importance of punctuality. But instead, she hurried to her car, and a moment later, her taillights were disappearing down Jefferson.

"Ok, baby," Theo said, laughing as he dodged an elbow to the face. "Show me the dance when we get home. Are you and Papi going to make a video for me?"

Auggie groaned quietly, and Theo shot him a smile.

He was opening the door to get behind the wheel, Theo still helping Lana into her seat, when tires squealed. Auggie looked up, and the old animal part of his brain reacted first: something big and something black rushing toward him out of the sunset. Adrenaline jolted through him. Then the car skidded to a stop, and the front of Auggie's brain caught up with him, and he stared at the black Chrysler, trying to make sense of what had just happened.

Theo said, "Get in the car, Auggie. We've got to go—"

But before he could finish, the silver Lincoln bumped over the lip of the parking lot and shot toward them. The driver braked hard and spun the wheel, and the car turned and slid across the asphalt toward them. The smell of burning rubber carried on the hot, heavy air. When the Lincoln came to a stop, it formed a vee with the Chrysler, the two cars working together to block Theo and Auggie in. Auggie was suddenly aware that they were alone. The rest of the strip mall was unoccupied and dark, the parking lot void of cars, and Terese's angry little face was now just a fond memory. It was dinnertime. It could be fifteen, twenty minutes before someone drove down this little stretch of Jefferson.

"Get—" Theo tried again.

But the door to the Chrysler opened, and a big man got out. In spite of the heat, he was dressed in a long-sleeved shirt and jeans. The ski mask and gloves rounded out the outfit. With the sun behind him, it was impossible to make out anything more than his size. Then he came around the front of the Chrysler, and Auggie saw the baseball bat.

"Get in the car and lock the doors," Theo said.

"No—"

"Keep Lana safe."

For a frozen instant, Auggie's brain rebelled. That was an impossible choice: to leave Theo to face this man alone, or to protect Lana. Then he knew it wasn't a choice, not really. He started to turn toward the Audi.

The Lincoln's front doors opened, and two more men got out. One was wearing a mask that made Auggie think of a cartoon rat. The other was, Auggie guessed, supposed to be a werewolf. The rat carried a length of steel pipe. The werewolf had a folding knife, three inches of steel that he spun. The blade turned faster than Auggie could track, and in the dying daylight, it became a ring of fire.

"Whatever you think is going to happen—" Theo began.

The man with the bat stepped forward and swung.

11

The bat moved so fast it cut the air, the sound raw and shredded.

Theo stumbled back. Too slow, his brain said. Too slow. The bat missed him, but only barely. The whiff of it passing felt like someone's hot breath on his cheek.

Auggie shouted something, and a door slammed shut, and then the car alarm went off.

Out of the corner of his eye, Theo saw the men in masks—a rat and a werewolf—moving in. The rat went for the passenger door, while the werewolf, knife spinning like a carny doing a trick, came at Theo from the side. That was an old move, older than humans, ganging up, taking turns. It was going to be a dogfight, Theo realized. And the old part of him, the part that had fought on a hundred different nights, in a hundred different bars, with broken bottles and pool cues and chains and fists—the old part of him raised its head, sniffed the air. The old part of him, a far-off part of Theo, wanted to fuck around.

The one with the bat came again, but it was a feint, and Theo knew it. At the last moment, Theo turned toward the werewolf. The knife solidified, became the tip of a spear made out of the werewolf's extended arm. The stab fell short of Theo. When he pulled back for another thrust, Theo stepped in. He closed the distance between them and punched the werewolf in the throat. The feel of the rubberized mask collapsing under the blow was strange. The secondary sensation, of muscle and cartilage compressing, was not. The werewolf gagged and hacked, falling backward, and the knife clattered against the asphalt.

Auggie was still shouting, and now Lana was crying and screaming, the sound distant and low. Some of that was the glass and steel surrounding her. Some of that was the thunder in Theo's ears. He ducked to recover the fallen knife, and some combination of senses—the feel of displaced air, the hum of movement—alerted him. At the edge of his field of vision, the baseball bat came toward him.

Theo moved back, but not fast enough. The blow caught him on the shoulder, and it was like someone had shoved his arm into a bucket of ice. There was a faint, buzzing discomfort almost like a vibration, and then numbness. That's not good, a part of his brain registered. The werewolf was still on his hands and knees, vomit burbling out of the openings in the mask, and the knife was still there, a little lick of light. The one in the ski mask stepped forward again, and Theo moved back. His ass connected with the Audi's side panel. Lana was still screaming. There was a noise like a bag of sand hitting the ground, and Theo realized that had been Auggie.

Favoring his arm, Theo slid along the back panel. The one in the ski mask followed, matching Theo's pace. The bat came up again, the way they taught you to hold it playing baseball. That said something, but Theo's brain was too scrambled to make sense of it. All he knew, in that fuck-around part of himself that was awake and hurting and vibrantly alive, was it was a stupid way to hold a bat in a fight. You were trying to clobber somebody, beat their brains out; you weren't trying to hit a knuckleball.

Risking a glance, Theo checked on Auggie. That awful sound of something hitting the ground had made Theo expect the worse, but Auggie was standing. It looked like the Audi was doing some of the work to hold him up, but he was standing. Blood stained one sleeve, and under the soft brown of his skin, he was pale. He had his fists up; he'd taken a lot of kickboxing classes, and dragged Theo to one or two of them, and Theo recognized the pose.

The sound of a step clipping the asphalt made Theo turn. The man in the ski mask tried to take Theo's block off with a giant swing, and Theo dodged. The bat hit the Audi, and there was a popping noise as the side panel flexed. Theo repeated his maneuver from earlier, closing with the man. He cut the distance between them to less than a foot, putting size and speed behind the elbow he threw.

But the man with the ski mask was smarter than his friend—or maybe all that mattered was that he was bigger. He took the elbow center mass, and then he clubbed Theo on the side of the head with one big fist. The first blow rocked Theo to the side, but it didn't take him down. The second one came in just as fast, and he hit the asphalt.

From a long way off, Lana was still screaming, and then the thud of something striking flesh came, and Auggie whimpered.

Theo tried to get up. A sneaker came out of the darkness, and then Theo's mouth was full of blood, and he was down again, staring up at the purpling sky. A flock of birds, small in the distance, drew a dark vee like two brush strokes.

The man in the ski mask crouched next to Theo. He rested the end of the bat on Theo's chest and said in a too-deep voice, "Stop asking questions."

The birds had grown in Theo's vision. They were spreading their wings, taking up the whole sky now like ink bleeding across a page. That was why, at first, he thought it was a dream.

"Hey, ass-breath."

For a moment, Theo was sure he had blood on his brain, because that sounded like North.

"I don't think you should say ass-breath." And that was definitely Shaw. "It's not polite."

"Who cares if it's polite? He's a fuckwhistle. If he's got ass breath, I'm going to call him ass-breath."

"Well, right, I understand. But it might be a little bit, well, homophobic."

"It's not."

"But it might be."

"It's not."

"I don't want to get into the weeds about this, but let's say, you know, he enjoys getting his salad tossed. Maybe it's with a man. Maybe he's a dark, mysterious man with raven-black eyebrows and—"

"It doesn't matter if he likes somebody eating his ass. I'm not talking about that."

"You're kind of referring to it."

Some of the darkness in Theo's vision folded again. The birds—if there ever had been any—had flown on. The asphalt was warm under his head, and the blood in his mouth made him want to be sick. He could see, now, that the man in the mask had gotten to his feet again.

"I'm saying he has ass breath. If anything, in that situation, he's the one tossing salad."

"Right, but—"

"And who says he's eating another guy's ass? Maybe he's a totally normal, straight vanilla type who only has sex with his eyes closed. The straights can eat ass too."

"Ok, yes, but when you use the word 'normal,' you're actually kind of kink-shaming—"

"What the fuck is going on?" the man in the ski mask shouted.

"Shut the fuck up," North said. "How about that for what's going on?"

"It is kind of rude when you interrupt," Shaw said. "Especially when I'm defending you."

"Get the fuck out of here," the man in the ski mask said.

"You know what?" Shaw said. "He does kind of look like a fuckweasel. Oh, actually, I saw a video about an inflatable toy called a fuckweasel—"

"He's a fuckwhistle, donkey-tits. Why the fuck would I call him a fuckweasel?"

"—it had this tail that was, like, velour, I think, or maybe—no! It was Duvetyne! A Duvetyne tail—"

"I said get the fuck out of here! You want some of this?"

Something like a giggle was working its way through Theo, and he had to fight it, had to struggle to keep himself centered. Auggie still needed him. Lana needed him.

"Let me tell you something," North said. "Do you know how many hours I've spent in the car with him over the last two weeks? Do you have any fucking idea? And he gets to pick the music half the time. I had to listen to some shit-for-brains with his own podcast shilling some shit called 'colon broom' for six hours. A six-hour fucking infomercial in my car. And this numbnuts subscribes to the fucking podcast."

"It sweeps your colon clean," Shaw said with what Theo thought might have been pride. "Imagine someone taking a rake—the gardening kind, not the leaf kind—through your large intestine. Oh, it should be called 'colon rake.' I'm going to call Dr. Dimitrov and maybe I can be a guest on his show!"

"This. This is what I'm talking about. So, you're asking me if I'd like the opportunity to beat the shit out of a trifecta of ass-breathed chumps who pick on old men and little kids? Yes. That's a definitive yes. I would absolutely fucking love it."

"It's all the dairy," Shaw said. "His moon hormones are totally out of whack; that's why he's so aggressive."

No one, it seemed, knew what to say to that.

The man in the ski mask finally spoke. "We're done here."

"No," North said, "you're going to stay right there and wait for the cops."

The pause lasted only a heartbeat. Then the man in the ski mask broke and ran for the Chrysler.

North let out a wordless shout, and steps hammered the asphalt. Theo rolled onto his hands and knees. The world spun with him, and for a moment, he thought he'd go back down again. But then everything steadied. The man in the ski mask dove into the Chrysler and yanked the door shut, and North reached him a moment later, shouting as he pounded on the glass. The Chrysler tore out of the parking lot, thumping over the curb at the turn.

A scream from the other side of the Audi made Theo lurch to his feet. The werewolf was gone, presumably inside one of the cars already. The man in the rat mask kicked Shaw away from the Lincoln long enough to pull the door shut, and then the Lincoln sped after the Chrysler. Neither car, Theo noticed, had license plates.

Then he saw Shaw, really saw him. A crushed velvet smoking jacket (maroon, of course), and a ruffled shirt, and then a pair of shorts that Auggie would have loved because they were smaller than most of Theo's underwear. Across the back, Theo saw when Shaw turned, were the words TACTICAL PANTIES.

It's one of those things in your brain, Theo thought. You get hit in the head, and blood pools, and you die. I can't even think of the word. Probably because I'm dying.

Hematoma—that was it.

"Get back here, you fucking fuckweasels!" North shouted after them.

"I knew it was fuckweasels," Shaw said. Then he squinted at Auggie and said, "What's that?"

Auggie shook his head.

"It's his ear," Shaw announced. "Auggie ripped off his ear."

"No, he fucking did not," North said as he stomped around the Audi. "That's an ear lobe, dumbshit. Anybody can rip off an earlobe."

Auggie let out a ragged laugh. "He had an earring under that mask." He laughed again, and it made Theo think of horses rolling their eyes. "I just grabbed him and didn't let go."

North clapped Auggie on the shoulder, and Auggie staggered. "Not bad, Fun-size."

12

The police came. John-Henry came. An ambulance came. All of it playing out in front of Kidz Academy.

Theo sat on the back of the ambulance while Frannie, a paramedic he'd known for years, checked Auggie out. Whatever reserves Theo had started with, they were gone now. He was shaking, unable to stop. He kept hearing that sound, the heavy thump of the blow, Auggie's cry of pain, Lana's screaming. She was sitting on Auggie's lap now, unwilling to let go of him and, in the process, making Frannie's job that much harder. Frannie was a pro, though. She talked to Lana while she worked, and Lana seemed content to snuggle into Auggie's chest and eat the M&M's Frannie had given her.

The sound of Auggie hitting the asphalt.

Lana's trapped screams.

Theo tented his hands over his nose and mouth and tried to control his breathing.

When a hand fell on his shoulder, he startled, eyes snapping open. John-Henry studied him. Light moved over his face; the lazy circles of emergency lights created a perpetual ripple of shadows. Blue. Then red. Then nothing.

"Do you feel up to talking?"

Theo nodded, and he looked over his shoulder.

"Go on," Auggie said, shifting Lana's weight. He winced as Frannie cleaned an abrasion on his elbow. "We're good here."

Theo stood. His legs shook, and he knew John-Henry hadn't missed that—probably didn't miss much, ever.

John-Henry led him down the length of the strip mall, away from the milling bodies of law enforcement and emergency responders, toward the dark, empty storefronts at the other end of the lot. Then John-Henry stopped at a bench.

Theo shook his head. "I'm fine."

A partial smile touched the side of John-Henry's face. "I'd like to sit down if you don't mind. I've been on my feet all day."

Theo wanted to think about that, but exhaustion had snowed out everything in his head. He nodded, and they sat. Voices carried to them from the men and women who had responded to North and Shaw's call. The words were indistinct. Someone laughed. A car rolled past on Jefferson, slowing to rubberneck at the scene. Old cigarette butts filled a stone planter next to the bench, their smell mixing with the whiffs of diesel exhaust and, closer up, Theo's own sweat.

"I'm sorry," John-Henry said.

Theo rubbed his eyes. "What?"

"I'm sorry, Theo. I'm—I'm incredibly sorry. I'm sorry I didn't listen to you. And I'm sorry for how I reacted."

Theo shook his head. He felt like someone had slowed him down, like he was moving at half the speed of everything else in the universe. "What?"

John-Henry offered him a tight smile. "You told me. You told me something was happening. And I didn't listen."

"Hold on. This isn't your fault. You certainly don't need to apologize."

"It feels like I do. It feels like I about got you and your family killed."

My family, Theo thought. And he remembered the spin of the car sliding out of control. Lana screaming. But that wasn't right; he tried to separate the two moments. She'd been too young to scream in the accident. He waited for the fear that always came first, and for the anger that, more and more frequently, had become a way of living with the fear. He felt nothing. Every fuse blown. He'd hiked a burn the summer before, when Auggie suggested he take a day for himself. Not a big one because wildfires weren't a huge problem in Missouri. But he remembered the desolation, the emptiness. Everything burned away, and char lifting on the wind.

Somehow, he heard himself say, "This was not your fault."

John-Henry nodded, like he was willing to let the point go; his face, though, said otherwise. In that smooth, professional tone, he said, "Why don't you walk me through what happened?"

Theo did. And when he finished, he said, "I honestly don't know what would have happened if North and Shaw hadn't shown up."

"Do you think they were trying to kill you?"

Theo scrubbed his face. "I don't know."

"You said one of them had a knife."

"He did." Theo tried to replay the fight, but it was a blur of impressions: vivid, snapshot moments, and then fragments of other sensory details. "I don't know. They might have been trying to kill us, but if they were, they were pretty incompetent. The one said something at the end about asking questions, so I think it was a warning. They were trying to scare us off."

"From what?"

Theo blinked. "From this—this investigation. That sounds silly, but you know what I mean."

"Yes, but I'm asking, which investigation? Do you think this has something to do with the Cottonmouth Club? You were there last night; is it possible someone came after you? Or do you think this is about looking for Shaniyah? Or for Leon? I know those things feel connected, but the reality is that you might be dealing with multiple perpetrators."

The snow-out in his brain made it hard to think. Theo knew he should have recognized that; he should have started trying to puzzle it apart as soon as the fight was over. He struggled for an answer and finally said, "I don't know."

John-Henry nodded. "Frannie says she doesn't think you have a concussion. She says Auggie's fine except for some scrapes. I think you might want to go to the hospital anyway, though, and get yourself checked out."

"No." Shaking his head, Theo spoke over John-Henry before the man could press the point. "Lana's had a rough night. She needs to go home. She needs her routine."

After a moment, John-Henry gave a nod. He stood, and he didn't say anything when Theo struggled to stand—the combination of exhaustion and his bad knee stiffening up. They moved slowly back down the length of the strip mall, toward the maelstrom of lights. Auggie was a silhouette, but Theo would have known him anywhere. He was carrying Lana, never mind that she was ten and that she must have been killing his arms and back. Her head was tucked into his shoulder, and he leaned his head against hers, rocking her slightly as he walked.

"He's really good with her," John-Henry said.

Theo nodded. He felt it again, like some other Theo was walking through the burn, mile after mile of blackened rubble, wings of ash rising, hovering, drifting away. He had felt, during some parts of that hike, like he was floating.

"I'm going to have a patrol car on your house again tonight," John-Henry said as they approached Auggie. "How do you feel about houseguests?"

Theo barely heard the question. "I can hold her."

Auggie shook his head. "She just fell asleep."

"Do you want to sit down? Why don't you sit in the car?"

Shaking his head again, Auggie gave him a small smile. The bandage on his arm looked so small, so insignificant—a part of Theo wanted to believe that Auggie had given himself worse in those damn kickboxing classes.

"She's too big for you to carry," Theo whispered.

"I'm fine," Auggie whispered back. Then Lana murmured, and he walked off, rocking her as he said something in a low voice.

"He's kind of a wundersquirt," North said as he and Shaw joined them. "Ass-kicker, baby-whisperer."

"Plus he's so pretty," Shaw said.

"He's not that pretty," North said.

"He's basically got perfect human male features," Shaw said. "I mean, people would kill to look like him."

"He's a runt."

"You said he has a beautiful smile."

"I said he's got an ok smile because you wouldn't stop talking about how pretty he is." North's volume was rising. "I never said he had a beautiful smile."

Shaw's pause had to be deliberate because his tone was different when he said, "You know what, though? I actually prefer blonds."

"Don't do that."

"I do. I mean, I don't even care that Auggie is a perfect human specimen. I like guys with these weird clumps of blond fur—patches, patchy fur—"

"Listen here, you son of a bitch: it wouldn't be patchy if you didn't think it was a hilarious prank putting Nair in my body wash! And for the record, he's not half as pretty as John-Henry." Then he squared his body with John-Henry's and said, "What?"

John-Henry, somehow, managed to keep a straight face.

"You've got something to say?" North said.

Shaw was giggling helplessly into the lapel of his smoking jacket.

"Not particularly," John-Henry said.

"I was stating a fact," North said. "And for the record, you've got the personality of shit that's gone through a blender."

"Maybe I should go to the hospital," Theo said. "Maybe I do have a concussion."

"Don't worry," John-Henry said. "I get that feeling pretty much every time I'm around them."

"Is everybody ok?" The question came from Tean as he and Jem hurried across the parking lot. An officer moved to intercept them, but John-Henry waved him back.

Jem glanced at Theo and then around the parking lot. "What happened?"

"Daddy went street fighter," North said.

"One of them was a werewolf," Shaw said. "Theo hit him in the throat. And Auggie ripped off a rat's ear."

Tean blinked and reached up as though he might straighten his glasses before stopping himself.

"He didn't rip off an ear," North said. "It was a lobe. Not even all of one."

Jem looked past their group to Auggie, still walking Lana around the lot, and said, "Respect."

When Theo glanced over his shoulder, Auggie grinned and then hid his face in Lana's dark hair, whispering something to her.

"Oh my God," Shaw whispered. "My ovaries."

"That's how you look with the girls," Tean said to Jem. Then, to Theo, he said, "You can always tell when somebody's a natural with kids."

"You should see him when they wrestle," John-Henry said.

"They're going to explode," Shaw said. "My ovaries are literally going to explode."

"For fuck's sake," North snapped, "we get it. Old Man River got himself a wundertwink."

"I thought he was a wundersquirt."

"He can be two things!"

"You know," John-Henry said mildly, "Theo's actually younger than me."

"Oh, we know," Shaw said. "You can totally see it."

"Uh. Ok."

"It's your skin. Well, mostly it's all the lines, which is why I say Auggie—"

At that point, mercifully, North clapped a hand over his mouth.

Jem wore a huge smile, revealing slightly crooked front teeth, and a laugh rode the crest of his voice when he asked, "So, what happened? Emery told us to get over here as fast as we could; I think he's staying with Evie and Colt."

They went through all of it from beginning to end, and as they did, the crowd of responders dwindled. The ambulance left after Frannie had checked one last time that Theo and Auggie didn't want a ride to the hospital. Then the officers left, and as their spinning lights shut off, the parking lot fell into the buzzing, yellow haze of a lone security light.

When Theo had finished, he noticed Auggie standing next to him, without Lana. "Asleep," he whispered. "In the car."

Theo nodded.

"How'd you two end up here?" Jem asked North and Shaw. "Pretty nice timing."

"Yeah," North said. "It reminds me of the time I saved your ass at that fucking resort."

"Actually," Shaw said, "Jem saved you, remember, because your trick knee gave out because you'd been slathering it in Bengay—wait, was it because you'd been slathering it or hadn't been slathering it? How much slathering had you been doing?—and that guy was going to stab you, and Jem smashed him with a clock." He turned toward John-Henry and beamed. "I used a phone like a morning star."

"The details aren't important," North snapped.

"The universe sent me a psychic distress call," Shaw said. "That's how we reached you in time."

"Yeah, right after you got your asses handed to you," North said. "We were driving back into town and saw one of those dickweeds flip around to follow you. We both had a weird feeling about it—"

"That was the universe."

"—so after a few minutes, we doubled back. Let me guess: you two stuck your noses where they didn't belong, and you almost got yourselves killed doing it."

Theo grimaced. Between the exhaustion and the headache, it was hard to think clearly. "I don't know. Something doesn't make sense. I don't know why they would have come after us."

"Theo, what's done is done, but I think North and Shaw might be right." John-Henry put his hands on his hips. "You went there, and you asked about this girl, and somebody started running his mouth. Then he freaked out, and he pointed out Auggie to somebody dangerous. Now we're here."

"But he didn't recognize Shaniyah's name," Auggie said. "And he didn't say anything really incriminating. I mean, something about a wild weekend, but that's basically their whole marketing angle—I mean, nobody's going to start investigating them because one guy brags about a wild weekend."

"A normal person might not find that statement troublesome," Tean said, "but someone with a guilty conscience might read a lot more into it.

He might have heard what he said and, because he knows what went on in that club, immediately jump to the worst possible scenario."

"He's a piece of shit," Jem said like he was clarifying, "and he's a guilty piece of shit, so he's jumping at shadows. And whoever he told probably doesn't mind tying off a loose end, just in case."

Auggie looked at Theo, and Theo saw the helplessness there, the frustration. It mirrored his own. "We've gotten too fixated on the Cottonmouth Club," Theo said. "There's more happening here."

North opened his mouth, but when John-Henry shook his head, he shut it again.

"How about this?" John-Henry said. "You and Auggie kicked the hornet's nest, and now they're mad. That's a good thing."

"Because they're going to make stupid mistakes," Jem said.

"Like this amateur bullshit," North said. "In a fucking Kindercare parking lot."

"It says Kidz Academy," Shaw said. "He has trouble with cursive. Well, reading in general. Last week, I had to read an entire report to him."

"Because you wrote it in invisible fucking ink! And I'm the one who graduated college—"

"That one right there?" Shaw said. "That's a Z."

Theo caught the flicker of something on Jem's face—a sudden tight, blankness that seemed strangely defensive—and then Jem noticed him looking, and the mask changed, for a single moment, to something else. Anger, maybe. A look Theo had seen on students' faces before, the kind of fixed dislike some of them, especially boys, brought to the classroom of a known faggot.

But then the look was gone, and Jem turned away, tilting his head to listen to Tean whisper in his ear.

"It was amateur," John-Henry said. "Tonight. But we know they've made successful hits before, and since they didn't succeed tonight, they'll try again."

"We'll stay with Theo and Auggie," Tean said. When everyone looked at him, he ducked his chin, but his voice was firm as he added, "I can stay up and keep watch, and Jem knows how to handle himself if—if something happens."

"If that's ok with you," Jem said to Auggie.

Auggie looked at Theo again, and Theo answered, "We don't want to put you out." But Auggie was still looking at him, and he could see what Auggie wanted him to say, so he said, "Yes. Thank you. That would be great."

The relief actually made Auggie's body bend slightly.

"For the next few days," John-Henry said, "you and Auggie are going to lie low."

"While we take care of these pieces of shit," North said.

"They messed up. This is Wahredua; they attacked you here. That means this is my investigation now, and that means I can bring the whole department to bear on the Cottonmouth Club. I'll talk to the sheriff, too; he might have contacts I don't. We're going to work this piece by piece, starting here and following it straight back to the club, and then we're going to take that place apart." He paused, and he said to Theo, "I want to apologize again for earlier. And I want to tell you that you and Auggie did a good job."

Theo nodded. He was too tired for anything else.

"It's like a scene from *Bad Boys*," Shaw said. "Oh, do you think Martin Lawrence ever got a sunburn in his ass crack because he was trying to tan for this Chouteau bro who was going to toss his salad —"

North didn't even hide it: he just twisted one nipple savagely through the ruffled shirt, and Shaw squealed.

"One of you say something," North said to the rest of them, red in his cheeks. "I fucking dare you."

"North," Shaw wailed, both hands over the wounded nipple. "What if I'd been lactating?"

Tean opened his mouth like he might respond to that, but he stopped when Jem elbowed him. Instead, he said, "Theo and Auggie need to go home. They need rest. Lana needs to be in her own bed."

Theo nodded again. He remembered the emptiness of the burn. Coming out of the green of hickory and pine, the smell of the duff warming up under the sun, and then the reek of old smoke and char. The emptiness had been big enough, he remembered thinking, to swallow him up.

"Come on," Auggie whispered, touching his arm.

Theo nodded, and they went home.

13

The house was dark, and Jem tried to go first.

"Just in case," he explained.

Theo tried to say no politely. He tried to say that it wasn't necessary. Jem kept insisting, until finally, Theo said, "It's my goddamn house."

Jem nodded, but the corners of his eyes tightened as he stepped back.

While Auggie carried Lana upstairs, Theo led Jem and Tean to the living room. He turned on lights as he went. For a moment, as they stepped into the living room, before he found the switch, they could see out through the sliding glass doors to the deck. Everything was dusted with silver: the patio furniture Auggie had spent so much time deliberating over; the grill Theo needed to clean; the maples bent over the creek; the water, like someone had drawn a line with mercury. Theo thought, in that moment, he could hear the babble of the creek. And then the lamps sprang to life, and the doors became a mirror, and Theo saw himself in the glass.

He told Jem and Tean to help themselves from the fridge while he checked on Auggie. He went upstairs and reached the second-floor hallway as Auggie was emerging from Lana's room. Auggie held a finger to his lips and shut the door, and then he led Theo into the guest bedroom. He shut that door too, and then he turned on the light and began to check everything: the bedding, the closet, the dresser drawers.

"They don't need to stay over," Theo said.

Auggie glanced up, and something changed in his face. He nodded.

"Nothing is going to happen to you or Lana while I'm in this house."

Auggie sat on the edge of the bed. He smoothed the blanket, his gaze turned down. Then he looked up again. "What about you?"

"I'll be fine."

Auggie nodded.

The silence stretched out between them.

Theo broke first. "So, I'll tell them they can go."

"I'd like them to stay."

Theo thought he could hear the creek again. His jaw cracked when he said, "Ok."

"You haven't slept in two days, Theo. We were literally just talking about this. You need a good night's sleep, and you can't get that if you're worried about staying awake and keeping us alive."

"I said ok."

"What's the problem? I thought you liked them."

Theo didn't say anything.

"They're doing us a favor," Auggie said. "They just want to make sure we're ok."

"Right," Theo said. "Because I can't."

"Hey—" Auggie said.

But Theo left before he could finish. He left the door open behind him because he didn't trust himself to shut it quietly.

In the combined living space at the back of the house, Tean sat on the couch, paging through a book of poetry Theo had picked up—Frank O'Hara. He looked up when Theo entered the room, one finger marking his place in the book. Jem leaned against the counter, a White Rascal in one hand. His lips moved silently as he read something on his phone.

"You're all set," Theo said. "The guest room is at the top of the stairs."

"I'm sorry we're intruding," Tean said.

"Don't apologize to him," Jem said without looking up from his phone. "We're doing him a favor."

"I'm apologizing because of the circumstances," Tean said.

Jem made a noise, but he didn't reply.

"Do you need anything?" Theo asked. "We've got spare toothbrushes—"

"We're fine, thanks." Jem swiped on his phone. "We're going to stay down here. Keep an eye on things."

Tean gave his husband a look, which Jem either didn't see or ignored, and then turned to Theo. "Do you need anything? Is your head ok?"

Theo nodded. "I'll be in our room."

In their bedroom, he stripped and examined each article of clothing before dropping it into the hamper. He expected to find blood. He expected to find oil stains. The knees of his jeans were a little scuffed, and a dirty patch marked the back of his shirt. He found himself waiting for the smell of smoke, but there was nothing but sweat, a hint of detergent.

He showered, and after, he opened the door to clear the steam. The bedroom was empty. Theo put on deodorant, found a pair of sleep shorts, and stumbled putting them on. His knee was always worse when he was tired, and worse still when he'd been skipping his exercises. He caught a stranger in the mirror, and his pulse spiked before he realized he was seeing himself. He turned and looked again. Hair wet from the shower. A long red mark ran diagonally across his shoulder and back where the bat had connected. When he moved that arm, it still pinged at him. On his chest, a triangular bruise was already forming, shaped almost like an arrowhead, and Theo guessed he'd taken a punch that hadn't registered during the chaos of the fight. But it was the eyes, really. He looked away from his eyes and got busy finding a shirt.

By the time he'd pulled on an old Wroxall tee, there was still no Auggie, so he let himself out into the living room. He found him on the couch. Auggie's sleeve was rolled up, and Tean was applying a clean bandage while Auggie furiously wiped away tears.

"It's going to be ok," Tean was saying in a low voice. His bushy hair gave him a slightly wild edge, but the way he moved, the way he touched — he was always, as far as Theo could tell, so gentle. "Everyone's been through a lot —" He stopped when he saw Theo.

Auggie looked up and wiped his face again. He met Theo's gaze and held it, and Theo looked away first.

"Is your arm ok?"

It took a moment too long for Auggie to answer. "Fine. The bandage kept coming off, so Tean's fixing it."

"All done," Tean said, rolling down Auggie's sleeve. "Keep this arm dry while you shower, though. I can help you tie a garbage bag around it if you'd like."

"I can do it," Theo said. He got a garbage bag from under the sink, and by the time he stood up, Auggie was gone again.

Tean gave a significant look at the doorway to their bedroom.

"Where's Jem?" Theo asked.

"He wanted to look around outside." Tean offered a small smile. "I know that doesn't mean anything to you, but it's a sign of how seriously he's taking this."

"Thank you. Again."

"You can trust him," Tean said. "He won't let anything happen to your family." Then he gave another small smile. "Plus he knew I'd be suitably impressed. He did undermine himself a little when he made me list every snake in the state, even the non-venomous ones, before he'd go out there in the dark."

Theo tried to smile, but he couldn't find one, and after a moment, Tean's smile faded too.

"Goodnight," Tean said quietly.

Theo nodded and went into their bedroom. The water was running in the shower, and when he stepped into the bathroom, Auggie was naked. He leaned over the sink, his back to Theo, every line of his body defined with muscle. Theo stepped up behind him. The garbage bag rustled in his hand.

"Are you mad at me?" Theo asked.

Maybe it was his breath on Auggie's skin. Maybe it was proximity, that was all, the way one body senses another. Goose bumps spread across Auggie's back. Then he shivered. The word was almost not a word when he said, "Yes."

Theo leaned in and kissed the back of his neck, and Auggie shivered again.

"I'm sorry," Theo whispered.

The next words were thick: "I know."

"I'm scared."

Auggie made a noise, and Theo realized he was crying, but somehow he said again, "I know."

Theo let the garbage bag fall. He slid an arm around Auggie's waist and hugged Auggie against him. Theo was surprised to find himself hard when Auggie's ass bumped against him, and he was even more surprised, in that distant corner of his brain, that he could be hard and not know it, that his own body could be a surprise to him. He slid a hand down, over the hint of stubble since Auggie had last groomed down there, and Auggie was hardening too.

"We could have gotten killed," Auggie whispered. "Lana could have gotten hurt." His voice broke.

Theo shushed him. He nuzzled Auggie's neck, and Auggie whimpered. He was fully hard now—young and healthy, his body trained and toned. Theo scraped his beard over Auggie's neck because he wanted him to make those noises again. Auggie was shivering, still crying, and Theo tightened his hand so that Auggie couldn't thrust or hump.

"You were such an asshole," Auggie said through the tears.

"I'm sorry."

Auggie shook his head. Tears fell, and some of them hit Theo's arm, hot as embers.

"You were so good tonight," Theo whispered, and then he mouthed at Auggie's neck. "You were so good. So smart. So strong. So brave. You fought off that son of a bitch. You ripped his fucking ear off."

He could feel it, the way Auggie's body responded to the words, the way his muscles softened. In the mirror, Auggie looked the way they used to paint saints: eyes half closed in ecstasy, lips parted, face alight. Even the tear tracks only made him more beautiful. But he whispered, "Just a lobe."

Theo chuckled. He kissed Auggie's ear, and Auggie tried to buck then. Theo held him tighter. "You were so good with Lana. So good. You're perfect, did you know that? And I love you so much."

Auggie's breathing was ragged. He rolled his head to one side, and Theo kissed him again. When Theo started to move his hand, Auggie squeezed his eyes shut. It didn't take long—he moaned as the orgasm hit him, and the tension in his jaw showed his effort to remain quiet. Then he sagged against Theo, his breath hitching like he might start crying again.

He didn't, though, and after a few long moments, he opened his eyes and found Theo in the mirror. "Your turn."

Theo kissed the side of his head. "Not tonight."

Auggie looked like he might protest, but he didn't. He turned around and pressed his lips to Theo's. When he pulled back, he brushed his fingers through Theo's hair and looked into his eyes.

"Let's get this arm covered," Theo finally said. "And you can clean up."

While Auggie showered, Theo wiped down the counter. He went back into the bedroom and stripped off his tee. In the dark, under a thin sheet, he listened to the water shut off, and the everyday sounds of Auggie moving around the bathroom, conducting his nightly routine. Then the bathroom light switched off too, and the soft sounds of Auggie's steps came through the darkness. The bed dipped, and then Auggie was there—warm from the shower, smelling clean, with a hint of sandalwood.

Theo was asleep before Auggie had finished lying down.

He didn't dream, not at first—or if he did, the dreams were in those dark-down places, and they didn't reach his conscious mind. But then he was dreaming, and the dream was of fire: a forest ablaze, and Theo running as the flames chased him. His skin crackled in the heat. Smoke filled his throat. The fire was even a noise: the vast, rushing breath of air being drawn in, so loud it swallowed everything else.

He sat up. Sweat soaked the sheet; his legs were roasting, but now, in that groggy state between sleep and waking, his chest and arms were freezing as cool air brushed damp skin. For another moment, he could hear the fire, the roar of it. And then his brain clicked on, and he saw the fan, which Auggie liked for a little white noise. He tried to take deep breaths, but his chest rose and fell unevenly, and he could hear the edge at the end of every sound, the whine that was almost a sob.

A hand at the small of his back made him flinch. Then Auggie began to rub slowly.

Theo found his leg in the dark and patted it. He managed a cracked whisper: "Sorry."

Auggie made a sleepy noise.

Lying down again, Theo discovered the bedding was soaked through with his sweat. He thought about getting up to lay a towel down. Then he thought about closing his eyes.

Auggie's hand came to rest on his belly. He wiggled his thumb back and forth a few times.

"Go back to sleep," Theo whispered.

"If you'd had a mind-blowing orgasm like me," Auggie murmured, "you'd be sleeping just fine."

A quiet laugh escaped Theo.

"What's up?" Auggie asked.

"Nothing. A bad dream. Go back to sleep."

But Auggie propped himself on one elbow. It was hard to make out anything but an outline in the dark. "We've made a lot of progress in the last few years," Auggie said, and the tone was teasing, but there was something hard underneath it. "How about you don't throw it all away by going back to bad habits?"

In the living room, the TV was on—not loud, but in the silence, Theo could hear the low buzz. He tried to think of what to say, how to say it. The dream was still there; he could feel it breathing down his neck: the devouring heat, the smoke, the white scream of it.

Throat thick, Theo said, "They were here, Auggie. In our house. Our home."

Auggie was quiet for what felt like a long time. Then he let out a breath that seemed to be agreement.

"I don't care what John-Henry says," Theo said, the words pouring out of him now. He sat up. "I don't care if he thinks they've got a line on the Cottonmouth Club, or if they think the four of them can handle it while we stay safe at home. Someone was here, Auggie. Someone came here looking for something, and I don't think they found it. And if I'm being totally honest, I don't know if any of this is connected back to the Cottonmouth Club. Something is seriously wrong, and I'm not going to sit here while someone comes after our family."

Auggie was an outline cut from the darkness of the room. Like paper. Like velvet.

"What do you think we should do?" Theo asked. "Tell me what to do, and I'll do it."

Auggie's laugh screwdrivered through the void. "Come on."

"What do you mean come on? I'm not repeating bad behaviors. I'm asking you, aren't I? We're partners. This is a joint decision."

"I don't know."

"You have an opinion, and I want to hear it."

"I said I don't know."

"Then I want to hear the points you're weighing on each side."

Auggie made a vexed noise. "You know that's annoying. I know you know, and you do it anyway." He hooked his arms around his knees. "I don't like what's going on with you."

"What?"

"I don't know; that's the problem."

"I'm fine, Auggie."

"You slept—" They both looked at the clock's glowing display. It read half past ten. "Less than two hours, and you woke up from a nightmare on the verge of a full-blown panic attack."

"It was a bad dream. I'm fine."

Auggie made that noise again.

"But?" Theo asked.

"But what?"

"But you agree. You don't think this is about the Cottonmouth Club either."

"I think—" He stopped, and his voice softened. "I think this is an impossible situation. They're doing the best they can."

"But you think they're wrong."

Auggie's silence felt like one of those deep-dark places below dreams, but finally he said, "I think whatever is happening, it's more complicated. I think they're only focused on one part. What's been happening, it doesn't add up to something simple and neat. It's messy. There are lots of loose threads. I'm not saying they're wrong, but I think they're missing some of it. Maybe something important." He was silent again, and then he said, "Theo, I meant what I said: I'm worried about you."

I think something's wrong with me.

The words were on the tip of Theo's tongue; he was opening his mouth to say them. And then he stopped. The darkness made him dizzy, like his body couldn't tell up from down. He breathed with artificial slowness, and then he shifted to the edge of the bed and stood. The dizziness went away, and with a kind of abstract dreaminess, he thought, Never mind. It was all fine the whole time.

"We need to talk to Tean and Jem."

14

Neither Tean nor Jem liked the plan.

"I don't think John-Henry wants you leaving the house," Tean said. He pushed his hands through his hair, making it wilder than usual. "In fact, I know he doesn't, because he specifically told me you weren't supposed to leave."

"Too bad," Theo said. "This is important."

"Plus—" Jem said, pausing to toss a piece of popcorn into the air and catch it in his mouth. To judge by the chips and cookies spread out on the countertop, he'd conducted a very successful raid on the pantry. "—you'll probably get yourselves killed."

"We'll be careful," Auggie said.

Jem rolled his eyes and caught more popcorn.

"Let me call John-Henry—" Tean began.

"They're working tonight," Theo said. "Don't bother them."

"Let them go," Jem said. "If they die, maybe we'll get this house."

Tean shot him a dirty look.

"What?" Jem said with a laugh. "Squatters' rights."

"We're just going to talk to someone," Auggie said. "Have a conversation. That's all."

"The teacher?" Tean asked, standing as Theo moved past him. "John-Henry already tried. He's not home."

Theo paused long enough to give him a look. "He's giving you updates?"

Raising his chin, Tean said, "We're part of this too."

"Where is he now?"

Tean hesitated.

"They headed back to Auburn, didn't they?" Theo said. "To the Cottonmouth Club. Fine. I know where Dalton is, and I'm going to have a chat with him."

"If you know where he is, you can tell John-Henry—"

"Tean, we're going." Theo tried to blunt the sharpness of his words. "I appreciate what you're trying to do, but we're going."

The only sound was Jem crunching another piece of popcorn.

"Lana should sleep all night," Auggie said, "but if she wakes up, she's got some books by the side of her bed that she likes. She might be hungry, too; she didn't eat."

Tean nodded. His dark eyes looked miserable behind the glasses. "I think you're making a mistake. You barely slept, and you've been through a lot today. I think your judgment might be impaired."

"I appreciate you saying that," Theo said.

"That's how smart people say fuck off," Jem said and shook his bowl of popcorn.

Theo shot him a look, and he was distantly aware that Tean was sending some not-so-happy energy toward his husband as well.

"Is that a pistol in your pocket," Jem said with a smirk, "or are you just happy to see me?"

"I assume you're going to call John-Henry and tell him what we're doing," Theo said as he tugged at his oversized t-shirt, trying to hide the outline of the gun.

"I think he needs to know," Tean said quietly.

Theo nodded.

"I'm sorry," Tean said.

"Don't apologize," Jem said. "Think about this great house we're going to get."

Theo opened his mouth, but Auggie caught his arm and nodded toward the door.

"Call us," Auggie said, "if you need us."

"Could you pick up some more beer?" Jem called after them. "Maybe something Mexican?"

"He's doing that to annoy you," Auggie whispered as he continued to nudge Theo down the hall.

"Great. He's doing a great fucking job."

Outside, the night had cooled—relatively speaking, anyway. The air was still thick, but not oppressively so. The porch light hung in a hazy ring of humidity. They made their way to the Audi, and Auggie got behind the wheel.

"The community theater," Theo said.

Auggie made a noise like something had clicked, and they drove. Wahredua was a quiet town, with the notable exception of the area around the college. The clock on the dash was nearing eleven, and the streets were empty under the wash of streetlights. They passed Sunburst Laundry, the windows soaped with the design of a rising sun. They passed Wildcat Outfitters, where an animated bullseye winked at them from the sign—each ring illuminating in turn until the bullseye was visible, which then proceeded to flash at them before going dark again. They passed a lonely cinderblock storefront that had been empty as long as Theo could remember, with the words REPLAY COMPUTERS on a faded sign above the door.

The community theater was an uninspiring brown building with hardboard siding and a flat roof, and it looked like something a bureaucrat had dreamed up—hell, probably a committee had been involved. A dozen cars were still in the parking lot when they arrived, and although most of the building was dark, Theo could see lights on deeper in the building. They left the Audi and tried the front doors, which were locked.

"Want me to try calling?" Auggie asked, already pulling out his phone.

Theo shook his head and led the way around the side of the building. He had been to enough plays here—on his own, with Auggie, and with students—to know the layout of the building. They followed a sidewalk past more of the darkened windows, and then a ramp led down to an exit-only door propped open with a brick, because in the past, Theo guessed, one too many actors had been locked out after a smoke break. A wedge of light from inside forced back the darkness. Voices spilled out, and then a burst of music, and then laughter.

When Theo stepped inside, they stood backstage. The set showed a Depression-era apartment building with a Juliet balcony. A woman and a man leaned against the railing, kissing.

"No, no, no!" Theo recognized Dalton Weber's voice. The drama teacher appeared a moment later, climbing onto the stage. He looked a little less like Pat Sajak right then—bags under his eyes, the suggestion of a squint, what looked like dust tracked across his button-up. Waving a rolled-up sheaf of papers toward the balcony, he shouted, "She has her back to the audience, her back. Your ass! Is that easier to understand?"

The woman on the balcony huffed and squirmed a little more.

"Your ass!" Dalton had clearly come from the playing-to-the-back-row school of acting. "Your fat ass!"

"This window is the size of a Kleenex box!" the woman shouted back at him. "We won't both fit!"

Dalton looked like he was going to respond to this, but at the same moment, a waifish boy pranced up to him. The boy looked like eighteen going on thirteen, with flaxen hair and a creamy complexion, and for a moment, Theo thought it was Leon Purdue. But after that first impression, he could see the differences: not the same face, not at all, but a look. And then he thought, A type.

The boy whispered something to Dalton, and Dalton rolled his eyes—playing to the back row again. He touched the boy's arm. The boy giggled, but he didn't pull away. Dalton said something else, and the boy nodded and hurried off.

"Take five," Dalton announced. And then, pitching the words up to the couple on the balcony, he snapped, "Figure it out!"

Dalton headed toward the opposite end of the stage, and Theo started after him. Auggie walked at his side, glancing at the set.

"Dick," the woman said, but not quite loud enough for Dalton to hear.

"What crawled up his ass?" the man said.

"Nothing he liked," the woman said, and they both laughed.

"Didn't they use a window in the movie version?" Auggie asked.

Theo was surprised to feel himself smile. "They did."

"Not exactly his own artistic vision, then."

"Not exactly."

"Some creative genius."

Theo laughed, and that surprised him too. "Honestly, I'm kind of grateful. It's hard enough to get the kids to understand what's going on. Doing it like this makes it easier for them to understand why Claudio would believe Hero is cheating on him. You stage it for them, and they get to be part of the process—they see Hero's servant in the window, they think she's Hero, they make the same mistake Claudio does because, of course, that's the whole point."

"Misunderstandings," Auggie said as they pushed past a black curtain.

Dalton was a few yards ahead of them, elbowing open a door. He stepped out into the hall, and the door swung shut.

"Misunderstandings," Theo said. "Claudio and Hero, of course. And Benedick and Beatrice; they're the epitome of a misunderstanding—they even misunderstand themselves, the way they think they hate each other and don't realize they're actually in love."

"I believe a certain someone once got an article published in *Shakespeare Quarterly* about characters in Shakespeare coming to know themselves."

"This is going to be hard for you to believe, but teenagers aren't actually as impressed by that as you think."

Auggie faked a gasp.

This time, Theo grinned.

Maybe it was a couple of hours of sleep. Maybe it was the sex—being able to touch Auggie again, be with him again. Maybe his body had finally recovered from the adrenaline purge. Maybe it was simply doing something again, instead of feeling helpless and afraid. Whatever it was, Theo felt like his head was clearer than it had been in a while. He caught Auggie looking at him, and their conversation from earlier echoed back to him, the things Theo had wanted to say.

Auggie was still looking at him, a question forming in his face, so Theo said, "And that article wasn't about *Much Ado*."

It was a moment, nothing more. A pause. And then Auggie gave him that goofy grin and rolled his eyes, like everything could be normal again.

A shout from the hallway made Theo put an arm out to stop Auggie. Auggie made an annoyed noise. Theo inched forward, moving closer to the door, listening. Raised voices filtered through the steel, but Theo couldn't make out the words. He nudged the crash bar, inching open the door, and paused as his eyes adjusted to the dim light of the hallway.

Dalton stood facing a blond woman Theo recognized from earlier that day—he had seen Ambyr outside Leon Purdue's home, where she had been arguing with Leon's mother about something. She had changed clothes since the last time he'd seen her, and she now wore a black crop top and a leopard-print skirt worn low enough to expose what was clearly a G-string. Theo thought that might disqualify her, on technical grounds, from being called Leon's stepmother—well, that and the fact that she couldn't have been more than two years older than the boy. As Theo watched, she passed something to Dalton, and Dalton shoved it in a pocket.

"Don't piss me off," she said. "I'm sick of your bullshit."

Dalton rubbed his cheek, and with a kind of retroactive shock, Theo realized that Dalton had been the one who had cried out, and that the shout he had heard through the door had been pain. Dalton looked on the brink of tears.

If Ambyr noticed, she didn't seem to care. She pulled out her phone, already checking her hair, and tapped the screen a few times. Holding the phone at eye level, she said, "So, I just got some cash, and now I'm going to get crunk!" She gave a little scream and then laughed for the camera. "Oh my God, that's so cringe, but I had to do it—"

As though on cue, the blond twink came down the hallway. The way he popped out from behind the corner of the next intersection, and the furious expression on his face, told Theo he'd been eavesdropping, and he hadn't liked what he'd heard. He was carrying a paint tray that still held bright pink paint—Theo thought maybe he'd seen a similar color used for the flowers on the set pieces.

Ambyr was too busy laughing for her audience to notice that the twink was dead set on a collision course. He crashed into Ambyr, and the paint tray hit her in the belly. A few drops spattered the floor, but the twink's aim had been true, and most of the paint went onto Ambyr.

She screamed.

At first, it was wordless outrage. And then it escalated, rising higher and louder as she processed what had happened.

"You ruined my stream!" Ambyr swung a fist at the boy. It wasn't a serious attempt to hit him, more an outburst, maybe even a reaction. But it still caught Theo by surprise. "You ruined everything!"

She burst into tears, plucking at her ruined clothing with her free hand, spreading paint to her fingers. Theo had spent enough time around Auggie to know the light on her phone meant she was still live. Her crying turned into sobs, and then she shoved past the boy. She kicked the fallen paint tray with one sandaled foot, and it skittered across the hall with the sound of a tin can, leaving streaks of paint across the carpet. A moment later, the sound of Ambyr crashing into one of the doors echoed down the hall, and her weeping faded.

Dalton stared in the direction Ambyr had gone.

The blond boy shifted his weight uncertainly. "Um, Mr. Weber, I'm sorry—"

A half-formed laugh fell from Dalton's mouth. He rubbed his chin, and then another laugh, a real one, came. His gaze shifted to the boy. "That was excellent, Ross. Excellent!"

Ross ducked his head, but he grinned. "She was being such a bitch. She can't talk to you like that."

"Yes, well." Some of the humor faded from Dalton's face, and he looked sallow again, too tanned, skin massaged with too many creams. "You have to do something for me. You have to pretend you didn't hear any of that, all right? Forget all about it. She's not a nice person. And the next time she comes, you'll have to stay clear—she holds a grudge."

"Oh, I'm not scared of her. I can be a bitch too."

"For my sake, dear one. For my sake."

Ross's smile got bigger, and he lowered his head to hide it.

"Now, we've got to hurry and clean this up before it sets. If the theater fines us for the carpet, we'll be sunk. Chip-chop, love. Run and grab something."

Ross turned and jogged back the way he had come.

As the sound of his steps faded, Theo pressed out into the hall. Dalton had his phone in one hand, and he was doing something, a little smirk pasted onto his face. He looked up, and a string of reactions flashed across his face: shock, fear, and then the oily unctuousness that Theo remembered from staff meetings.

"Well, hello, Theo." He shoved his phone into his pocket. "What are you doing here?" A little laugh. "Did I miss a PLC meeting?"

The pills made a bulge in the pocket of his tight jeans. And for a moment, Theo remembered: the way one fit under his tongue, the weight of it, the edges pressed against sensitive muscle and membrane. The relief as it began to dissolve, his brain anticipating the relief before it could make its way through his bloodstream. The tension, and then the release. Like a key. Like his body and mind were a series of locks waiting to be opened.

It was the dream, he told himself. The sleepless nights. It's knowing what this piece of shit has done. Theo had a million reasons, and he lined them up for himself, neat as you please. But what he remembered was how the pill, once it had absorbed enough of the moisture in his mouth, began to crumble, and the secondhand rush it gave him, knowing it would dissolve faster, knowing he'd get more of it, knowing he'd get it faster.

He punched Dalton in the mouth.

The theater teacher went down. He did it the way he did everything else, stagily, his legs flying up, his arms windmilling, like he had trained his body to the consummate peak of theatricality, and now, in a moment of genuine distress, he couldn't turn it off.

"Theo!" Auggie barked.

Dalton warbled a cry, part pain, but mostly disbelief.

Theo bent and grabbed the collar of his button-up. Sometimes you had to use the hair, if you wanted them to play along, but with someone like Dalton, someone who was scared and who was—aside from the drugs and, most likely, the abuse of a minor—a good citizen, someone who went along to get along, usually a shirt was enough. Even in the bad old days, even in claptrap bars and shithole saloons, guys who thought they were rough and tough, lots of them were that kind—in a classroom, Theo would have called it prosocial, or conformist, or a dozen different things. Right then, though, he just knew it on instinct; that part of him was awake again, scenting violence in the air, raising a shaggy head.

His instincts were right: instead of lying limp and forcing Theo to drag him, instead of fighting back, Dalton scuffed along with his legs, trying to keep up—and, in the process, inadvertently helping Theo drag him toward the bathrooms.

"What the hell are you doing?" Auggie asked.

When they reached the door, Theo hit it with his shoulder, and then he held it open with his heel while he dragged Dalton inside. Dalton was still making those baby-bird cries, reaching back to bat at Theo's arm, his touches butterfly light. Theo got him a little farther into the bathroom. It was an older style, done in blues and greens that suggested home décor circa *The Partridge Family*, with little square tiles covering the floor and halfway up the walls. Easier to clean, Theo thought as his foot smudged a drop of blood that had fallen from Dalton's mouth. The mirrors were rectangular and banded in stainless steel, and Theo looked away from the thing moving in them. He changed course again, shoving Dalton toward one of the stalls.

"Theo! Hey!" Auggie's voice wasn't Auggie's anymore. He caught Theo's arm. Theo rounded on him, but Auggie stayed where he was, face set with a challenge. "What in the world—"

"Wait outside."

"No, I'm not going to wait outside. What's wrong with you?"

"Then let go of me."

Maybe it was something in his voice. Maybe it was whatever had clawed its way up out of the past, that feral thing from the bad old days. Auggie's eyes got wide, and he released Theo's arm.

Dalton was on his hands and knees, one hand on the door to a stall. "My tooth," he was saying. Theo couldn't see his face, but he could see three drops of blood clustered together on the tiles. "I think you chipped my tooth."

Theo moved behind him. He grabbed his collar again and forced him forward, into the stall. The toilet was the old kind, long and deep. It looked clean, or as clean as a toilet ever got.

"Theo," Auggie said, and he sounded lost and far off, and that made sense because the part of Theo that heard him, the part that understood the timbre of Auggie's voice as fear—fear for you, that part of him recognized, he's afraid of what's happening to you—was down at the bottom of a well again. In the deep-dark place. Staring up toward that little circle of light and order and sanity, where Auggie's voice drifted down to him.

"Tell me about Leon Purdue," Theo said.

Dalton twisted around, clawing at Theo's arm now, squealing, "Let me go, let me go!"

The key was to use your knees to control their body, to collapse their elbows if they tried to brace themselves. That had been another lesson from the bad old days.

Water splashed. Dalton thrashed. His feet drummed against the tile.

The pull, when it came, was so much stronger than Theo expected that it moved his whole body. He came off balance, lost his grip on Dalton, and thudded into the side of the stall. The toilet paper holder dug into his hip. Pain didn't make its way down to the deep-dark place, but it registered as a distant red light.

Auggie's face was inches from Theo's, and in a whisper shout, he demanded, "Are you out of your mind? You're going to kill him!"

Theo reacted without thinking. He broke Auggie's hold. Auggie stumbled into the stall partition, and at first, the only thing on his face was surprise. Then it closed, folding hurt and rage into smaller and smaller parcels until there was nothing left. And from that place inside himself, deep down at the bottom of that hole, Theo tried to say he was sorry.

But what he heard himself say was "I told you to wait outside."

Auggie's eyes looked liquid, but he didn't cry. He pushed off from the partition, and his steps splashed away. A moment later, the door breathed shut on its closer.

Dalton was sputtering and crying. Water dripped. It was like waking, like someone had turned a switch and Theo was back at the front of his brain again. The world pressed in on Theo: the faint hint of urine, the echoes coming back from the tile, the ache in Theo's knee, in his hand. He'd need to ice it. Auggie was always kind about packing the ice; he knew just how Theo liked it when his knee was acting up.

Theo dragged himself back from those thoughts. He turned his attention to Dalton, who was starting to cry in earnest—humiliation and fear working on him now as the initial shock wore off.

"This is the second time," Theo said, and he tried to make the words hard, but what he felt was tired and old and sick of himself. "There won't be a third. Tell me about Leon Purdue."

"I didn't do anything," Dalton said, crying harder. "I didn't even touch him. He needed a place, that's all. I swear to God! I didn't do anything!"

"He needed a place to stay."

"His parents divorced. He was emancipated. He wouldn't stay with his mom, wouldn't tell me why, so he was staying with Merlin and Ambyr. Then they got into a huge fight, and Merlin threw him out."

Merlin, the wizard of shitty dads, Theo thought. And Ambyr, dealer and part-time influencer.

"And?" Theo asked.

"He was at the Pretty Pretty one night. I knew he was underage; I wasn't going to mess with that. Plus, he'd been a student, and you never know. But he came up to me. He wanted to talk, that's all. He told me."

Dalton wiped his face. "I'd had a few drinks. I thought I was being nice. And he was so sweet."

"And it was the perfect setup: your live-in twink, on demand."

"No! I didn't—I wouldn't have done that."

"I find that hard to believe."

Dalton looked up at him. With his hair lying in scraggly strands against his scalp, and his concealer ruined by the water, he looked old. "He's a child!"

"What happened?"

"He left."

"Come on, you're going to have to do better than that."

"I swear. I swear to God! I came home from school one day, and he was gone. All his stuff was gone. He packed up and left."

"Where'd he go?"

"I don't know."

"All right," Theo said.

When he started to move, Dalton squeaked and drew back, trying to wedge himself between the toilet and the side of the stall. "I'm telling you I don't know! His dad! Merlin!"

"He went back to Merlin?"

"No! I told you they got in a huge fight, right? Well, Merlin said he was going to kill Leon. And that wasn't a joke. He really would have killed him; that's what Leon told me. So, he was going to leave. He wanted to move out west. LA. He wanted to be an actor. We were always close because he wanted to be an actor." The last of Dalton's dignity crumbled, and he started to weep, hands outstretched toward Theo—half pleading, half warding off. "Please, I didn't do anything!"

It had none of the over-the-top dramatics of Dalton's earlier performances. In a way, it was probably what Dalton aspired to—or, at one point in his life, had aspired to: the charge of raw emotion like a live wire, fear making the air spark.

Theo reached for Dalton again, ignoring his wail of protest and his feeble kick. He flipped him over and reached into his pocket and took the pills.

"Clean yourself up," Theo said. He let himself out of the bathroom.

Auggie waited farther down the hall, arms crossed, back stiff. He looked over as Theo approached, and his eyes were flat and hard. "Did you kill him?"

Theo wanted to close his eyes. Instead, he said, "No."

"Good. I guess that's something."

"I'm—"

"If you say you're sorry, Theo, I'm going to leave. Do you understand me?"

Theo swallowed. Finally, he managed a nod.

"I am so fucking sick of you being sorry," Auggie said, and he sounded like he was out of breath, like he'd been running and running, and his body had burned up all its fuel. Trying to get to you, a part of Theo thought. Trying to save you. Auggie pressed his hands to his eyes. When Theo put a hand on his shoulder, Auggie shrugged him off, dropping his hands, and stared out at him from behind the tears. Then he punched Theo in the chest—not hard, not really, but Theo remembered the way Auggie had stumbled into the partition.

"Auggie," Theo whispered.

"You are such an asshole." The words had a trembling quality that Theo knew Auggie would hate; he hated anything that made him sound young, and right then, he sounded young and hurt and broken-hearted. "I'm so sick of you right now."

"You're right. I am an asshole. You're right to be sick of me."

Auggie dashed at his eyes again with his arm and took a deep breath.

"Let's go home—"

"While you were off acting like a colossal dick," Auggie said over him, "I sent that kid away, the one who was supposed to clean up the paint. I decided you probably wouldn't want to be interrupted while you were committing murder."

"I wasn't going to kill him."

"Are you even for real? Theo, you were a fucking zombie in there. If I hadn't pulled you off him—"

He cut himself off, and Theo wondered about that. About all the things they couldn't say to each other. He should have said, again, *I wasn't going to kill him*, but he didn't say that either.

"Please, Auggie—" was what he settled on.

But Auggie spoke over him. "Anyway, I told him I was from the theater, and we were just going to replace the carpet squares, and then I offered to help him carry the cleaning supplies back to the closet so that he wouldn't walk in on you. Come on."

He led Theo down the hall, and they took a turn that led them into the backstage portion of the building. Auggie stopped at the first door and pointed to a small plaque that said CUSTODIAL.

"Ok," Theo said. He opened the door, and sure enough, it was a custodial supply closet. "What am I missing?"

"The plaque, Theo. Look at the plaque."

Theo gave it another glance, and then he remembered: Shaniyah's video, the montage of recordings from the theater, and a plaque identical to this one—only it had said TRAP ROOM, not CUSTODIAL.

"Jesus," Theo said.

Auggie nodded.

"Good work, Auggie. God, really good work. That's amazing."

It was a cheap tactic. Theo meant the words—as usual, Auggie had shown his intelligence and resourcefulness, and he'd made an important connection. But he also knew the effect the words would have on Auggie.

Or at least, the effect, they usually had.

"Don't do that," Auggie said, the words cold and clipped. "Don't do that again until I tell you it's ok."

A stage door opened, and music flooded the hall. Someone was playing a lute and singing, "Hey nonny nonny." Someone else shouted good-naturedly, "Let's get the hell out of here."

"Auggie—"

"Did you hear me?"

The stage door shut hard, and the sound of metal on metal thundered down the hallway.

"Yes," Theo said.

Auggie turned and started down the hallway again.

The door to the trap room was at the far end of the hall, and it was clearly marked, just as it had been in Shaniyah's video. When Theo tried the handle, it was locked, but it was an interior lock, barely a step above a thumb lock. He got out his insurance card, because that one would be easy to replace if it got damaged, and forced it between the door and the jamb. Then he brought it up, quick and hard, at the same time that he yanked on the handle. The door popped open.

Muscle memory, he thought, and suddenly he wanted to laugh. Or maybe cry. It was hard to tell. The bad old days.

The air that wafted up had a faint, foul note that sent pins and needles through Theo. He nudged the door, opening it a few more inches, and more of the fetor seeped up to them. He remembered hearing—it felt like ages ago—that Emery and John-Henry had once found a body under a stage.

"I think you should call the police," he said.

Auggie shouldered past him and started down the stairs. Theo counted to five and went after him.

The flight of stairs was longer than Theo expected, doubling back on itself once, and the stink grew stronger the farther they went. Emergency lights provided enough illumination to pick out each step, but details were lost in the shadows. Auggie, for example. In that low illumination, from lights mounted high on the walls, he looked smaller than he actually was. Compressed. Like something had pushed and pushed and pushed until he was, somehow, less. Something, maybe a sound, made Auggie turn his head, and the sudden familiarity of his profile went through Theo—a puncturing relief that he didn't have words for.

When they reached the trap room itself, Auggie felt around for the lights, and then they came on: banks of fluorescents flooding the space with light. It was a large, high-ceilinged room, and overhead, the occasional sound of a footstep echoed through the stage floor. The trap room itself was surprisingly full of what appeared to be theater miscellanea: stacks of plastic totes, one of them filled with brightly colored wigs; a pallet with what appeared to be the pieces of a chandelier (*Phantom of the Opera*, Theo thought); a mocked-up player piano that was nothing but cardboard and a few one-by-fours.

The stench was strong enough that Auggie pulled his shirt up over his mouth and nose, and Theo followed suit. They moved deeper into the maze of boxes and shelves. The fluorescents' hum registered barely at the edge of hearing, like something Theo felt in his teeth more than actually heard. Overhead the footsteps stopped. The silence began to build.

They maneuvered around a piece of set (what appeared to be the exterior of *The Addams Family* mansion, if Theo didn't miss his guess), and Auggie stopped. In the wall ahead of them was a service elevator, where a large plastic tilt truck waited on casters. The tilt truck was the kind of thing a lot of custodial departments had, a multipurpose conveyance for whatever you could throw inside it. A leg was hooked over the side: bare brown skin, white Nike sneakers.

"I'll check," Theo said.

But Auggie started forward again, and the only thing Theo could do was follow.

Shaniyah had been his student. She'd been to their house. He would have said he'd recognize her anywhere. But what was left in the tilt truck wasn't Shaniyah, not anymore. He didn't recognize the clothes—the knit cutout shirt that seemed too mature for a girl who had giggled while playing with Lana, the polka-dot skirt that hung askew on her now. The bloat of decomposition had started, distending her features, but in other ways, she looked shrunken—her eyes collapsed into half-open sockets, her cheeks hollow. Someone had duct-taped her mouth shut. Flies buzzed and settled on the foam leaking around the tape.

Auggie gagged once, and then he turned toward the way they'd come.

Theo started to follow, and then something caught his eye—a hint of orange at Shaniyah's finger. He forced himself to lean over the tilt truck. It was a bit of fuzz, the kind of thing you might pick up if you had long nails and caught them on a sweater the wrong way. Or, Theo thought, if you were struggling with someone who was trying to kill you.

He went after Auggie. As he started up the stairs, he left the lights on for Shaniyah.

15

Auggie lost track of the hours he spent being interviewed: first at the theater, explaining what had happened to a red-faced uniformed officer he didn't recognize; then to Detective Palomo, who arrived in jeans and a Cubs t-shirt, her long, dark hair tucked under a newsboy cap; and then at the station, to Palomo again, and then to John-Henry. He had arrived hours later, the expression on his face grim. He hadn't said it, not then, but Auggie knew he'd been out at the Cottonmouth Club, some ninety minutes of driving back roads and state highways.

He asked the questions Palomo had asked, and Auggie and Theo gave the same answers. For now.

"Detective Palomo tells me that Dalton Weber appears to have been assaulted," John-Henry said. "She says you told her you don't know anything about that."

Theo's gaze was fixed on the table.

Auggie said, "No."

"She says that, according to your statement, you talked to Mr. Weber."

"That's right."

"But you didn't talk to him about Shaniyah Johnson."

"John-Henry, we've done this a million times," Auggie said.

"Did you talk to him about Shaniyah Johnson?"

Auggie groaned.

"No," Theo said and rubbed his face. "We asked him about his relationship with Leon Purdue."

"According to statements from crew members, Mr. Weber had a conversation with a blond woman this evening."

"Yes," Auggie said. "Her name's Ambyr, and she's Leon's stepmom, or his dad's girlfriend, or something. And she's a drug dealer. And she hit him—Dalton—we're pretty sure. I don't understand why we're going round and round about this. Isn't it obvious what happened? Dalton had something going with Leon. It ended, or it went wrong, or something happened. And then Shaniyah showed up and started asking questions, and Dalton decided to get rid of her. Why haven't you arrested him?"

For a moment, the anger in John-Henry's face was a tamped-down heat, like banked coals fanned until they were on the brink of flames again. He got up and left the interview room. Then he came back, and he shut the door hard.

"This is just us talking. We have arrested him, Auggie. He's being interviewed right now by Detective Palomo. And for the record, she's good at her job, and she doesn't buy for a second that Dalton Weber ended up in his current condition because Ambyr Hobbs slapped him." His attention shifted to Theo. "You're lucky Dalton isn't saying anything—and I mean that literally, not anything—because otherwise you'd be looking at an assault charge, Theo. Minimum. Jesus Christ, what got into you?"

Theo shook his head. He put a hand on the table, still staring down, and ran his thumb along the edge.

John-Henry rubbed his forehead, and some of the tightness drained out of his body.

"You arrested Dalton?" Auggie asked.

"Yes."

"Um. Why?"

Dropping his hand, John-Henry fixed Auggie with a look.

"I mean if you want to tell us," Auggie said in a rush.

"We arrested him because, as I told you, Palomo is a good detective. As soon as she saw those fibers under Shaniyah's nails, she used every officer she could get her hands on. They've been picking through the garbage at the theater and at Dalton's apartment for the last couple of hours."

"They found a match?"

"They found a match." But John-Henry sounded tired. "An orange cardigan. According to some of the cast and crew, he's worn it recently. As recently as last week; that's the best guess."

"That's great, right?" Auggie looked at Theo, who was still staring at the table. "I mean, you've got a motive, you've got physical evidence linking him to the body." He stopped. "What's wrong?"

"Why?" Theo said quietly.

John-Henry nodded.

"Why kill her?" Auggie said. "We already know—"

"Why leave her body in the trap room?" John-Henry said. "Why toss your sweater in the dumpster behind your house? Why kill her at all?"

"She was asking questions about Leon."

"Right, Auggie. She was asking questions. She was a teenage girl playing sleuth on her phone. Which, by the way, is still missing, along with her bag."

"You don't think Dalton did it?" Auggie let out a disbelieving laugh. "Are you kidding me?"

Theo shook his head.

"I don't know," John-Henry said. "I think the scenario you've laid out is possible. Hell, Auggie, it's actually plausible. I think a prosecutor can make this one land. But something feels off about it."

"He won't answer any questions," Auggie said. "Doesn't that tell you something?"

John-Henry shrugged.

"Theo?" Auggie asked.

It seemed like it took a long time for Theo to rouse himself, and then his eyes met Auggie's only briefly before skating away. "I don't know."

"Well, who the hell is going to know, then? You're the one who talked to him."

"He told me he didn't touch Leon. That much, I believe; he was…"

"Terrified?" John-Henry suggested dryly.

Theo rolled one shoulder. "But I didn't ask about Shaniyah. I don't know."

"Why?"

Theo's expression was blank.

"Why didn't you ask him about Shaniyah?" John-Henry said. "I thought that was the whole point."

Theo had a decent poker face, but right then his distress was clear.

"Things got out of hand," Auggie said. "We got as much as we could out of him." John-Henry gave Auggie an appraising look, so Auggie hurried to add, "Look, Dalton is a creep. Maybe it's technically true that he didn't do anything with Leon, but he still had a teenager, a former student, sleeping at his house. And I know how he was looking at that boy tonight at the theater. And his vibe is super creepy. The drugs, too—what about the drugs?"

"He must have flushed them," John-Henry said, "or stashed them; he didn't have them with him when Palomo brought him in for the interview."

Auggie let out a frustrated noise. "So, what? You're going to let him go."

"Of course not. I told you: it's a solid case, and for all I know, Dalton really did kill that girl. But there are things about it I don't like. I'm hoping some of that will get cleared up as we go along. If he's guilty, we're going to put this case together nail by nail."

"What about Shaniyah's aunt and uncle?"

A yawn caught John-Henry. "Palomo's going to inform them. She would have done it already, but they found the cardigan, and things took off. I offered, but she still wants to do the notice. It's going to be a long night for her, especially with Gray still on leave." He stopped another yawn with his fist.

"Did you find anything?" Auggie asked. He didn't have to say *at the Cottonmouth Club*.

John-Henry shook his head. "We checked the lot; the vehicles you described weren't there. We tried a few other places out there—bars, clubs, anywhere those guys who attacked you might have gone. But this is a needle in a haystack situation. They could have gone anywhere. They could be holed up at home with the garage door down. We'll pick it up tomorrow and grind it out: traffic cameras, witnesses, vehicle registrations. It won't be fun, and it definitely won't be fast, but at least we've got something to follow. We'll track them down, and we'll figure out the connection to the Cottonmouth Club. It's just a matter of time."

Auggie nodded. The jittery energy running through him seemed to have evaporated, and now his head had that unfamiliar lightness that came from exhaustion, the sense that he was detached from his body.

"I'm sorry, for the record," John-Henry said.

Theo raised his head.

"I should have listened to you." Frustration—and what sounded, to Auggie, like a mixture of self-recrimination and discouragement—ratcheted down John-Henry's voice. "You told me something was wrong, you asked me to keep looking. God, I feel like a broken record. You were right."

"John-Henry—" Auggie said, and he looked at Theo.

"This isn't your fault," Theo said. "She'd been dead for days—before we even knew she was missing. And Shaniyah's aunt and uncle kept telling you everything was all right. You did listen to us, and we appreciate that. There just wasn't anything you could do."

"That's what you told us," Auggie said. "You didn't have any options, and you were right."

"Yeah, well." John-Henry's smile was only the corner of his mouth. "It fucking blows to be right sometimes."

He walked them out of the station. The small hours were surprisingly cool, and the air smelled like the river.

"Is it—" Auggie stopped. "I mean, Shaniyah's aunt and uncle. Does anyone care that they lied?"

"People care," John-Henry said. "The question is what will happen to them."

"What will happen to them?"

"Nothing," Theo said, and his voice had a vacant quality.

"We'll see," John-Henry said. "It depends on what they actually knew, why they insisted she had gone home. For the love of God, as awful as it sounds, they might have believed they were telling the truth."

An engine puttered on the next street over, and the sound faded to a buzz.

"Get some rest," John-Henry said.

They went home. A groggy Tean waited on the couch. Jem, asleep, had his head in Tean's lap.

"She slept all night," Tean said. "Emery called. Are you ok?"

Auggie nodded. He got ice from the freezer, packed it in a plastic bag, and wrapped a towel around it. Theo floated behind him like a shadow, reaching out and pulling back. Theo, the awkward ghost, Auggie thought, and it was the kind of joke that left his ears ringing. He went into the bedroom and left the homemade ice pack on Theo's side of the bed. He was undressing when Theo came into the room.

Their eyes met. Theo opened his mouth. And then he looked away, and he shut it again.

Auggie crawled under the covers. He thought he heard the rustle of plastic, the clink of ice, the rasp of the towel. He thought Theo said something like "Thank you." He thought, maybe, the sun was coming up. Somewhere, was his last, fleeting thought. It's coming up somewhere.

16

When Auggie woke, the room was full of indirect light—seeping past the blinds, filling up the empty space with a golden weightlessness that meant afternoon. His body ached, and he was still tired, but sleep was already miles off. Theo was gone, and lying there, Auggie considered the state of the bed, the shape of Theo's pillows, and wondered if he had slept there.

He dragged himself to the shower, and without a garbage bag—or Theo to help him cover his arm—he had to settle for splashing around and doing his best to keep his bandage dry. The hot water still felt good, washing away some of the aches. He did his hair quickly, brushed his teeth, and decided he was eighty percent back to being human.

In the living room, Tean was sitting on the floor, playing Fashionista Fillies with Lana. He was, from what Auggie could deduce, trying to braid the mane of one of the fillies, which for some reason had Lana in helpless giggles. Jem lay on the couch in stockinged feet, reading a battered paperback that, when Auggie glimpsed the cover, he could have sworn was an old *Goosebumps*.

"You're up," Tean said.

Lana saw him, squealed, "Papi!" and got to her feet with a steadying hand from Tean. She crashed into Auggie, and he scooped her up long enough to kiss her cheek.

As Lana started in on an explanation about their game—something to do with the fillies actually being unicorns, which she seemed insistent that Auggie understand and remember—Tean said, "Can I make you something to eat?"

"I got it," Jem said a little too quickly. He bolted up from the sofa and shot toward the kitchen.

"I don't mind."

"No, no, no," Jem said—and he actually waved a hand at Tean, like somehow that might stop him. "You've been playing with Lana all morning; it's my turn to chip in."

"Where was this attitude when the girls needed their soccer clothes washed?"

"Scipio and I were guarding the backyard!"

"We've got a widow on one side of us," Tean told Auggie, "and a family with four little kids on the other."

"Mrs. Drake is a holy terror. She tried to spank Scipio." The outrage in Jem's voice made Auggie smile in spite of himself, and he had to hide it when Jem turned to face them across the room. "And the Magleby boys are ruining my rhododendrons!"

"It's a lilac bush," Tean said in that same tone to Auggie. "And since when does guard duty involve beer and pretzels?"

"Teancum Leon!"

"Those soccer uniforms are disgusting."

"The pretzels are for Scipio because he's so vigilant!"

"He was literally sleeping under your chair."

"Because he was full of pretzels and he'd worked so hard!"

Auggie's smile grew, but it felt borrowed, and it faded quickly.

Jem seemed to notice; his gaze sharpened on Auggie, and he asked, "Eggs ok?"

"Eggs would be great. Have you seen Theo?"

Jem and Tean traded a look.

"He went out to work in the yard," Tean said.

Something about the tone caught Auggie. He looked at Tean.

After a moment, Tean picked up one of the fillies, turning her in his hands. "That was a while ago. He, um, didn't sleep very long."

"He didn't sleep at all," Jem said. "And he looks like shit."

"Jem!"

"He does. All haggard and red eyed."

"He was tired."

Jem shrugged. "He looked dead."

Giving Lana another kiss, Auggie set her down. She dropped down next to Tean, already talking to him about the fillies again—insisting, Auggie was aware at the corner of his mind, that now the unicorns had to fight each other for some reason.

"Why don't you sit down—" Tean tried.

"I'll be right back," Auggie said. He touched Lana's head, her hair silky under his fingers, and let himself out onto the deck. The sun struck him, and the angle felt wrong, already too late in the day for having just woken up. The afternoon was sweltering, the air still. Even the silver maples seemed to feel it; they hung listlessly over the creek, where the water was barely a trickle. On good days, Auggie thought, when a breeze lifted the leaves, they caught the light like foil.

Theo was digging a trench along the side of the house. He had, to Auggie's count, eight different shovels in a heap, all different sizes, with blades of different shapes. He had the mattock, too—Auggie knew the word because he'd called it a pickaxe one too many times, and Theo, ever so gentle, had finally, quietly, said, *It's called a mattock.*

As Auggie approached, Theo rose up. He was wearing a black t-shirt in spite of the heat—the Eagles one, the one with the sleeves cut off. As Theo reared back, the mattock coming up and over his head, the muscles in his arms lengthened, his arms long and corded, glistening with sweat. The way the shirt clung to his back showed the muscles there too, the powerful vee of his torso. He shifted his weight, one leg coming back, a strong, thick thigh exposed as the terry shorts rode up. And then the mattock came down. Theo breathed out harshly—an explosion of breath. He did it again. And again. And again. Chunks of earth flew up as he yanked the mattock free. His breathing became uneven, labored, and he lost his balance. His shoulder checked the side of the house, and the mattock rested between his legs, and he trembled, like the wall was the only thing holding him up.

Auggie wasn't sure what gave him away, but Theo said, "You're up."

"Hey."

Theo turned around slowly. Dirt speckled his face and neck and arms, and sweat ran so thickly that at first, Auggie mistook it for tears, running in muddy paths down his cheeks. He ran his forearm over his face. "How are you doing this morning?"

"Afternoon." Auggie's mouth moved mechanically into a smile. "I'm all right. I could use some more sleep."

"Stick around a couple of hours."

"How are you?"

"All right."

"Hot out here."

Theo wiped his face again.

"Why don't you come inside?" Auggie asked. "It's too hot for this kind of work; you'll make yourself sick."

Theo nodded. "Sure. Give me a few more minutes."

Sweat was beading on Auggie's hairline now, damp at his temples. He'd somehow picked a spot in the sun, and the light was scorching the back of his neck.

"What if you just came inside for a glass of water? Have you had anything to drink today?"

Theo gave him a strange smile, and it took a beat for Auggie to recognize it as indulgent. "I'm almost finished."

"Ok."

Theo rested the heel of his hand on the mattock. He had strong hands, strong fingers, with golden hair on the back of them. More dirt flecked the hair there, and a red line showed where Theo had grazed himself with the mattock or one of the shovels. He probably hadn't even noticed it. He's like that, Auggie thought. He'd come in once from clearing brush, a slice up the back of his leg running from ankle to knee, shoe and sock bloody, and he hadn't known until Auggie made him stop so he could clean it up.

"It's just," Auggie said, and he wondered if he was the one who needed a drink of water, "it's really hot. I don't want you getting sunstroke."

The sun danced on Theo's face. It turned his hair and beard into a blaze, the red and gold and copper too bright to look at, so that Auggie wanted to close his eyes.

"I need to get this done," Theo said. "I'll be inside in a bit."

Auggie nodded. He turned and headed back inside. Something hung in front of him, something like a sunspot, moving wherever he turned his head. It was like being blind, a little. He fumbled with the slider to get back into the house, and then the air conditioning hit him, freezing the sweat on his nose and cheeks. Lana was still talking; unicorns had switched to princesses, and in the background, an episode of *She-Ra* was playing. He was aware of Tean and Jem watching him, although he couldn't see their faces, not with his eyes all screwed up. He'd stared at the sun once because Chuy had dared him to—stared until Fer had come out and slapped him upside the head for being so stupid—and it had been a little like this. Fer had been so mad. And then Auggie thought: Fer would be so mad.

"Is it ok if she watches TV?" Tean asked. "I didn't know if you had a time limit."

Auggie nodded, staring through the shifting sunspot in the direction of Tean's voice. And then he heard himself say, "I'm going to catch up on some stuff in the office. If that's ok."

The silence was a little too dense before Jem said, "Sure."

In the office, Auggie shut the door behind him. The blinds were up, and he checked the windows by touch, making sure each one was latched. He had to make sure now. That had gone on his mental list of all the things not to do. Don't change lanes too quickly. Don't brake too hard. Don't leave a candle burning. Don't let Lana out of your sight.

He sat at his desk. In those natural disaster movies—the dumb ones he still kind of liked, even though he knew they were trash—they could show you all sorts of stuff, do all kinds of cool things with special effects. He could see it in his mind now: a flood rushing through a narrow canyon, gathering speed and momentum, knocking down everything in its way. It was on a path to obliterate a city, of course. All that water, all that energy, all that destruction. And it only had one way to go.

He didn't cry because that was on the list too, but he groped around until he found the tissues, and he pressed them to his eyes. His face was hot and puffy, and after a couple of minutes of that, he couldn't breathe through his nose, so he had to suck air through his mouth. And then the worst of it was over. The water reached the end of the canyon. All that pressure released. And the city? He couldn't remember. He couldn't remember the movie, either. Probably not *Sharknado*, he thought.

He tossed the soggy tissues into the wastebasket, grabbed fresh ones, dried his face. He was good at planning, good at organization, good at understanding patterns. He'd used those skills to build his own social media platform, and he used them now for businesses and influencers, to help other people. Hell, he used them to help Theo, who couldn't balance the checkbook to save his life. Not that Auggie had ever balanced a checkbook, actually, but he did keep track of their money.

And right then, his mind was already busy assessing new data, translating it, adjusting plans—scrapping some, making new ones. Things were going to get better. They'd arrested Dalton for Shaniyah's murder, and in the light of day, with a few solid hours of sleep behind him, Auggie didn't know why it had felt so wrong the night before. And now that Shaniyah's murder had been cleared up, things would start going back to normal. Nobody would break into their house. Nobody would attack them in a parking lot. Nobody would send Theo into that place Auggie couldn't follow, because he didn't know the way, and even if he had, didn't know how to bring Theo back. Leon Purdue had gone to California, and Shaniyah Johnson was dead, and the mystery of the missing kids was over.

The more Auggie said it to himself, the easier he breathed.

In a few weeks, after everything had calmed down, Auggie would talk to Theo about therapy again. It had helped—a lot—when they'd started dating. And couples' therapy, too. They probably needed that as well. The anger, that was part of it. Theo had never been an angry person, but over the last year, he had been angry so often. And part of it, Auggie knew, was from trauma—they'd been through so much together, and Theo had been through even more on his own. But part of it, Auggie thought, was something else. And whatever the causes were, they needed to address them. And they would. Together.

But at the same time that the conscious level of Auggie's brain was building a new future, another layer of his mind, barely brushing the edge of consciousness, was saying, He's never going to get better, and he's never going to change. Not in the ways you want. Never. He's never going to want another child. He's never going to want to get married. He's never going to want more than what you have now. Images swam at that level of near-consciousness: the float trips and campouts that would never happen; the trip to Disneyland Auggie had, at some level wanted to recreate from his childhood; the look on Fer's face when Auggie told him he was going to be a grandpa, and the other look, when Auggie finally said, *Because you raised me* or *Because you're the closest thing I've ever had to a dad*.

He was moving before he realized what he was doing, opening the top drawer, taking out the surrogacy paperwork. He rolled toward the shredder. It was ok, he thought. Life went on. And he had a good life. A very good life. He was, after all, happy.

A knock came at the door, and Tean called, "I know Jem just made you eggs, but I think Lana might be ready for an afternoon snack, and I thought maybe an early dinner would be better for everyone."

Auggie dropped the papers next to the shredder, in the pile of everything else he needed to shred. He left the office and went to take care of his family.

17

The dream wasn't one that Theo could put into words. It was a sense of twisting darkness, of something powerful grappling with him. Even asleep, he was aware of his body aching.

The day had been brutal: the work in the sun, the pounding headache, the cored-out sensation of fatigue like nothing he could remember. After showering, while he was sitting at the table, eating some sort of taco Jem had cooked, he'd caught his head nodding, like he was about to fall asleep. I'm getting old, he thought. And he wanted to say it to Auggie, because it was the kind of thing he'd love, but then he remembered that awful gulf between them, the one that had opened over the last few days, and he found himself staring at Auggie, unable to speak, until Auggie had finally said, "Theo?" Said it in that way he had, kind and loving and concerned, like nothing was wrong, even though Theo knew everything was wrong. Knew because he'd messed it up himself. And finally Theo had shaken his head and finished his taco, and the moment had passed.

Now, though, wrestling with smoke and shadows, he was aware of consciousness seeping in as sleep receded.

And then he heard the shout.

He sat up, heart racing, and a part of his brain told him he'd imagined it. Dreamed it. But Auggie was upright too, barely more than a shape in the darkness, his breathing rapid.

Then it came again: "Theo!"

Jem's voice.

"Lana," Theo said as he scrambled out of the bed, and he felt more than saw Auggie nod.

His first move was to get the gun. He dropped to the floor, found the safe, and entered the combination—thankfully, not one of those spinning wheels, just buttons that were easy to identify and press. The lid popped open, and he grabbed the pistol and the magazine. He shoved the magazine home as he got to his feet.

"Theo—"

"Get Lana and go."

Jem shouted again, wordless this time and full of outrage. And pain. There had definitely been pain.

Their bedroom connected with the combined living room and kitchen, and when Theo threw open their door, he had only an impression of the room: the darkness, the flicker of a candle Auggie must have lit after Theo went to sleep, the moonlit deck on the other side of the windows.

Something moved at the periphery of Theo's vision, and Jem shouted — a warning, this time. Theo threw himself to the side. Something barely missed him—a knife—and then Theo hit the coffee table, and his bad knee gave out.

He landed hard on the coffee table, flat on his back, the slap of skin on wood registering for a millisecond before the breath exploded out of his lungs. His body had gone into overdrive, and he was distantly aware of Jem shouting. A shape all in black loomed over Theo. The man—that was how Theo thought of him—raised something. Not a knife, Theo saw. A sickle, the metal matte black. Not some old farm implement—this thing was clearly tactical, minimalist, made with the kind of beauty designed for violence. He thought of the smoke in the dream. Then the sickle flashed down, and Theo was still gasping for air, too slow.

Auggie shouted, and the man in black staggered. Kicked from behind, Theo decided. The man spun around, the sickle in one hand and—now Theo could see—a matching matte black knife in the other. A trench knife, with the long, double-edged blade and the knuckle dusters. Theo rolled onto his side, trying to get up. He could see Auggie now, in nothing but the gray modal trunks that looked like water, sheer and clinging to him, as he backpedaled. He might as well have been naked, every vulnerable point exposed. The man lunged, and Auggie stumbled back.

Then Jem was there, and something spun in his hand, whistling in the darkness. The sound of contact came—a hard, thunking sound—and their attacker howled. The sickle swept out, then the knife, but Jem danced back. Something long and silver flashed in his other hand, warding off the other man long enough for Auggie to get clear.

Theo got to his feet. He'd lost the gun, and a quick, panicked scan of the room showed him it was gone.

"Get out of here," Jem said.

It took a moment before Theo realized the command was meant for him and Auggie. Auggie was already moving, circling behind Jem toward the hallway that would take him to the stairs. Theo backed toward the kitchen, taking advantage of the precious seconds Auggie and Jem had bought him. He gave one last look for the gun, and then he turned to the kitchen.

"Ok?" he called to Auggie.

Auggie nodded, the movement a blur in Theo's adrenaline-warped vision.

"Lana! Lana!"

Auggie kept running toward the hallway, which Theo took to mean that Auggie had understood him. Theo brought his focus to bear on the fight. At the edge of his field of vision, Jem was giving ground to the man in black, moving slowly, fencing with that long, silver sword. Not a sword, Theo thought. But he couldn't come up with anything better. In a few moments, Jem would run out of room—he'd hit the dining table, or he'd corner himself, and then he wouldn't be able to dodge the black steel.

Theo grabbed the chef's knife, the twelve-inch one, from the magnetic strip. He hit the lights, and suddenly he could see. The man in black had done a good job: a close-fitting cloth mask, long sleeves, gloves, nothing to give away his identity. But he was small, Theo thought. Short, with a whipcord frame. Maybe Auggie's height, but with less mass than Auggie packed.

His size clearly wasn't holding him back. Jem held what looked like a telescoping antenna—not a sword. He was bare chested and barefoot—Theo realized, distantly, so was he—in nothing but those gray-and-purple vintage Adidas shorts he loved. A red line ran diagonally across Jem's chest, and blood curtained across his belly.

"Fina-fucking-ly," Jem panted. "Could you stab this bitch in the back, please?"

Theo yanked open a cabinet and took out the lid to the stockpot—the biggest lid they had. Then he started toward the son of a bitch who had come into their home.

The man slowed his advance on Jem, repositioned himself to keep Theo in his field of view. If the possibility of two opponents bothered him, he gave no sign of it. His stance was loose, almost relaxed. The sickle looked like it was hanging from one hand, and although the knuckle dusters meant his grip on the trench knife was tight, his whole body looked liquid.

"We're going to fuck your shit," Jem said. He was grinning, his eyes bright with a wildness Theo hadn't seen before. "I sell real estate, and do you know how fucking cutthroat the Salt Lake market is? And him? He teaches teenagers."

Theo inched closer, hoping to use Jem's patter as cover, but faster than Theo could believe their attacker spun toward him and swung the sickle. Theo barely got the lid up in time.

He might as well have been holding a sheet of paper. The blade of the sickle tore through the steel before catching. Theo yanked, trying to pull the sickle from the man's grip, but the man twisted his body, and instead, Theo lost the lid. The attacker dropped the weapon to his side, trying to shake the sickle free of the lid, and lunged at Theo with the knife.

Jem darted in, the antenna whipping so fast that it blurred. It caught the man on the side of the head, and he expelled a furious breath. Jem pressed the attack, slashing over and over again with the antenna, and the man reacted instinctively, trying to pull out of Jem's reach.

Theo saw the opening and took it. Their attacker's lunge had left his arm partially extended, and now, while his attention was turned to Jem, Theo dropped his own knife to grab the man's wrist and forearm. He forced the man's arm down and brought his knee up, driving it into the man's arm. Theo didn't care if he broke the man's arm or if he simply forced him to drop the knife—he'd take whatever he could get.

For a moment, it seemed to be working. With the sickle trapped in the pot lid, Jem raining down blows, and Theo breaking his grip on the knife, Theo had the barest flash of a thought: we're winning.

Then it all went wrong.

The attacker stomped on Jem's foot, and Jem fell back, howling. Theo tried to take advantage of the man's momentary imbalance, and he managed to drive him back a few steps. But without Jem to distract him, their attacker brought the sickle up, still trapped in the stockpot lid, and swung it in an arc at Theo's head.

Theo twisted, trying to get away from that black metal. The stockpot lid saved him.

Caught in the lid, the blade of the sickle couldn't reach him. But the lid struck Theo instead, and the force of the blow rocked his head sideways. Theo's grip on the man's arm weakened, and he fought to keep hold.

Jem, meanwhile, had somehow stayed upright, and his face was wrought with fury. Their attacker's attention was still focused on Theo, having dismissed Jem—too early, as it turned out. Theo watched now as Jem took advantage of the opening. He staggered forward, one hand knifing out, something small and black visible between his fingers. Whatever it was, it sank into the man's side, and Jem repeated the movement, stabbing in a frenzy over and over again.

The man screamed. The noise was half startlement, half pain. Theo was still holding the man's arm, still trying to wrest the knife free. Now, the man moved with the pressure Theo was applying. The sudden lack of resistance meant Theo stumbled, and his bad knee failed him again. As he lost his balance, their attacker spun into the movement, so that he passed Theo. He kicked backward as he moved, the sole of his boot connected with Theo's back, and Theo grunted as breath exploded out of him. Then he crashed into Jem, and they both went down.

Jem fought to separate them, trying to get free, and Theo flopped onto his back. He still couldn't catch his breath. He tried to help Jem, to disentangle himself from the other man, to get to his feet. But the signals from his brain to his body had been short-circuited somewhere, and all he could do was lie there, arching his back, struggling to get air.

Above them, the man appeared again, sickle and knife finally free for their bloody work.

Then he staggered and let out a muffled shriek.

Theo got onto his side, and he stared in disbelief as Tean brought Theo's cane back for another blow. The vet's hair was wild, his eyes huge, and fear painted his face in broad strokes, but he swung the cane again, and the thud of wood against flesh seemed to reverberate inside Theo's head.

As the attacker rounded on Tean, the vet fell back, giving ground and holding up the cane in a fending off gesture. But the man didn't go for Tean. He let out a furious noise, and then he turned and kicked something resting next to the kitchen island. In the melee, Theo hadn't noticed it, and now he saw that it looked like an old metal gas can. Liquid sloshed as the can tumbled toward the front of the house. Some of it arced out and sprayed the walls. When it hit the floor, more of the liquid flowed out across the floor. It wasn't water—Theo could tell from the way the light hit it—and then he smelled gasoline.

In another smooth, almost contemptuous movement, the man slapped the candle still burning on the island. It flew across the room and landed in the spreading puddle of gasoline, and flames burst into life.

The wave of brightness and heat made Theo flinch back, and by the time he recovered, the man was gone.

Jem was already getting to his feet, shouting something over the noise of the flames as he stumbled toward Tean. Tean was saying something back. Fueled by the gasoline, the fire caught easily, spreading along plaster and wood, lapping at the carpet. The heat made Theo's skin itch, already hot enough that he felt like he had a sunburn.

And then his brain connected the rest of the dots.

The hallway.

The stairs.

Auggie and Lana.

He took a step toward the inferno, and the heat made him feel like his skin was peeling back. He held up a hand. His brain searched for alternatives, anything but the fire. A fire extinguisher. He knew they kept a fire extinguisher—

Something dark moved on the other side of the flames, and then a shape hurtled through the blaze. It was like something dark and primal— something beyond the rational fears of the front brain. And then it staggered and hit the ground, flames licking at it as it rolled.

Tean moved first, dropping onto his knees and grabbing a pillow to beat out the flames, and Theo lumbered into motion then, his body too slow. Jem helped too.

A blanket. A burning blanket, Theo thought.

And then Auggie was staring up at him, Lana still clutched in his arms, her face buried in his chest as she cried uncontrollably.

Theo felt something break inside him, a dam that had been holding back a flood, and he started to weep as he wrapped them in his arms.

18

Later, in Emery and John-Henry's basement—which had been turned over to Theo and Auggie and Lana, without so much as a word of complaint from Colt—Auggie lay quietly and waited for Theo to stop shaking.

It had been hours. The police had come. The fire department. The ambulance. Statements made while the fire engines pumped water and men and women fought the flames. Theo and Jem and Auggie and Lana in the ambulance.

Now, in the darkness of the basement, with Lana asleep on the couch while Theo and Auggie took the floor, Theo gripped the blanket and trembled, and Auggie tried to figure out what to do.

A man had come into their home, and Theo hadn't been able to stop him. Auggie knew what that meant for him. Even with Jem, who had fought like a dervish, Theo hadn't been able to do anything but slow him down. Auggie closed his eyes. What he had seen of the fight had been brief, but he remembered the matte black of the sickle rising like a crescent moon.

Theo was still shaking.

Auggie rolled onto his side. His hand found Theo's arm, and he ran his fingers up and down slowly.

After a while, Theo whispered, "You need to sleep."

"Look who's talking."

Theo didn't answer.

"It's ok," Auggie said. "We're here. We're safe. Let go of it for a little while, Theo. Let go of it until tomorrow."

"Ok," Theo said.

Auggie made a shushing noise.

"Ok, you're right," Theo said. "I'm fine. You need to sleep."

Lana made a restless noise and tossed on the couch.

Auggie found his hand. He worked Theo's fingers loose from the blanket, and then he slotted his between them. Theo had nice hands—strong hands, callused, hard. His fingers tightened around Auggie's until it hurt.

"Stop," Auggie said, and his voice was a little more serious this time.

"Are you sure you don't want to go to the hospital?"

"You heard Frannie," Auggie said. "It's a little bit of skin on the back of my calves, and it's not any worse than a sunburn."

"How's the pain? Has the lidocaine worn off?"

Lana made that noise again, her little body twisting under the blanket.

"Come on," Auggie said, squeezing Theo's hand. "We're going to wake her."

Theo nodded, barely more than an impression of movement in the dark. The blanket rustled as Auggie sat up, and then he tugged on Theo's hand, and they made their way upstairs.

They crept to the top of the stairs, and in the kitchen, Auggie eased the door to the basement shut. The main floor of the house was dark and quiet; the sound of uneven breathing from the living room announced North and Shaw's presence. Everyone gathered under one roof, Auggie thought. In case someone came again.

Auggie let them out into the garage. The air was cool in the small hours, and the smell of grass clippings and motor oil was strangely pleasant. Normal smells, Auggie thought. Everyday smells.

Auggie turned on the light. The space was cramped with the Mustang and the Odyssey pulled into their spots, but he found a cooler, and he sat Theo on it. Then he sat on Theo's lap and wrapped Theo's arms around him. He was aware of Theo's heartbeat, of it beating faster than he could count. He was aware of Theo, too. The warm solidity of him. The smell of his hair. The familiar feeling of being safe in his embrace.

"If I catch that other Theo tonight," Auggie murmured, "the one who likes to beat up on you, I'm going to kick his ass."

Theo laughed quietly and kissed the side of his neck.

"Thank you, by the way, for never making me drive a minivan." Auggie heard the possible implications and rushed to add, "I didn't mean it that way."

Theo nodded against him.

"It's just that they're so…gross."

"Uh huh."

"You, on the other hand."

"I'd be perfect in a minivan?"

"I was going to say, if you want a Mustang, we're getting you a Mustang."

"I think Mustangs are wasted if you try to drive under thirty miles an hour."

"But you'd be so hot, Theo. I mean, you are so hot, objectively. But I can just see you sitting in one, window down, one big brawny arm hanging out, your hair flowing in the breeze. Oh God, you'd probably get a farmer's tan, and then you'd get fired because I'd keep you in bed all the time for sex."

"I already have a farmer's tan, if you'll recall. You like to point out the exact spot where my t-shirt and shorts cover me. I believe your usual line is 'I can't believe how white you are.'"

Auggie made a noise that was low and filthy, and he said, "You're right. I hope we can survive on one income."

"We might have to downgrade. I'm not sure our homeowners' insurance covers homicidal maniacs."

"It covers arson, Theo. I already checked. And the house wasn't destroyed. There's some fire damage, and we'll have to clean it up, maybe have some of it rebuilt. But we're going to be fine. Our home is going to be fine. We're going to be fine."

Theo tightened his arms around Auggie, and Auggie grabbed him back, his hands wrapping around Theo's arms, pulling him even closer.

After a while, Theo said, "I'm ok, I promise. I'm better now. Thank you."

"You still haven't given me an answer about the Mustang."

Theo kissed the side of his head.

"Maybe we can borrow John-Henry's," Auggie said as he stood. "For a night."

"For a night?"

"We'll clean it super good."

"Auggie."

"He never has to know."

Theo let Auggie help him up. He kissed him. And then he said, "I'm sorry for—for how weird I was acting yesterday."

Auggie was quiet until it was almost too long. But then he said, "It was a weird day, Theo."

He followed Auggie back inside, and the murmur of voices stopped them in the kitchen.

"—because, dumbass," North was saying, "Auggie looks like a squealer. We would have heard them."

"You're drawing conclusions way too early," Shaw said. "In the first place, he might have gagged Auggie. In the second place, maybe Theo's the squealer."

"That doesn't make any sense. Either way, we would have heard something." In a grudging voice, he added, "Unless they're still waiting for Old Man River's Viagra to kick in."

Shaw's head appeared suddenly above the sofa, and even in the dark, Theo could tell he was looking at them. "Are you still waiting for your Viagra to kick in?"

"Mother of fuck," North said, and he sat up too, another silhouette in the darkness. "How long have you two been creeping on us?"

"I think it's a little creepier," Theo said, "to be lying in the dark discussing our sex life."

"Also, not that it's anybody's business," Auggie said, "but Theo doesn't need Viagra."

"Ok, Auggie."

"Like, he really doesn't need it."

Theo gave him a look that Auggie pretended not to see in the darkness.

"Like sometimes I wonder which one of us is twenty-five and which one of us is thirty-five, just based on—"

"Ok," Theo said. "That's enough right there."

North made a disgusted noise.

Shaw said, "That's so sweet."

"Are you guys awake?" That voice was Jem's and as best Auggie could tell, it came from the top of the stairs. "Thank God. Tean, they're awake." He moved down the steps. "I was going crazy up there. Tean said I had to stay upstairs, and it only took me ten minutes to memorize all of Shaw's credit card numbers. Oh, Shaw, by the way—I found your wallet."

Something tumbled through the darkness, and Shaw caught it. In a voice of wonder, he said, "North, he found my wallet! I didn't even know I'd lost it."

Lights sprang on, and North, shielding his eyes, said, "That's because he stole it, because he's a fucking shitheel. For fuck's sake, could you warn somebody? My fucking eyes."

Tean appeared a moment later. The vet wore a pajama set—shorts and a matching short-sleeved top—printed with tropical plants and monkeys, and nobody had to tell Auggie that Jem had picked it out for him. Jem looked comfortable in a pair of mesh shorts and a white tee, which was almost identical to North's sleepwear. Shaw, of course, wore a sleep mask pushed up on his forehead, a cropped mesh tank, and crocheted rainbow booty shorts. The fact that they were crocheted meant that every time Shaw moved, he was sixty percent naked. What was really remarkable, though, was that Auggie could have sworn he hadn't seen the man with any luggage.

"We couldn't sleep," Tean said.

"He's saying that to be polite," Jem said. "I couldn't sleep. Whatever they gave me is wearing off, and that cut itches like a bastard."

"Watch your fucking language in front of the kid," North said, nodding at Auggie.

"You need to—" Theo began.

But Auggie made a shushing noise and shook his head.

"Are you going to creep over there all night, Shortstack?" North asked. "Is Daddy about to put you to bed?"

Taking Theo's hand, Auggie tugged him toward the living room.

Jem had moved the coffee table against the wall, and he sat there now, playing with a deck of cards, sending them flying one from one hand to the other, and then sending them back again, the movements so practiced that he didn't even seem to be paying attention. Tean sat on the floor next to him, arms around his knees. North had taken the armchair, and he smiled at Theo and shot him the bird. Shaw was sprawled out on the sofa, but he sat up and moved over, making room for them. Theo and Auggie sat, and then, with a smirk for North, Auggie shifted over to Theo's lap.

North groaned. "You're killing me, half-pint."

Auggie brought one of Theo's arms around him, gave North a smile like butter wouldn't melt in his mouth, and rolled one shoulder in a shrug.

"Because, John, I think knowing whether these troglodytes are robbing us blind is preferable to ignorance, although I'm sure—" Emery stopped at the top of the stairs. He wore pajama pants and a Death Cab for Cutie t-shirt that looked like it might pop off him if he breathed too hard.

"No," North said. "Whatever it is, fuck off."

"What are you doing?" Emery asked. "Why are you all awake?"

"We're planning an epic heist," Jem said. "It's going to take all six of us, but we've got an elaborate plan to break into your house and steal every one of these priceless DVD documentaries."

Tean swatted his leg.

"You're already in my house," Emery said.

"Phase one accomplished."

"In the first place, those DVDs are far from priceless, with the exception of *Whiskers and Whispers: Kompromat, Perestroika, and a Soviet History of Cats*, which is surprisingly rare—"

"Very surprisingly," Shaw said.

Emery threw him a dirty look and opened his mouth again, but a hand rested on the back of his neck, and a moment later, John-Henry appeared. He wore a tank top, sweatshorts, and white tube socks, and Auggie was surprised again, the way he always was, by the dark lines of ink that covered John-Henry's chest and arms.

"Everything ok?"

"We're planning a heist!" Shaw announced.

For whatever reason, that made John-Henry grin, and he started down the stairs. "I couldn't sleep either."

"Great," Emery said, but after a moment, he followed. "Maybe I'll call around, see if the clown college can send over a few more people, really round out my night."

"They can't," Shaw said promptly. "I already asked."

"They've got their clown college finals tomorrow," Jem said.

"They're going to be up all night," Auggie said, "throwing pies, spraying each other with seltzer, getting in and out of tiny cars."

"John," Emery said, "I want to apologize for every time I called you a comedian, because clearly I had set the bar too high."

"Also, fuck you," North said with a grin. He flipped Emery off and then, slowly, inverted his hand so his middle finger pointed in the general direction of his dick.

Auggie couldn't believe it, but for a moment, he was sure Emery was fighting a smile.

"Did you know," Shaw said, perking up, "saying 'I want to apologize' isn't actually the same thing as apologizing?"

"Did you know that if that crochet were slightly looser, your dick would be poking out?"

"I did!" Shaw sounded breathless with excitement. "North said the exact same thing."

"No," North said, "I didn't."

"He said it would be the first ever ball doily!"

"That's incorrect," Emery said, "doilies are made of lace—" He cut off, glaring at Shaw, who beamed back at him.

John-Henry rubbed his shoulders. "Come on. Let's go back to bed."

"Don't go," Jem protested, and he did another flourish, sending the cards springing from one hand to the other. "If you go, Tean'll make me go back to bed, and then I'm going to scratch my chest like a motherfucker."

"I should have bought those safety mittens," Tean said. "The kind for newborns."

"Or the sex ones," Shaw said, "like he's your dog-slave."

Tean made a noise that sounded like he might have swallowed his tongue, and Jem lost control of the cards for a moment. North looked like he was about to lose it, and when he coughed into his fist, it didn't really sound like coughing.

Auggie couldn't help the grin that was growing. "Do you know any tricks?"

"Oh, sure," Shaw said. "I'm an empath, which means I can sense people's emotions—"

"Wonderful," Emery said. "Can you sense anything right now?"

"—and I'm a level nine psychic. No, wait! North! I'm level ten now, which means I now have access to retrocognition."

"Fan-fucking-tastic," North said. "Does level ten come with a wand or fairy wings or a unicorn's cock ring?"

"What's retrocognition?" John-Henry asked.

"It means I can see the past. Things that happened to me. Things I experienced."

"Everyone does that," Emery snapped. "It's called memory."

"That's great," North said, rubbing his eyes. "That's really fucking great because now maybe you'll be able to find the fucking remote when I want to watch TV for one fucking hour at the end of a very fucking long day."

"I'm not very good at it," Shaw said. "And I still think the remote might be a transliminal remote, which means it crosses a psychic threshold when you're not being a good boyfriend and don't spend enough time with me—"

"Don't spend enough time with you? I spent four fucking days on a stakeout with you riding my Jockeys, and for the rest of you, no, that is not a fucking expression."

It was strange seeing it spread through everyone else: the way Theo's face opened, a smile hiding behind his beard, and Jem's broad grin; how Tean leaned against Jem's leg, the corner of his mouth curving; John-Henry's smile was the same stunner he used every day, but it had a richness and depth that Auggie had only ever seen when the man turned off the sparkle and let himself be himself; even Emery wore one of those near-invisible smiles.

"I'd love to see your retrocognition," Auggie said, "but I was asking Jem."

Jem grinned and did another of those moves that made the cards leap from one hand to another. He gathered them again, held the deck in one hand, and then did something. It was hard to follow because his hand moved so quickly, but a card sprang out of the deck and flew into his other hand.

Shaw gasped.

Auggie applauded—and he lowered the volume when Emery glared at him—and everyone else joined in. Jem bowed from where he sat on the coffee table and then knelt on the rug, and Tean scooted back to give him room to work. In one broad sweep of his arm, Jem spread the cards in a perfect semicircle. Then, without missing a beat, he brought one finger back, flipping the cards face up in a single, smooth movement. Auggie couldn't help himself; he applauded again.

"That one's actually easier than the first one," Jem said with a grin that exposed the slight crookedness of his front teeth. "But people love it."

"He's teaching Colt," Emery said.

"Colt's got good hands," Jem said as he gathered the cards again.

Emery looked unbearably proud of that, and Auggie noticed John-Henry was careful to hide a smile.

"He's already pretty good at lifting wallets," Jem said absently. The expression on Emery's face didn't look quite as pleased, but before he had a chance to respond, Jem held out the deck of cards, spread open now in his hands. "For my last trick, I'll need a volunteer."

It was Shaw, of course. Not that anybody had any question about that. He knelt in front of Jem, and as the crochet shorts stretched in the new position, Auggie found himself seeing a whole new side of Shaw.

Until, that was, Theo put a hand over his eyes.

Auggie laughed, and when Theo let him pull his hand down, he saw that Theo was smiling—a big, real smile, the first one Auggie had seen from him in what felt like weeks. Auggie kept hold of his hand, pulling it to bring Theo's arm around him.

"Now, I'm not a psychic," Jem said, "but I do know a tiny bit of magic."

"Is it apportation?" Shaw asked. "The puppy apports into our bed sometimes, but it only happens when I go to sleep first and North and the puppy stay up to watch TV together."

"I want you to pick a card," Jem said.

"The queen of spades."

Laughing, Jem shook his head. "Draw a card and don't show me. You can show everybody else."

"You're going to look in a reflective surface," Emery said.

"I'll keep my head down," Jem said.

"Your peripheral vision—"

GREGORY ASHE

John-Henry shushed him, and Emery fell silent.

Shaw drew a card and showed it around—somehow, he had gotten the queen of spades. After everyone had seen it, he said, "Ok."

"Go ahead and put it back in the deck. Perfect, thank you." Jem shuffled the deck a few times and then he repeated his move from before, spreading the cards in that broad semicircle. This time, however, they were face up, and Auggie's eyes went immediately to the queen of spades. Jem studied the cards for a moment, and then he said, "I'm going to need some help. Do we have anybody here born in February?"

Shaw's hand shot up, but Jem looked at Auggie. Auggie grinned in spite of himself and raised his hand.

"You're already doing such a good job helping me," Jem told Shaw. "I'm going to need a little more help, though. You, sir. Could you come over here?"

"You're going to watch for a reaction," Emery said. "You're going to point to cards and judge by his expression—"

"For Christ's sake," North said, "be quiet." After the flash of annoyance on North's face, Auggie was surprised to see childlike wonder spreading across his features as he turned his attention to the cards again. But maybe not so surprised, Auggie thought as he knelt next to Shaw on the rug. Because he felt it too. The anticipation. The thrill that was building slowly.

"You don't have to do anything," Jem said, "except picture the card in your mind."

He leaned forward, and he ran his finger along the edge of the semicircle—not touching the cards, but moving his finger back and forth, a slow, almost hypnotic pendulum, like he was waiting for the charge.

"One last thing," Jem said, his face screwed up with concentration or frustration or effort—maybe all three, and Auggie realized, suddenly, how good Jem was at this, how remarkable, and how he had hidden it from all of them. Then he noticed Tean watching, and the glow on Tean's face, and he thought, Not all of us. "I need you to say alakazam. At the same time, all right?"

Auggie met Shaw's eyes. Shaw's mouth was trembling, and Auggie realized he felt it too—the urge to laugh—the silliness, yes, but also the excitement of it all.

"Alakazam," they said, and they were a little off.

"You can do better than that," Jem said.

"Alakazam."

"Come on."

"Alakazam."

172

He didn't even see Jem do it, not really, and he was sitting right in front of him. One moment, Jem's hand was still moving in that same low, lazy arc. The next, the cards began to turn, flipping face down one by one in a seamless ripple, until only one card lay face up.

The queen of spades.

"Bullshit," Emery said.

Everyone burst out laughing. Auggie kept staring at the card and looking at Jem and glancing over his shoulder at Theo, who wore a broad, open grin and was shaking his head. That was how Auggie felt too, the head-shakingness of it. The wonder of it. Jem settled back again, a tiny grin on his face.

"How did you do it?" Emery asked.

"Magic."

"There's no such thing as magic."

Shaw launched himself across the cards to wrap Jem in a hug. Jem laughed and rocked back and maybe only Auggie saw it, but Shaw whispered something, and Jem's face softened as he hugged Shaw back.

"It was magic," Shaw said. "It was real magic, and you saw it."

"That was fucking awesome," North declared.

Tean leaned forward to squeeze Jem's arm.

"Very cool," Theo said.

"I'm not letting you or Colt anywhere near my wallet," John-Henry said, which made everyone laugh again.

"Do your trick," North said, nudging Shaw with one foot.

"No," Shaw said, "it's no good—"

"Do it!"

"Do it," Auggie said. "We'd love to see it."

"It's not as good as Jem's," Shaw said.

Jem gathered up the cards, did a quick—and flashy—shuffle, and handed them over. "Any magic is good."

Shaw hunched over the cards, hiding them with his body. When he sat up again, he held them out toward Emery.

"No," Emery said.

John-Henry sighed and pushed him forward.

With a glower, Emery took a card. While keeping it hidden from Shaw, he showed it around the room—the ace of hearts. Then, when Shaw was ready, he handed it back, and Shaw slid it into the deck.

"It's not as good," Shaw whispered, glancing at Jem.

"It's magic," Jem said with a grin.

Shaw brightened, and then he held out the deck and fanned it open. Only one card was face down. He proffered the cards again; Emery sighed and plucked the face-down one out of the deck. When he turned it over, it was the ace of hearts.

"This is bullshit," Emery said.

"I watched him," John-Henry said. "He put it in the deck the right way."

"It's all bullshit."

Auggie did a quiet (very quiet) whoop and applauded, and the others followed. North even leaned forward to grab Shaw from behind, and it was somewhere between a hug and a half-Nelson.

"Very smooth," Jem said as he took the cards back.

Shaw looked so happy Auggie honestly thought he might cry.

"John can do that," Emery said.

"No, I can't," John-Henry said with a grin. "But I wish I could."

"Do your thing."

"That's not exactly the same."

"I'll get the watermelon."

"The watermelon?" Auggie asked.

But Emery was already moving into the kitchen, and when he came back, he had a whole watermelon. He moved the coffee table into the center of the room, set the watermelon on top of it, and waved John-Henry forward.

"This is not a card trick," John-Henry said, "and I'm apologizing in advance because this is just something we'd do when we were kids and we got bored. And I'm realizing right now that I need to explain that this was before smartphones. No comments from the peanut gallery, please."

Auggie mimed zipping his lips.

"Stop stalling," Emery said, "and start showing off."

For whatever reason, that made John-Henry grin. He accepted a single card from Jem, held it between two fingers, and flicked. It spun through the air with startling accuracy, but it glanced off the watermelon.

John-Henry shrugged and spread his hands. "Like I said—"

"Oh for fuck's sake," North said, "do it again."

So, John-Henry accepted another card. That one went wide, cartwheeling wildly to the left. He rolled his eyes and shook his head.

Theo said, "One more; you've got this."

John-Henry's grin went for rueful, but he accepted a third card. He sent it flying, and it sliced right into the watermelon and stuck there, the card quivering.

The cheers went up before Auggie could open his mouth. John-Henry was laughing, and his face was flushed as Emery pulled him in for a kiss.

Auggie didn't realize he was looking for Theo until their eyes had locked. Theo was still smiling, and something about the crinkle of his eyes, something about the wry set of his mouth, answered a question that Auggie hadn't even known he was asking.

"I don't know a single card trick," Theo said, easing himself up from the couch, "but if you've got balls, I can do a little juggling."

"More than a little," Auggie said. "He's really good."

Shaw made a noise like that had somehow been adorable, and North rolled his eyes, and Tean clutched Jem's hand, and suddenly Auggie's face was hot.

John-Henry said, "Be right back," and headed toward the garage.

"If you've got balls," North said. "Eight gay dudes and not one of you lazy motherfuckers made a joke."

"Oh, question," Shaw said, "As North's body succumbs to the ravages of age—this is a question for the senior members of the group—is it normal for them to get all stretched out and saggy and wrinkly?"

"Open your mouth," Theo said to Auggie. "See what happens."

Auggie had to hide his grin by pulling up his shirt.

Jem whispered something to Tean that made the vet turn an intense red.

"How saggy?" Emery asked. Laughter broke up the room again, and Emery scowled. "It's a legitimate question."

"This is the best I could do," John-Henry said as he came into the room. He held out four tennis balls, a baseball, and a couple of softballs. "I didn't know how many you needed."

"You're overestimating my abilities," Theo said, but he took the tennis balls and moved to the center of the room. He gave Auggie an unreadable look, and then the balls began to fly. There was a wobble at first, an unsteadiness that Auggie could track even as the balls spun through the air. And then Theo seemed to find his rhythm, and when he spoke, his voice was surprisingly easy. "Jem, do you mind?"

"I got you," Jem said, scrambling over to the sofa. He watched Theo's rhythm, and then, with a smoothness that made Auggie think of all those cards turning over one by one, he pitched the baseball to Theo. Theo caught it, and the baseball went into the rotation. After a moment, he said, "Ok."

Jem sent one of the softballs toward him, and Theo added that to the mix. Then, when Theo prompted him again, he tossed him the final softball. The balls whirred through the air. Theo's face was a mask of concentration, but also of what Auggie would have called pleasure. Auggie's eyes stung, and the intense need to cry came over him. He blinked rapidly and took deep breaths. The other guys, he was aware distantly, were applauding.

The quality of the applause changed, and North muttered something that sounded impressed, and Auggie had to wipe his eyes to see what was going on. Theo had changed the pattern, and now the balls wove in a pattern overhead, and all Auggie could do was stare. He'd never seen this before—juggling, sure, which Lana loved. But never this complicated. Never this...good.

"Ready?" Theo asked.

A startled look crossed Jem's face, but he stood. "Yep."

The balls started to move between them, faster and faster. And then Shaw was on his feet, saying, "Can I try? Can I?"

Laughing—when was the last time Theo had really laughed, Auggie wondered—Theo said, "Get ready."

Jem must have known what to do because the balls slowed, and then one of them flew in Shaw's direction, and to Auggie's—and probably everyone's—surprise, he caught it and sent it flying again. They found their rhythm, the three of them trading little comments in their own private world.

Pushing John-Henry forward, Emery said, "John wants to play with you boys, but he's too shy to ask."

John-Henry grinned, a blush bright in his cheeks, shooting a half-amused, half-embarrassed look back at his husband, but he didn't object.

"Coming your way," Theo said.

When John-Henry caught the ball, he burst out laughing, and Auggie watched the years drop away.

As the four continued juggling, shouting out warnings and heads-ups, joking, trying to impress each other—Jem, in particular, had a tendency for trying to show off, and more than once it meant he almost lost control of a ball or missed the next one. Auggie scooted back until he bumped up against the recliner; he glanced back and caught North giving him an amused look before turning his attention back to the jugglers. Tean moved next to them, and then Auggie was surprised to see Emery take a seat on the sofa.

"He learned how to juggle for baseball," Emery said. "His coach said it would improve his fielding."

John-Henry's gaze remained fixed on the balls, but a startled look crossed his face.

"Come on," Emery said with what almost sounded like amusement. "You can't be that surprised."

For an instant, John-Henry spared him a look, and the force of the love in it staggered Auggie. Then Jem called out wordlessly, and John-Henry's attention whipped back to catch the next ball before it fell.

Auggie was so caught up in what he'd seen in John-Henry's face that he almost missed North saying, "Shaw tried out for—"

"No," Shaw said, voice rising in protest, "no, no, no!"

"—and got rejected by a circus the summer after junior year."

"No, I—God damn it!" He fumbled a ball, and Theo swept out a hand to send it spinning back into the rotation. "North!"

"They told him he made the other performers uncomfortable."

Auggie laughed, and he was shocked to hear a quiet chuckle from Tean. When he glanced over, the vet was smiling as he watched Jem. Then his eyes cut to Auggie, and for a moment, it seemed that Tean hesitated. Then he blurted, "Jem lets the girls catch him when he does tricks for them."

"Traitor!" Jem called. "They legit catch me. I would never—mother of God!" That last bit came as John-Henry sent a ball wide and Jem scrambled to catch it.

Auggie knew how Theo had learned to juggle. He had known since the first time he'd seen him do it to entertain Lana. The empty hours in a logging trailer. The empty years of Theo's life, as Auggie thought of them, although he'd never put it to himself in exactly those words before. When Theo had been lost, adrift. A time, Auggie knew, that he wouldn't want Auggie telling everyone about.

So, instead Auggie said, "We went to a Sigma Sigma party my senior year, and Theo was trying to teach my friend Orlando how to juggle, and he ended up getting Orlando run over by an ATV."

Theo burst out laughing as he snagged another ball out of the air. "That's a lie! Orlando shouldn't have been showing off, trying to walk backward while he juggled, and those doofuses shouldn't have been on a four-wheeler anyway."

"It was amazing," Auggie said, laughing. "Orlando was fine, thank God, but you could literally see the tire marks for a month."

"Hold up," North said from behind Auggie. "Theo pledged Sigma Sigma?"

"Uh, no," Theo said. "Not exactly my scene."

"Ha ha," Auggie said. "I made possibly the worst frat bro ever, considering I spent more time reading Shakespeare with my boyfriend—"

"Yeah, yeah," North said over him. "You were a hot nerd. We get it. Dude, we pledged Sigma Sigma. Shaw and I."

"Uh—"

"This means we're literally brothers," Shaw said, and the note of glee in his voice was worrisome.

"Not literally—"

But before Auggie could get the rest of it out, North attacked him from behind. It didn't feel like precisely the right verb, but Auggie's brain couldn't come up with anything better while he was being put in that weird half-nelson hold-slash-hug that Shaw had earlier been a victim of.

"Lil-bits!" North said, tightening the hold as Auggie squirmed. "Way to fucking go!"

"What the fuck is going on down here?" The voice came from the stairs, where Colt stood. The teenage boy, lanky in shorts and a tee, glared down at them while he rubbed his eyes.

"Hey bubs—" John-Henry tried, but he cut off when Colt turned the glare on him.

"We were simply—" Emery began, but the words seemed to dry up in his mouth.

The only sound for a moment was the whoosh and slap of the balls flying through the air. Then, between the two of them, Jem and Theo collected them, and the game was over.

"There are children in this house," Colt said. "Did you think about that? Little kids who need their sleep. Biscuit's whining in her crate, you know."

"Bubs—"

"Bunch of grown-ass adults acting like it's a fucking slumber party."

"All right," Emery said.

"I've got fucking school in the fucking morning!"

"I said all right. You made your point. And you've used up your quota of righteous indignation, so I suggest you quit while you're ahead."

For another moment, Colt glowered at them. Then a cocky half-smile slipped out, and he padded back upstairs.

"Good God," North said, releasing Auggie and then ruffling his hair. "He is going to be fucking terrifying as an adult."

"Thank you, North," John-Henry said. "Now I can have nightmares about that."

"Does his boyfriend know?"

"I wish," Emery said. "Frankly, the whole thing would be much more tolerable if he tore a few strips off Ashley's hide now and then. Instead, he just melts every time Ashley looks at him."

"Gee," Auggie said, remembering how John-Henry had looked at Emery. "I wonder what that's like."

Maybe Emery heard it in his voice, or maybe he was aware of it, at some level, because he directed a dark look at Auggie.

"Can all you motherfuckers get out of my bedroom," North said, giving Auggie a little shove on the back of the head, "so I can actually get some fucking sleep?"

Jem helped Tean up, and the two of them slipped upstairs, and John-Henry and Theo returned the balls to the garage. Shaw got on the sofa and fussed with the blankets and asked Emery to tuck him in.

"That's right," John-Henry said, steering Emery toward the stairs. "Just pretend you didn't hear him."

"Night, little bro," North said as he pulled a blanket over him.

"Uh, actually, that one's got some weird associations for me," Auggie said.

North cracked an eye. A crook of a smile appeared. "Night, Lil-bits."

"That one's not exactly better."

North scratched his nose with his middle finger.

"But," Auggie said with a sigh, "I guess I'll take it."

Theo was waiting by the stairs, and they went down together. In the dark, they fumbled around until they were lying under the blanket together. Theo looped an arm around Auggie and pulled him against his chest. His beard was soft against Auggie's neck, and his body was warm from the juggling. One moment, Auggie was telling himself he'd never fall asleep, and the next, darkness crashed over him like a wave.

But from somewhere a long way off, he thought he heard Theo say, "Thank you."

19

The next morning, in the calm that came after the rush of everyone else leaving the house, Auggie sat in the kitchen, reviewing Shaniyah's videos, while Tean babied Jem.

"It's not that the cut is itchy," Jem said. "It's scratchy."

"Itchy and scratchy are the same thing," Tean said. "And I don't know how McDonald's is supposed to help."

"The sausage has a naturally soothing oil. Like the kind we give Scipio for his coat."

"In the first place, that's salmon oil, and it actually is good for you because of the omega-3 fatty acids, among other things. In the second place, McDonald's grease is definitely not good for you—"

"It's good for my coat."

"—because it's the kind of fat that clogs your arteries."

"It's right here," Jem said, tracing a line across his chest. "This is where it's the scratchiest. Where I got cut."

Tean made a helpless noise.

"Risking my life to defend a helpless child."

"I hope that was for Lana," Auggie said without looking up from his phone, "and not me."

"In a burning building."

"Oh my gosh," Tean breathed.

Auggie had a number of good tricks up his sleeve, and he would have put himself in the running for some seriously good puppy eyes, but Jem put him to shame.

"One," Tean finally said in a helpless voice. "One sausage biscuit."

"And a hash brown," Jem put in quickly. "For my coat."

Tean made that noise again.

"And a coffee, but the really good one from that place on Market Street."

"You are lucky that I love you."

"And remember that fudge cake we tried —"

"Jeremiah."

"Doctors say it's good after you get stabbed. For, um, antioxidants."

"You did not get stabbed —"

It wasn't even fair, not really. Auggie almost felt bad for Tean. All Jem did was wince, like he'd felt a twinge of pain, and Tean's breathing changed, accelerated. And then he said, "You jerk."

"It's nothing, really, just a maniac with a sickle tried to gut me —"

"Fine." Tean kissed the top of Jem's head. "And tomorrow, why don't I back a cement truck full of gravy up to the house?"

"Actually, Emery was telling me about this place, Big Biscuit —"

Auggie couldn't help the smile growing on his face.

"Please don't let him cook any bacon," Tean said to him as he headed toward the front of the house. "I'll be back as soon as I can."

Auggie spared Jem a look, and Jem grinned back.

"I honestly don't know how you do it."

"He's the kindest human being in the world." Jem shrugged. "So, it's easy. What've you got there?"

Auggie scooted over and angled his phone so Jem could see it. "Videos from Shaniyah."

The steps to the basement creaked, and a moment later, Theo appeared. Lana came behind him a moment later; she could do stairs like a champ now, even with the brace.

"Where's Evie?" she asked.

"In her room," Jem said. "Hold on, hold on. Give me five."

Lana held up her hand for a high five, and Jem slapped palms lightly and then said, "I meant five tickles," and Lana squealed with laughter and ran away before he could grab her.

"Shaniyah?" Theo asked, glancing at the phone.

"Uh, yeah," Auggie said. He worked his thumb along the side of the phone's case.

Theo nodded and moved over to the coffeemaker.

"I was thinking," Auggie said. "You know, after last night."

"Someone is still out there. Still trying to tie up loose ends. And it's not Dalton." Theo's words were clinical as he poured coffee into a mug. "I agree."

When he put the carafe back on the warming plate, it clicked a little too loudly.

"When we went to the Cottonmouth Club," Jem said slowly, "the night someone shot and killed DeVoy—I've been thinking about it. I think it was the same guy who was at your house last night."

Theo breathed out, hard, and said abruptly, "In case it matters, I checked the security cameras at our house. I sent everything to John-Henry."

"Oh my God, I didn't even think—" Auggie began.

"You can't see anything useful; just somebody in black breaking into the house." Auggie opened his mouth again, but Theo said over him, "Can't even tell if it's the same person who broke in earlier." Then he stalked off toward the living room and the sounds of the girls' laughter.

Jem let out a breath and raised his eyebrows.

Auggie shook his head, fighting the urge to comment. Finally he said, "Why didn't he bring a gun? Why not just shoot us last night?"

"Because he was going to torch the place." When Auggie didn't say anything, Jem added, "The cuts and stuff, nobody would be able to tell because the bodies were burned. It would look like an accident, like you died in a fire. It's harder to do that if they find bullets in the bodies."

"Jesus," Auggie said.

Jem shrugged.

There didn't seem to be anything else to say about that, so Auggie went back to the videos. He played Shaniyah's final piece, the one that she had made before she had been killed: the footage of Keelan and Leon fighting in the high school commons; the play rehearsal at the community theater; the party. Now that he knew who he was looking at, he recognized Ambyr doing her stupid dance—and, in the process, making a total fool of herself as she fell and exposed herself. He guessed Merlin was the one going after Leon, screaming.

"This was on TikTok?" Jem asked.

"No, she never posted it. Never posted any of it, actually."

Jem wrinkled his nose. "People watch that stuff?"

"Oh yeah. You don't?"

"There are some barbers I follow, and some lifestyle ones. And then all the random animal ones. I'm trying to teach Scipio how to sing like this one Lab I found. Oh, and then those stupid challenges, even though Tean says I'm encouraging bad behavior. But it's hilarious when these dumbass teenage bros slap each other in the face or shoot each other with paintballs in the 'nads or even the old standbys, like the shaving cream in the hand, that kind of stuff."

"Yeah, the challenges are lit right now. You wouldn't believe how many companies want to get in on it. But I tell them it never goes the way you want—the people doing this kind of stuff, the ones who make it go viral, are idiots, and they'll do something that ends up making your product look bad. Like the stuff with Tide pods, for example."

Jem gave him a considering look and asked, "How about this stuff? Do companies want to do this?"

"God, I bet the true crime networks and TV shows would love to find a way to capitalize on it. Actually, that's not a bad idea. But the amateur stuff on TikTok, what these people call investigations, they're not actually doing much investigating—not really."

"Ok."

"I'll give you an example. The video we just watched, that's the exception—Shaniyah had exclusive recordings of people fighting with a kid who disappeared. That's a legit investigation. But a lot of what you'll see on TikTok is stuff like this." He scrolled through the contents of Shaniyah's drive and found another video.

In this one, Shaniyah spoke while a series of screenshots appeared. "So, I've come across some scary stuff connected to Leon Purdue's disappearance. Take a look at his public Spotify playlist. Back in June, the first six songs were by Orville Peck. But look now—he's got three by The Cure, and one by The Smiths. If you listen—" A snippet of music played. "—you can hear that's some seriously depressing shit. It's obvious that something significant happened in Leon's life in June, and it changed things for the worse. No one has explored the possibility of suicide, and it makes you wonder why."

"Uh, maybe because nobody cared he was missing," Jem said. "For real? That's a TikTok investigation?"

"I mean, there's a whole range, but yeah, a lot of it is stuff like that. They'll analyze people's posts on social media, looking for clues. Did they change their profile picture? Did they post something vague, something that can be interpreted a million different ways? Did they follow an account, or unfollow an account, or like a post?"

"That's nuts."

"Oh yeah, it's crazy."

"But people like it?"

"It's definitely got a following." Auggie was quiet for a moment. "Shaniyah was so smart. So talented. I mean, if she'd approached me with this, I don't know what I would have told her because honestly, it's right up her alley. She wanted to do smart, creative work, like that piece about social media and teens, the one she was originally working on. But this is even better. She could have been a kickass journalist, but maybe she would have been something else." He stopped because it felt melodramatic to say, *But someone took that away from her*. It was enough, for Auggie, that he knew it.

"I want to talk to the dad," Theo said from the opening to the living room. He held his coffee like he'd forgotten about it, and in the background, Lana and Evie's excited voices carried clearly. "Merlin Purdue. I want to talk to him."

Auggie nodded, but he said, "He wasn't exactly receptive the last time we tried."

"He's the one we haven't talked to yet, so I want to talk to him."

"Who's this guy?" Jem asked. "What's the problem?"

"This boy who went missing, Leon. His dad's name is Merlin—"

"No shit?"

"It really is. He and Leon's mom split up in the spring, and that's when Leon got emancipated. A few months later, Leon had vanished. Merlin's in that montage—he's the guy fighting with Leon in the final clip."

"And Dalton told us that they'd had a fight," Theo said. "He told us that Merlin threatened to kill Leon."

"According to Leon," Auggie said, and when Theo gave him a look, he added, "That's important, Theo. We don't actually know that it happened."

Theo made a noise that could have meant anything.

"So, make him want to talk to you," Jem said with a shrug.

"Wouldn't that be nice?" Theo muttered.

"I'm serious." Jem laughed at whatever he saw on their faces. "People aren't that complicated. Figure out what he wants. Or what he's afraid of. And use it to make him talk to you."

"Like what?" Auggie asked.

"I'm not saying you're wrong," Theo said, "but the problem is, we don't know anything about Merlin except that he split up with his wife and went after a much younger—and, from what I've seen of her, a shallow and vicious—woman."

"There you go." Jem rolled his eyes when neither of them spoke. "He's, what, fortysomething? He's starting to get a dad bod. His glory days in high school or college or whenever are behind him. His life's a dud. So, he shakes everything up. Tries to party like he's twenty instead of forty. Hooks up with a girl half his age. That's everything you need to know."

"What am I supposed to offer him? A young sex worker?"

"Do you have one?"

The question hung in the air until Auggie realized it was serious. "Uh, no."

"Guys like that, they want money, they want youth, they want status. Whatever the high school version of cool is, they want that. And they're afraid of losing it, of being left behind, of facing the fact that they're old." Jem sat back and spread his hands. "This one is easy."

"I appreciate—"

"Holy shit," Auggie said.

Jem cocked an eyebrow. Theo moved his hand around his mug. The ceramic was printed with the words STILL GAY.

Auggie grinned. "I think I've got it."

20

The trailer park was located on the outskirts of Wahredua. The city peeled back slowly, sad little frame houses giving way to undeveloped land, the occasional ag field—soy, so much soy this year, Theo noted, and he wondered what his father and Jacob had decided to put in. Then a sign that said DIXIELAND PRIVATE COMMUNITY and, below it, A FAMILY FRIENDLY PARK.

"You see it, right?" Auggie asked.

"Yes, Auggie."

"It's not just me."

"It's not just you."

"I know you don't want to hear me say California," Auggie said. "But can you feel me thinking it? As an innocent, vulnerable little brown Latino boy being taken against my will to Dixieland?"

"You're driving."

"Under duress."

"There's a firehouse back that way," Theo said, "and they're a Safe Space. You know what that means?"

Auggie rolled his eyes.

"You can surrender a child there, no questions asked."

Another big, dramatic roll of his eyes before Auggie pulled up his t-shirt to chew on the collar, turning to study the trailer park again.

It had the look—perhaps the name was proof—of something that had outlived its time. The asphalt roads were worn away, eroded in places until they drove over rutted dirt; a hundred yards later, they would hit a buckled patch, or a pothole, or a skin of gravel that had been dumped in a half-hearted attempt to fill in the pavement.

The trailers themselves didn't look any better. They passed a white trailer with one aluminum wall bowed out, and it made Theo think of canned goods, the kind of bloat that told you the food had spoiled. Another trailer, a pink that might have been delicately beautiful under the algae covering it, stared at them with window-eyes made crazy by broken miniblinds. They rolled past a doublewide with its skirting scrolled back, and something darted through the shadows before Theo's brain caught up and said, Raccoon. A Coke machine, the old-fashioned kind with the opener built in, sat on the side of the road. On the next street, a little girl with vacant eyes walked a fat old tabby on a leash, only the cat had stopped to sit and was attacking its balls with its tongue.

Theo had gotten the address for Merlin Purdue's trailer from the school's online learning management system; apparently, they'd updated Merlin's address after the divorce but before Leon had gotten himself emancipated. The trailer itself was a single-wide, turquoise on the bottom, white on the top, without curtains or blinds in the windows. In the late morning sun, it made the place look abandoned, but the Thunderbird in the driveway suggested otherwise. Someone had planted sunflowers, and they stood cockeyed in too-small pots, leaning against the trailer.

"I guess he's home," Auggie said.

"We'll find out."

They left the Focus on the side of the street and climbed the steps to the tiny deck. When Theo knocked, the door rattled in its frame, and Auggie looked at him.

"That wasn't intentional."

"It's a curse, being so strong."

"All right."

"It's all those muscles."

Sometimes it was better to ride it out in silence.

"I'm surprised you don't just explode out of your shirts when you flex."

If he counted to ten, maybe. Although Auggie would probably love that.

"It was all that jocking around you did with the guys last night," Auggie said. "And the showing off."

"You started that nonsense last night, and I only went along with it because—" Theo miscalculated; he glanced at Auggie's face, saw the wide eyes, the hint of hurt, and finished, "Because I love you, and because we all needed to blow off some steam."

"I knew I had better puppy eyes than Jem."

"Excuse me?"

"Nothing."

"They don't tell you it's like an ancient curse," Theo said as he knocked again, and this time, he didn't care that the door shook under his fist. "It's like calling Bloody Mary or—"

"Or saying the name of He Who Must Not Be Named."

Theo spared him a look. "You let one undergrad into your house, you feed him one Dorito after midnight, and that's it, the end, there's no getting away from him."

"Didn't you make me watch a movie about that?"

Yes, Theo thought. Silence was definitely better.

He readied himself to knock again, but the door swung open. He'd seen Merlin in the short video clip on Shaniyah's account, but seeing him in person was a different experience. He was shorter than Theo expected, with a strong jaw and dark, wavy hair that was, Theo thought, suspiciously free of gray. Merlin Purdue had none of his son's waifish build; he was thick with muscle, and he had a kind of juiced-up fullness to his face that made Theo think of every guy on *Jersey Shore* (which Auggie, of course, had forced him to watch). When he saw them, his eyes narrowed.

"What?"

"Good morning," Auggie said. "Am I speaking to Mr. Purdue? Mr. Merlin Purdue?"

"I go by Merl," he said. "And I'm working—"

"This will just take a moment, Mr. Purdue. Mr. Harris—" He tipped his head toward Theo. "—and I were wondering if you wanted to make any comments about the disappearance of your son."

Under the bronze of whatever tanning agent Merlin used, his face took on red. "No. Now get the fuck off my property—"

"Then we can run the episode with your partner's comments and simply have the narrator explain to the audience that you were unwilling to participate in the episode?"

"What episode? What the hell are you talking about? What did Elise say? She's a fucking bitch, are you going to tell the audience that?"

Auggie looked at Theo, and Theo swore silently and promised himself, for the hundredth time, he would never, ever, ever again fall for puppy eyes, or innocent eyes, or simply darkly beautiful eyes, which had a way of making him do all sorts of stupid things.

"Mr. Purdue," he said in his best English accent, "I represent a program called *Lost Lads*, which runs on Acorn TV. We're doing an episode on the disappearance of your son, Leon."

Merlin stared at him for a moment, and then his gaze swung to Auggie. "He got something wrong with him?"

Theo had never seen Auggie die from humiliation and, at the same time, fight the giggles.

"He's English," Auggie said in a choked voice. "Acorn is a British network. I'm his local guide, you know?"

"We'd like to hear your side of the story to run alongside your partner's," Theo said.

"He doesn't sound British," Merlin said.

Theo gave up and went with "How about this? How about I practice my American accent?"

"That's your American accent?" He shook his head. "All right." Auggie looked like he was losing the war against the giggles, but Merlin spoke again before Auggie could fall apart. "I don't care what Elise told you. She's a lying bitch, that's what you can say."

"You're talking about your ex-wife?" Auggie said. "No, Mr. Purdue, we're talking about—let me see." He looked at his phone for a moment. "Ambyr Hobb."

Merlin's jaw loosened, and then his whole face darkened with a flush. "What'd she say?"

"That's not how this works, Mr. Purdue. We can't repeat the comments of our interviewees; that's what makes the program so exciting."

"If you'd like to comment—" Theo said.

"That stupid cunt," Merlin said. "Where the fuck are her brains?" He looked up, eyes reassessing them. "You told her she'd be on TV, didn't you?"

"It is a television program," Theo said.

"God fucking damn it."

"If this is a bad time, or if you'd like us to simply run the episode with the information she gave us—"

"No," Merlin said. He stood there a moment, his hands braced on the jambs, and the pose made Theo think of Bible illustrations, Samson in the temple. Or, maybe, an old movie. Laurel and Hardy, and one of them stuck in a doorway. "It's got to be fast."

"Not a problem," Theo said.

"Buddy, give it a rest with the accent."

Fortunately, he'd already stepped back inside before a tiny squeak escaped Auggie.

Theo glared at him. "Why in the world do I have to be English?"

"Because," Auggie said, "if you were American, and it was an American show, he'd wonder why he'd never heard of it before."

"It could have been Canadian, Auggie. It could have been a new show that had never aired before. For hell's sake, it could have been an English show we were porting over."

"Huh," Auggie said with a glimmer in his eyes as he stepped toward the front door. "I didn't think about that."

Theo had been inside his fair share of trailer homes. He'd lived in a few, as a matter of fact, and none as nice as this—and that was saying something, since Merlin Purdue's fell somewhere on the spectrum between outdated and rundown. It had brown walls, brown carpet with a pattern that made Theo think of the tabby licking its balls, brown countertops in the kitchen that adjoined the living area. A little patch of checkerboard linoleum near the front door presumably gave guests a space to kick off their shoes before ruining the tabby-print carpet, and Theo could see matching linoleum in the kitchen. It had the smell of an old place that hadn't been cleaned well, or perhaps, really, ever—the accumulated oil and skin cells and dander of everyone who had passed through here, engrained in every surface. A TV, a microfiber sofa, and a matching microfiber recliner made up the living room set. The only addition that might be considered personal was the poster of a Thunderbird, which looked wrinkled, and maybe a little tattered at the edges, like something Merlin might have toted around for a long time before finally hanging it up. The protective plastic sheet over it gave back their reflections.

Merlin gestured to the sofa as he dropped into the recliner, and he swiveled to face them. "Do you want something to drink? I've got beer and water."

"No, thanks," Auggie said. "Did you know English people drink their beer warm?"

Merlin turned a look on Theo like he was an alien, and Theo, because nothing had worked so far, went with the only thing he could come up with: "Cheers."

Auggie actually rubbed his eyes at that, but he recovered quickly. "Mr. Purdue, this is just a preliminary conversation. We like to get the whole story, and then we'll refine your talking points for when we record the interview. Would you be able to join us in our affiliate studio in St. Louis? We'd pay for the travel, of course."

"Yeah, yeah. What did she tell you about Leon?"

Auggie traded a look with Theo. "I'm sorry, Mr. Purdue, but we already told you: we can't share that information. It would ruin the, uh—"

"Integrity," Theo said.

"—the program's integrity."

"If she said I hurt him, that is fucking bullshit. He cries about everything. He said one time I broke one of his nails." He sat back, scoffed, his whole body communicating that this was beyond belief. "Are you recording this?"

Auggie set his phone on the arm of the sofa and tapped the screen. "Why don't we start—"

"He's a pansy, all right? I know that. It's twenty-twenty. Fine, he can do whatever he wants. Go climb a dick, that's his business. But it's the mouthing off, that's what I won't stand for. I broke a fucking nail? So the fuck what? Pick up your fucking room like I told you. Do your fucking homework. How fucking hard is it to be polite to your fucking stepmom?"

"Leon and Ambyr didn't get along?" Theo asked.

"Didn't get along? Jesus, they were like cats in a bag. I told both of them, I'm only going to live with one crazy bitch, so figure this shit out. The next day, Leon moved out. Mr. Emancipated. Fine, I told Ambyr. If he thinks he's a fucking adult, he can be a fucking adult."

"When was this?"

"Oh, June, I'd say."

"You haven't seen your son since June?"

A little more color came into Merlin's face, and he sat forward. "What the fuck is that supposed to mean?"

"We're trying to confirm the timeline," Auggie said. "That's all."

"He wanted to leave. I didn't throw him out."

No, Theo thought. You just made it impossible for him to live here.

"This was in June?" Auggie asked.

"What was I supposed to do?" Merlin said. "Beg him to stay? Get on my fucking hands and knees? He would have loved that, let me tell you."

"Mr. Purdue—"

"Are you paying Ambyr?"

"No, we don't pay—"

"Of course not. She's doing this because she's pissed I wouldn't pay for another fucking round of headshots. Give me a fucking break. We're in the asshole of Missouri, and she's mailing headshots like she's Meg Ryan."

Auggie blinked—with a dark squiggle in his gut, Theo realized there was a high possibility Auggie didn't even know who Meg Ryan was—but all he said was "About your son—"

"She's doing this to get back at me. Making me look bad because she's mad I won't pony up. You can't use the stuff she told you if it's a lie, you know that? I could sue."

"Did Leon—"

"Did she say I hit him? Because it's one thing to abuse a kid, and it's another thing to straighten them out. If you had kids, you'd know. Sometimes you've got to give them some of this." He held up his hand. "It's for their own good. Did she tell you that? That he'd mouth off to anybody, and somebody had to teach him the world wasn't going to let him get away with that."

For a strange moment, Theo felt like he was seeing double. His brain played out for him an imagined version of Leon's life, the slow-motion shattering of innocence and trust and safety, the realization that he was different, and that this difference was part of why he was unloved. And, at the same time, he saw Auggie. Auggie adjusting Lana on his hip, even though she was too big to carry like that anymore. Auggie in a state of intense focus, his nose scrunched as he tried to figure out the clips for her hair, because he was determined to get her ready for school without Theo's help. Auggie walking through fire. And something was growing inside him, a realization that he couldn't quite put into words, a kind of horrified awareness that he had made a mistake, perhaps a tremendous one, and he didn't know if he could make it right, because it might be too late.

"Mr. Purdue," Auggie was saying. "This isn't productive. Why don't you start from the beginning? We're trying to tell the story of Leon's disappearance, and this is your chance to tell us your version of what happened."

"My version is the truth."

"That's all we want."

Merlin dropped back in his seat. The recliner made a soft, exhaling noise, and in the silence, something ticked farther back in the house. When Merlin spoke again, his voice was thick, and Theo couldn't untangle the emotion there—rage, maybe; fear; or, possibly, grief. "That stupid bitch. She got us into this. The drugs." He stopped and looked up at the ceiling of the trailer, the textured resin panels with rusty water stains. "That fucking club. I never should have let her take him there."

"What club?" Theo asked, although he thought he already knew the answer.

"She's the one who introduced him to that kiddie-diddler. I told Leon to stay away from him. I said I didn't care what that fucker promised him; they weren't going to put Leon in any movies, and they weren't going to make him a star. That's not how the world works. I tried to teach him that." He looked up. He looked lost.

"Back up. Are you talking about Dalton Weber?"

"I said this piece of shit is twenty, thirty years older than you, and you want me to believe he's making movies in this shithole? Give me a fucking break. I told him. And you know what he did? He laughed. He said I was old. I was stupid and old and pathetic. And he said, 'Look who's talking,' or something like that, meaning Ambyr because he didn't understand that Ambyr and I are adults, and we're in love." Maybe he heard the dry, mechanical quality of the words. Maybe it was something else, something inside that made him stop. He let out a raspy laugh and rubbed the bridge of his nose. "We were at some fucking teeny-bopper party. They still have them out on the back forty, did you know that? Me, forty-five years old, and I'm in some old lady's field trying to do a keg stand like I'm in college again, and Ambyr high off her tits and trying to do that fucking dance, like I've got any fucking clue what it is or why it matters, and Leon in my face telling me she's pathetic, telling me I'm a joke. What I told you, when I said I'm only living with one crazy bitch, it had been that day, the day before, and he was mad. He wanted to come back at me, and he did. Told me everything he thought about me to my face. I'm a piece of shit. I'm an abusive asshole. I'm old and sad. I went after him. Because he was right. I could see he was right. Jesus Christ." He let his hands drop to his lap, and he clasped them there, the pose schoolboyish. "My own son making me see what a fucking loser I am. I tried to take his fucking block off." He made that noise again that wasn't really a laugh, and he shook his head.

"And what happened?"

"He ran. He was already emancipated, so it's not like I could stop him, could I?" The question was a challenge, but he dropped his eyes quickly, and he clasped his hands more tightly in his lap.

"When was that?"

"Like I said, June. End of June."

"And you haven't seen him since?"

Merlin shook his head. To Theo's surprise, though, he started speaking again. "And then that Black girl started coming around, asking questions. What happened to Leon, where's Leon, when was the last time I talked to Leon? So many fucking questions. I told her he was gone, that was all I knew. But he went with that creep, I know he did. Nobody has to tell me. Jesus Christ, he's seventeen years old. What the fuck does he know about anything?"

"What happened when Shaniyah came to interview you?"

"Oh no. No way. I didn't do anything to her. She came, she asked her questions, showed me that fucking video. Then she left. You can ask Ambyr if you don't believe me—she was here for the whole thing."

"Mr. Purdue, where were you last night?" Auggie asked. "We stopped by to conduct this interview, but you weren't home."

He tilted his head at the change of subject. "Kansas City. I have some accounts out there, and a couple of times a year, I drive out, take the guys to dinner, sometimes take them somewhere after dinner, make sure they know we appreciate their business."

"Did you spend the night there?"

He nodded, but he said, "What's going on? Why are you asking about that?"

Theo opened his mouth to ask if they could circle back to something Merlin had said before, but before he could, the door opened. Ambyr stepped into the trailer. She was holding up her phone, shaking out her blond hair, and saying, "I know I'm disgusting right now, but do you see what I mean about how my hair is cuter with that new smoothing serum—"

With the automatic air of someone checking a room, she glanced over at them and stopped. Her phone hand drifted down, ruining the shot. Her gaze went from Merlin to Theo to Auggie, and horror appeared in her face.

"You stupid bitch," Merlin said, pushing himself up from the chair. "What the fuck did you tell them?"

Ambyr didn't stick around to answer. Theo wasn't sure he'd ever seen someone run in wedges before, but that girl knew how to do it. She sprinted out of the trailer, her steps thumping down the deck. Merlin, shouting, ran after her, and a moment later, an engine grumbled—throaty and muscular and undoubtedly the Thunderbird.

"Jesus," Auggie said with a half-laugh. "What the hell?"

Theo shook his head. He got up and shut the door. A high, whining sound suggested that the trailer's air conditioning unit was struggling to catch up. He stood there for a moment. Then he flipped the deadbolt on the door.

"What he said about Kansas City," Auggie said, "do you think he was telling the truth?"

"It'll be easy enough to check. John-Henry will only have to make a couple of calls."

"He could have driven back, though, right? It's, what, a couple of hours away?"

Theo nodded as he started toward the kitchen.

"It doesn't necessarily mean he's not the one who attacked us last night," Auggie said.

"No, it doesn't."

Auggie let out a sigh. "We'd better hurry. I'll start in here."

They worked quickly. Theo wouldn't have liked to admit it, but they hadn't lost any of their rhythm, and they worked well together. It could be one of those articles that came across his feed sometimes, some glitch in the algorithm: "Strengthen Your Relationship by Committing Burglary— Together!" had a nice ring to it.

The only thing of interest that Theo found in the kitchen was a glass pipe that had clearly been used for meth; it still had a faintly burned smell, and it made the hair on the back of Theo's arms stand up. He left it where it was, in one of the wobbly drawers, and made his way back to the bedroom.

It was a sty: dirty plates and bowls were stacked on the dresser, alongside clothes and accessories and tangled charging cables. Garbage littered the floor—empty bottles, plastic wrappers, Starbucks cups. The bed was unmade, and to judge by the ash tray and the lingering reek of weed, at least one of them enjoyed a jay before bed. He began working his way through the filth. He wished he had gloves.

From the hallway came Auggie's cry of dismay and then, "Theo, this bathroom is disgusting."

"You can take the other bedroom instead; I'll do it."

"No, I'll do it." The faint sounds of Auggie's search came: the sound of a cabinet door opening, the click of plastic, the rattle of what Theo imagined was the shower door sliding loosely in its track. Auggie's voice came as a surprise. "Remember when you made me clean the bathroom?"

"I didn't make you clean the bathroom." Theo hesitated. "Ok, I maybe didn't handle that too well. In hindsight."

"I'd never been woken up before by someone putting a bucket of cleaning supplies on the bed."

A chuckle broke out of Theo, and Auggie laughed a moment later. Theo gave up on the dresser and started kicking through the clothes on the floor. Nothing there except more trash—he found one of those stupid tumblers Auggie wanted, the kind that cost forty dollars and were just a glorified white girl cup with a lid, under one pile, and he wondered if Auggie would object to taking that one instead of spending good money on yet another trendy drink container. Then he worked the bed, and under the mattress he found almost a whole ounce of meth in a plastic baggie. He checked the other bedroom, located at the far end of the trailer, and found clothes— clothes in the closet, clothes on the floor, piles of new clothes with the tags still on them. And a green screen. And a ring light. He recognized, from Auggie, the basics of a studio.

GREGORY ASHE

When he got back to the bathroom, Auggie was prying on the outlet covers, testing to see if any were loose.

"Normal stuff," Auggie said, waving a hand at the plastic prescription vials in the cabinet. "Are you going to have to start Lipitor when you turn forty?"

"I'm going to ignore that."

"Do you remember you were really focused on the grout that one day? You made me use a brush and everything."

"I'm going to ignore that too."

Auggie gave him a goofy grin. "What'd you find?"

"Meth. And a pipe in the kitchen. And it smells like they smoke weed."

"Everyone smokes weed." But then Auggie's voice changed, and he said, "Except responsible adult types."

"Uh huh."

"Like us."

Theo scratched his beard. Then he said, "God damn it."

Auggie sighed and nodded. "Nothing, right?"

For a moment, Theo wanted to argue the point. He wanted this whole—well, escapade, to put it in politest terms—to have been worth something. But there was no sign that Merlin had been behind the attack on them the night before, no indication that he had the training or skills or, if Theo were being frank, the physical capacity for a fight that had brought Jem and Theo, even working together, to the brink of defeat. He thought about the juiced-up look of Merlin's face, the swagger in how he carried himself. The height was right, if what Theo remembered of the attacker the night before could be trusted, but nothing else seemed to line up. And there was nothing else here that might point them in a helpful direction—no sign that Leon had ever lived here, much less of where he might have gone or what might have happened to him.

Theo shook his head. "Nothing."

21

On the drive back to Emery and John-Henry's house, Auggie said, "It's ok."

Theo had been silent since they'd left the trailer.

"He was scared, right?"

Theo looked out the windshield, face set.

"When we told him Ambyr had talked to us, he freaked out." Auggie tried to inject enthusiasm into the words. "That means something."

"It means he has a teenage son who disappeared, and, whether Leon was emancipated or not, he's afraid his trailer-park-daddy lifestyle is about to come to a screeching halt."

"Ok, first of all, you never get bitchy, and I'm absolutely living for this."

Theo could get some seriously stormy eyebrows going when he tried, it turned out.

"And second, Trailer Park Daddy is, like, a thing now, and you and I are going to lean into it."

"No, thank you."

"Theo, come on. You've already got those red shorts. And I bet if we got you a wifebeater and a beer, one of those lawn chairs, and we let you sit out by the creek. You could scratch your balls. Oh, God, we need a trucker hat, but a good one that says 'merica or God's Gift to Women or something like that."

"How about some music?" Theo said.

Laughing, Auggie fought him off from the radio, and Theo let him win. It was nice to see a hint of amusement behind Theo's beard. Only a hint, but still.

"It's going to be ok," Auggie said. "We tried something, and it didn't work out. We'll try again."

"Christ, Auggie, I don't know if it's going to work out. We can't live in Emery and John-Henry's basement forever. Jem and Tean can't have sleepovers at our house for the rest of their lives."

"To be fair, I think Jem would actually love sleepovers for the rest of his life."

"This is such a fucking mess. Someone is trying to kill us, and we have no fucking idea why, let alone who they are or how to stop them."

Auggie drove another hundred yards, the tires whispering between them. Then he said, "That's not entirely true. We know that whoever came after us last night, they're trying to stop us because we're looking into Shaniyah's and Leon's disappearances. We don't know the rest of the details, not yet, but we know this all started when Shaniyah disappeared, and somehow, it's connected to Leon's disappearance as well."

Theo nodded. It looked like he was trying to hold back, but then the words burst out of him. "I just—I just can't do this, Auggie. It's hard enough at school. I watch these kids show up, day after day, and they're children, they're practically infants, and they're so full of life, wanting to grow and have happy, healthy, fulfilling lives. And some of them will. And others, they drag themselves into the classroom, and they don't have clean clothes, and they haven't bathed, and if they don't get the free breakfast at school, they haven't eaten since lunch the day before. Some of them, you can see it in their eyes, the mixture of fear and this intense desire for someone to love them and keep them safe."

"Hey—" Auggie tried.

"And then there are the ones who have learned to put up this hard shell, to protect themselves, and they're so angry because they're so scared. It's bad enough to see that every day. It's bad enough to know that for an hour at a time, I'm responsible for them, and nothing—absolutely fucking nothing—I do can make up for the shit they go through when they walk out of my classroom. But this? Elise Purdue was practically a nothing, a nonentity. She didn't even know the last time she texted her son, and she couldn't be bothered to worry about what happened to him or where he'd gone. That might be worse than Merlin, and that's really saying something considering he was busy trying to live out a teenage fantasy of his own, and getting Leon out of his way was part of making sure the fantasy could last a little longer. For fuck's sake, Auggie, he sat there and told us he knew about Dalton and Leon, and he didn't do anything because it was easier not to, easier to keep pretending he could have some stupid second chance at being a kid. Shaniyah's aunt and uncle would rather lie about where she was than look bad in public, never mind that their niece, whom they were responsible for, was lying dead in a basement, and some motherfucker had put tape over her mouth. Even Keelan, that little shit. I mean, he has no parental supervision, and he's going to go through life thinking fucking is the answer to every emotional problem. Jesus fucking Christ. I love Lana, and I'm grateful for her every day, but I look around, and I want to know what the fuck is wrong with this world."

They were rolling up to a stoplight, and the sound of the Focus changed as they slowed. In the intersection, a man wearing a purple t-shirt that said MARVIN'S MINISTRY was shaking a Big Gulp cup as he approached each car at the light.

"I'm sorry," Theo said, voice subdued now. "I know you want kids, and I know we—we've talked about this, and I know there are a lot of happy, healthy, well-adjusted kids."

"Do you feel guilty about Lana?" Auggie was surprised by his own question, which had come out of the dark storm inside his head, out of a place he couldn't point to, much less name. Even more surprised by his tone, by the evenness of it, the steadiness, the sureness. Because inside, everything was windblown, but that voice sounded like a rock.

Theo put his hand up like he might scratch his beard, but then he didn't. The light changed. They started forward again. When Theo spoke, it was so low, wound tight with bitterness, that Auggie could barely hear him over the sound of the car. "I was driving, wasn't I?"

Auggie blinked his eyes to clear away the tears, and he focused on pulling in deep breaths, drawing the air deep, breathing into his belly. Pilates. He thought, in one of those Pilates classes, they had done this.

As they drove, the city reassembled itself: pole-barns, a chicken coop made out of asbestos siding, a donkey tied to a clothesline and pissing in the mud, and then the Citgo, a Dollar General, a shopping cart jammed sideways in a corral. Each item, Auggie tried to capture whole, to hold it in his head, to leave no room for anything else.

Maybe because he wasn't thinking about anything—or trying not to, anyway—was why his brain finally had a chance to catch up with what he'd heard.

"Theo?"

When Auggie risked a look, Theo had his eyes closed, his head back. His color was bad, and his breathing shallow, and Auggie wondered, again, how long Theo could keep doing this. Not only the sleepless nights. But carrying everything. For everyone. Forever.

"I'm sorry," Theo said, the words thick, "but I need a minute."

Auggie weighed his options. Then he said, "What if he wasn't talking about Dalton?"

Ten seconds passed. "What?"

"Well, think about it. He kept saying 'that kiddie-diddler,' and obviously, we both assumed he meant Dalton because, well, gross. But isn't that kind of strange? I mean, Merlin said he told Leon to stay away from that guy, and he said he tried to warn Leon about what that guy really wanted."

"He said the guy was older, twenty or thirty years older. That sounds like Dalton."

"But—this is going to sound stupid, so don't judge me—wouldn't he have called Dalton by his name? I mean, I'm not saying Merlin was father of the year. I don't think he knew who Leon's teachers were. But Wahredua isn't a big town, and if Leon got involved with someone here, especially someone from school, it feels like—well, it feels like Merlin would know who it was. Even if he just called him 'that theater teacher' or something like that." Silence. Auggie could feel his heartbeat in his face. "Never mind, that was stupid—"

But Theo sat up, his eyes opened. They were that soft, watercolor blue that Auggie had fallen in love with the first day Theo had walked into class. Ok, maybe not the first day. Not exactly the first day. Because Theo had been such a hardass about his no phones in the classroom rule. But even then, even when Auggie had been pissed off, he'd been struck by the color. A gentle blue, he thought now. And in his whole life, Theo had been given so little space to be gentle.

"We need to talk to Dalton," Theo said.

22

The Dore County Jail was attached to the sheriff's station, which in turn was part of the complex of government buildings on Jefferson Street. With the exception of city hall, with its classical façade and shining dome, the primary objective of whatever committee had designed the government complex seemed to have been, in Auggie's judgment, to showcase the period of Midwestern architecture when, for one shining moment, everyone had loved the color brown.

"Stop," Theo murmured.

Auggie laughed in spite of himself as he turned into the parking lot.

To be fair, the buildings weren't actually hideous—ok, maybe they were. But they looked like a lot of the town that had been developed at the same time: the low, single-story construction because land was abundant; the flat roofs; the windows with some sort of thermal coating that tinted them yellow. It was the kind of stuff that someone had been proud of because they could tag it with the words *affordable* and *sensible* and *on-budget*. Auggie wondered, not for the first time, if architects had a high rate of suicide.

They waited in the station lobby. Aside from the deputy at the desk, the only other occupant was an old man with a sour onion smell. He was picking at a scab on one elbow, and he was wearing Minnie Mouse slippers that looked decidedly too small for him. He caught Auggie looking and snarled—a little, lips-pulled-back snarl—and Auggie decided now would be a good time to look at his phone.

"Sorry about that," John-Henry said when he came through the doors. Then he saw the old man and said, "Hi, Wallace."

"It's my .22," the man said. "And they're my squirrels."

"Well, let's see what the sheriff has to say about that." John-Henry continued across the lobby to join Theo and Auggie. "I had to make a couple of phone calls after we talked."

"Are you sure this is going to work?" Theo asked. "We don't want to put you in a bad spot."

"The sheriff seemed fine with it. He was very accommodating about the room, and anyway, it's my investigation. If I want to bring in a couple of civilians to help, that's my business. Here we go."

Auggie turned around to see Sheriff Engels emerge from a hallway. The sheriff was a trim man with a silver mustache and silver hair, and he gave Theo and Auggie a nod before turning his attention to John-Henry. It gave Auggie a chance to study the sheriff more openly. He looked older than Auggie's initial assessment; it showed in his face, but only when you really looked—his movements, his energy, they all suggested a vigor that Auggie wasn't sure was entirely real. Not too long ago, the sheriff had lost his only son to a deranged killer, and Auggie wasn't sure anyone came back from that, not at any age. Look at Theo, a quiet voice said inside Auggie's head.

"Do you need anything from me?" the sheriff asked.

John-Henry shook his head. "Thanks for arranging this."

He led them to a cinderblock room with a scarred and battered table that had a metal bracket bolted to the top of it. The chairs were tubular, with orange upholstery that was pilled from too many asses. Across the room, a steel door connected to another part of the building—presumably, the jail itself. Auggie had visited the jail before, but never this room—he'd been thinking of the general visitation room, which was long and narrow and divided into cubicles with reinforced windows and telephones.

"Lawyers use this room to meet with their clients," John-Henry said to the question he must have seen on Auggie's face.

"And law enforcement uses it for questioning," Theo said.

"Sometimes."

John-Henry motioned for them to sit, so they did, and then Auggie could see where someone had scrawled the name DONNY on the table, going over and over the name in whorls of blue ink. A bit of adhesive-backed paper was wrapped around one chrome table leg—a leftover bit of nametag, maybe. The smell of the place was stronger—a watered-down artificial perfume that made him think of floor cleaner, and something else that he couldn't name but was like a film on his tongue.

The sheriff waited long enough to see that they were settled, and then he left. When the door closed behind him, the room seemed to seal itself off from the rest of the world. The silence tightened until Auggie thought his eardrums might pop.

"Are we being recorded?" Theo asked.

"No," John-Henry said.

"That's why law enforcement only uses it sometimes for questioning."

"That's one of the reasons." He gave them a cool look. "You're convinced that Dalton knows something he's not telling. He has a legal right to counsel, and he's also got the right to remain silent. He's not going to talk to you if he's got a lawyer glued to his side while we record the circus. But, on the other hand, if he tells you something and I'm not recording it, I'm going to get my ass burned. This is what we call a calculated risk, and I'm doing it because I was wrong earlier."

Auggie wasn't sure how many police chiefs across the world were capable of a sentence like that, but he thought the percentage wasn't high. "It's going to work. There's something weird, something he's been keeping secret."

"I'm sure there is, Auggie. There always is. But one of the things you learn when you do this job is that everyone keeps secrets, and they're not always worth ferreting out."

The door across from them opened, and Dalton came into the room, followed by a deputy—moon-faced, cheeks red. The kind of kid who had grown up eating a lot of dairy, Auggie thought. Then Auggie's attention moved back to Dalton. He wore prison scrubs, and he looked thinner than Auggie remembered. During the short time he'd been in jail, he'd changed drastically. His forehead and eyes were lined, his hair lank, his cheeks sallow even under a scruff of beard. Auggie was a little surprised that there was little sign of the violence from Theo's questioning at the community theater—a swollen nose was the worst of it. The real changes were from fear. And, of course, withdrawal. Dalton's eyes came to rest on them before darting away again, scanning the room, and then came back. They darted away again almost immediately. Remembering the community theater, the sweeping gestures, the voice projected to the back row, Auggie wondered how much of this was real. If it was a performance, then this was Dalton's role of a lifetime.

The deputy connected Dalton's cuffs to the ring set in the center of the table and said, "Need anything else?"

John-Henry shook his head.

"Just buzz when you're done." He nodded toward a button on the wall, and then he let himself out. A moment later, a bolt thudded home.

For a moment, Dalton sat there, shoulders curling in, and the pose made Auggie think of a crushed bug.

Then John-Henry stood. "I'm going to step outside, Mr. Weber. These men have some questions for you. As always, you have the right to refuse to answer them." John-Henry gave Theo and Auggie a last look, and Theo nodded. John-Henry let himself out of the room, and Auggie had that feeling again of the silence tightening around them.

Auggie broke it. "Mr. Weber, we'd like to ask you some questions."

Dalton's eyes flicked toward him. Then they came back to Theo before sliding away again.

"They're about Leon," Auggie said. "We spoke to Leon's father, and he said something we didn't understand. We're hoping you can help us."

"Dalton," Theo said, "are you listening?"

Auggie fought the urge to dry his hands on his jeans. "Do you know anything about Leon meeting an older man? Another older man, I mean. Not you."

Seconds ticked past. Theo leaned forward and said, "You're making a mistake right now. The best thing you can do is answer our questions."

"I'm not talking to you," Dalton said. His voice was constricted, like he could barely get the words out. "You piece of shit."

Theo let out a slow breath. "I'm sorry for what happened." He stopped and started again. "I'm sorry for what I did. I crossed a line."

Dalton let out an indignant squeak. He sat a little straighter, and a hint of color came back into his face. "You're sorry?"

"I know that doesn't—"

"You put my head in a fucking toilet!" The words exploded out of him, and they kept coming. "And now I'm here! Do you know what it's like here? I can't think. I can't think!" And then, like he couldn't hold the rest back: "I'm going to die in here!"

Theo looked down. The light from the fluorescents left little crescent shadows under his eyes. Not deep shadows. Barely anything at all, really.

"Mr. Weber—" Auggie tried.

"You're sorry?" Dalton said. "You're so fucking sorry? You've got to get me the fuck out of here!"

"Mr. Weber—"

"Tell them I didn't kill that girl! Tell them I didn't do anything!"

"Shut up!" Auggie barked.

Dalton pulled his head back, the movement oddly snakelike. The cuffs rattled on their chain. Theo looked over to examine Auggie.

"Shut up," Auggie said again, leveling out his voice, "and listen to me very carefully. You think what Theo did to you was bad? You didn't like getting pushed around a little? You didn't like getting a swirlie? What do you think is going to happen when you get convicted of murder, Dalton? For murdering a teenage girl to cover up the fact that you were molesting a teenage boy?"

"I wasn't—"

"Do you know what they do to guys like you in prison? They're going to cut your dick off and choke you to death with it. That's not an exaggeration. They might rape you to death while they're at it. That's your future if you don't get your head straight right now."

Dalton stared at him. The hint of color had drained away, and his lower lip trembled. Theo was still staring, and then, to Auggie's horror and surprise, his eyes crinkled at the edges.

Before Theo could ruin everything, Auggie said, "Merlin Purdue said he warned his son to stay away from, quote, 'that kiddie-diddler.'"

"I told you," Dalton said, "I never touched Leon. He slept at my apartment. He was sweet. But we never did anything!"

It was the way Dalton said it, the shrill protest, the indignant raise of his chin, that gave him away. Betrayed by his own dramatic talent, Auggie thought. He tried not to roll his eyes.

"You're dodging the question," Theo said. "Which means you do know something. You know we're not asking about you. We're asking about someone else. Who did Leon meet?"

The change came again—one costume discarded, another pulled on. Dalton shrank in his seat and shook his head.

"Do you want to try that again?" Theo asked. "Someone killed Shaniyah Johnson because she was investigating Leon's disappearance. Right now, you're the best candidate. They'll put someone on the stand, some forensic expert, and he'll tell them all about the fibers under Shaniyah's fingernails, about the match to your cardigan, about the fact that someone tried to get rid of the cardigan, to destroy the evidence. They'll put another expert on the stand, and he'll tell them about the tape over her mouth, about how that symbolizes that killer's motive to silence the victim, to keep her from revealing any secrets. They'll put somebody up there to talk about your childhood, and why you're attracted to teenage boys, and they'll use the word predator. And brick by brick, they're going to wall you up, Dalton."

Dalton made a choked sound and shook his head again. He squeezed his eyes shut. Once again, Auggie had the sense that this, perhaps, was the truth—or as close to it as someone like Dalton Weber could come.

He said, "You know who we're talking about. Why won't you tell us? If you're protecting someone—" He stopped because he thought of the Cottonmouth Club, the ooze of brown light, the man named Gideon saying something about the weekend before. He thought about the person who had come into their home and tried to kill them. "If you're scared, Dalton, the police can protect you."

"Ha!" The sound wasn't amused; it was a bark of scorn and derision. But Dalton shook his head, and he blinked his eyes clear. A single tear ran down his cheek. He shouldered it away, cleared his throat, and sat up again. "If that's what you think, you've got no idea what you're talking about."

"Then tell us," Theo said. "Tell us what's going on."

"These are dangerous people. These are bad, bad, dangerous people. And they can—they can get you anywhere, don't you understand? Maybe you're right. Maybe they'll convict me, and maybe I'll go to prison, and maybe those things, what you said, that'll happen to me. But that's better than what they'll do, all right?"

Theo shook his head. "If it's witness protection—"

Dalton barked that laugh again, and Theo sat back and looked at Auggie, helplessness scribbled across his face.

"You cared about Leon," Auggie said. "Nobody else did. Not his mom. Not his dad. They couldn't be bothered with him when they were married, and they had even less time for him after they got divorced. You took him in when he needed a home. You were good and decent and kind to him. And someone did something to him, Dalton. Something horrible. I don't know you, but I don't think you're the kind of person who's willing to let that happen, especially not to someone like Leon."

His face crumpled. Tears came. He shook his head again. It went on for a minute, and then another, and then he exhaled sharply several times and wiped his eyes on his shoulder because he couldn't bring his hands up that high. When he spoke, there was only the slightest roughness to his voice.

"There's a place," Dalton said. "The Cottonmouth Club."

It was like electricity, like someone had plugged in a cord. Every part of Auggie lit up. Goose bumps knitted his forearms, and the faint brown hairs there stood up.

"We know it," Theo said.

Dalton frowned. "Ambyr...took us. I mean, I knew Leon from school, and I knew Ambyr because—"

"Because she was your dealer," Theo said.

With a shrug, Dalton continued, "She introduced us to the Cottonmouth Club. Leon wanted to make some money, and she said she'd vouch for him. I wanted to make sure Leon would be ok."

Theo's face tightened at that, but all Auggie could do was hear the words the way Dalton said them, to think about what they said about all the years of loneliness and desire and helplessness.

"Leon thought she was going to set him up dealing drugs," Dalton said, "but that wasn't it. Ambyr—you've met her?"

"She made an impression," Theo said drily.

"She does the drug thing, but she's not—she's not serious about it, if that makes any sense. We met when she was in a musical I put on at the community theater. *Evita*. She can't sing a note, by the way. But the drugs are an easy way for her to make money, and she's your standard issue basic white bitch, so she doesn't get hassled by the police. Anyway, if you've met her, you know she's all about her influencer career. So, of course, she wasn't really trying to help Leon. She was trying to help herself."

Auggie frowned. "I don't understand."

"There was a man there. At the Cottonmouth Club. Ambyr's supplier had introduced them because the guy was looking for talent, and he thought Ambyr might be interested. Well, Ambyr didn't want it, what the guy was offering, but she wanted to step up the ladder—this guy said he might have other projects down the road, and he could put her in touch with people, that kind of thing. So, she gave him Leon."

"What did he want?"

But Theo was the one who answered. "Porn."

Dalton nodded. "They shot one video here. I don't know where; Leon didn't want me to come, and I—I was trying to respect his independence. As an adult."

Theo didn't say anything, but Auggie watched it sweep across his face: the incredulity, and then the anger that broke after.

"He came back home." Dalton stopped. He shook his head, and for a moment, Auggie thought he'd squeeze his eyes shut again. "He was so proud of himself. It had gone so well. He was going to be a star." He stopped. His throat moved once, and his clasped hands twisted, like he was trying to hold on to something. Or like he was trying to let go. "It was all he could talk about. And I tried to talk to him about it. I tried to be supportive because nobody had ever been supportive, and because it's important to be sex positive with young people."

"And because he was so happy," Auggie said.

Dalton made a little broken noise and nodded. "But I tried to tell him. You can't do acting as long as I have without hearing a little about the industry. Some people do all right. Some people are all right. But other people...aren't."

"And this guy?" Theo asked. "The one who wanted to put an underage boy in a video?"

Dalton shrugged.

"Jesus," Theo said.

Easy, Auggie mouthed.

But Theo sat back hard in his seat, and the tubular legs groaned. His cheeks were red behind his beard.

"Enough," Auggie said quietly.

"He was a child—"

"Theo."

It looked like it took a tremendous amount of effort, but Theo stopped and looked away.

Dalton had watched the exchange with a dull-eyed helplessness, and now he turned that empty gaze on Auggie.

"What happened?" Auggie asked.

"This man had another video to shoot. Another opportunity for Leon. More money. Maybe, if it went well, a studio contract. But it meant moving out to California. Right then."

"When was this?"

"The weekend of Fourth of July."

The end of June, Auggie thought. Everyone had said the end of June.

"I couldn't even pretend to be supportive," Dalton said. "I told him he was taking too big a risk. I told him he didn't know anyone out there, didn't have anyone who could help him if the deal turned out to be bad, or if this guy wasn't who he said he was, or if he got sick. We fought. It was a huge, ugly fight. He said ugly things."

Auggie could imagine; he thought about Merlin, about how Leon had known, instinctively, where to set the knife and how to twist it.

"I left because I couldn't stand to be there anymore. When I came back, he was...different. The Leon I knew. He was sweet. He apologized. He cried. We decided we were going to figure it out. I can retire next year; we'd move out to California together, and I'd have my pension, enough to keep us off the street while he started his career." Dalton stopped. He shut his eyes again, but this time when he opened them, they were dry. Dry and lusterless. And, Auggie thought, unseeing. "He was lying. I finally decided, later, he was lying because he was trying to be kind to a pathetic old man. The next morning, I woke up, and he was gone. All his stuff, gone. He'd left in the middle of the night."

That pressurized silence was back again, making Auggie's ears throb. He tried to look at Dalton, but the grief there was like an open wound, and finally Auggie had to turn away. He met Theo's gaze by chance, and he couldn't read what he saw there. Theo touched his leg, and Auggie nodded, surprised to find himself on the brink of tears.

"Do you know this man's name?" Theo asked. "What he called himself? His company? Did he give Leon anything?"

Dalton shook his head, but he said, "I saw him. Just once, but I've got a good eye for faces."

"You're saying you'd recognize him?"

"You have to be good at faces," Dalton said. The words were numb. "If you want to direct, you have to be able to remember them. But you don't understand, these people—" He cut off, and what he didn't say hung in the air.

Finally, Theo said, "It's your choice. But if you're telling the truth, this is your only way out."

"Chief Somerset is a good guy," Auggie said. "He'll keep you safe."

Dalton shrugged and looked off toward the corner of the room.

"We'll tell him you've decided to share some information," Theo said. "You're doing the right thing, Dalton."

"I'm doing the stupid thing," he said without looking at them. "As always."

"Did Leon have a ring?" Auggie asked. The question popped out of him before he'd realized he was going to ask it.

Now Dalton did look at him. "A ring?"

"A class ring. From Wahredua High."

Dalton nodded slowly. "Yes."

"If I showed you a picture—" Auggie scrolled through the images on his phone until he found the photo of the ring that Jem had recovered along with a collection of other stolen and illegally transported items.

Dalton made a soft noise. He reached for the phone, but the cuffs caught him, so he leaned in for a closer look.

"Is that Leon's ring?"

"Yes. Where did you get this? What happened to Leon?"

"Are you sure?" Theo asked.

"I don't know. I think so; I don't know. Did something happen to him? I told him not to go with that man."

"We don't know," Auggie said. "That's what we're trying to find out."

They stood and moved toward the door. Theo hit the buzzer, and it sounded distantly. Dalton looked smaller inside his scrubs, as though the interview had stolen something from him.

When he spoke, it sounded like he was talking to himself. "It wouldn't have worked even if he'd stayed. I know that. He was nice to me, but he didn't feel the same way. There was always that other boy. He'd let Leon go for a while and then reel him back in, and every time, Leon let him."

"What boy?" Theo said. "Keelan?"

"It was sad, really. I tried to tell him it wasn't ever going to work out. Keelan liked fooling around, but that's all—anybody could see that. Of course, Leon was convinced there was more. Deeper feelings and all that." A laugh bubbled up. "And yes, I'm aware of the irony, but at least I knew how Leon felt about me. What he didn't understand, though, was that it wasn't just that boy. It was his mom. Even if Leon had stuck around, she would have made sure nothing ever happened between him and her son."

"Who are you talking about?"

The deputy entered the room, keys jingling, and Dalton stood to be led away. "Baylee Vasquez. Do you know, I honestly believe if she'd ever caught them, she would have killed Leon?"

23

"That was good," John-Henry said. "That was really, really good."

"Excellent work," Sheriff Engels said.

In the sheriff's office, after their debriefing, Theo felt exhausted. The physical and emotional toll of the last few days, sure, but then this. Dalton. His terror had been hard enough to experience secondhand; this was a man Theo knew, and although they hadn't been friends, it was still somehow worse because Dalton wasn't a stranger, someone Theo could explain away without a second thought as a pervert and a deviant. Even worse, though, was hearing him talk about Leon, and learning—even though it seemed impossible—that the campy theater teacher who lusted after teenage boys might have been the closest thing to a parental figure in Leon's life. Certainly, Theo thought as he ran through the cast of asshats they'd encountered in the last few days, he was the only one who had genuinely cared about Leon. Then he thought of Shaniyah and added, While he was alive. He tried to scrub that thought out as soon as it came, because maybe Leon was still alive, and maybe he was healthy and happy somewhere. But when he closed his eyes, he saw the terror in Dalton's face, and beyond it, a shadow—the man who had taken Leon away from Wahredua.

"We're going to get started on this right away," John-Henry was saying, and Theo forced himself to open his eyes again. "We've got a connection between Leon and the Cottonmouth Club. We've got Dalton as an eyewitness. We'll start working on taking that place apart, finding the weak links, the ones who will talk if we apply the right pressure. We've got six-packs we can show Dalton in the meantime, in case we get lucky. Some of the sex offenders, don't you think?"

Engels nodded; it took Theo a moment to realize six-packs referred to packs of photos of previously convicted individuals.

"You did good," John-Henry said. "This is solid. This is golden, actually. And we're going to run with it."

"Now," Engels said, "you boys need to go home and get some sleep, because you look dead on your feet."

John-Henry walked them out, chatting about something—about Lana and Evie, Theo thought, although it was hard to track the conversation. He left them at the door and hurried back, obviously excited to get started now that the investigation had legs.

When Theo caught Auggie's expression out of the corner of his eye, he was surprised to see a frown.

"What?"

"What about Shaniyah?"

Theo's eyes had that gluey feeling that came from too little sleep. "Shaniyah?"

"All right, some mysterious man offered Leon a chance to make porn. Let's say Leon went with him, and that's why he disappeared. If the guy was telling the truth, if it was a semi-legit offer and Leon's out there in California living his best life, then why would someone kill Shaniyah? And more importantly, why would they kill her here, in Wahredua? I mean, it's not like she showed up on the studio doorstep and announced they were using underage models. But the other version doesn't make any sense either—if the guy's dirty, if he was lying to Leon and still took him, why kill Shaniyah? Leon's gone, and there's no way Shaniyah could have made that connection to whoever this guy was. I mean, Dalton was the only one who knew the whole story, and he wouldn't tell us until his own life was on the line; there's no way he told Shaniyah. So, it's the same question: why kill Shaniyah, and why kill her in Wahredua?"

It took a moment for Theo to make sense of what Auggie was saying. His brain had that same tackiness as his eyeballs, like his thoughts were gummed into place. Finally he said, "You think Keelan's mom killed her? Why? Because she stumbled onto something else?"

"I don't know. I think we know—kind of, partially—what happened to Leon. But we don't know who killed Shaniyah, or why, and the answer is still here, in town."

Theo wanted to say no. He wanted to go home and sleep; this had started because no one had known where Shaniyah was, and no one had seemed to care. Now they had found her, and they had found another missing boy on top of that, and he wanted, for one moment, with a feeling like claws tightening in his gut, to be done. To go back to his normal life, his safe life, where he could minimize risks, control things, protect his family.

But the vision rose of Shaniyah in their living room, laughing. Of Shaniyah showing him the video Auggie had helped her edit. Of Shaniyah talking about the future, laying out multiplying possibilities as she combined colleges and majors and career paths, like watching a kid play with train tracks.

He nodded. "Let's go talk to Mrs. Vasquez."

24

As soon as Auggie started the car, Theo fell asleep. It was kind of adorable, really; he and Lana slept the same way, heads hanging forward, bouncing a little as the car rocked over uneven pavement. The inside of the car was sweltering, and Auggie turned the Focus's air conditioning all the way up. Outside, heat waves shimmered above the asphalt, making it look like the spinning sign of Riverside Burgers was floating. The river was the only thing that looked cool, like someone had drawn it with a slate marker, the currents hard-edged with white where the sun caught them.

Keelan's house was a big, expensive-looking brick home on a street with other big, expensive-looking homes, and Auggie's first thought, on seeing the three garage doors facing the street, was of a slot machine. The street was empty except for the Focus. No one driving. No one working in the yards. Maybe this was the kind of place where everyone paid someone to do the yardwork; that was kind of the vibe, anyway. Auggie tried to remember what day it was, tried to figure out if everyone was at work. Thursday? Friday? God, was it possible it was only Wednesday? It felt like it had been months since they'd started looking for Shaniyah. Years.

When they rolled over the lip of the driveway, Theo sat up, his lips making a dry sound as he craned his head.

"We're here," Auggie said.

Theo made another noise that suggested his brain was still booting up. Then he said, "God, sorry."

"Don't be sorry; you're tired."

"You've got to be exhausted too."

"I'm young."

It took a beat, but then Theo rubbed his eyes and said, "Here we go."

"And virile."

"Now might be a good time for you to explain if this is a compare/contrast exercise."

"And I did six Red Bulls and a Five-Hour Energy before my bros and I hit the club."

"What is happening? Am I still asleep? Is this a nightmare?"

Auggie grinned, and to his relief, Theo smiled too. Only barely, but it was there. Then his smile flattened out and he said, "Do you want to explain your intimate knowledge of prison shankings, by the way?"

It took a moment for Auggie to realize he was talking about what Auggie had said in their interview with Dalton. "Oh. Fer watched a lot of Oz."

"That was—how old were you?"

"Eight. Nine. I don't know. It's not like I understood it, you know. I went back and rewatched it when I was fifteen or sixteen because I knew he loved it."

"Oh my God," Theo said and scrubbed his face.

"Did another piece of the puzzle just fall into place?"

"I'm not going to answer that," Theo said and got out of the car.

When Theo rang the bell, a chime sounded deep inside the house. Not your standard ding-dong—this one was a melodious chime that went on for almost five seconds.

"Do you think people want to ring it again as soon as they hear it," Auggie asked, "just because they know how annoying it must be?"

"Your teenage hooligan is showing."

Auggie fought down the grin as the door opened.

Baylee Vasquez had that dark olive skin that suggested both genes and a tan, and her makeup and hair suggested a great deal of time and undivided attention. On their first—brief—meeting, Auggie had gotten the impression of someone with a PTA mom's boundless energy, but now, as the honey-colored eyes flitted toward him and then back to Theo, he wondered if that wasn't a mask for someone else. Girls learned that, he thought. Even more than boys, they learned how to wear masks early in life.

"May I help you?"

"Mrs. Vasquez, my name is—"

"I know who you are."

Somewhere in the distance, a lawnmower rumbled to life.

"We'd like to talk to you," Theo said. "About your son."

"I see. And what's going to happen if I call Principal Wieberdink and ask why one of her teachers is on my doorstep with his...partner?"

She didn't turn the word into a sneer, not exactly, but the pause wasn't a hesitation—it was more like a slap. A warning, Auggie thought, before she brought out the claws. Yes, he thought, as those amber eyes fixed Theo again. Someone else is back behind that mask.

"I don't know," Theo said. "I took a personal day. I suppose Principal Wieberdink can say whatever she wants. In the meantime, I'd like to talk to you about the relationship between your son and Leon Purdue."

"I don't know what you're talking about. What relationship? They were friends."

"It's more believable," Auggie told her, "if you breathe a little between sentences."

Dusky color bloomed in her cheeks as she turned toward him and opened her mouth.

But Theo spoke first. "Mrs. Vasquez, this isn't a joke. We need to have this conversation, and we need to have it right now. Either we can have it out here on your front step, where the neighbors can hear, or we can have it inside." He wiped his forehead and added, like a peace offering, "Where it's cool."

Maybe it was Botox. Maybe it was fillers. Maybe it was cheap plastic surgery. Whatever it was, it seemed to have left the muscles of her face fixed; nothing showed there except whatever was moving at the back of her eyes.

"All right," she said and moved aside.

They stepped into the entry hall, where air conditioning licked Auggie's nape, and she shut the door behind them. Inside, the house matched the exterior: cold and pristine, with maple floorboards, an accent table in French country blue, white walls that hinted at another shade of blue. A sideboard in the next room had brass fleur-de-lis accents. The mirror over the mantel had a gilt frame. An Art Deco lamp added lines, a spot of masculine energy to keep everything else from becoming too much. The family portrait, though, was the best part—oil, Auggie decided, not a photo, and done by someone with a reasonable amount of talent. Baylee stood on one side of Keelan. His father—Ray, Auggie wanted to say—stood on the other. They each had a hand on one of Keelan's shoulders. It was a nice touch, Auggie thought, how the artist had really captured the family dynamic. You could tell just from looking at the painting that between the two of them, they were about to rip the boy in half.

Baylee led them to the sofa and took an accent chair. She was wearing yoga pants and a white top, and she straightened the top now, adjusting it across her shoulders. "You'll have to forgive me if I don't offer you anything to drink."

"That's all right," Theo said in the teacher voice Auggie had come to know. "We won't take much of your time. When did you learn that your son was sexually involved with Leon?"

"I don't—"

It was the teacher voice again: kind but firm. "Answer the question."

It worked on Auggie. It worked on more people than Auggie would have thought, actually, and it worked on Baylee. "And I suppose if I don't, you're going to tell everyone about this." Before they could respond, she continued, "A few months ago. I came home early—" She stopped herself. "I told Keelan I didn't want him having friends over when I wasn't home. That was the end of it."

Theo nodded. He didn't say what he must have been thinking: that Keelan would have kept doing whatever he wanted, because there was no one to stop him, no one to care enough to make sure. "You didn't discuss it with Keelan?"

The look she turned on Theo was pure horror.

"Did he know?" Auggie asked. "Even if you didn't talk to him about it, do you think he figured it out?"

"I don't know. And I don't know why it matters. It was a—a phase, and that boy was a terrible influence on Keelan. And it's none of your business. I'd like to know why a couple of grown men have so much interest in a teenage boy. Maybe this is something I should be discussing with the police."

"You may need to discuss it with the police, Mrs. Vasquez," Theo said. "It might come to that. Do you hate gay people?"

"Don't be ridiculous."

"Come on," Auggie said. "You can barely look at us, and you can't even talk about Keelan and Leon being involved."

"I'd like you to leave now. And I think I will be calling the police. I'd like to know why you were with my son at the ice rink. If this is some sort of—of grooming—"

"That's enough," Theo said in that teacher voice again.

Baylee's whole body went still, but she stopped talking.

"A girl named Shaniyah Johnson was looking into Leon's disappearance. Did she talk to you?"

Plastic clicked. A motor came on. Auggie startled at the noises, and then he had to suppress a laugh as he spotted the Roomba leaving its docking station to patrol the house for dust that might have escaped its notice.

"Please," Baylee said, her voice soft and crushed. "Please leave."

"Did you talk to Shaniyah?"

"I want you to leave."

"Did you know someone killed Shaniyah? Someone didn't want Shaniyah telling people something, something she'd learned. Someone didn't want a secret coming to light. And so they killed her."

The words hung in the air. Everything felt frozen, like they'd all become part of the perfect Vasquez dollhouse. Then the Roomba bumped into the sideboard, and a decorative candle wobbled, and the world spun into motion again.

"Don't be ridiculous," Baylee said. "I would never—" Some of the force came back into her voice. "I want you to leave right now. Get out, or I'm calling the police."

"The police are going to talk to you, Mrs. Vasquez," Theo said as he stood. "You can be sure of that. And they're going to ask the same questions. And they're going to ask your husband. And they're going to ask Keelan. And they're going to ask Keelan's friends. And every secret you think you can keep, it's going to come out into the light. Get ready for it."

Auggie stayed on the sofa, and he waited until Baylee looked at him. Then he said, "I think you love your son a lot."

She stared. Her cheeks were red, and she looked on the brink of tears, but the mask had fallen away, and the woman facing him now was iron.

"I don't know if it helps you to hear that Keelan actually isn't gay. Or, at least, that's not how he identifies. I think he'd probably call himself straight. There are a lot of explanations for what was going on between him and Leon. It might have been just for fun. It might have been, like you said, a phase. It might be—actually, it definitely is—part of Keelan figuring out who he is and what he likes. He might be bi. He might not ever want to put a label on it. He's growing up at a time when he's got a lot of options. I think that's a good thing; I think you should too."

She was silent for a moment. Then she said stiffly, "I don't understand what you're saying."

"I didn't come out until I was in college, but when I was a teenager, I did what Keelan did. I tried things out. I told myself it was just for fun."

"So, you're saying he is gay."

Would that be so terrible, Auggie wanted to ask. Would it be such a horrible thing? He could see, looking into her face, that for Baylee Vasquez, it would be. He didn't know why. Religion, maybe. Or social standing. Or some knee-jerk reaction to the life she'd envisioned for her son. But Auggie didn't think he'd ever know, and he wasn't sure it mattered.

"No, I'm saying I'm gay, but when I was Keelan's age, I was just trying to figure out who I was. That's not really the important part. The important part is that, even if you're happy and well-adjusted and confident, which Keelan seems to be, it's scary. Because there's a lot of pressure. And because you don't know how people are going to react. And you're worried something might be wrong with you. Teenagers feel those things even when they're a hundred percent straight; they all go through that uncertainty, the scariness of not knowing who they are and being afraid to find out."

She swallowed and pulled at her shirt again, but her eyes didn't leave Auggie.

"One thing that helped me was my brother. He made sure I knew that he didn't care who I loved. If I was straight, fantastic. If I was gay, great — he already had all sorts of jokes."

Her eyes cut away. "Keelan knows we love him."

"If you want to hear the flip side of the coin," Theo said, "my family didn't want anything to do with me when I came out. I was in my twenties, and it took me that long because my parents let us know, in no uncertain terms, what would happen if any of us turned out to be gay. You want to talk about unhappiness and uncertainty? That's how you mess a child up."

"Ray and I have never—never told Keelan anything like that." She seemed to catch herself and added, "We would never."

"You don't have to say it," Theo said. "Kids pick up on it. It's not hard to tell you don't like gay people, Mrs. Vasquez. Your son has picked up on it; you can be sure of that. And that means he feels like he has to hide this from you. In the long run, kids who can't talk to their parents about their romantic and sexual lives pay a high price. They deal with a lot of internalized negativity, a lot of shame. They begin sexual activity without the knowledge they need. Some of that has to do with safe sex, but some of it is just about picking partners and making good choices. If you love Keelan—and I agree with Auggie, I think you do—then you need to get a handle on how you feel about gay people, and then you need to have a conversation with him. Maybe the first real, open conversation you've ever had with him."

"And it's going to be awkward as fuck," Auggie said.

For some reason, that made her laugh, and she wiped her eyes and shook her head. She was silent for so long that Theo finally held out his hand to Auggie and said, "We'll see ourselves out. If you change your mind—"

"She came here." The words were thick, and Baylee fanned herself with one hand as she swallowed. "That girl. Shaniyah. She came to the house one afternoon. Keelan was gone, thank God. That's all I could think. Thank God.

Thank God he's not here. She wanted to talk about—about Leon. Like you said. About Keelan and Leon. And I just…couldn't. I couldn't. I couldn't sit in my kitchen with a girl I didn't know, sit there with a girl saying these awful things about my son."

Silence pooled in the room. Auggie could see it: the argument escalating, Baylee's fear making her lose control, the final moment when anything was better than facing the truth about her son. She might have grabbed something heavy. They were in the kitchen; she might have picked up a knife.

"What did you do?" Theo asked.

"Do?" Baylee sounded surprised by the question. "I made her leave."

Auggie sat forward. "You made her leave?"

"Of course. I wasn't going to sit there and listen to that. To be accused of doing something to Leon so that he'd leave my son alone. I asked her to leave, and I warned her that if she came back, I'd call the police."

"And?" Theo asked.

"And what?"

"What happened the next time she came to the house?" Auggie asked.

"She didn't. She never came back. I didn't see her again until the party."

"What party?" Theo asked.

"The back-to-school party. On Saturday. On Mrs. Renshaw's back forty." She stopped and looked at them. "The high school kids like to have their parties out there—"

"We know about the parties," Auggie said. "What do you mean you saw Shaniyah there on Saturday?"

"I saw her."

"Explain," Theo said. "From the beginning."

Baylee shifted in her seat, picking at the upholstery, her nails making a soft popping sound as she worried a stitch. "Keelan went, of course. He's very popular. He gets invited to everything. He has a very good group of friends, and they're all very responsible, and I'd much rather know what they're doing and where they're doing it than be left in the dark. And that's what would happen, you know? If I put my foot down, Keelan would simply do it anyway, only I wouldn't know. I wouldn't be able to make sure he's ok."

"Mrs. Vasquez."

"I was taking them beer. It's just beer."

"You drove out to Mrs. Renshaw's property?" Auggie asked.

She nodded.

"And?"

"You've been out there? So, you know how people park all over the place. I drove around for a while, trying to find Keelan and his friends. And I saw her. Shaniyah."

"Where?" Theo asked. "What was she doing? How did she look?"

"She'd passed out," Baylee said, a hint of the vicious smugness seeping back into her voice. "She was drunk. That's why I noticed her; he had to pick her up and put her in the car."

"Who?" Auggie asked.

"Her uncle. The one she lives with."

25

The Johnson family lived in a side-split house, in a neighborhood of side-split houses, with old concrete roads spider-webbed with tar and lawns that had mostly gone to crabgrass. Their house had wood siding on top and brick below, with river rock around the foundation. No weeds, no mess. Someone had tucked a little wooden bench under the house's overhang. The gray paint was peeling, and there was a little heart cut out at the center.

When Auggie knocked, he asked, "Is anyone going to be home? It's the middle of the day."

"They're still grieving."

"Not if they killed her they aren't."

"If they killed her," Theo said drily, "they're lying low and hoping everyone thinks they're grieving."

The door opened, and Tiera Johnson looked out at them. She was an imposing woman, taller than Auggie and much bigger, her Afro gathered in a powder blue wrap. She looked at him for a moment, her face not registering, and then she seemed to startle awake. "Mr. Lopez? Dr. Stratford?"

"Hi, Mrs. Johnson," Theo said. "I'm so sorry about Shaniyah."

"Thank you."

"We wanted to come in person to tell you that. She was a special girl, and we both loved having the chance to work with her."

Tiera nodded. "We appreciate that you tried to help her."

It took Auggie a moment to separate those words out from this moment, to remember that Tiera wasn't talking about the investigation, about whatever Auggie and Theo had accidentally unleashed on their family. She was talking about a college admissions essay. She was talking about something that seemed from another lifetime.

"I'm sorry for your loss," Auggie said. "I see my fair share of people Shaniyah's age, people who are driven, people who want to do smart, creative work. Shaniyah really stood out—she was so passionate about what she did."

"Thank you for saying that," Tiera said.

An Amazon van hummed down the street and stopped, and a driver got out and slammed the door. He was talking too loudly on a Bluetooth headset. "No way, man, no way, not while Colby owes me twenty bucks."

"If that's all," Tiera began.

"Could we come in?" Theo asked. "We need to talk to you. And to Mr. Johnson, actually, if he's home."

"He's always home," Tiera said, but she pushed the door open wider, and Auggie followed Theo into the house.

Inside, the house wasn't what Auggie expected. Oh, it was standard enough—the walls that neutral grayish brown that had been so popular for a time, the white-upholstered sofa and loveseat that looked nice but not too expensive. But what struck Auggie was the casual disorder: a pile of laundry on the sofa, waiting to be folded; jelly jar glasses on the coffee table, one with a gold bracelet hung over the lip; empty cardboard boxes piled in the corner, the kind that suggested the Amazon van had visited this house a time or two. It wasn't dirty, exactly. But it was a kind of chaos that suggested nobody picked up around here—at least, not unless they were forced to.

"Could you take your shoes off, please?" Tiera said, pointing to a pile of footwear near the door. "We don't wear shoes in the house."

But you leave dead daisies in their vase, Auggie thought as he heeled off his sneakers.

"Could we speak to Mr. Johnson too?" Theo asked.

Some emotion tightened Tiera's expression—a species of anger, although it was gone too quickly for Auggie to decide what had been behind the anger. She moved to the stairs and called, "Cleve? Dr. Stratford is here to talk to us." Silence echoed back to them. "Cleve?" Then, to Theo and Auggie: "He's not feeling well."

"We really need to talk to him," Theo said. "We'll try to keep it brief."

That same emotion flickered on her face again. "I'll be right back."

In stockinged feet, they sat on the loveseat. Tiera's steps moved through the house, and then came the sound of a door opening. Tiera said something too low for Auggie to make out, but the intensity behind the words carried clearly enough—the low-vibration argument of a couple that can't tear into each other the way they really want to. The final words, though, cracked through the house: "Because I said so! Get off your ass and get down there!"

A moment later, the steps moved toward them, and Tiera descended the stairs. She was smoothing the front of her shirt, not looking at them as she said, "Now's not really a good time, Dr. Stratford. We appreciate you coming, and we appreciate what you did for Shaniyah. Maybe we could do this another day."

Auggie thought about how she had said, *Thank you for saying that*, and *We appreciate that you tried*, and *He's always home.*

"Shaniyah didn't talk much about her life here," Auggie said. "In Wahredua, I mean. Was she happy here?"

For a moment, Tiera didn't seem to know what to say. "She was a teenager; you know how they are."

Auggie did know. He'd been one himself, as a matter of fact—and a part of him could hear Theo adding, *And not too long ago*, which made him want to smile. "She never said why she moved here. She was from Kansas, right?"

"She moved here, Mr. Lopez, because she couldn't stop getting in trouble. She got in trouble here too, it turned out."

Auggie tried to keep his face expressionless, but he could see Theo's shock.

"Are you talking about…what happened to her?" Theo asked.

"I'm talking about all of it," Tiera snapped. It was like something giving way, the words rushing out of her. "Not coming home. Lying. Partying. Boys. She had to be little miss, like she was the adult and the rest of us were children, like we were bothering her. When she wasn't fooling around, everything was about her. Her college. Her videos. I've never seen such a selfish, self-absorbed child." She stopped, her eyes suddenly liquid, and said, "I guess that's what you wanted to hear, right? Everybody wants to hear me be a bitch because I'm just such a bitch."

"Mrs. Johnson—" Theo said.

"Well, I might be a bitch, but I did the best I could."

"Nobody's saying you didn't," Auggie said. "I didn't mean anything; I was only asking—"

"You saw her, what? Once a week? And she smiled, and she was polite; she always knew how to get people to do what she wanted. I'm sorry she's dead. I am. She was a troubled girl, and she made my life harder than it needed to be, and she never once showed me a drop of gratitude. I'm not saying I wanted anything bad to happen to her, because I didn't. But if you came here to watch me cry and hear me tell you how much we miss her, you can go home now."

"Tiera!" Auggie hadn't met Cleve Johnson before, but he assumed that's who the man coming down the stairs was. He was huge, all of it muscle, and he wore a black, satiny durag. His beard had a surprising amount of gray. His face, though, was what held Auggie's attention: a grayish cast made Cleve look half dead. "What are you talking about?"

"I'm telling them that whatever they came here for, they can just go. I'm not going to sit here and pretend—"

"Who's asking you to pretend?" His gaze remained on Tiera, as though he hadn't noticed them yet, or perhaps as though they didn't matter.

"I'm telling them the truth. I'm sure Shaniyah told them all about how I was a bitch. This is the proof, right?"

Cleve stared at her for a few more seconds. Then he shook his head and swung away from her to study Theo and Auggie.

"Sit down," Tiera said, taking a spot on the sofa. "They want to talk to us."

Cleve dropped down next to her and wrapped his hands around his knees. He had on what Auggie thought might be a championship ring—the letters KC, the gold plating and red enamel, the cubic zirconia in the shape of an arrowhead. And he thought of the bruise on Theo's chest. The strange arrowhead shape of it.

"I don't know how to ask this politely," Theo said, "so I'm just going to ask, and I hope if I offend you that you'll understand that's not my intention. Did Shaniyah go to a party Saturday night?"

Cleve started to shake his head, but Tiera said, "Yes. She snuck out of the house after I told her she couldn't go."

"Did you pick her up from the party?"

"Of course not," Tiera said.

But something was starting to come awake in Cleve's face. He was looking at them more intently, his eyes flat and unreadable.

"Mr. Johnson?" Theo asked.

Cleve stared back at him.

"I told you," Tiera said, "we didn't pick her up. She snuck out, and like we told the police, that was the last time we saw her."

No, Auggie thought. You told them she'd gone back to Kansas. You told everyone that everything was ok.

"Mr. Johnson," Theo said again in his teacher voice.

Tiera opened her mouth, but nothing came out. Cleve shifted on the sofa, springs pinging slightly as he sat forward, his body tensing as he moved to the edge of the cushion.

"Did you pick up Shaniyah from that party?" Theo asked.

"No," Cleve said.

"We went to bed like we always do," Tiera said. "We watched television and went to bed. What's going on here? Why do you keep asking him like that?"

"Someone saw you," Theo said. "They saw you pick up Shaniyah. They saw you put her in your car."

"What are you talking about? Cleve, what are they talking about?"

"They're mistaken," Cleve said. "You're upsetting my wife. I want you to leave."

"It wasn't a mistake," Theo said. "Why'd you go out there?"

"I won't tell you twice," Cleve said, and he started to stand, his hands gathering into fists at his sides.

"The ring," Auggie said.

The comment must have surprised Cleve—surprised everyone, for that matter, because they all looked at Auggie.

"It leaves a distinctive mark. Theo's got a bruise shaped just like that ring. Right here, on his chest. And let me guess: you drive a black Chrysler."

Cleve drew in several deep breaths. Then he started to push himself up again.

"What did you do?" Tiera asked.

"Don't worry about it," Cleve said. "I'm handling this."

"Handling this? What the hell did you do?" She slapped his arm. Then she slapped him again, this time on the back. "What the hell stupid kind of thing did you do?"

"He tried to kill us," Auggie said. "He would have killed our daughter. Him and his friends."

"No," Cleve said.

But Tiera moaned. She hit him again, harder this time, and Cleve twisted to get away. The movement carried him a step, and then another, until he formed the third point of a triangle: Theo and Auggie at one corner, Tiera at the other, and Cleve like a paper target at the end of a long lane.

Thoughts stormed across Theo's face. Then he looked at Auggie, the glance long enough and solid enough to send a charge through him, like someone had run through a room flipping every switch, all the lights blazing.

"What the hell are they talking about?" Tiera said. "We talked about this. You and I talked about this. We weren't bailing her out anymore. No more rushing out to fix her problems."

"What happened?" Theo asked. "What happened on Saturday night?"

"We agreed we weren't going to enable her bad behavior!"

"Will you shut up?" The shout started small and then grew into a roar. "Shut up! Shut the fuck up! I did this for you; don't you fucking get that?"

Tiera drew back as though he'd struck her.

"What did you do?" Theo asked.

"She'd had way too much to drink. She texted me to pick her up, and I wasn't going to say no—what was I supposed to do? Tell her to drive home wasted, hit a telephone pole? Enable her bad behavior? How stupid are you? We were responsible for her!"

Tiera held herself rigid. Her face looked like a wax mask.

"That night," Auggie said. "You went out there. And something went wrong, didn't it? What went wrong?"

Cleve stared at him, but it was like he was looking through Auggie. Then a laugh jolted through him. "You think I did something to her?"

"I think you cared about Shaniyah," Theo said. "But something bad happened."

"I wouldn't have hurt her. I never would have hurt her. Hell, I spent half my time making sure nothing bad happened to her, and the other half I spent putting out fires between the two of them." He nodded at Tiera. "From the minute she set foot in this house, they were going at it. You know what that's like? You know what it's like, going from this nice, peaceful life with the woman you love to—to World War Three? They couldn't walk through the room without going after each other. I just wanted it to be like it used to be." He seemed dazed, as though even he weren't sure of what he was saying. "I just wanted some peace and quiet."

"And Shaniyah was the problem," Theo said.

"What did you do?" Tiera asked stiffly. "What stupid thing did you go and do?"

"I didn't do anything!" Cleve's gaze seemed to sharpen, as though he were taking them all in again, and he stepped back once. "I wouldn't have hurt her! And I wouldn't have hurt you either." But that last part came out a little weaker than the rest of it, and Auggie remembered the baseball bat, the pipe, the knife spinning so fast the steel seemed to bend. "We wanted to scare you, that's all. You called here, you were asking too many questions. You were supposed to stop."

With what looked like an effort, Tiera pushed herself upright. The shakiness of her voice had gotten worse, and she leaned on the sofa, steadying herself with one hand. "Did you kill that little girl?"

The wound in Cleve's face went down to the bone. All he said, in a disbelieving whisper, was "Ti."

"What did you do? Tell me what you did!"

He shook his head once, blinking as tears welled up. Voice thick, he said, "She was—" He stopped. "She was dead. Already. When I got there. She had tape over her mouth. She'd tried to throw up, but the tape—" He stopped. Tears spilled down his cheeks, and he wiped them away. "There was nothing I could do. I sat there with her. I knew she was dead. I knew there wasn't anything anybody could do for her; she was already starting to get cold. And that party was still going, people everywhere, drunk and laughing and music blasting. It was like hell."

"Did you call emergency services?" Theo asked.

The pause lasted a long time. Longer than Auggie thought possible, until it felt like the air had drawn too tight it would snap. Then Cleve shook his head.

"You stupid man," Tiera said.

"She was already dead!" But that shout seemed to be the last thing he had left, because his voice collapsed, and his shoulders curled inward. "There was nothing anybody could do for her. And I knew if I called, I knew it would start trouble, and I just—I just wanted it to go away. I just didn't want to deal with it. We've dealt with so much. She was gone, and it broke my heart, but now it was just us again, and we could go back to being us."

He held out a hand to Tiera, and she stared at it from out of the wax mask of her face. When she spoke, the word was a strangled whisper. "You didn't want to deal with it?"

"Ti—"

"You didn't want to deal with it? With a dead child?"

"Nobody could do anything for her," Cleve said, but the words were almost a whisper, and his gaze dropped.

"I'm calling the police," Tiera said. She lurched away from the sofa, patting herself down for her phone. "That's what I'm doing. I'm calling the police."

Cleve's head sank.

"You're going to need to talk to them," Theo said. "One thing you're going to need to explain is why you decided to frame Dalton."

Seconds thudded past. Auggie thought he could feel the force of each one being nailed into place. "I don't know," Cleve finally said. "I don't know. I don't know. I went crazy. At first, all I wanted to do was get away from the party, so I got Shaniyah into the car, and I drove. I didn't even know where I was going except I couldn't go home. I kept thinking about how Ti would react, about how we'd fight, and then I remembered that guy."

"Who?"

"The theater guy. The teacher."

"Did you know Dalton?"

"No. Shaniyah had been doing that detective stuff. She showed us her videos. Showed me, I guess. She didn't like him, thought he'd done something funny with a boy. I thought—I thought if it was him, if people thought it was him…" He trailed off. His big hands hung empty at his sides, his chest rising and falling.

"You broke into the theater?" Auggie asked.

Cleve nodded. "She'd told me all about that place. I walked around for a while, trying to find the right spot. I just needed time. If I could hide her somewhere for a day or two…" But he didn't finish that thought, and Auggie thought maybe there wasn't an end to it; he knew how thoughts became fragmented when the brain was pushed to the extremes: fear, trauma, pain. Guilt.

"I thought you wanted people to believe Dalton did it," Theo said.

"I did! By the time I got her down to that basement, I knew I'd screwed up. Someone had seen me at the party, I was sure of it. Or I'd be on a video—that's all kids do these days is record themselves. And then it'd look like I'd done something wrong."

"You did do something wrong," Theo said. "You moved a body. You covered up a death."

"Man, you know what I mean!"

"So," Auggie asked, "what did you do?"

"I'd seen his sweater. The director guy's. When I'd been walking around, trying to find the right spot. So, I took it. I got some of it under her nails. Then I drove over to his apartment."

"Let me guess: Shaniyah had told you where he lived."

Cleve shook his head. "You can look that stuff up online."

In the background, Tiera was trying to explain the situation to a 911 dispatcher, but her sentences sounded choppy and uneven. More grief, Auggie thought. More guilt.

"I don't understand," he said. "Why didn't you just leave her?"

"I went crazy," Cleve mumbled, making himself smaller and refusing to look at them. "I just went crazy."

26

They waited until a pair of uniformed officers arrived. Then they waited some more for Detective Palomo. They told her the chain of events that had brought them to the Johnsons' home. She listened, said she'd have more questions down the road, and went inside. Before the door closed, Theo had a glimpse of the interior: Cleve still standing where they'd left him, arms wrapped around himself, hangdog. Tiera sat in the dining nook, tissues in one hand, a glass of wine on the table beside her.

Theo said, "Let's go home."

It wasn't until Auggie was pulling into their driveway that Theo remembered the fire. It wasn't that he'd forgotten it, exactly, but it had been pushed to the back of his mind. From the outside, the house looked fine. Untouched. But when he opened the car door and smelled the hot pavement and the mulch and the reek of old smoke, it came back to him. The madness of the fight, the slowly growing realization that even with Jem's help, he was outmatched, his family in danger. He could feel it, his whole body tightening as his exhausted system tried, once again, to flood him with stress hormones. He tried to think about the house. In stories, a house was never a house. In stories, a house was always a symbol for something more.

"I forgot," Auggie said. "Sorry, I was on autopilot."

"No." Theo pushed the door open the rest of the way. "This is good."

They walked around the outside of the house, the day's heat hammering them. Hot enough that everything had a slight shimmer to it, and sweat ran down the back of Theo's neck. The sides, the back—no sign of damage, although on the deck, Theo could see where the sliding door's frame was warped from whatever tool their attacker had used to gain entry. Fingerprint powder covered the exterior of the door, and Theo took it to mean that he didn't have to worry about messing up prints.

Inside, the stench of the fire was overwhelming, and Theo and Auggie went about opening windows. Theo remembered, like an old nightmare, doing all of this in reverse. After they'd first learned about the intruder. The way he'd walked the house. Patrolled. Policed. The way he'd checked every lock. How he'd made sure Auggie knew. And Auggie, because he was so smart and so sensitive, had known without Theo having to say anything that it was a punishment.

With the windows open, currents of thick, soupy air began to move through the house, and Auggie brought the fan from their room and started it going. Theo inspected the living room and kitchen first. A spot of blood on the tile suggested where Jem had been cut, but otherwise, the room looked untouched—the rumpled blanket on the couch where Jem had kept guard and, in the process saved their lives; the little bulb under the built-in microwave was still on, probably because Jem had kept it on as a nightlight; one of the accent chairs was pushed slightly out of place so that Lana and Tean had more room to play.

Together, they moved down the hall toward the front of the house. This was where the fire had caught, and the signs of it were everywhere: the floorboards blackened, the plaster charred, a wall light melted. The gasoline had burned fast and hot, but the fire had actually—in this case—been the lesser of the two evils. Even though putting out the fire had been a necessity, the water that the firefighters had used had destroyed the front of the house. It would be, Theo guessed, a gut job. Months. His heart was beating too fast, and his head had started to hurt. He wondered if he had high blood pressure; his dad and Jacob had high blood pressure.

"It's not so bad," Auggie said. His voice echoed back weirdly from the soggy plaster and warped boards. "It's actually not as bad as I thought."

Theo nodded.

"Want to go back to Emery and John-Henry's?" Auggie said.

"No, I'm going to—" Theo didn't finish the sentence, but he gestured at the hallway.

Auggie waited a beat, nodded, and took out his phone. "I'll call around, see if I can find anyone who can come out and give us a quote."

Theo nodded, and Auggie's steps moved toward the back of the house.

For a time, Theo just looked at it all, taking in the smell of char, the first hint of mold. His heart was beating so fast he felt sick. He moved into the office, not because he had any idea what to do, but because his vision was starting to go black around the edges. He had the weirdest feeling—non-feeling, actually, because he couldn't feel his legs. He dropped into Auggie's chair, which had been rolled over near the shredder, and leaned back. He closed his eyes. After a while, the hammering in his chest slowed. He rubbed his thighs and felt silly, immediately, even though his thoughts were syrupy and slow. Silly, but gratified, too, that he could feel his legs again.

He sat up, and he looked around the office—not looking for anything in particular, just taking in Auggie's typically neat workspace, the sense of something familiar and safe and normal. The thick packet of pages next to the shredder caught his eye, and he picked them up, turned them over.

AGREEMENT, it said at the top. And then, below, with blanks left to be filled in: *The following is an agreement made and entered into between* _____ *and* _____ *(Intended Parents), a married couple, and* _____ *(Gestational Carrier) and* _____ *(Gestational Carrier's husband), a married couple.*

There was more, but Theo couldn't read it. The words swam together. The headache was back, and he could hear his pulse in his ears, too loud for him to hear anything else.

Which was why when he realized Auggie was standing in the doorway, mouth moving, Theo couldn't tell what he was saying. After a while, Auggie stopped, and he looked more closely at Theo. Looked at the pages in his hand. And something rippled across Auggie's face. It made Theo think of something opening in the wind. A flag. A bedsheet. The way the wind caught it and hurled it out, snapped it so hard you couldn't read what it said.

"What is this?" Theo asked. That's what he thought he asked. The pound of his pulse in his head made it hard to tell. He had that feeling again that he was looking up at Auggie from somewhere else, the world narrowed to a circle like the mouth of a bag drawn shut. The bad old days. And bad old Theo.

"It's not—" Auggie stopped. He swallowed. "It's a template, Theo. It's a sample. That's all. I just wanted to know what it said." It all sounded so rational, so normal, until he blurted, "I'm sorry."

Neither of them said anything. The headache seemed twice as bad, and Theo wondered if there was still some sort of particulate matter in the air, something left by the smoke, maybe. Or perhaps some sort of toxic chemical that had been released when the paint had heated, or that cheap light fixture in the hall, or the old plaster. Something was wrong, that was all he knew. Something in the air. He couldn't seem to get any air.

"Please don't be mad," Auggie said. "I downloaded that before— before everything happened, and before I knew how strongly you felt about—about kids, and you've been really good about explaining your feelings, Theo, and I want you to know that I hear you, and you're the most important person in the world to me, and I respect you, and I love you, and it matters so much to me what you feel and what you think, and I wasn't trying to send any other kind of message by—by looking at that stuff. And I think you make a lot of really good points, and I'm with you, I really am, I mean, I understand, and I agree, about—about the kids thing, about not having more kids, about—" He looked lost. That emotion was still pushing against him, that invisible force rippling and snapping. When he finished, his voice was small. "—about everything."

Theo leaned forward. The chair creaked. The pages whispered against his knee.

Auggie flinched.

It was small. It was barely anything, and he was so good at controlling himself, so good at being whoever you wanted him to be—and, still too often, doing it without really thinking about it, without, possibly, even meaning to—that the movement was swallowed up a moment later in the earnest look he turned on Theo.

"I realize I shouldn't have ever downloaded that template—"

It was like Theo was hearing him from the next room. They lived here. This was their home. They could be at opposite ends of the house, and Auggie would be on the phone, and Theo could listen to his voice, not the words, just the sound of his voice, and think, This is home. This is my home. And he thought again that in stories, a home was never just a home. It was always a symbol of something else.

"Auggie," he tried to say.

"—and I never should have done it without telling you, without your permission—"

"Auggie, stop."

"—because I want you to understand that I understand that this is a partnership, and you're so smart, Theo, and you're so loving, and I know you want what's best for me—"

"Stop!"

The word came out louder than he intended. Harsher, too. Because it had been ripped from him. Because no matter how it sounded, it had hurt more coming out. The thunder in Theo's head was suddenly gone, and the nausea was back. His hands were trembling. He told himself to hold on to the pages, but he couldn't, and they fluttered down, one by one, to snow across the floor.

Auggie was crying. He wiped his eyes with his arm, and in a tiny, choked voice, he said, "I'm sorry."

And then he was gone.

27

Auggie had a good cry, if there was such a thing, in the hall bathroom. He almost made the mistake of going to the master bath, but then he had a vision of Theo coming after him, of being trapped in there. Of course, he could be trapped in here too, but this seemed less awful in comparison. Not their room. Not their bedroom.

But when he'd sobbed himself out and cleaned himself up, when he was drying his face with a towel and checking himself out, red eyed, in the mirror, he didn't hear anything. No creaking floorboards. No footsteps. Nothing that suggested Theo was even still in the house. He might have left, Auggie realized. An Uber. Or walking. The old joke, the one that still had a sting for Auggie, no matter how many times he and Fer and Chuy had tried to laugh it away, was the one about going out for a pack of smokes. He wouldn't leave Lana, Auggie told the face in the mirror. And the face said back, No, but he would leave you.

That threatened to bring on a fresh wave of tears, but Auggie blotted his eyes and let himself out of the bathroom. He made his way to the kitchen and found a beer, and he carried it out to the deck. Summer clamped down on him, but after being trapped in the claustrophobic stinking ruin of the house, the sticky, slow breeze felt like heaven. It smelled like the creek, and like the silver maples lining the banks, and like moss and green things that were growing. He opened the can and took a drink, and the beer was crisp and cold, and he couldn't remember the last time he'd had anything to eat or drink.

Ok, he thought. Damage control. His relationship experience was limited pretty much to Theo, and although they'd fought over the years — a few times, terribly — the bad fights, the really bad ones, were long in the past. And anyway, this one felt different, somehow. The look on Theo's face. He'd been so pale. So unresponsive. Like he hadn't been Theo anymore, but someone else. Or like Auggie hadn't been Auggie. That was probably it; he'd been staring at Auggie, not recognizing him.

Because, of course, for Theo, this was a betrayal. For Theo, for whom all the world's fears were bound up in their most terrifying form in one little girl, all his guilt and all his pain and all his loss captured in one tiny body, for Auggie to try to make it happen all over again—that was a betrayal. Perhaps the ultimate betrayal. And Auggie had known that, maybe, at some level. Known the fear. Learned, more recently, the guilt. But not until he'd seen Theo's face today had he fully understood what this meant.

With Dylan, a treacherous part of his brain said, there was always a way back.

Auggie wanted to shut down that line of thinking, but it was tempting. Dylan, his only other real relationship—if you could even call it that—had been domineering and abusive, controlling, threatening, had loved to play mind-fuck games. But he'd also reinforced something that Auggie had learned from his mother growing up: it was easier, in the long run, to manage people. To make sure they got what they wanted, or enough of it anyway, to keep them happy. To tell Mom she looked pretty. To talk about her next role, or the next role she was dreaming of, anyway. To put on little shows and performances for her and her friends. To appear like a magic trick when she wanted to show him off for the latest man. More importantly, to be absent when she wanted him to be absent.

With Dylan, it had been more of the same, only more intense. To say what Dylan said. To change whatever he was thinking as soon as Dylan changed, and never mention the change again. Auggie was wrong, and Dylan was right, and if he said it long enough and loud enough, there was always a way to patch things up.

You were right, Auggie thought. That's how he'd start. If Theo would ever listen to him. If Auggie didn't come home one day to find the locks changed and everything he owned on the lawn. No, no. I'm sorry. I'm sorry, that's how he'd start. You were right.

Behind him, the slider murmured along its track. Auggie didn't look back, but it was like someone had drawn a wire between his shoulder blades. Steps moved across the deck. Then they stopped, still a good way behind him.

"I know you're not ready to talk to me," Theo said, "but I wanted you to know that I'm ready to apologize whenever you're ready to…deal with me." He waited a moment—not a demand, but a courtesy. Then he said, "If you'd like me to leave—it's hot out here, Auggie. I'll go, so you don't have to stay outside."

A breeze lifted. It turned the silver maples, each leaf glowing as its pale belly caught the light. Then the breeze died, and the heat crashed over Auggie like a wave again. He needed to turn around. He needed to turn around right now. He needed to say something.

Theo took a step back toward the house.

Auggie looked over his shoulder, and there was Theo. Waiting. His flow of strawberry-blond hair flattened against his skull, the sun whiting him out like a spotlight, the way he stood, one arm folded low across himself, the other hand turned in toward his thigh.

"I needed some fresh air," Auggie said. "And a beer."

"God," Theo said, and so many things were packed into that one word. He gave a gruesome attempt at a smile. "You're always so much smarter than me."

Auggie tried words, but words were scarce, lost in the jumble of so many feelings. After a moment, when nothing came, he held out the beer.

Theo's steps clipped across the desk. His fingers brushed Auggie's as he took the beer, and Auggie felt the tremor in Theo's hand. He stood there a moment, and then the can began to shake visibly, and he said, "I don't think I can drink this without spilling it all over myself. I'm sorry."

To Auggie's surprise, that brought a smile. "Drink the beer, Theo. Don't drink the beer. Toss it in the creek. I don't care about the fucking beer."

Theo's answering smile was still that gruesome one, the one that made Auggie think of something twisted beyond what it could take, the whiteness of bone broken open. He rested the can on the balcony rail. And then, the words rushing out of him, he asked, "Are you afraid of me?"

This time, Auggie laughed. "Am I afraid of you?" But then he remembered his body betraying him, the desire to move back, to get away when he could see that other man rising in Theo's face again. "No. No, I'm not afraid of you. I'm tired, and I…reacted. That's all."

Theo made a noise that could have meant anything. The ripple of the creek filled the air, and now, in the distance Auggie thought he heard bees. "I don't know if this is the right time to apologize. I don't know if you want time or space or —"

He stopped when Auggie took the beer from him and set it aside. Auggie wrapped his hand around Theo's, so that they were holding the rail together. Theo's hand was so much bigger that it wasn't really fair. The dusting of red-gold hair on his knuckles caught the light.

"I am so sorry," Theo said in a low voice.

"It's ok."

"I don't—I don't think it is."

"It is, Theo. It will be. I knew that was going to upset you, if you found it, I mean. I understand a little better why you feel the way you do about having kids. About seeing the ones at school who aren't being cared for, how hard that is for you." Auggie wondered if he could say the next part because he knew it was the oldest, deepest cut Theo carried, the one that went all the way down and would never heal. But he said it because he had to say it right then, in this moment, or he might never say it later. "Because of Lana."

Theo nodded. He scratched his beard. Then he wiped his eyes. His voice was thick when he said, "How long have you been doing this?"

"Theo, I promise, the surrogacy thing, I was only reading about it. I knew it was a fantasy."

Theo nodded again, and the tears ran faster than he could wipe them away, but his voice came back clearer, more like the real Theo: resonant and low and assured. "This, Auggie. I mean this. How long have you been...handling me? You know what I mean. Telling me what I want to hear. Calming me down. I didn't see it until just now, how quickly you reacted, how you anticipated the blow-up, immediately went into damage control. How long?"

Auggie's silence lasted a beat too long.

Theo nodded and dried his cheeks. "Since the beginning?"

"No."

"Are you sure? Because I was in a bad place when we met, and I—" He laughed, and the sound had a rusty-hinge quality to it. "I don't know if I've gotten any better."

"Theo, no. I mean, we all do stuff like that in relationships, right? We get better at being in a relationship with someone, we know what sets them off, we know how to approach things. I hope I'm a little better at it than when I was nineteen and took my shirt off on your porch because I wanted you to have sex with me."

A wet laugh escaped Theo. "You've gotten a little subtler, yes. I think you're not answering my question, though. What I meant when I asked if you were afraid of me—God, I hope you know I'd never hurt you. Physically, I mean. But I meant this. Are you afraid of my...moods, I guess, for lack of a better word?"

Auggie thought about how it had been. Not always, but a year, maybe. Maybe a little more. The explosions of temper that came more and more frequently, with little warning or different triggers. The disagreements that escalated into cold, one-sided fury that sometimes took Auggie hours to recognize. The sleepless nights for both of them. That wire ran between his shoulder blades again, and he felt his breathing change.

"Ok," Theo said. "That's an answer."

"I love you, Theo. I'm—I'm worried about you, I guess. And I know I'm part of the problem. This is classic Auggie, in case you haven't picked up on it yet. I have this thing where I—I don't even know how to put it into words. My mom, I mean, she's a roller coaster, and growing up, every day, I was trying to play this game to be who she wanted me to be, and every day the rules were different, so I was always trying to catch up. It got better when Fer was older, when he could hold things together, but I bring a lot of that with me. Into our relationship, I mean. And I'm going to work on it."

Theo was silent so long that Auggie wondered if it had happened again: some word or phrase lighting a fuse that wouldn't explode for another hour or day or week. He shifted his weight, and the can clicked lightly against the rail, and he was aware, then, of how still the world had become around them.

"This might be an example," Theo said with a faint note of amusement, "of what you're talking about, Auggie. You're not responsible for any of this. I—" He stopped. When he spoke again, the words were labored. "My anxiety has been…worse. I don't know for how long. A year. A year and a half. It's hard to know because I wasn't keeping track of it, and it crept up on me. Some days I feel normal, or mostly normal, and other days, it's like—it's like I'm made out of all these different pieces that are fastened together, and someone just keeps tightening the bolts and screws. Me, I guess. I'm the one that keeps screwing everything tighter, ratcheting things down. Because I feel like if I let up for one second, everything is going to fall apart. I don't even feel like me. And then, later, when it's over, it feels like a dream, like it happened to someone else, except I'm exhausted, and a part of me knows it's going to happen again." He was silent again, and when the breeze rose, the maple leaves looked like they were doing cartwheels across the sky, incandescent for a heartbeat. "Nothing happened. That's what makes it so fucking frustrating. I don't know if it's just that I'm getting older. I don't know."

Auggie waited. When more didn't come, he said, "You made a lot of progress when you started seeing a therapist. Maybe it's time to think about that again."

Theo nodded.

"You can ask her about medicine, Theo. If it's getting worse, maybe a low dosage."

He nodded again. Then he worked his hand from Auggie's. He leaned against the rail, propping himself on his elbows, and covered his face. His breathing was deep and uneven. After a moment, he reached into a pocket and fished out a baggie. He pressed it into Auggie's hand without looking at him, and then he covered his face again.

Turning the baggie over, Auggie didn't recognize the pills at first. Then he remembered the night at the theater, Ambyr's deal with Dalton, and how he had left Theo alone with Dalton in the bathroom.

"Thank you for giving me these," Auggie said.

Theo's laugh was more like a sob.

"Did you take any?" Auggie asked.

"I wanted to."

Auggie waited.

"God, Auggie. I wanted to so bad."

"But you didn't."

The creek. The settling of maple branches. The bees.

"This time," Theo said. "But what if it's the same thing with whatever they want to dope me up with—"

"Ok, ok, hey. You're not the first person in this situation, all right? We'll talk to the doctor. We'll see what they say. Keying yourself up like this, though, that's not helping."

Hands still over his face, Theo nodded. But he said, "I just keep fucking up your life. I just keep fucking it up, over and over again."

The sound of the bees was louder, and Auggie thought of Vergil, of the Georgics, of *Henry V*. You taught me that, he wanted to say. You taught me how to love someone. You taught me how to share my body with someone. You taught me iambic pentameter, and you taught me how to hold a rifle, and you taught me how to dress for a real winter, and you taught me about myself. I was a kid, and I was spoiled and self-centered and immature, and I'd cocooned myself in a world that told me it was ok to be all those things. I would have kept being those things. I might have kept being those things forever. But like the best teachers, Auggie wanted to say, you showed me the path and let me find the end of it on my own. There was this part of myself that I never would have seen, never would have touched if I hadn't met you. The dark side of the moon. But you saw it. And because you showed it to me, I could see it too. You might have to go halfsies on it with Fer, but you taught me how to be a man. Fucked my life up? You gave me a life, Theo. You gave me myself.

He was still trying to put it into words, the enormity of it, when Theo said, "I know that maybe—maybe the last year and change has made you rethink wanting kids, Auggie. With me, I mean. I understand that I'm not a partner you can rely on—"

"Theo."

"—and I understand that you might not want me to be around your child, not if I'm so unstable—"

"Hey," Auggie said sharply. "Knock it off, or I'm going to climb inside your head and beat both of you up."

That, at least, made Theo drop his hands. He'd been crying again, and his eyes were red, but he gave Auggie a bent smile that looked a thousand times more like the real Theo than anything Auggie had seen in a long time. "Do you? Want kids, I mean?"

Auggie considered turning the question aside. They were both exhausted. They were both hurt and trying to make things better, and this might only make things worse. But for the first time in a long while, Auggie felt like he was talking to the man he had fallen in love with, and he wanted to keep that door open for as long as he could.

"I do have a kid, Theo. I have Lana."

"I know. You know that's not what I mean."

"But it kind of is. A little." Auggie had rehearsed what he'd wanted to say, his reasoning, his carefully articulated list. Gone over it again and again. Delivered some of it when they'd been fighting, just bits and pieces. And now, when he needed it, it was gone. He heard himself stumbling through his best attempt to put it all into words again. "You know about my mom. And, fuck, about my dad. And about Fer and Chuy. And I know you know. And there's this part of me that thinks about that, about all the ways my parents let me down, and I want to do better. And there's this part of me that thinks about Fer. And he is such a jackass, such a total, unbearable tool sometimes. But he's also the one who made a blanket fort for me when we were in this shitty little apartment, a one-bedroom where Fer and Chuy and I had to sleep in the living room. And every time Mom had a guy over, it freaked me the hell out. So, Fer built me this blanket fort, and sometimes he'd sleep in there with me, but most of the time, he slept right outside it because I moved around too much. On the fucking floor, Theo." Auggie's throat closed, and he had to wipe his eyes. "And I was this stupid little kid, so I complained that it was too dark, and he went out and bought me a dinosaur nightlight. With his own money, of course."

"Auggie." Theo reached for him, and Auggie surprised himself by letting Theo pull him into a hug. He dried his face on Theo's chest, and the rush of familiar smells—the laundry detergent, and Theo's sweat, and the green summer of their yard—made him snuffle a few more times.

But he pushed himself back—not enough to break free from Theo, but to give him space to talk again—and said, "I think about that, and I want to do that for a kid. And I love the idea that there's something I helped bring into the world, something that's going to live beyond me, something that's going to be different from me, separate, and still this piece of me living into the future. That's a miracle. And maybe it's selfish; I'm ok with that. I don't have to have a biological child, Theo. I love Lana. I can't imagine loving anyone more than I love her. That's enough for me. That's more than enough; it's everything."

Theo gave him a moment and said, "But?"

"There's no but." Then Auggie smiled. "But."

Theo groaned softly.

"But," Auggie said again, "I'd be lying if I didn't tell you something I've been struggling with. I didn't want to say anything because I know it's silly and dumb and all in my head. I want to preface that I know this is an Auggie issue, not an us issue. And I'm working on it, I promise. I probably wouldn't even say anything right now except I haven't been able to talk to you in so long, and then you went and showed me up by dramatically handing over those pills."

Theo froze.

"Such a production," Auggie murmured.

"You."

"You almost did a flourish with the baggie. Did you want to do a flourish?"

"I was—that was—Auggie, I'd been lying to you. About something that's been a big deal in our relationship in the past. I was making a statement."

"It would have been even better if you'd put them on the railing and slid them toward me, you know, keeping them covered with your hand—"

"You are such a brat," Theo said with a laugh, squeezing Auggie. He loosened his hold again immediately, rearing back to check Auggie, worry written around his eyes. Auggie grinned up at him. "I swear to God," Theo muttered. "Fer is right. You need to be spanked, like, regularly." Then he touched Auggie's cheek, drew his hand back, checked Auggie's face again. When Auggie leaned into his touch, he said, "What's this Auggie thing that I'm pretty sure is neither silly nor dumb?"

Auggie wanted to let it end there. To press against the warm, solid strength of Theo's hand, to feel Theo's arm around him, the sun hot on his neck like a brand. But he made himself speak. "The Auggie thing is, sometimes I—I feel like I'm just, you know, an add-on. I mean, you and Lana, you're a unit. I guess I want something like that."

He couldn't bring himself to put it all into words: that he knew Ian would never be exorcised completely—that he didn't even want him to be, but at the same time, he had the sense that he was always half a step behind a ghost. That when Auggie brought up marriage, Theo talked his way around it until he was practically a pretzel. That even though Auggie knew Theo considered him Lana's dad—or stepdad, or adopted dad, or whatever—there was nothing on paper about it. That his own family, growing up, had always been fractured, and some part of him, some remnant of that child, wanted his own family, a family that was whole and his and his own.

Theo's breathing had changed again, pitchy and uneven.

"That's not a comment about you," Auggie said. "This is an Auggie thing, remember?"

"God, Auggie, of course it's a comment about me. Oh my God."

"Theo."

"Oh my God."

"No, I didn't tell you this so that—"

"You don't feel like you're, what? That you're part of this family? That we're a family? That we're a couple?"

"No, of course that's not—"

"That you're a replacement or something for Ian?"

"Theo, I told you this because I needed to tell you. Not because I need you to fix it. Not because I need you to apologize. And you're going to make me mad if you keep trying to turn this into a Theo thing."

The struggle twisted Theo's good looks, and it clearly took an effort for him to smooth out his expression, to take a deep breath. He nodded.

"I'm going to work on it," Auggie said. "Do you understand me? We don't have to have a baby just because I'm having, I don't know, a teensy bit of an identity crisis."

Theo nodded again.

"I'd like some words, please."

That jarred a small smile out of him. "I understand what you're saying. But I also want you to know that I hear you, and I know that having a child is important to you, and I'd like to talk about it some more when I'm in a better place. That's not me putting you off. That's a promise, and I want you to hold me to it."

"We can talk about it. But I promise, it's not a deal breaker for me."

Theo nodded. "And I know you told me this is an Auggie thing—"

"No, stop, why can't you be the good kind of old, with dementia and you forget everything I say as soon as I said it?"

"I'm going to remember you just called me old, and I'm going to remind you about it the next time I hear something along the lines of 'But I need my big, strong man to carry in the groceries.'" Theo wet his lips. "You are my family. I want to say it so you hear it and you know it's true. You are my one love, my life, my everything. Anything that has let you believe differently is a failure on my part, and I'm going to do better."

Auggie blinked back tears, and emotion clotted his voice as he said, "You realize this is you ignoring all the stuff about this being an Auggie thing, right?"

Theo made a noise that sounded a little smug and a little amused, and then he tipped Auggie's head back and kissed him. The kiss was short and soft, and when Theo pulled back, the question lingered around his eyes. Auggie gave a nod, and some of the worry eased.

"I don't know what to do right now," Theo said.

"We're both exhausted. And if we go back to Emery and John-Henry's place, we're going to have to deal with North and Shaw."

Theo made a face.

"And Jem."

His expression screwed up a little more.

"I know, I know," Auggie said, laughing as he patted Theo's chest. "Could we just—could we lie down for a little while? In our room, I mean."

"I'd really rather stand out here in the blazing sun while I face the magnitude of how much I've screwed up everything important in my life." Something must have shown on Auggie's face because a little lopsided Theo smile came back. "See? Do you like it?"

"It doesn't matter if I like it, Theo. I'm the designated smartass in our relationship. It's a cross I carry."

Theo laughed quietly as Auggie led him inside, their index fingers hooked like the last link in a chain. Or, Auggie thought, the first link in a new one.

The house still smelled of smoke, but opening the windows had reduced it to annoying rather than overpowering. In their bedroom, Auggie hopped out of his shorts and turned himself out of his shirt and was down to his trunks by the time he reached the bed; Theo, of course, was still unlacing one shoe, grinning openly as Auggie bounced on the mattress.

"Is it an Auggie thing or a California thing," Theo asked as he started on the second shoe, "this ability to get naked in the blink of an eye?"

"I'd say you'll have to do some research, but you're limited to a sample size of one."

Theo made a noise of acknowledgment as he undid the waistband of his jeans.

"It's for your own good, Theo."

"Thank you."

"They'd eat you alive. Death by twink."

"Why does that sound familiar?"

He slid onto the bed, still in his t-shirt and boxers, and he was smiling too much at his own joke. Fortunately, he grunted in a gratifying way when Auggie slugged him.

They lay there awhile. It was cooler out of the sun, although not by much—with the windows open and the air conditioning off, the air was thick, almost steaming. Auggie's chest rose and fell. He couldn't smell the smoke anymore, not here. He could smell a hint of hair product on his pillow. He could smell Theo, the complex mixture of sweat and skin and a body he knew almost as well as his own. He got hard by degrees: his dick filling out, his nipples stiffening. Theo's breathing sounded different.

He opened his mouth to say something, and for the first time in a long time, embarrassment stalled him. He'd worked hard to get to where he wanted to be with Theo, and now all that progress seemed swept away, and he felt like a child again: unsure, maybe even a little afraid.

Theo rolled onto his side. Some of his hair had come loose and fell in his eyes, and his mouth made a line—not angry, not grim, but neutral. He put one hand on Auggie's thigh, and Auggie shivered. His fingers stuck lightly to Auggie's skin when he trailed them up. Then that big hand cupped Auggie's dick and balls.

"I've got kind of a situation," Auggie whispered.

Theo nodded.

"If you don't—I know it's a weird time—I promise we can just take a nap."

The corners of Theo's mouth curved slightly. "You know, I kind of had a feeling this might happen." He rubbed lightly, and Auggie shivered again. If it was possible, he got harder. It felt like months since Theo had touched him. Years. Theo's hand moved to his waistband, and he rolled onto his knees. His eyebrows arched in a question, and when Auggie nodded, Theo slid the trunks down. His eyes followed Auggie's body. He tossed the trunks aside, and then he put his hands on Auggie's thighs. Hard, strong hands. Auggie could feel himself leaking onto his belly, and when Theo slid his hands up an inch, back again, up an inch, back again, Auggie made a noise. Theo shushed him and whispered, "You are so beautiful."

Auggie blinked his eyes, but the tears spilled anyway, running down to soak into the pillow.

"Are you ok?" Theo asked. "Do you want to take a break?"

More tears fell as Auggie shook his head. "I want you to get naked, dummy."

For another heartbeat, worry lingered in Theo's face. Always so worried. Always so determined to keep Auggie safe. Then it melted into a new expression. Theo's grin had a distinct cockiness, and for a moment, Auggie could see what teenage Daniel Theophilus Stratford might have looked like. Theo shucked his shirt, and he worked his way out of his boxers. He was hard, his dick jutting out. When he touched Auggie again, Auggie spread his legs and let out a shaky breath.

Theo went down on him: Auggie's sex professor, still giving master classes in blowjobs. Auggie raked his fingers through Theo's hair. He tightened his grip. He pulled. Emotions stirred in him, a kind of turbulence made up of leftover anger and love and frustration and fear and animal sexual need. He pulled until Theo made a noise—not quite pain, but definitely discomfort. The world stepped back as the orgasm began, everything receding, and Auggie heard himself from a distance saying, "Oh shit, oh shit, oh shit."

And then it stopped. Theo sat back. He ran his knuckles under puffy lips, and his cheeks had red circles in them. A string of precum hung between the tip of his dick and Auggie's thigh, and a voice in Auggie's head said, This is what you do to him.

"Theo," he whined.

Shaking back the strawberry blond hair, Theo chafed Auggie's thighs again. Then he sat with his back to the headboard and said, "Come here."

Auggie grumbled. He swore. He made discontented noises so that there would be no doubt how he felt about the matter. The crack of Theo's hand against his bare thigh wasn't hard, not exactly, but it sounded like a gunshot, and Auggie squeaked. He bolted upright and, glaring at the smirk on Theo's face, crawled over to straddle him.

"That hurt!"

If anything, the smirk grew bigger. Theo rubbed the stinging spot—the sting was almost gone, to be fair, but that patch of skin had taken on a decidedly rosy glow. He didn't say anything, but he pulled Auggie closer, until their chests were almost touching, their dicks trapped between their bodies. Theo studied Auggie's face, and the amusement dropped away, the smirk faded. It felt like a slice of eternity, that indeterminate span of time when Auggie could see, in Theo's face, more. More of Theo. More of them. Then Theo kissed him again, longer, his hand light but firm on Auggie's jaw. Little adjustments, tiny repositionings, one of Theo's hands following the muscles in Auggie's back.

When Theo broke the kiss, Auggie felt oxygen deprived, drunk on the taste of Theo, on the taste of himself in Theo's mouth. Theo, however, seemed to be suffering no such problem. He licked Auggie's neck. And then he whispered, "I love you."

Auggie shivered like someone had run an ice cube down his spine. He managed a choked, "I love you too."

For some reason, that made Theo chuckle and shush him. He kissed Auggie's neck. He bit his earlobe. One of Auggie's legs was trembling now, like it couldn't hold him up, and Theo's hand moved from his back to his hip to steady him. His other hand cradled the back of Auggie's head, giving him no chance to break away.

"I want to tell you something," Theo said. The words were barely loud enough for Auggie to hear them. "I want to tell you how good you are for me. I know you told me not to do that, not until you tell me I can. So, I'm asking. Please?"

Auggie nodded drunkenly, his head loose and bobbing, his leg trembling faster.

"You're amazing," Theo whispered. "You're amazing with our daughter. You're amazing with me. You're so smart and funny and kind. You're gorgeous. Every day, I'm proud of you. I'm so proud of who you are."

Auggie moaned. He rutted into Theo's belly, his dick sliding across Theo's skin.

"I am," Theo said. "And I think about the last few days, about how hard you've worked, about everything you've done, about how you never give up. I can't believe how lucky I am to be with you, to get to spend my life with you."

It was meant to be one word, a single sound: "Oh." But Auggie's mouth broke it into two syllables, the second sliding lower. He was breathing like he was running. Running faster and faster because he couldn't slow down. He rocked his hips, Theo's hand there comforting him, following his rhythm. A race. Yes. He was racing his own body, racing toward the thing that was gathering in his toes, in his fingertips, in his belly. Theo licked the inside of Auggie's ear, and he made a choked noise as his body stuttered against Theo's.

THE GIRL IN THE WIND

Then he couldn't even manage words. He wanted to say, Touch me. He wanted to say, Not like this, but of course, he knew this was what Theo wanted, and giving Theo what he wanted—knowing Theo would be proud of him for giving it to him—was what made it so intense. He humped against Theo's belly. He was distantly aware of his hands clutching the headboard, of fighting the urge to reach down and bring himself off. He rocked, bucked, moaned. Theo bit his neck and sucked hard and whispered, "Give it to me. Right now."

The orgasm broke Auggie open. He couldn't have said if it felt good or if it hurt; it was so intense that it went beyond that categorization. He was conscious of it only in the aftermath, like catching a glimpse of it out of the corner of his eyes. At some point, his body had given up on supporting him, and he lay draped over Theo now, shaking. Theo had one hand between their bodies, moving furiously, and then he grunted. Heat splashed against Auggie's belly, and the tension in Theo's muscles slackened.

At first, the tears were barely a trickle, but then something unhinged inside Auggie, and he began to sob. He shook as he cried harder. Theo held him until the worst of the storm passed. Then, slowly, he eased them apart and helped Auggie lie down. He stroked Auggie's hair.

"Oh my God," Auggie muttered when he finally felt capable of speech. He dried his eyes on the pillow. "That's not my fault; you broke my brain."

Theo smiled, but he said, "How are you doing?"

"I'm fine," Auggie said. "Embarrassed. Alive. Temporarily satisfied."

That earned a chuckle, but Theo kept stroking his hair, kept watching him with those delicate blue eyes.

"I promise," Auggie said. "I'm fine." He tried to lighten his voice. "It's been a long time since I had a total breakdown after sex, right?"

"Lots of feelings," Theo said. "Lots of hormones. Crying after sex is perfectly normal."

"I don't know about normal, but I know, I know, please don't give me that look. I'd make a joke about you dadding out, but you know, it feels a little weird after you just hosed me down."

"Auggie," Theo said with what sounded like despair.

"Lots of feelings. You got that right."

Theo was quiet, his fingers whispering against the bristles of Auggie's short hair. Then he said, "I did get the impression you might be feeling some feelings when you tried to rip my hair out."

Groaning, Auggie pulled the pillow over his face.

"Do you want to talk some more? I know—I know there's still a lot to talk about."

"No, Theo. I do not want to talk right now. I want to lie here and be pleasantly sticky, and I want you to hold me, and I do not want to deal with the psychosexual ramifications of the fact that I tried to scalp you when you were giving me head. How does that sound to you?"

"I always forget that you're bratty after sex too. I think it must be like how moms forget how difficult childbirth was. I always convince myself a good fuck will take the edge off."

"Theo! Cuddles! Now!"

Laughing softly, Theo lay down, wrapped an arm around Auggie, and pulled him against his chest. The last thing Auggie knew before sleep claimed him was an awareness that Theo's breathing had settled almost instantly into sleep, and he felt weirdly victorious about that fact.

28

The next day, Auggie and Theo took Lana back home. Theo wasn't sure how Auggie had managed it, but he'd gotten three contractors to take a look at their house, and all three had assured them that the house was livable — although it would smell like smoke for a while. Theo had made sure to thank Emery and John-Henry for the place to stay, but he wasn't sure he'd been able to hide his relief. The Hazard and Somerset household was currently at max capacity, and Theo wasn't going to miss the jack-in-the-box, I-just-popped-in-to-argue-about-split-infinitives experience of living with Emery Hazard. He also wasn't going to miss sleeping on the floor, although, of course, it hadn't bothered Auggie, who still slept like he was sixteen.

They spent most of the day cleaning and moving Lana's bed down to the living room since, as soon as a contractor was available, the front of the house was going to be off limits while the fire damage was being repaired. By the time evening came around, neither of them wanted to cook, so Theo picked up takeout from Taco Amigo. Lana must have still been exhausted from all the transitions, not to mention playing with Evie, Shaw, and Tean, and she actually fell asleep with a taco still in one hand.

Auggie cleaned her up and put her to bed. Then he and Theo retreated to the bedroom.

"I guess we're going to be spending a lot of time in here," Theo said.

Auggie waggled his eyebrows. He was, of course, already halfway naked. And he was down to his trunks by the time Theo finished that thought.

"I'd love to," Theo said with a low laugh, "but I've got to get ready for tomorrow."

"God," Auggie said, tossing himself down on the bed, "real life is the worst."

That made Theo laugh again.

He was vaguely aware that Auggie was working—which, because this was Auggie, looked a lot like Auggie scrolling mindlessly through social media—while he got his laptop set up. He began reading through the sub reports from the days he'd missed at school, checked his planner, tried to consider how to move things around. Some activities he could cut, and some he could compress, but the days he'd been out had still put him behind, and he'd be playing catchup for the foreseeable future. Especially, Theo realized, once he saw the email chain from the other Language Arts teachers.

"You've got to be kidding me," Theo muttered.

Auggie flopped onto his back. "What?"

"Nothing. Sorry."

"I'm literally looking up TikTok challenges. Do you know how stupid these are? One of them is the Tide Pod one, which is just horrible. But then there's this one where all you do is slap your friend as hard as you can in the face. Big surprise, it's all boys, of course, and it's just so stupid. I mean how immature can you be? When I was their age—" Auggie cut off. Horror swam into his face. "Oh my God."

Theo cracked a grin.

"Theo, did you hear me?"

"I heard something."

"But did you hear me? Did you hear the words coming out of my mouth?"

"It's ok, Auggie. It happens to the best of us."

Arm over his eyes, Auggie somehow managed to give the impression of flopping even though he was pretty much already totally flopped. "I'm dead. I'm old and ancient and dying and dead."

Laughing, Theo rubbed his leg and turned back to his computer.

"Ok, no, I'm sorry," Auggie said. "Before I shriveled up and became an ancient stick-in-the-mud, you were going to tell me something. What happened? Did that racist old sub show up again? Oh God, it's not another of Emery's white papers, is it?"

"No, I gave him a dummy email address, and I only check it once a month. It's the other Language Arts teachers; they're still going to see the play."

"What? What play? *Much Ado about Nothing*?"

"That's the one."

"But Dalton's in jail! And it's a crime scene!"

"You don't have to tell me."

"Theo, I'm sorry."

"Don't be sorry. It's fine—it'll be a rush to get through the play before we go see it, but the kids will have a good time."

"Because it's a field trip and they get out of school."

Theo laughed. "Well, yes, that's probably the main reason. But they'll enjoy the play more than they expect, the ones who actually watch it. And they'll understand more of it than they expect too. They always think it's the language that's going to trip them up."

"Oh my God, I'm having flashbacks from the war."

When Theo tried to pinch his leg, Auggie giggled and squirmed away.

Smiling in spite of himself, Theo said, "I'll stop. You can go back to work."

"No, tell me. I mean, the language is hard, especially for the ones who struggle with reading. But that's not the real problem?"

"Well, that's the immediate problem, especially when we're reading it. But like I said: once they see the play staged, they'll understand a lot more than they expect. What's actually harder, in my opinion—"

"It's like freshman year all over again."

"Never mind."

Propping his chin on his fist, Auggie grinned. "Are you kidding? This is literally my fantasy. Do you still have that button-up?"

Theo grabbed a pillow to put between them, but, of course, Auggie bulldozed through it the way he'd bulldozed through, well, pretty much everything else that had stood in his way.

"What's actually harder," Theo said because Auggie was still waiting with that eager-beaver expression on his face, "is helping them understand the culture, the characters, why Claudio would break his relationship off with Hero over a lie, and why Hero could conceivably die from the shame, and what the hell is going on with Beatrice and Benedick."

"They need to see all the asses. You need to show them the movie with all those naked butts so they'll get it."

"This conversation is officially over. Please play on your phone."

Flopping onto his back again, Auggie started scrolling as he murmured, "Yes, Dad."

He only laughed when Theo whapped him with the pillow.

"The thing that's really hard to understand in that play," Auggie said in the distracted tone of someone only half-focused on what they were saying, "is Don John. He doesn't even have a reason for the shit he pulls except that he wants to ruin everything."

"The kids actually get pretty interested in that. Shakespeare has several villains whose crimes seem to be without any motivation, and we have a good conversation about psychopathy and what is evil."

"I'm sure the parents love that."

"I don't send home handouts."

"You should tell them about narcissistic personalities because: a, that's definitely Don John, and b, that's all the rage on the Tok these days." He didn't actually gasp or choke or swallow his tongue, but he sat up so fast that for a moment, Theo thought something was wrong. Before he could ask anything, though, Auggie turned a wide-eyed gaze on him and said, "Theo, I think I know what happened."

29

The next afternoon, in a parking lot outside a Panera in Columbia, Auggie tried to keep his nerves from showing. The restaurant was a standalone building in a strip mall parking lot. Cars filled the lot, and people streamed into the Panera. It wasn't just crowded; it was bustling. The lunch rush. Lots of people meant, Auggie and Theo hoped, the situation wouldn't get out of hand. But a part of Auggie also recognized that lots of people also meant the potential for lots of collateral damage.

"We should wait," Theo said. The gun—Ian's gun—was hidden under a baggy Cardinals t-shirt. John-Henry had returned it after one of his officers had recovered it from their house after the attack. Auggie felt like he could see it in spite of Theo's best efforts to hide it, like the gun was somehow magnetized and drawing his eyes, or like the tiny adjustments to Theo's posture gave him a map to the gun's location. "We don't have to rush into this."

"We don't have time to wait."

"They have phones and email and ways to reach police in other states."

Auggie shook his head, but what he said was, "It's going to be fine. We're going to keep it calm and cool, and we're going to stick to the plan."

"I can call North and Shaw—"

"Theo." Auggie forced himself to soften his voice. "They're watching Lana and Evie, and that's a good thing because there's still a maniac out there who wants to hurt us. Jem and Tean are back in Auburn following up on the tiger necropsy. Emery's been hired on by John-Henry to help the police department as they work with Dalton to ID the man who took Leon. Everybody's busy, Theo. There isn't anybody else."

"That's ridiculous. There's the Highway Patrol, the Columbia police department—you can't tell me John-Henry wouldn't reach out to them."

"We don't have time. Ambyr already left Wahredua. She's not going back. And she's not going to stick around in Columbia, either. We don't know where she'll go or what she'll do, and maybe you're right, maybe the police could track her down and pick her up, no problem, and in a couple of weeks she'd be back here to stand trial for murder. But what if that doesn't happen? What if she has a new ID, or she stays off the radar, and we never see her again? Or what if she gets rid of her phone, or deletes the videos, or—I mean, do you want her to get away with murdering Shaniyah?"

Theo let out a frustrated breath. "We could follow her—"

"Theo, please. We're almost there; let's finish this. We just need her phone."

The silence swelled with Theo's struggle. Finally, he clutched Auggie's hand, still wrapped around his knee, and squeezed hard.

"We're going to do this," Auggie said.

"Be careful."

"I'm always careful."

Theo was probably feeling too many feelings to roll his eyes right then, but he did stare at Auggie with a shell-shocked look that was kind of insulting.

Auggie slid out of the car, leaving it running for Theo; the swampy heat bore down on him, and sweat broke out across Auggie's face, under his arms, down his back. He crossed the parking lot. The sun was directly overhead and so bright that it gave the world an unreal quality, like everything was in high definition. Auggie felt like he might be floating.

Inside, a wall of cool air met him with the smell of fresh baked bread and cinnamon. It seemed impossibly loud: the clink of flatware on ceramic, voices calling in the kitchen, people ordering, kids screaming as they zoomed past. The line to order stretched to the door, and the woman next to Auggie gave him a side-eye as she bellowed into her phone, "I can't hear you!"

Auggie moved into the restaurant, heading toward the armchairs gathered around an electric fireplace. Digital flames danced back and forth behind the glass. Maybe that was comforting, Auggie thought, when you didn't feel like you were being simmered inside your own skin. Maybe he should come here and sit by the fire and be creative.

Ambyr sat in one of the armchairs, her attention glued to her phone. She hadn't seen him yet, which was good; Auggie didn't want her to run, and he thought that might be an option. It had been easy enough to lure her out of hiding—he'd simply used the Instagram account for his marketing agency, where he featured a lot of the work he did with clients, and sent her a DM. She'd responded in twenty minutes. Yes, she was interested in affiliate marketing. Yes, she was interested in doing sponsored content for

Detox Gash. She loved Detox Gash. Detox Gash was amazing. Which was interesting, since Auggie had invented Detox Gash—their five-minute-old profile described them as "a lifestyle brand geared toward empowered AFAB-bodied individuals." He'd spent twenty minutes trying to work in some lyrics from Pussy Riot until Theo had taken his phone away and made him go to sleep.

So, it had been easy to get her to come out of hiding for a meeting with an agency rep who just happened to be in the area. And it was easy to get her to send him some of her content. Detox Gash wanted shock value. They wanted eyes. Now, Auggie had almost everything he needed. Almost.

As he took a seat in the armchair facing Ambyr, he gave a final look around. The setting wasn't exactly private—in a place like this, that wasn't a possibility. But he was glad Ambyr hadn't chosen a booth or a table; the only other person in the seating group was a woman with a baby carrier next to her. The baby was asleep, and the woman was holding her phone to her mouth in what was apparently a life-or-death attempt at speech-to-text, saying, over and over again at eardrum-shattering levels, "Dyson hairdryer, Dyson hairdryer."

Ambyr looked up, and Auggie smiled at her. Her face kaleidoscoped: shock, then fear, and then a geometry of emotion Auggie couldn't quite name. She was frozen for a moment, and then she reached for her purse and started to stand.

"Sit down," Auggie said. She was still standing, so he lowered his voice, and added, "You already sent me the evidence I need, Ambyr. I know you murdered Shaniyah, and I can prove it; that part is over. So, you might as well sit down and talk to me."

He wasn't sure about the logic, but Ambyr sank back into her seat. She looked past Auggie, with one last vestige of hope, said, "So, I don't understand. Is there really a marketing gig?"

It took Auggie a full five seconds to process that before he said, "No. I made that up."

"Oh my God." Ambyr dropped back in the chair. "I knew it. I knew it was too good to be true. Everything bad happens to me."

"Everything like the video Shaniyah had of you? The one she showed you? The one you knew she was going to post everywhere?"

Ambyr glared at him and hugged her purse closer.

The young mom or babysitter or whoever she was leaned forward, as though that might help, pronouncing each syllable with distinction: "Dyson hairdryer."

"This one," Auggie said, and he opened the video they'd found in Shaniyah's cloud drive. He only played the important part, the stuff at the end: the party on the back forty, with the stripes of lights shifting in time with the music, the drunken teens, Merlin and Leon shouting at each other. And in the background, Ambyr. It had been easy at the time to overlook her; Auggie felt like he could cut himself a little slack. He hadn't even known who she was the first time he'd seen the video. Ambyr had been literally in the background, of the investigation and of the video, and the fight between Merlin and Leon had been the focus of Shaniyah's recording. But there it was, what Auggie should have seen the first time: Ambyr, wasted, trying to do one of the dances that was so popular on TikTok—Auggie was pretty sure it was the Savage Love dance. Except that Ambyr, because she was on the brink of passing out, fell mid-dance. Her cutoffs slid down, and even over the pulse of the music, her fart was distinctly audible.

"Give me that!" Ambyr snapped, leaning forward.

Auggie pulled his phone back, shaking his head. "That's the video. If that went live, if people saw that—hell, if Shaniyah did something like tag you—your social media career would be over, right? Dead in the water, before you even got started. And you knew it. You didn't remember the party, I'm guessing—I don't know how you could after getting trashed like that—but she came to Merlin's trailer and showed you. And that's when you knew. She told you she was going to post her investigation. And you couldn't let that happen."

Ambyr stared at him, her lips peeled back, her breathing shallow.

"That's why you broke into our house," Auggie said. "Because you knew I was helping Shaniyah with her college project, and you thought she might have left copies of the files with me. That's why you stole my laptop. And I'm assuming you took Shaniyah's phone and destroyed it or got rid of it. But what I don't understand is do you seriously not understand the idea of cloud storage?"

"I'm leaving. And I didn't steal anything or kill anyone."

"Yes, you did. I don't think you meant to kill her. In fact, I bet you were relieved when they arrested Dalton—you'd been wondering, I think, if your little prank had gone wrong, but when they charged Dalton, that was the answer. It wasn't your fault. Somebody else did it."

Ambyr shook her head. "I don't know what you're talking about."

"Ambyr," Auggie said gently, "you sent me the video. I told you: it's already over."

He played the video, the one she had sent to his agency account. The one for Detox Gash, the one that showed AFAB individuals being empowered, being wild, being fun. It was dark in the video, with only the phone's flashlight to provide light. In the background, music played, a boy cheered, voices mingled together. Mrs. Renshaw's back forty. The back-to-school party. Where Merlin and Ambyr had gone, of course, because they were both trying to live out a fantasy.

Shaniyah's face filled the screen. She was clearly unconscious, passed out from too much beer and weed, maybe something stronger. She had been grieving, Auggie thought, a wave of pity crashing over him. Her heart broken because she hadn't gotten that big scholarship. She had done what most kids did. They coped, and they made bad choices.

Ambyr's laughter came from the video, and the video wobbled, presumably because Ambyr was trying to hold the phone steady while doing something else at the same time. A moment later, it was clear what she was doing: one hand appeared on screen, holding a strip of duct tape. She pressed it into place over Shaniyah's mouth, making sure it was good and tight, laughing harder. Then the video faded to black, and a tag appeared on the screen: #tapechallenge. Not exactly genius-level marketing when it came to the name of the challenge, but no one had ever accused Ambyr of being a genius.

Ambyr's eyes were wide. She was still taking those shallow, rapid breaths. "That doesn't mean anything. That could be anyone. A friend sent me that."

"I don't think you meant for her to die," Auggie said. "But you're still responsible, Ambyr. She was unconscious. She vomited. She asphyxiated."

"I didn't do that. I didn't do anything!"

The last words were a shout, and the mom with the baby carrier gave them a dirty look before repeating, "Dyson hairdryer" into the phone again at full volume.

Auggie nodded. He was surprised, in the moment, to feel sorry for Ambyr. Her panic and pain and fear were clear, and he knew that the night could have played out a dozen different ways. There were so many ways people were stupid, so many ways they were reckless, so many things they did for attention.

"Shaniyah kept screenshots of the messages you sent her," Auggie said. "This whole thing would have been easier if she hadn't changed your name in her phone, but she still kept the screenshots, and the police will be able to match those to the records from your phone. They'll be able to match the video to your phone. It's over, Ambyr. What you can do right now—the best thing you can do—is leave here with me, and we'll go straight to the police station. You'll tell them what happened. Explain it was an accident. But you've got to tell them, Ambyr; if they have to track you down, they're not going to believe it was an accident."

Music. Voices. A man chewing so loudly it sounded like he was smacking his lips next to Auggie's ear. The blood drained from Ambyr's face, and she wobbled slightly, clutching her purse again as she tried to stand.

"It wasn't my fault. She should have listened to me. She should have—she should have deleted that video as soon as I told her. She shouldn't have been such a bitch. She was such a bitch!"

"Excuse me," the mom said, "some of us are trying to work—"

"You need to calm down—" Auggie said at the same time.

Ambyr drew a knife from the purse. For a moment, Auggie struggled with the ridiculousness of it, the improbability. It was a big chef's knife, maybe twelve inches, and the way she drew it out of the tiny purse made him think of a magic trick. He felt something rising inside him like a laugh. And then Ambyr slashed the air, and Auggie leaned back. The mom screamed. And Ambyr grabbed the baby carrier.

The movement must have jolted the infant awake because she—in a moment of engrained sexism, Auggie decided based on the baby's pink onesie—began to wail.

The mom screamed and lunged at Ambyr. Ambyr gave another chopping blow with the chef's knife, and the mom fell back. She screamed again, and this time there were words: "My baby!"

"Stay away from me!" Ambyr shouted, waving the knife at Auggie. Then she pointed the blade at the baby carrier. "Everyone stay away from me."

Auggie held up his hands as he stood. His movements felt agonizing slow. He played this game with Lana sometimes called slow-motion, and it was exactly what it sounded like. They played it sometimes until Lana was giggling so hard she fell over; Theo usually had to leave the room halfway through because, of course, they always did it when he was trying to work. All of that flashed through his mind, and that weird not-laugh surged up inside him again, and he realized he was tasting the edge of terror.

"Everybody stay back," Ambyr said, the point of the knife drifting back toward the infant. "Everybody stay where they are!"

In the background, something poppy and saccharine continued to play, but otherwise the restaurant had gone silent.

"This is a mistake," Auggie said. "You're making things worse for yourself."

"My baby," the mom said, still trying to push herself up. It seemed to be impossibly difficult for her, and Auggie knew what that felt like: when shock and fear turned you into a prisoner inside your own body. "Please. My baby."

"Stay back!" Ambyr shouted again.

With another wary glance, she started to move backwards. No one else seemed to know what to do. An old man was trembling so hard that his tray, complete with two bowls of soup, looked like it was about to fall out of his hands. A middle-aged woman in a power suit with albatross-winged shoulder pads had her hand halfway inside a trash can, like she'd been paralyzed in the midst of throwing something away. Under one of the tables, a little boy was crying, his sobs cranking higher and higher with each second.

Auggie gave Ambyr a full beat, and then he started moving after her. "Ambyr, put the baby down. All you have to do is put the carrier down, turn, and run out that door, and nobody's going to come after you."

"You're going to come after me! You said everybody was going to come after me! Well—well, fine! Come on!"

"Please don't do this. You don't want to do this."

"Why couldn't she just delete those videos? Why doesn't anything ever work out for me?"

The last words pitched into a scream. Maybe she thought Auggie had come too close because the knife slashed out at him again—the blow erratic, verging on uncoordinated. Then she lurched back again, her chest heaving, toward one of the single-wide exit doors.

Auggie kept going. He couldn't hear the poppy background music anymore. Something rushed in his ears. Something huge. Much, much bigger than he was.

"Stay back!" Ambyr said with another of those wild slashes. She bumped the door, still moving backwards, and forced it open. "If you follow me outside, I'm going to cut her up!"

Behind Auggie, a woman moaned, "No!"

Auggie held up his hands to show he wasn't following. Ambyr stumbled through the door, pausing half a second because it fell shut behind her and caught on the baby carrier. Then she got it open once more and yanked the carrier free. The infant was still wailing, and maybe that was why Ambyr glanced down, some final, automatic reaction to a baby's sound of distress. That was why she didn't see the blow coming.

Theo must have been pressed to the side of the building, waiting for a clear shot, because as soon as the door began to close again, he kicked

Ambyr hard enough to send her stumbling. She cried out, the sound muffled by the glass, glanced around. A Ford F-150 was trying to turn into a parking spot; the driver must not have noticed the fight between Theo and Ambyr. Ambyr turned toward the incoming vehicle and threw the baby carrier directly in front of it.

Theo dove toward the baby.

Ambyr ran.

Auggie shouldered open the door and ran after her.

A horn blared. Theo shouted. The baby was screaming. The Ford's engine rumbled. The choking, humid heat of midday closed around Auggie, and on top of that, the heat pouring off the big truck felt like a hammer. He had a momentary impression of Theo crabbing backwards, on hands and knees as he hauled the baby carrier away from the truck, but the horn blatted again, and it didn't seem to be rolling forward anymore. Then Auggie locked his gaze on Ambyr, who was tearing off down the parking lot, and put on the gas.

He was young. He was fit. He was wearing shoes designed for running—ok, designed for looking dope, but still, technically running shoes. And Ambyr was trying to sprint in four-inch heels. He was less than ten feet behind her by the time she stopped at a beat-up Impala.

Somehow, even though he didn't feel like he had any breath in his lungs, he managed, "Ambyr, stop!"

She turned. The knife came out. It streaked through the air, catching the sun, a bright line.

He was moving too fast. He'd put on all that speed, and now he couldn't hit the brakes hard enough.

When it sliced open his face, it felt like a tug—hot, and then cold, and then nothing. The knife continued past him.

How bad? The thought was immediate. It was almost overpowering, forcing its way to the front of Auggie's brain, demanding all his attention. My face, he thought. My face. How bad is it?

But he forced the thoughts down. Ambyr was shaking, her lips pulled back in a silent snarl as she stared at him, but she still had the knife. His blood was dark in contrast to the steel's glow. My face, he thought.

She didn't know what she was doing; he could see that. Not just the murder, the bizarre attempt at a hostage and an escape. Not even her laughable attempts to establish herself as an influencer. This, right now. The knife.

Ambyr screeched and lunged. As soon as she moved, Auggie recognized the half-hearted effort, knew that she wouldn't actually reach him. All those kickboxing classes. All the self-defense workshops. Hell, even the Street Queen videos from years ago, the ones Fer had loved sending him. All the ways he'd trained himself and his body never to be weak again, never to be a victim. And he was correct; the move had been a feint or a threat, and before the knife reached Auggie, Ambyr began to draw back, already shifting her weight onto those ridiculous heels again.

Auggie had done the kick so many times, his body flowed into the movement without him having to think about it. A lead kick, which meant with his front leg. One of the three basic kicks in kickboxing. He'd done how many of these at this point? Hundreds? Thousands? All the power he generated with his back leg and his core traveled the length of his body and exploded out of him when one (in Theo's unfair opinion, very expensive) sneaker connected with the side of Ambyr's head.

She made a weird, ducklike noise, almost a quack, and rocked against the Impala. The knife fell from her hand, her legs folded, and she lost her balance on the heels. As Ambyr fell, Auggie kicked the knife away. Then he dropped down, flipped her over, and pinned her to the concrete. She was shaking really bad, he thought. And then another part of him noticed the blood dripping onto his arms, and he realized, no, the shaking was him.

"Auggie!" Theo's shout. "Auggie! Aug—"

Glancing over his shoulder, Auggie spotted Theo. And he saw it, the moment Theo saw the cut.

"Oh Jesus, Auggie," Theo said, crouching next to him.

"I'm fine."

"Oh fuck. Oh fuck."

"Theo, I'm fine." He tried to smile, but his face didn't seem to know how to do that anymore. "Help me hold her until the police get here." He was going to say something else, but then the world tore free of its moorings, and Auggie found himself leaning against the Impala, trying to keep himself upright against the backwash of dizziness. "I'm fine," he mumbled. Hands. Theo's hands, keeping him upright, holding him here, in the last spot of solid ground. Which, of course, was with Theo. It would always be with Theo. "I'm fine."

30

The police. The hospital. The police again. Finally, when the police had completed their interview, when they had confirmed they had Ambyr's phone and the recording Auggie had made of their conversation, they released Theo. He had a scrape on his hand from the fall he'd taken, trying to get to the baby carrier before it went under that truck.

Auggie was with a plastic surgeon.

He wasn't sure how long he spent pacing corridors. The thing inside him, the thing eating him from the inside out, had a name, Theo knew, but giving a thing a name—in this case, at least—didn't make it any better.

Jem, of all people, kept him company. The other men had all shown up at the hospital, but when that thing gnawing at Theo drove him out of the waiting room, Jem was the one who came with him. Theo knew he said something. Something like, *I'm fine* or *You can go back to the waiting room.* Maybe more. But Jem just tagged along, a paperback folded open in one hand, reading as they walked.

And then that thing inside him, the thing eating him up bite by bite, broke through some internal dam, and Theo started to sob. He ducked into a stairwell, and then he couldn't move anymore, could barely stay there, hands on his knees, shaking as sobs tore him apart. Jem was there for that too. He stood there and rubbed Theo's back. And then, when the flood had drained out of Theo, they sat on the top step, and Jem slung an arm around Theo's shoulders and read his book while Theo held his head in his hands.

After a while, eyes burning, Theo managed to sit up a little straighter. He tried to knock some of the roughness out of his throat. Then he said, "Goosebumps?"

"*Night of the Living Dummy,*" Jem said and turned a well-worn page. "It's the best one."

Hand on the rail, Theo stood. He was vaguely aware, under the strata of other emotions, that he was embarrassed, and he said, "Thank you. For, you know."

Jem nodded. He stood and tucked the book into the pocket of some ridiculous vintage shorts—some sort of iridescent purple with pink trim, which went nicely, Theo guessed, with the pink font on his t-shirt. It said, PATRICK SWAYZE, and sure enough, there was a picture of Swayze himself below the words.

"You know something Tean had to teach me? I mean, I guess he's still teaching me, since we agreed I'm technically still feral."

The words meant something, but Theo's exhausted brain couldn't track them.

Jem smiled. His front teeth were slightly crooked, and it made him look younger. And, of course, like he'd be a hell of a lot of trouble—which, Theo supposed, was correct. "You're not in this on your own."

Theo nodded.

"Want to go find a snack?" Jem asked. "Do you think they have pretzels? The soft ones, not the gross hard ones."

"I...don't know."

Jem was quiet for a moment. Then he said, "Maybe this isn't the time, but I wanted to say I'm sorry." Theo glanced at him, and Jem shrugged. "For being...well, a major asshole, I guess. When we met." He couldn't seem to look Theo in the face as he continued, "I've got all this stuff about reading and school, and you were so smart and confident, and I acted like a huge piece of shit. So, I'm sorry."

It seemed impossible to Theo that they could be having this conversation right then. He could only process it in bits and pieces, his mind lurching toward Auggie every few seconds before Theo tried to pull himself back to this moment. Somehow he managed to say, "It's ok."

Jem did look at him now. "Plus I had no idea you were such a badass."

Theo's smile felt dry and cracked.

"He's going to be ok," Jem said quietly. "We're going to get through this together, all of us."

"I know."

A man in scrubs hurried past them, texting on his phone, and he left silence in his wake.

Jem broke it by saying, "Tean would say we should go back. I guess we should go back."

Theo nodded, and he let Jem lead him back to the waiting room.

They didn't have to wait much longer. Auggie appeared, escorted by a nurse. The nurse was telling Theo things, explaining how to care for the wound, change the bandages, something about the stitches. But the words breezed through Theo; all he could see was Auggie. A huge bandage covered one side of his face, and he looked ashy, his eyes smudged with exhaustion. But he looked back at Theo, and one side of his mouth smiled.

"Mr. Stratford," the nurse was saying, "do you have any questions?"

"No," Emery said. "He doesn't. We'll pick up the prescription, and I'll go over the instructions with him after he's had some rest."

That seemed to satisfy some obligation that Theo could only register at the periphery of his consciousness. He was aware, as they left the hospital, that John-Henry was going back to work—now, of course, to deal with the aftermath of everything with Ambyr. Jem and Tean piled into a car with North and Shaw. And Emery got behind the wheel of the Audi, which meant Theo could sit in the back seat with Auggie.

They drove. Columbia's light pollution faded behind them, and then they were in the true dark, the deepness of limestone cuts, under walls of hickory and oak and pine. Everything that Theo needed to say ran through his head like words on a ticker tape that wouldn't stop printing, wouldn't give him a chance to catch up.

"Stop," Auggie murmured, tucking his head into Theo's shoulder. He rubbed Theo's belly. "Please. Stop."

He was asleep in a few minutes.

When they crossed the Missouri, the tires rumbled over the bridge, and the waters were black and wide except where reflected light floated like pancake ice. No stars. The sodium and halide coruscation of Jeff City. The dark again, movement: a branch bending, outstretched wings, the curve of a white-tail's neck.

Emery parked in front of the house and killed the engine. They sat there in silence, and then the headlights clicked off.

"Let me get Auggie in bed," Theo said, surprised by the rasp of his words, "and I'll drive you home."

"I'm going to stay here tonight. Tean and Jem took Lana for a sleepover with Evie."

Theo nodded and let that flow past him. He woke Auggie and helped him into the house, into the residual reek of fire and scorched plaster and singed wood. In their bedroom, he undressed Auggie and helped him under the covers, and then he stripped down to a t-shirt and boxers and stretched out beside him. Auggie's hand came to rest on his belly. That was good; his hand was an anchor, while everything else in Theo was electrified, spinning on a thousand rotors and propellers, every inch of him trying to take flight.

The knife.

The baby carrier skidding toward the wheels of the truck.

Auggie's face. The curtain of blood.

He could hear his labored breathing in the darkness. He thought he saw lights, colors, in the darkness of the room. Spots that floated on the edge of his vision and faded when he turned his head. The pancake ice lights of the river, he thought. Floating out in the blackness.

And then the old, treacherous part of his brain stirred. Because there was a way to feel better. He'd given Auggie the pills he'd taken from Dalton, and what had Auggie done with them? It didn't matter. Theo was done with that. Done with all of that. He'd promised Auggie. He'd promised Lana, although not in so many words.

Auggie had put them in his pocket. That was clear in Theo's memory. He'd put them in his pocket after Theo had given them to him.

It didn't matter.

And then they'd come into this room, and Auggie had stripped down the way he always did.

It didn't matter.

And Theo doubted Auggie had worn the same pair of jeans today, which meant yesterday's pair was on the floor where Auggie had left them.

It didn't matter.

But Theo was already sliding out from under Auggie's hand, settling his feet on the floor, his mind going dark—all lights off, everything powered down. It was easier not to think about it. Easier not to think anything; he was long past the time when he had to make excuses.

He found his phone and, with the help of the flashlight, searched the floor. He found Auggie's jeans from the day before, groped the denim, turned the pockets inside out. Nothing. A little spark of panic. Had he flushed them? No, Auggie wouldn't flush them. He might have hidden them until he could dispose of them responsibly. Where? Auggie was smart and creative, but he didn't have an addict's experience with hiding the good shit. In a drawer, maybe. But nowhere Lana could reach them—

And then Theo stopped. His brain was still dark, everything shut off, the place abandoned, because it was easier to live with himself that way. But that animal part was still awake. And the animal part knew he didn't need to find where Auggie had hidden the pills because the doctor had given Auggie a script for Percocet, and Theo was sure one of the guys had filled it, not knowing that Auggie would have refused the script, not knowing that Theo would have given in to Auggie's wishes.

In that moment, he was aware of himself: crouched in the dark, on the floor, half-naked, driven by something he was too afraid to look at in the light. No names, he thought. Tonight was the night of things he left unnamed.

He made himself stand and let himself out into the living room, and he was so quiet, so careful, easing the door shut so that Auggie wouldn't even stir.

Emery sat on the couch, reading a piece of paper in the light from a single lamp. It took Theo a moment to realize the page was from his lesson plans. Emery looked up, and those amber eyes glinted in the semi-dark.

"Everything ok?"

Theo nodded. Then, because more seemed to be required, he said, "He's uncomfortable."

Emery said nothing.

"It's not bad yet, the pain, but we want to stay ahead of it."

After a moment, Emery nodded.

"He's—he's fine, really. He doesn't even want to take something."

"I see."

"But I'm going to make him. Because he needs to sleep."

Another of those fractional pauses. Another nod.

The conversation opened like a void under Theo, and he blurted, "How about you? Do you need anything?"

Emery shook his head.

Theo made his way to the kitchen island, where a white paper bag from the hospital pharmacy waited. He found the vial of pills and extracted two. He returned the vial, and the rustle of the paper bag was too loud in the house's stillness.

On the way back to his room, he tried not to look at Emery.

"Theo," Emery said.

At the bedroom door, Theo said, "Yeah?"

"I do have a question about this lesson plan."

His fist tightened around the pills. They were round, but the edges still cut into his palm. He thought he could feel his heartbeat in his hand. He could say no. He could say tomorrow. He could open the door, and in the darkness, open the cage, and then the bad old days really would be back again.

"Theo," Emery said, his voice surprisingly gentle. "Sit down."

Theo wasn't sure how long the internal wrestle lasted, but he sat.

"Leave the pills on the coffee table," Emery said with the sound of someone warming up. "This is going to take us all night. Let's start with what has to be an intentional simplification of gender roles and societal expectations in the play. It's hard for me to imagine why you'd willingly choose to minimize the significance of those elements, but the only other explanation is that you're an idiot, so I'd like you to explain yourself. Then, once we've covered that, I think it would be interesting to hear your defense of the laughably incorrect proposition that this play is a proto-feminist piece."

Theo hesitated.

Then he started talking.

The argument lasted until dawn, and it ended, like most of his conversations with Emery, in a stalemate. When Theo finally stood, his back popping, Emery gave the pills a glance and then looked back at Theo.

"I think—" Theo had to stop and start again, his voice thick. "I think he'll be ok."

Emery nodded. "I think so too."

31

The next day passed in a quiet that was almost lassitude. Theo slept some, trying to catch up on the night he'd lost, but knowing Auggie was awake drove him out of bed. But Auggie only sat on the couch, scrolling through his phone. When Theo asked, he didn't want to eat. When Theo insisted, he complied. He made faint sounds of discomfort when Theo helped him change the bandage on his face. Theo tried to hurry, but Auggie warded him off, preventing him from placing the new bandage. He sat there, studying the stitched cut that ran from jaw to nose. His dark eyes looked bottomless.

"What did the plastic surgeon say?" Theo asked when Auggie finally let him place the bandage.

It took a while before Auggie spoke, and his voice had the barest hint of an edge, like the first sign of a weapon being drawn. "He said there's a lot they can do."

The hours accumulated, drifting around them as they sat on the couch, Theo pretending to read, Auggie pretending to look at his phone.

The knock at the door jolted Theo upright, and he hurried to answer it. Jem and North stood on the porch.

"Come on," North said. "We're going to get dinner."

"Dinner?" Theo said. He heard himself, heard how he said the word like he'd never heard of the idea before, but the endless summer day and the lack of sleep had made him lose track of time.

"Emery insists he's smart," North said to Jem. Jem gave a slanted grin. "Me, I don't see it." A little too loudly, he repeated, "Dinner, Gramps. Dinner."

Theo looked over his shoulder. Auggie lurked at the end of the hall, his dark eyes empty, his face white. We make our own ghosts, Theo thought to himself, and then we tie them down so they can't get away.

"Jesus Christ," North said and shouldered past Theo.

"North—" Theo said.

"Let's go, pocket rocket," North said as he reached Auggie. And then, in one easy movement, North scooped Auggie up onto his shoulder and carried him, fireman-style, toward the door.

"Are you crazy? He's hurt, put him—"

Then Theo realized Auggie was laughing. Giggling, really. It must have hurt, judging by how his cheek creased and the bandage pulled, but if it bothered Auggie, it didn't stop him.

North slapped Auggie's butt and grunted. "What the fuck are you feeding him? All right, giddy up!"

And with that, he did this bizarre two-step that some distant, non-horrified part of Theo's brain recognized as an imitation of a horse's gallop, and charged toward the door. Auggie broke out in a laugh, a real one.

"North, stop, he's—"

But North galloped toward the car in the driveway, and Auggie's laughter floated back to them.

With a grin, Jem said, "I hope you're not expecting the same treatment."

Theo stared at him. Then part of his brain seemed to start up again, and he said, "I've got to—he can't be so rough—"

But Jem caught his arm, the touch loose, but solid. "North's a jackass, but he's not a moron. He's not going to hurt Auggie or let him get hurt."

After a moment, Theo nodded.

"Maybe some shoes," Jem suggested in a strangely kind voice, and Theo realized he must look like he was out of his mind. "For both of you. Also, I changed my mind: I can offer you a piggy-back ride, but that's the best I can do."

It was all unreal. It was beyond unreal, like Theo had stepped through the nightmare of his life into...what? Wonderland? But there was no sign that he was going to wake up, or that, if this were a stroke, his brain was about to go off-line completely. So, he grabbed his New Balance and Auggie's Jordans.

When he got back to the door, Jem seemed to have trouble meeting his eyes. "So, um, Theo, listen, one thing before we go: whatever the guys tell you, they're full of shit. I did not say I had a crush on your beard."

That seemed to require a response, but the best Theo could do was nod. It must have been enough because Jem relaxed, beamed at him, and led the way to the car.

Theo ended up in the back seat of the GTO. North had the top down, and although the day was hot, and the damp, heavy air crowded them like a living thing, once they started driving and the wind picked up, it felt surprisingly good. Theo hadn't realized how much he needed the fresh air. He looked over. Auggie's face was still creased with a tiny smile, his short hair rustling in the wind. When he noticed Theo noticing, his smile opened a little wider, and he turned his body to lean against Theo.

It was later than Theo had realized, closing in on eight, and when North pulled into the Cock of the Walk parking lot, it was almost empty. Emery's minivan was there, and John-Henry's Mustang. The smell of deep fryers mixed with car exhaust and something fresh and light, whatever North used to clean the inside of the GTO.

"Seriously?" Theo asked. "Cock of the Walk?"

"The squirt picked it," North said as they got out of the car. "If you've got a fucking problem, take it up with him."

North and Jem started toward the restaurant. Theo opened his mouth to call North back.

Auggie's hand caught his and squeezed once.

"I'm going to say something," Theo said. "He can't talk to you like that."

"Theo, he's just giving me crap. Believe it or not, he says that kind of stuff because he likes me. Swap all the stuff about me being short for jokes about butt stuff, and you've basically got Fer."

"I'm familiar with the idea of guys giving each other grief, Auggie, believe it or not. I don't like him talking to you like that. He takes it too far, and he's being an asshole."

Somehow, Auggie was still smiling, and Theo remembered, for a moment, what he had looked like only minutes before: the wraith at the end of the hall, the darkness where his eyes should have been, that horror superimposed on the man in front of him, the one Theo loved.

"Well, yeah," Auggie said, the smile growing again. Lopsided, Theo saw. Because his damaged cheek wouldn't respond, not fully. "Have you met North?"

Theo didn't have an answer for that, so he let Auggie lead him inside.

Emery and John-Henry had taken a table at the back with Shaw and Tean. John-Henry gave them a nod and a smile; Shaw knelt on one of the benches and waved with both hands. He was, for whatever reason, wearing a fuzzy shirt that Theo immediately thought of—and could only think of—as a Muppet pelt. Evie and Lana were running in circles, and although Lana squealed, "Daddy!" when she saw them, she didn't break away from her game with Evie.

"So much for absence makes the heart grow fonder," Theo muttered.

Auggie laughed quietly and leaned into him again.

The other men joined them, and they lined up at the register to place their orders. Somehow North got Auggie in a headlock, and after Theo fought down his initial, knee-jerk reaction to stop them, to insist that Auggie stay where he was, where Theo could keep an eye on him, he was able to let North haul Auggie away, where they immediately fell into a conversation with Jem and Shaw. Tean and Emery were talking about something, and John-Henry got in line to order.

For the first time in what felt like years, a weight lifted off Theo. A rush went through him, his eyes stinging, and he forced himself to take deep breaths, to focus on this moment. The inside of the restaurant was fragrant with fried chicken and hot biscuits. Music played softly in the background. Kacey Musgraves, "Rainbow." Theo was only able to name the song because John-Henry had turned Auggie on to it, and then the song had played nonstop in Theo and Auggie's house for a week. Auggie and Lana even had a dance for it, a slow, silly waltz: Auggie holding Lana with one arm, his other hand clasped with hers as they spun around the living room.

"Sir?" The girl behind the counter wore braces and pigtails, and Theo vaguely remembered seeing her at school, although he thought—hoped— he'd never had her in class. He realized that somehow he'd lost track of time, and now he was the last one left; the others had made their way back to the tables at the back. In fact, when Theo checked, North was trying to smack Auggie in the head with an empty cup, while Auggie ducked and laughed.

"What would you like, sir?"

The question registered at the periphery of Theo's awareness, and the answer went through him: his skin tightening, goose bumps breaking out, the feeling like white waters were racing through him, like his body weighed nothing, like his spirit or his soul or his mind was a doorway for something vast that came and went, and in its wake, he was different.

"Sir?" the girl asked again.

Somehow, Theo managed to order. He paid. He took his receipt and clutched it because he couldn't feel his fingers. Couldn't feel anything, really, below the cloudiness in his head. Instead of making his way back to the tables, where Shaw was finger-combing Emery's hair and Emery kept jerking away and snapping at him, he stayed near the counter and waited for the food. Because, if he were being honest, he thought his legs were going to fold.

The same girl brought two trays to the counter and, when Theo started to reach for them, called out a number. The way she looked at him managed to penetrate some of the fog in his brain, and he realized it wasn't his order.

John-Henry clapped him on the shoulder. "Everything ok?"

"What? Oh, yeah. Just waiting for the food."

His smile was gentle. "You can wait with us, you know. This place isn't that big."

"Right," Theo said. He even managed a laugh.

North was shouting at Jem, and Jem was grinning as he tossed a phone to Emery—presumably, North's phone. North spun toward Emery, but to Theo's distant surprise, Emery only grinned and did a slick, behind-the-back pass to Auggie, who in turn did a little jump and an overhand shot to Shaw, who—because he was Shaw—immediately shoved the phone down the front of his shorts.

North bellowed in outrage.

"They're a lot," John-Henry said with another smile. "I don't blame you." He waited a moment, and when Theo didn't say anything, he added, "I'm glad Auggie picked this place; I've been trying to get Ree to try it for years, but he hates the name so much."

Theo managed to smile back, like that was an answer.

Something, though, must have shown through the mask because John-Henry frowned. "I know the last few days have been a lot. If you need anything, I hope you'll tell me."

"We're fine. We're going to be fine."

John-Henry watched him for another moment. Then he smiled, nodded, and carried his food back to the tables.

The girl called another number, and this time, North stomped to the counter as he shouted over his shoulder, "Because if I wanted my phone to smell like your sweaty balls, I would have done it myself." His gaze swiveled to Theo, and he snapped, "You need a wheelchair or something? Why the fuck are you still up here like a weirdo?"

Fortunately, he didn't wait for a response. He collected his food, went back to the table, and after unloading one of the trays, immediately started trying to smack Shaw in the face with it.

The girl called the number, and this time, a beat too late, Theo realized it was his. He carried the tray to the tables in the back. He still felt like he was floating, like his head had been cut off. He wondered if anyone could tell. Maybe North had been right; maybe he did need a wheelchair.

But he managed not to fall on his way back, and he slid into the seat next to Auggie. Auggie flashed him a quick smile and grabbed the box of chicken tenders, which he set out for Lana, along with her mac and cheese and her drink. She tried to unwrap the plastic fork herself, and Auggie, laughing, took it from her. Theo kept seeing them waltzing around the living room. He kept seeing the look on Auggie's face.

"I know you're still working on identifying who took Leon," Tean said, "but does this mean—I mean, do you think everyone's safe? We know Ambyr wasn't behind the attack on Theo and Auggie, but someone came into their home and tried to kill them."

"And someone tried to kill us," Jem added, "in case anybody forgot."

"How could we forget?" Emery muttered. "You're still in my fucking guest room."

"No work talk," North said.

"I think we're close," John-Henry said. "Really close. The attacks all go back to the Cottonmouth Club, and Dalton is sure he can identify the man who took Leon. If he's telling the truth about Ambyr putting them in contact, then she'll be able to corroborate the identity. Once we have this guy, whoever he is, I think we'll be able to pressure him into identifying more people involved in this operation, whatever it is."

"Human trafficking," Shaw said, and perhaps for the first time Theo could remember, his face was dark. "We've seen something like this before."

"No work talk," North said again, more loudly.

"That seems likely," John-Henry said. "But we won't know for sure until Dalton gives us our guy."

"No work talk," North said, "or are you mother—" He stopped with a glance at Evie and Lana. "Are you deaf?"

"North was deaf once," Shaw said. "I had to repeat everything for him. Oh my God!" He let out a delighted laugh. "You guys were there!"

The conversation broke up again. Auggie bent down to ask Lana something, and she was pointing to the mac and cheese—lately, mac and cheese had been a touchy subject, because apparently there was only one correct kind, and it came out of a box. Auggie nodded as he listened. The smile was still there, barely a tracing on his mouth. He was so young, so resilient, so full of life. Happy in spite of everything he'd been through. His face, Theo thought. Why, God, did it have to be his face? But somehow, because he was Auggie, he was still here, his smile lopsided now but still making everything better, every moment of Theo's existence better.

He leaned over and whispered, "I love you."

Auggie craned his head, startled, and then the corner of his mouth crooked up. "I love you too."

Theo sat back. His heart was thudding in his chest. It hadn't been the right thing. That hadn't been the right thing to say, not at all. Lines from the play ran through his head. *Much Ado About Nothing*, didn't that seem to fit? Benedick saying, *I do love nothing in the world so well as you: is not that strange?*

And Benedick saying, *The world must be peopled.* And Benedick saying, *I am not as I have been.*

Clutching his shirt, Theo fanned himself. He was sweating, he realized. And the lights were too bright. And he suddenly was sure he was going to be sick. Part of him was aware that Tean was watching him, a worry line between his eyebrows. Shaw was watching too, and then, for some reason, he started to grin.

Theo tried to swallow. He tried to take a deep breath. Nothing was working. He caught Auggie's arm in one hand, and Auggie looked over again. This time, concern tightened his eyes. "Theo, is everything—"

Trying to keep his voice low and steady and not-freaking-the-fuck-out, Theo said, "Marry me."

Auggie stared at him. The plastic fork drooped in his hand. "What?"

"Please. Please marry me." Too late, Theo remembered to add, "I love you."

Across the table, Shaw made a noise like that was the sweetest thing he'd ever heard.

"Oh my gosh," Tean said.

"Because, dick-breath," North was shouting at Jem, "a phone is someone's personal property, and I don't care if your only talent is playing grabass—"

"What did you say?" Emery asked.

"He asked Auggie to marry him," Shaw announced.

The silence that followed was like a place for Theo to fall into. Auggie was still staring at him. Everyone, it turned out, was still staring at him, except Lana, who was pushing her mac and cheese away, and Evie, who was eating fries from Emery's plate.

"Is it too late for Auggie to say no?" North asked.

"Oh my gosh," Tean repeated, and he wiped his eyes and looked at Jem.

"That's amazing," John-Henry said.

"What the f—freak is so amazing about it?" Emery asked. "Asking him while he's still got a mouthful of fried chicken."

Auggie covered his mouth, but you could still see the smile everywhere else. His eyes were wet. His face was shining.

"What are you waiting for?" Emery asked. "Do it properly."

"I don't—" Theo's heart was pounding so fast that he wondered if he was about to pass out. Or maybe this was what a heart attack felt like. "I didn't—"

"A ring!" Shaw said. He worked a gold band from his finger, and a stone caught the light. "Amethyst," he said as he handed it to Theo. "For Auggie's birth month." With a shy smile, he added, "Mine too."

"How—" Auggie started to ask, but then he just grinned again. He was starting to cry.

"In a fucking fried chicken shack," Emery muttered, but he quieted when John-Henry shushed him.

"Maybe on one knee, Pop-pop," North said, "if that's not too much trouble."

Somehow, Theo ended up on one knee.

"Just tell him how you feel," Tean was saying.

"You've got this," John-Henry said.

"And maybe remember to breathe," Jem said wryly. "I forgot that part when we did this."

For some reason, that made Tean laugh.

Emery squeezed Theo's shoulder, and Theo fought the rush of tears.

The music in the background changed to another of Auggie's favorites: Leon Bridges, "If It Feels Good."

"I love you more than anyone in the entire world," Theo heard himself saying. "You're my best friend. You're Lana's dad. Her favorite dad." A chuckle ran through the other men. "You're so smart and talented and creative, and you're the most loving person I've ever known. You brought me back to life." He had to swallow. "You've been with me through— through everything." And he saw, in Auggie's eyes, that Auggie knew what he meant. Knew enough of it, anyway, even though he couldn't know all of it. "I can honestly say I wouldn't be here without you. If I hadn't met you." He smiled, surprised that he still could, and heard himself add, "If you hadn't been so goddamn persistent." Another laugh rolled through their gathering. "I should have done this years ago because I want to spend my life with you. August Paul Lopez, will you please marry me?"

Auggie started nodding halfway through the question, tears running down his face, and when Theo finished, he blurted, "Yes."

Theo slipped the ring on his finger. Somehow, it fit. Then he kissed Auggie, and for a few precious heartbeats, everything else fell away.

When they broke their kiss, North was saying, "Brought me back to life. You know he's talking about his ancient dick, right?"

The other men crowded around: shaking hands, clapping shoulders, hugging—Shaw's hug lasted well over a minute—and, of course, congratulating them.

"Fer," Auggie said, still wiping his eyes. "Oh my God, I've got to call Fer."

Theo grinned. He was about to say something about that—about possibly needing a new identity, or at the minimum, a bomb shelter—when he noticed John-Henry had pulled away from the group. He stood with his phone pressed to his ear, and his face was empty with shock that was slowly clouding into anger.

The mood spread through the group like a contagion. Voices fell off. Silence hardened around them, and they were all looking at John-Henry, waiting, when he lowered his phone. Waiting, Theo thought. Waiting, because somehow, at some level, he thought he knew.

"The details aren't clear," John-Henry said, the words clipped with his fury, "but there was an incident in the county jail. Ambyr Hobbs hanged herself."

"Jesus," Jem said.

"It gets worse. Someone killed Dalton Weber in his cell tonight. And they murdered Sheriff Engels in the process."

The Spoil of Beasts

Keep reading for a sneak preview of *The Spoil of Beasts*, book three of Iron on Iron.

1

Shaw tried to make sense of the words.

There's been an incident.

Ambyr Hobbs hanged herself.

North's hand squeezed Shaw's shoulder, and Shaw felt himself sink down into the moment. It was surreal, sitting in the Cock of the Walk, with country music playing in the background and the smell of fried chicken hanging in the air. John-Henry still stood with the phone pressed to his ear; Emery sat next to Evie, the frozen amber of his eyes catching the light in a way that made them glow. Auggie leaned into Theo, happiness crumbling to ash behind the bandage on his face. Theo wrapped an arm around him, expression grim.

"Jesus," Jem said.

And then John-Henry spoke again. Even before the words came out, Shaw felt their force—destabilizing, undermining, like backwash dragging grains of sand out from under their feet.

"It gets worse. Someone killed Dalton Weber in his cell tonight. And they murdered Sheriff Engels in the process."

Tean shook his head. "That's not—" He stopped, but they all heard the word he hadn't said: *possible*. Because, of course, it was possible. Shaw only had to look at John-Henry's face to see the reality of it.

"I've got to go in," John-Henry said to Emery.

"Go," Emery said. "We'll be fine."

John-Henry ran for the door. In the background, the music changed to Dolly. "Wildflowers."

"We should—" Emery stood, scanning their table and then looking around the restaurant. Night made mirrors out of the windows, and in the glass, Shaw saw a group of frightened men. "Are the children done?"

"Lana's finished," Auggie said in a numb voice.

Pain flashed in Theo's face, but he nodded.

"Come on, baby," Emery said, lifting Evie.

"Where's Daddy?" she asked.

"He had to work," Emery said, and he sent a meaningful look toward the other men. "And we need to go home now."

"I'll check the parking lot," Jem said. Tean held on to his arm for a moment, but Jem slipped free and pushed off from the table, jogging not toward the exit, as Shaw had expected in that first moment, but toward the kitchen. The girl who had taken their order said something like she was trying to stop him, and Jem said something back. It must have worked, whatever it was, because the girl laughed and waved him on, and a moment later, Jem disappeared from view.

"Guess being slipperier than goose shit has its advantages," North grumbled.

Tean's face creased with displeasure, and Shaw elbowed North.

"Uh, that was quick thinking," North muttered.

"Oh my God," Shaw said under his breath.

A moment later, Tean's phone buzzed, and he answered it on speaker.

"Clear," Jem said.

"Are you sure—" Emery began.

"If Jem says it's clear," Tean said, "it's clear."

Shaw waited for the argument, but Emery only nodded. Carrying Evie, he headed toward the door. Auggie copied the move, picking up Lana even though she was definitely too big to be carried. It didn't stop Auggie, though, and he followed Emery. Theo was a step behind, his hand on Auggie's shoulder. North motioned for Shaw to go ahead with Tean, and he brought up the rear as they filtered out of the restaurant.

The summer evening was hot and waiting for them, like a wet cloth pressed against their faces. It was hard to believe that it was past eight, but the sun had almost set, and in spite of the peach-colored arc in the west, the parking lot had fallen into shadow. It was mostly empty.

"Our house," Emery said. "Everyone."

"We don't have—" Theo began.

"It's not a discussion. Theo, Auggie, you're with me. North, Shaw, are you good?"

"Good," North said.

Theo and Auggie hurried toward the minivan, where Emery was already loading Evie into her booster seat. North herded Tean and Shaw toward the GTO, where Jem waited, hands in his pockets.

Inside, the car smelled like American Crew hair gel and the faint hint of cleaner, whatever North had used last time, and maybe, possibly, just barely, the faintest whiff of cigarette smoke. The engine rumbled to life, and North eased the car forward.

"He thinks someone's going to try to kill us," Tean said. Under the GTO's growl, he was barely audible. "Doesn't he?"

Jem said, "Let 'em. We fucked them up last time."

"Last time," North said, "you and Theo barely got out with your lives, and Theo and Auggie's house burned down."

"It didn't burn down," Shaw said, "not entirely."

"And that time, the killer didn't even bring a gun. How well do you think you're going to do if four guys step out of an alley with shotguns?"

"We've managed to stay alive so far," Jem said.

"Because you're lucky. How long do you think you're going to be lucky?"

"We've stayed alive because—"

But when Shaw looked in the rearview mirror, Tean was shaking his head, and Jem cut off.

"Exactly," North said.

"North," Shaw said.

North grimaced, and his attention seemed to settle on driving. They rode the rest of the way in silence.

Instead of hotdogging it, as usual, North hung back a few car lengths and let the minivan lead them to the Hazard and Somerset home. He pulled up in front of the house as Emery was still guiding the Odyssey into the garage.

"I'll clear it," Jem said.

"We'll clear it," North said.

"But I'm lucky," Jem said, "and you're just an asshole."

North barked a laugh. He waited by the side of the GTO after he got out, and when Jem climbed out, North tried to swat him on the back of the head, which made Jem laugh in turn. Their laughter faded, though, as they headed toward the dark house.

Shaw traded a look with Tean. "Do you understand boys?"

Tean touched his glasses like he wanted to resettle them. "They're nervous, and they're finding outlets for that nervousness." Then a tiny smile curled the corner of his mouth. "But no. Not in the slightest."

They waited in silence. Shaw's mind began to branch and fork, a labyrinth of possibilities. First and clearest was the one North had suggested: men in the dark, men in masks, waiting with shotguns to deliver a rain of death. But it could be so many things. Gas filling the house, waiting for a single spark to explode. Or the man again, the one with the sickle, who had come before. He pictured North caught off guard, North with nothing to defend himself against that black blade sweeping out of the darkness—

Tean touched his arm, and Shaw flinched.

"You need to take deep breaths," Tean said. "You're hyperventilating."

Shaw nodded and tried to breathe through the chaos of his own mind. For a moment, the frustration was worse than the fear itself: the old, familiar dismay that no matter what he tried—psychotherapy, psychedelics, weed, meditation, even exercise—he was a victim of neural wiring.

But the breathing helped, some, and after a moment, Tean dropped his hand.

Lights went on in the house, and then the front door opened, and North signaled. By the time Tean and Shaw stepped inside, Shaw could hear Emery and the others in the kitchen, where they'd entered through the garage. The house itself looked untouched: no vandalism, no destruction, no ominous threats or messages. It felt right, too, although Shaw knew North would dismiss that as woo-woo; the house still felt safe, comfortable, like a home.

"All good," Jem said.

"For now," North said. "Let's make it through tonight before the victory jackoff."

"So, cool fact, I actually didn't know victory jackoffs were a thing until literally right now, which means I've wasted, like, at least eight of them—"

"Go on, sweetheart," Emery said from the living room. "You and Lana go upstairs and play. I'll come check on you in a minute."

The little girls' voices faded in time with their steps. North led their group into the living room.

Theo and Auggie stood near the stairs, Auggie clutching Theo's hand like his body weight was an anchor to keep Theo from going after their daughter. Emery stood in the center of the room, head down, face empty. North dropped onto the couch, and Shaw joined him. Tean stayed near Jem, close to the entry hall.

"Is North right?" Tean asked, breaking the silence. "Is someone going to try to kill us tonight?"

"We don't know that," Shaw said.

"They'd be stupid not to," North said.

"We don't know what they're doing. We don't know anything."

"We know somebody tried those bozos." North nodded at Jem and Tean. "And someone tried to kill those bozos." He nodded at Theo and Auggie. "And tonight, somebody killed the motherfucking sheriff. So, I'm

GREGORY ASHE

going to go out on a limb and say somebody's cleaning up, and we're part of the mess."

"We have no idea what really happened tonight—"

Emery's head came up, and he broke in, saying, "North's right."

"Put that on a fucking plaque," North said.

"We had two leads that could connect us back to illegal activity at the Cottonmouth Club. Both of those leads are now dead. The sheriff is dead. And those three deaths took place inside a secure facility. We don't know everything, but we know enough: someone is tying off loose ends, and we—in particular, Theo, Auggie, Jem, and Tean—are a bundle of loose ends."

Shaw opened his mouth. Then he shut it again.

"Who's doing this?" Jem asked. "That's what's driving me crazy about the whole thing. It was one thing when we thought we'd stumbled onto a wildlife trafficking ring. And then—and then Theo and Auggie got caught up in it, and it turns out it's more than animals; they're trafficking people. But who's doing this? We don't have names. We don't even have faces. We've got a psycho in a mask, but that's one guy."

"That's not the real problem," North said.

"It felt like a pretty real problem when he tried to gut me." Jem touched his chest, where a cut was still healing.

"He came into our home," Theo said, his voice flat. "He tried to kill my family."

"North is—" Emery seemed to hear himself and managed to say, "—not wrong."

North snorted.

"The real issue," Emery said, "is whoever conducted these killings tonight, they have a reach and influence beyond our original estimation. This isn't a group of amateurs who have found a way to profit from illegal activities. We're dealing with people who are organized, who are ruthless, and who can strike into the heart of a law enforcement facility."

"Where's Colt?" Tean asked.

"Ashley's." Something in Emery's voice eased. "He's fine; I called on the drive over."

North rubbed his eyes. "Anybody want to go to Tahiti?"

Auggie raised his hand.

"What are we going to do?" Shaw asked.

Emery looked at him, but instead of answering, he reached into his pocket and took out his phone. He spoke quietly as he moved into the kitchen.

"You two should go home," North said with a glance at Tean and Jem. "Hell, I wasn't joking about Tahiti. Go to Tahiti."

Jem scratched his beard, but Tean shook his head. "They killed my friend."

"Our friend," Jem said.

"They were trying to kill us, and they killed her instead. We're not running away from that."

"Even though we don't exactly have unlimited vacation days. Well, I do. But that's because I'm a reprobate."

"We talked about this," Tean said, his voice dropping as he turned toward Jem. "It's my choice—"

"I know, I know, I know." Jem held up his hands. "Look, this is my fault. I'm the one who screwed up. I'm the one who got these fuckers after us."

"It's not anyone's fault," Shaw said.

"It's kind of his fault," North said. He twisted away from Shaw's elbow. "What? It is."

"It's not," Auggie said. "We stirred the pot too."

"He's being kind," Theo said. "I dragged him into this."

Auggie shook his head, but he didn't press the argument. After that, no one seemed to have anything to say. Silence gathered; it was thick in Shaw's throat, and he wiped his eyes and laid his head on North's shoulder. Emery's voice was a low rumble in the background. And then that ended too.

His steps moved back toward the living room, and everyone turned toward the sound. Emery looked at them, face grim. "John asked me to come in."

Theo glanced at Jem, who nodded, and said, "We'll keep an eye on things here."

"Good," Emery said, his voice suddenly dry. "Because he wants North and Shaw to come as well."

Acknowledgments

My deepest thanks go out to the following people (in alphabetical order):

Jolanta Benal, for lending her keen editorial eye to the all-but-final version and teaching me, in the process, barbecue (not barbeque), for her gentle "should bes," and for bonding with me over the singular of biceps.

Savannah Cordle, for catching all the times I mixed Leon up with someone else, for pointing out that Auggie needs to worry about marriage earlier, and, as usual, for giving me some of my favorite comments ever ("also, this is interesting").

Fritz, for sharing his insight into the students of this story (especially Keelan) and being generous enough to understand when I took creative license; for his help clarifying the timeline (and, of course, that important personal day!), and for catching so many of my errors (and being patient enough to point out that I'd dropped the ball on the acknowledgments).

Austin Gwin, for catching my typos, for his kind words about the "talent show," and for remembering Lana needs her dinner.

Marie Lenglet, for reminding me that Lana has grown, for remembering that Theo and Auggie have met the Breakfast Club before, and for (among so many other things), researching small versus large intestine.

Raj Mangat, for pointing out what Theo and Auggie would have seen on the video, for suggesting some more appropriate language in key places, and for raising so many other good concerns—most of which, I hope I've addressed!

Cheryl Oakley, for her feedback on Ambyr's visit to Shaniyah's house, for reminding me to introduce Auggie, and for pointing out that Theo and Auggie wouldn't stop to eat!

Pepe, for straightening out several key details in the timeline, for asking wonderful questions (about Auggie's injury and so much more), and for all the careful attention that made the story clearer, more consistent, and generally better.

Nichole Reeder, for spotting missing endmarks and superfluous words, for continuity help, (as always), and for asking that excellent question about how much they've told John-Henry.

Tray Stephenson, for spotting that stray Kaden, for spotting my missing words, and for his kindness about Auggie and Theo's growth.

Mark Wallace, for keeping track of my speakers (and slip-ups), for catching so many of my typos, and for lending his reader brain with his insightful comparison of the first two books in this series.

Wendy Wickett, for catching so many of my typos and missing words, for her suggestions that improved the story's clarity and flow, and for tracking so many continuity issues (not least of which was Biscuit, and the story of the man licking the dog's nose!).

Last but not least, thanks to Christine, Connie, Crystal, Juli, Keren, and Raye for their help putting the final polishes on this manuscript!

About the Author

For advanced access, exclusive content, limited-time promotions, and insider information, please sign up for my mailing list at **www.gregoryashe.com**.

www.ingramcontent.com/pod-product-compliance
Lightning Source LLC
Chambersburg PA
CBHW052031240626
47153CB00006B/2041